KU-682-656

DIAMONDS
are for *Sharing*

Raye
MORGAN

Nina
HARRINGTON

Shirley
JUMP

MILLS &
BOON

All the characters in this book have no existence outside the imagination of the author, and have no relation whatsoever to anyone bearing the same name or names. They are not even distantly inspired by any individual known or unknown to the author, and all the incidents are pure invention.

All Rights Reserved including the right of reproduction in whole or in part in any form. This edition is published by arrangement with Harlequin Enterprises II B.V./S.à.r.l. The text of this publication or any part thereof may not be reproduced or transmitted in any form or by any means, electronic or mechanical, including photocopying, recording, storage in an information retrieval system, or otherwise, without the written permission of the publisher.

This book is sold subject to the condition that it shall not, by way of trade or otherwise, be lent, resold, hired out or otherwise circulated without the prior consent of the publisher in any form of binding or cover other than that in which it is published and without a similar condition including this condition being imposed on the subsequent purchaser.

® and ™ are trademarks owned and used by the trademark owner and/or its licensee. Trademarks marked with ® are registered with the United Kingdom Patent Office and/or the Office for Harmonisation in the Internal Market and in other countries.

Mills & Boon, an imprint of Harlequin (UK) Limited, Eton House, 18-24 Paradise Road, Richmond, Surrey TW9 1SR

DIAMONDS ARE FOR SHARING
© Harlequin Enterprises II B.V./S.à.r.l 2013

Her Valentine Blind Date © Helen Conrad 2008
Tipping the Waitress with Diamonds © Nina Harrington 2010
The Bridesmaid & the Billionaire © Shirley Kawa-Jump 2008

ISBN: 978 0 263 90288 4

025-0413

Harlequin (UK) policy is to use papers that are natural, renewable and recyclable products and made from wood grown in sustainable forests. The logging and manufacturing processes conform to the legal environmental regulations of the country of origin.

Printed and bound in Spain
by Blackprint CPI, Barcelona

HER VALENTINE
BLIND DATE

RAYE MORGAN

LONDON BOROUGH OF WANDSWORTH

9030 00003 3622 9

Askews & Holts	25-Apr-2013
AF ROM	£6.99

Raye Morgan has been a nursery school teacher, a travel agent, a clerk and a business editor, but her best job ever has been writing romances—and fostering romance in her own family at the same time. Current score: two boys married, two more to go. Raye has published over seventy romances and claims to have many more waiting in the wings. She lives in Southern California, with her husband and whichever son happens to be staying at home at that moment.

CHAPTER ONE

BAD timing.

Max Angeli shoved the single red rose he was carry-ing into his pocket as he flipped open his mobile and barked a greeting, resigned to the certainty that whatever he was about to be told was going to create a new level of chaos in his life. First problem—the dance club he'd just walked into was too noisy. Lights swirled and the heavy drumbeat of sensual rhythms pounded. The brittle clink of crystal liquor glasses vied with high-pitched feminine laughter to fill the air with a sort of desperate frivolity. He already despised the place.

"Hold on, Tito," he said into the phone. "Let me get to a spot where I can hear you."

He could tell it was his assistant on the other end of the call, but he couldn't understand a word he was saying. A quick scan of the crowded lounge located the powder room and he headed for it. The sound level improved only marginally, but enough to let him hear what Tito was saying.

"We found her."

Max felt as though he'd touched a live electric wire. Everything in him was shocked. Closing his eyes, he tried to take it in. They'd been searching for weeks, with no apparent leads, until this last tip that his brother's ex-girlfriend, Sheila Bern, might have traveled by bus to Dallas.

His brother, Gino, had died just months before. Sheila hadn't surfaced at the time, but she'd contacted Max months later to say she'd had Gino's baby. When he'd asked for proof that the baby was indeed his brother's, she'd vanished again. He'd almost given up hope. And now, to hear that she'd been found…

"You found her?" he repeated hoarsely. "Are you sure?"

"Well, yes and no."

His grip hardened on the mobile. "Damn it, Tito…"

"Just get over here, Max. You'll see what I mean." He rattled off an address.

Max closed his eyes again and memorized the information. "Okay," he said. "Sit tight. I've got to get out of this blind date thing I got myself involved in. I'll be right there."

"Okay. Hey, boss? Hurry."

Max nodded. "You got it." He snapped the phone shut and turned back to the noisy room, tempted to head straight for his car and forget the woman who was waiting for him somewhere in all this annoying crush of revelers. But even he couldn't be quite that rude. Besides, his mother would make him pay. She might be sitting in a terraced penthouse in Venice at the moment, but she had ways of reaching across the ocean to Dallas and turning on the guilt machine. Even though she was American, he was the Italian son, and he'd been raised to value keeping his mother happy.

Hesitating on the threshold, he scanned the room and searched for a woman holding a red rose—the match to the poor, straggly item he'd belatedly retrieved from his suit pocket. All he needed to do was find her and let her know something had come up. Simple. It should only take a minute.

Cari Christensen bit her lip and wished she could drown her red rose in the glass of wine that sat untouched in front of her.

"Five more minutes," she promised herself. "And then, if he's not here, I'm going to drop that rose into a trash basket and melt into the crowd. Without that, he'll never know who I am."

He was almost half an hour late. One half hour. That ought to be good enough. She'd promised her best friend, Mara, that she would go through with this, but she hadn't promised to spend all night at it. She sighed, carefully avoiding eye contact with any of the interested males shouldering their way past the bar, wishing with all her heart that she was home snuggled up with a good book. Mara meant well, but couldn't understand that Cari wasn't looking for Mr. Right. She wasn't looking for mister anyone at all. She didn't want a man. She didn't want a relationship. She didn't even want a husband. She'd done that once already and it had turned her life into a living hell.

"Once bitten, twice shy," was her motto. She had no intention of going through that sort of heartbreak again.

But how could Mara understand that? She'd married her childhood sweetheart, settled down in a cute little ranch house and had two adorable kids. Her life was full of piano recitals and pictures on the refrigerator and picnics and kittens. Cari's marriage hadn't turned out that way. They were two very different people, despite the fact that they had been best friends forever.

"Some people find the golden ring swimming in their cereal in the morning, slip it on their finger, and go skipping through life," was how Cari tried to explain it to Mara. "And others drop it in the sand at the beach and spend the rest of their life digging to get it back."

"That's just silly," Mara had retorted. "Do you think my life is perfect or something?"

"Yes, Mara, I do. Compared to mine, it is."

"Oh, Cari." Mara had taken her hand and held it tightly. "What happened with Brian and…and the baby…well, it was just horrible. It shouldn't have happened to anyone, much less someone like you who deserves so much better." She blinked rapidly as tears filled her dark eyes. "But you've got to try again. There's someone out there for you. I just know it. And once you find the right man…"

The right man. Was there such a creature? Even Mara didn't know the details of what her marriage had really been like. If she did, she might not be so quick to try to throw her back into the deep end of the pool.

"Mara, will you please give it up? I'm perfectly satisfied with my life the way it is now."

"Oh, Cari!" She sighed tragically. "I can't bear the thought of you sitting at home sniffing over old movies on one more Valentine's Day."

Was that what this was all about?

"Wait! Hold it. I don't give a darn about Valentine's Day. It's a made-up holiday. Who cares?"

"Don't try to fool me, Cari Christensen. I know you better than that."

"Mara, no!"

"You need a man."

Mara looked so fierce, Cari had to laugh. "I don't know why I let you be my friend."

"Because you know I'm looking out for what's best for you."

Cari sighed. She knew she was beat. But she had to pretend to fight on. "I don't need anyone looking out for me."

"You do, too. I'm your assigned fairy godmother. Get used to it."

"No."

Mara, of course, wouldn't give up at all, and that was why Cari was sitting here in the Longhorn Lounge, holding a sad little red rose and waiting for a man named Randy who Mara had assured her was the exact match for her.

"Just wait. He's special. You'll be surprised."

So she was doing this for her friend. She planned to smile a lot and act interested in Randy's tales of male world conquests, eat a nice dinner in the dining room here at the lounge, get a headache about time for ordering dessert, make a nice apology and head for home. From then on, her answering machine could take care of things for her. And maybe Mara would give up. After all, she'd tried.

The door opened and a man entered, opening his cell phone as he came. Tall and dark and dressed in a beautifully cut suit instead of the jeans and casual shirts most of the men here wore, he grabbed the attention of a lot of onlookers. Something about the way he held himself drew the eye. Or it might just have been the fact that he was the most ruggedly handsome man she'd ever seen this side of the cinema. His thick, dark hair was exquisitely cut and yet managed to give the impression of being a bit long and a bit careless—as though it had just been ruffled by a renegade breeze or a lover's fingers. His broad shoulders strained the silk suit as he turned, and the knife-sharp crease in his slacks only served to emphasize the muscularity of his thighs. A Greek statue brought to life and disguised in a modern business suit.

She shivered, and then had to smile to herself. One thing was certain, this couldn't possibly be her man Randy. And she was glad of that. In her experience, high-powered, incredibly handsome men were the worst kind. But she had to admit he had his attractions.

Eye candy, they called it. Lucky she was on a diet.

She pulled her attention away and looked at her gold watch. One more minute and she would be free.

"Sorry, Mara," she would say on the phone to her friend tomorrow. "He didn't show. Consider it a sign. And don't think you're going to get me to do this again."

A shadow fell over her and she looked up to find a rather beefy-looking man in a Stetson and tight jeans grinning down at her.

"Hey, little lady, why don't you let me buy you one of them fancy drinks with the umbrellas and fruit and such?" he suggested, all swagger and no appeal.

Inwardly she groaned, but she had enough control not to let it show. "No, thank you, cowboy," she said, trying to remain pleasant as she slid down off the bar stool and turned toward the door. "I was just leaving."

"No need to rush off," he said, effectively blocking her exit route. "Why, you're as pretty as a cactus flower, ain't ya'?"

She flashed him a tight smile and lifted her chin, letting him know she was no pushover. "And just as prickly, honey. Better stand back. You don't want to get stuck."

His face darkened. "Now you listen here…"

But just as suddenly as the cowboy had appeared in her line of sight, he now faded away, because someone bigger and more impressive had come into the picture, and everything else seemed to melt around them. She felt his presence before she saw him and she pulled in a quick breath, almost a gasp. Slowly, she raised her eyes.

Sure enough, it was the man she'd seen coming in the doorway a few minutes before—the man she'd been so sure could not have anything to do with her or her life. He was standing before her, holding out a bedraggled red rose, and asking her a question. Her mind seemed to go blank. She swayed. And she couldn't hear a word he was saying.

"What?" she asked numbly, looking up at him as though she were blinking into the sun.

Max was caught between interest and annoyance. He wanted to get this over with and get out of here, but he'd already bungled things. He'd managed fairly easily to find this pretty lady with the head full of blond curls and a frilly little black dress. Her attire revealed a figure that was full and rounded in all the right places and legs that made looking worthwhile.

But the problem was, he couldn't remember her name. His mother had said it often enough, over and over, whenever she told the old story of how the Triple M Ranch had been swindled from her family. This was the daughter of the woman who had done his mother dirty—but what was her name again? Something-something Kerry, wasn't it?

"Miss Kerry?" he repeated when she didn't hear him the first time.

"Oh!" she said, looking shell-shocked. "You can't be— I mean— Are…are you…?"

"Exactly." He waved the rose at her and nodded toward the one she held. "I was hoping we would have some time to get to know each other tonight," he said smoothly. "However, sadly, it is not to be. Sorry to do this to you, but something has just come up and I'm going to have to take a rain check."

"Oh."

He stopped, nonplussed. She seemed rather sweet and she was definitely embarrassed. Not what he was expecting. Was she taking this as a sort of rejection? Well, he supposed that made sense from her point of view. But instead of the arrogant siren he'd imagined from the tales his mother told, a woman whose ego probably had too hard a shell to be bruised in any way, she took this personally. Did she think he'd taken one look and decided she wasn't worth wasting time on? Despite everything, he didn't want to hurt the woman.

"My mother sends her best wishes," he said, his gaze flickering appreciatively over her pretty face. Interestingly, she wasn't his usual type. He tended to favor fashion models—long, cool ladies who were decorative and yet mature enough to know the score. Young innocents wanted to fall in love all the time. That sort of clingy attachment was neither in his nature nor in the cards. He'd spent a lifetime observing the human condition. In his opinion, falling in love was for suckers who were in denial and hoping for a fairy tale. He considered himself too hard-nosed to fall for such nonsense.

But there was something appealing about this young woman just the same. She looked intelligent and quick, even though she was gaping a bit. Her eyes were a brilliant shade of blue, framed by thick, dark lashes and accented by a pert nose that seemed to have a dusting of freckles just for spice. Her hair, the color of spring sunshine, was a stylishly tangled mass that kept falling over her eyes, making her reach up to push a way through in order to see him clearly.

Hardly what he'd expected. From what his mother had told him, he'd been sure he was going to dislike her intensely. Now he wasn't so certain.

"I'm hoping we'll be able to do this another time," he said, actually meaning it. "May I call you tomorrow?"

"Oh," she said again, her lovely crystal eyes enormous as she stared at him. "I...I guess so."

Her vocabulary wasn't extensive. Or maybe he'd been a bit too brusque. His friends and employees had accused him of that more than once, and he regretted it. He didn't mean to be rude.

But he had no time for this. Shrugging, he gave her a cool smile and turned for the exit. He was almost out the door when he remembered the stupid rose in his hand. She might as well have it. After all, what was he going to do with it?

Turning back, he found her still watching him, wide-eyed. Something about the look in those huge blue eyes...

"Oh, what the hell," he said impetuously. Leaving her behind would be like telling a puppy you didn't want him to follow you home. "Why don't you come along? We'll stop and grab something to eat somewhere else."

He congratulated himself right away. It was a good

idea. Yes, that way he had the original obligation out of the way and yet didn't do any damage to the hope of a future relationship. At the same time, he wouldn't feel quite so guilty when he called his mother later. Brilliant!

"I…well, maybe…" Cari cleared her throat.

She wasn't sure why she couldn't seem to get a full sentence out. This wasn't like her. But the fact that the man was so diametrically different from what she'd pictured had completely thrown her for a loop and she was taking some time to get over her shock. For the moment, she seemed to be putty in his hands, and the next thing she knew, she was hurrying out of the club with one of those same hands planted squarely between her shoulder blades. She was going with him, or so it seemed. She glanced back, not sure of the wisdom of heading into the dark of night with a stranger.

But he was Mara's husband's cousin. At least, that was what her friend had claimed.

The funny thing was, as she looked back at the noisy club, she thought she'd caught a flashing glimpse of a red rose being carried by a tall, sandy-haired young man with glasses. But everything was happening so quickly, she hardly registered that sight. And her companion tended to fill up her attention. So she went along with him, half skipping in her wobbly high heels to keep up, as they hurried to his long, low and very flashy car.

"Oh, my gosh," she said as he opened the door to the passenger's seat for her.

"It's a Ferrari," he said, frowning slightly. "Surely

you've seen Ferraris around town. I thought Dallas was crawling with them."

She nodded as she sank into the luxurious leather. "Of course. I've just never been in one before," she told him, then winced. Maybe she should have kept that to herself.

He lowered himself into the driver's seat and leaned forward to punch the address they were aiming at into the GPS, then turned to look at her with one slick eyebrow raised. "From what I've heard of your background, I would have thought fast cars and living in luxury were right down your alley."

She frowned at him, puzzled. Did he have her mixed up with some other blind date? "Who would have told you a thing like that?"

He gazed at her for a moment, then shrugged, looking reasonably adorable in his faux bewilderment. "Texas," he muttered, starting the car. "This place always surprises me."

And that statement surprised *her*. She was about to mention that Mara had said he'd grown up outside of Galveston, but her power of speech got lost as she noticed again just how incredibly good-looking this man was. Everything about him screamed wealth and power. His suit had probably cost more than her secondhand car. His gorgeous black hair, his wonderful tanned skin, the way his thighs swelled against the fabric of his slacks, all created a picture guaranteed to set off the female heart rate. His shirt was open at the neck, revealing more tanned skin and just a hint of crispy, crinkly chest hair. If she were the swooning type, she'd be out cold by now.

But she wasn't, she reminded herself sharply. Not her style at all. And there was another thing. All this embarrassment of hunky male riches didn't add up somehow. Mara's husband was basically a cutie, but to think that he had someone like this in his family boggled the mind.

But it was too late to say anything, anyway, because the low, slinky sports car had taken off like a rocket. As her body slammed back against the soft leather seat, she felt as though she had to hold on for dear life, her heart in her throat.

The car came to a stop at a light. She gulped in a mouthful of air and turned sharply toward him, letting him know she hadn't loved it.

"Wow. Do you always drive like this?" she asked a bit testily, pushing her hair back with one hand. "If so, you must have a permanent seat named after you at traffic court."

He seemed surprised by her strong voice and point of view, but laughed.

"I'm just trying this baby out. I picked her up at the showroom earlier today and I wanted to see what she can handle." He grimaced. "But I don't know the streets around here very well, so I think that will do it. Sorry. I should have warned you."

He gave her a lopsided grin, feeling no chagrin at all over the pleasure that surge of power had given him. But his grin faded as he looked at her.

That crazy, curly hair kept falling down over her eye and he had the oddest impulse to reach out and brush it back for her. The thought made his fingers tingle. He found himself looking at where her tiny, shell-like ear was peeking out from among the curls, and then staring at the smooth, creamy skin of her neck and imagining his lips there and his tongue…

The car behind them honked and he realized the light had turned green. He turned his attention back to his driving. But his mind was on the woman next to him in the car. Something about her tickled his fancy in a strange and unfamiliar way.

And suddenly her name came back to him. Celinia Jade Kerry. How could he have forgotten a name like that? Celinia Jade. Rather a mouthful, wasn't it?

"Mind if I call you C.J.?" he asked her a bit sardonically.

She blinked, truly puzzled. "Why would you do that?"

"For short. It's easier to remember."

She frowned, her nose wrinkling. "But…"

He turned the car onto the freeway and they were off again. Her words disappeared in the roar of the engine, and he had to merge with a tangle of speeding traffic, which didn't leave him time to ask her to repeat them.

Funny, but now that he thought about it, his mother had told him Celinia Jade Kerry would fit right in with the type of woman he usually dated—the sort his mother, Paula Angeli, actually tended to roll her eyes at.

Not that she knew C.J. very well, but she did know the woman's mother. Or had, years ago.

"Betty Jean Martin was her name before she married Neal Kerry, the man who stole my family's ranch," his mother had told him over morning cappuccino just days ago. They'd been sitting on the terrace of her Italian home, overlooking the Venice canals. "She was my best friend, but when she married Neal behind my back, she became my worst enemy."

He'd nodded, having heard the story so often, it was a family legend. He had a sneaking suspicion that his mother had thought *she* was going to marry the man—before her friend Betty Jean had whisked him to the altar—and that in that way she would have been able to get her ranch back. All things considered, he couldn't be too sorry that hadn't happened at the time. Besides, his mother had met his father, Carlo Angeli, shortly after, and her life had changed for the better, at least monetarily. That often happened when one married a millionaire.

Still, Max knew the marriage hadn't been a happy one. His father had rarely been around, and his affairs with the wives of his best friends were legendary. His mother's life had been wrapped up in her two sons—and in bittersweet memories of a childhood on the Triple M Ranch outside of Dallas, Texas.

"I'm sure Celinia Jade will be just what you're used to," his mother went on, waving the letter that had come from the daughter of her old friend. "I still keep in touch with enough old Texans to know what's going on. She's a clotheshorse with nothing on her mind deeper than the latest hemlines and whether her newest shade of lip gloss makes her mouth more kissable. Sound familiar?"

"Have you been listening in on my phone conversations again?" he'd teased her.

And that was when she'd rolled her eyes.

"Don't you get it, Mama?" he told her with loving humor. "I don't date women for their conversation."

"Then you'll probably get along perfectly with the young Miss Kerry." Paula had frowned, looking at the letter again. "It's odd to hear from her after all these years. And to have her ask to come visit us."

"And just lucky timing that I'm leaving for Dallas in a few days and can check out the situation." He looked at her, noting the dark circles under her eyes. She'd been looking more frail lately. Ever since Gino had died. It broke his heart to see her this way.

"What do you suppose she wants?" he'd asked casually, though he was pretty sure he knew.

"Money." His mother sighed, shaking her head of graying curls. "The word is she's in deep financial trouble. Her parents are both gone now and she's spent her way through what little they left her. She's looking at you as one big old ATM machine, I have no doubt."

"Interesting," he'd murmured, a plan developing in his head. "You're sure she still has the Triple M Ranch?"

"Oh, yes. She'll never give that up. Who would?" She winced and he knew she was remembering that her own family had done exactly that—something she could never forgive. "But she probably needs funds to keep it running."

"A loan?"

Paula laughed. "Hardly. She'd never be able to pay it back. My guess?" She smiled at her son. "She asks a lot of questions about you in her letter. I think she'll try to get you to marry her."

"Many have tried," he noted dryly, only half joking.

"But no one has come close yet," she agreed with a sigh.

He'd grunted noncommittally, thinking it over. "Call her," he suggested. "Put her off about her coming here, but tell her I'll be in town and would like to meet her. Set up a rendezvous."

She nodded reluctantly. "What are you planning?" she asked.

He smiled at her. "Mama, you know property acquisition is my specialty. I plan to talk her into selling us that ranch you loved so much."

Her eyes sparkled for just a moment, but she shook her head. "She'll never do it."

He shrugged. "We'll see."

"Oh, Max, do be careful. Don't let her charm you. If she's anything like her mother was…"

He'd dropped a kiss on the top of her head as he started for the door. "I'll give her that old famous Texas sweet talkin' you taught me all about when I was a whippersnapper. She'll be begging to turn the ranch over to us in no time."

Looking back at her as he reached the door, he could see a sad, faraway look in her eyes and knew she was thinking about Gino, his older brother who had died a few months before. That look on her face brought a catch to his throat. He would do anything to bring the joy back for her. Anything.

And that was the mission that had brought him to Dallas.

CHAPTER TWO

"So, TELL me, C.J.," Max said, looking sideways at Cari as they exited the freeway and turned into a dark, spooky-looking industrial area. A quick flash of lightning lit up the horizon, then disappeared as quickly as it came. The air was electric with possibilities. "How's life out on the ranch these days?"

She eyed him and shook her head. His conversation was becoming more incomprehensible to her. Her little house could be called ranch-style, but she certainly wasn't running any cattle in the yard.

"What ranch?"

The ranch your family stole from mine, he thought cynically, his mouth twisting. Are you going to pretend that never happened?

But aloud he said, "The ranch you live on, of course."

She shook her head. What in the world had Mara told this man in order to get him to spend an evening with her? She knew her friend was subject to occasional flights of imagination, gilding the lily, so to speak, but this was ridiculous.

"I don't live on a ranch," she told him firmly. He might as well know the truth.

"Ah. I suppose you're just a normal, everyday Texas girl." His voice belied his words. His sarcasm was showing.

But she nodded vigorously, becoming exasperated. "Yes, I am."

He chuckled. "What is it with you Texans? The popular myth is that you're all such big talkers, but all the Texans I meet are always trying to pretend they're just average folks, no matter how filthy rich they are or how much land they own."

She was at a loss. Surely Mara hadn't pretended she was from a wealthy family—a wealthy ranching family. Mara knew better.

"But we *are* mostly just average folks," she said defensively.

"Hah. *Se non è vero, è ben trovato.*"

The things he was saying were odd enough, but even odder was the fact that she was beginning to detect what sounded like a faint Italian accent, and that last outburst seemed to seal the deal.

"You know something?" she said accusingly. "You don't sound like a Texan."

"*Grazie,*" he replied with a casual shrug. "I'm only half-Texan, after all. I hope you can forgive my mistakes."

"Oh." Half-Texan! And the other half was evidently

Italian. How had Mara missed that tiny detail? She bit her lip, wondering if she'd offended him.

"So what did it mean, what you said a minute ago?"

He smiled at her. "I said it's a good story, even if it isn't true."

Before she could express fresh outrage, his phone chimed. He pulled it out of his pocket and looked at the screen.

"It's my mother," he said, sounding surprised as he pulled over to the side of the road. "She's calling from Venice." He flipped his mobile open.

"Your mother?" Cari gaped at him. She'd heard Italian men were attached to their mothers, but this was ridiculous.

"Sì, Mama."

He said something into the phone in what she assumed was Italian. It sounded like Italian. It even looked like Italian. Cari couldn't catch anything she recognized, but she watched the whole thing, fascinated. There was a lot of near-shouting and gesticulating, and suddenly he pulled the phone away from his ear and said, "Would you like to speak to my mother?"

She gazed at him in horror. His mother? Why on earth would she want to speak to his mother? What would she say?

"Not really," she said, shaking her head vehemently.

He said something else in Italian and clicked the phone shut. Turning, he eyed her narrowly.

"So the old resentments still live, do they?" he noted,

his gaze pinning her to the back of the seat with its dark, stormy intensity.

"What are you talking about?"

"The fact that you wouldn't speak to my mother."

Oh, this was just too rich. She'd signed on for a few hours of hopefully friendly conversation with a strange man, meal included, and that was about it. There had been no extended-family privileges implied in the deal. Now she was getting annoyed. Really annoyed.

"What am I supposed to talk to your mother about?" she asked heatedly, then waved a hand in the air. "I suppose I could give her a critique of how her son handles blind dates. But I'd hate to be insulting at this early stage of the evening."

He laughed, his gaze traveling over her face appreciatively. She glared at him.

"But listen," he said, his grin changing to a thoughtful frown. "I don't know what she's talking about. She says someone called and left a message that I was late to meet you." He shrugged, making a face and looking at her for confirmation. "I wasn't late. I was early."

She held his gaze. "You were late."

His frown deepened. "So you were already calling people and complaining that I wasn't there as early as you were?"

"I didn't call anyone." She couldn't have called anyone. She had a sudden picture of her phone, attached to the battery charger, still sitting on her kitchen counter where she'd left it. Darn. That made her feel naked and unprotected. A girl needed a good phone, especially when she was on a crazy and confusing blind date like this one.

"Well, somebody knew about it and called my mother."

Cari began to feel as though she were on a rapidly moving merry-go-round with oddly formed horses and scary faces leering at her out of the shadows. This entire date was becoming more and more surreal.

"Let me get this straight. Your mother's in Italy. Why does she care about whether you were on time to meet me or not?"

He gave her a slow smile and a long look, one that made her feel strangely languorous. Funny, despite how annoyed she was, she had to admit this was one sexy man. Given a chance, he could turn on the charm and wipe away most of her irritation.

"Because she's a caring person," he said smoothly. "And she wants us to get along well. For old-time's sake."

As she puzzled that over, his phone rang again. Max saw that it was Tito and barked, "Go," into the receiver.

"Where are you?"

"About a block away. I'll be there in a minute." He glanced at Cari. She seemed absorbed in the view outside her window. "Does Sheila know I'm coming?" he asked softly.

"Well, no."

"Why haven't you told her?"

"Well…"

"Have you filled her in on the parameters of the situation?"

"Actually, no."

"Why not?"

"Listen, boss, like I told you, she's not exactly here."

"But you said…"

"The baby's here."

That struck him like a thunderbolt. The whole point of this operation had been to find the baby. Gino's baby. Finding Sheila was secondary, but he hadn't expected them to be separated.

"I'm almost there," he said, signing off and dropping the mobile into the center bay. He turned to look at Cari. Why had he brought her along again? Hmm.

"Where are we going?" she asked, thinking maybe she should have established things like this before she'd agreed to go along with him.

"To take care of some…personal concerns." He put the car in gear. He'd thought he was going to be confronting his brother's ex-girlfriend, trying to get the truth out of her as to whether she'd had a baby with Gino. Now he knew she wasn't there. But a baby was. What did that mean? He was going to assume the baby was Gino's until someone proved different.

Turning to check for traffic, he pulled the car back into action.

"It should be right around this next corner. Ah, here it is."

"This is it?" Cari gazed at the run-down apartment building and frowned. Loud music was coming from an upper bank of windows. A dog was rummaging in a pile of papers near the entryway. One of the street-lights was broken, casting a pall on the area. She thought she saw someone withdrawing into the shadows across the street. This was not a neighborhood she would have ventured into if she'd been doing the driving.

"I thought we were going to get something to eat," she mentioned hopefully, thinking a nice bright restaurant on a busy street would be better than this gloomy place.

"We will." Leaning forward, he looked up at the ugly building and frowned. "I just have a little business to take care of here. I'll make it quick. Wait here."

No way. Cari looked at the empty street and shivered. "Actually, I think I'd rather go where you're going."

"Your choice." He shrugged. "Come along, then."

As he got out of the car and looked at the neighborhood, he couldn't really blame her. He didn't know Dallas well, but he was pretty sure nice neighborhoods didn't look like this. He couldn't leave her on her own out here, no matter how well he locked up his fancy car.

On the other hand, he didn't want her intimately involved in his family business. There was already too much family mixed into all this. Maybe it hadn't been such a brilliant move to bring her along after all.

He gazed at her speculatively as she came to join him, noting again how her riotous hair spun a magical frame around her appealing face. The ruffles of her bodice shimmered, giving her movements a fluid look, and her short, filmy black skirt followed suit with a flirty tantalizing style. There wasn't a hint of slick sophistication about her, just down-home, sexy woman. The sort of woman who made you think of crisp clean sheets on a big, wide bed. Was he allowed to think about her that way?

That made him laugh a little. What would his mother say?

Oh, Max, do be careful. Don't let her charm you. If she's anything like her mother was…

That was what she'd said, but he knew she didn't really think he would do anything hasty. Oh, she was serious about getting the Triple M Ranch back, but what she really wanted was for him to charm C.J., bewitch her, work on her emotions and manipulate her into selling it back to his family.

He'd been confident. From what he'd heard of her, he'd assumed this daughter of his mother's old rival would be just the sort of woman he was used to, beautiful and spoiled, born and bred to the flashy nightlife and the party scene where those with money tended to play. From what he'd seen so far, his read had been way off. Could he handle a woman like this? Was a little charm going to do the trick? Looking down into her clear, intelligent eyes, he had to admit this wasn't going to be as easy as it had seemed from across the Atlantic.

And what would happen if he let her follow him into the apartment he was planning to visit? The last thing in the world he wanted was a witness to his pending interview with whatever he would find there. A cool gust of a breeze chased leaves from between the buildings and brought the smell of pending rain. She shivered and he glanced up the driveway, noting where Tito had parked his white rental sedan.

"I've been thinking," he said, giving her his most winning smile. "Things aren't working out quite the way I'd thought they would. More complications have arisen than I expected. I'm going to have my assistant drive you back to the club. You can wait for me there. Tito will take good care of you."

She flashed him a look and raised her chin. "Forget it. I'm not switching partners at this late date."

His head went back as though she'd hit him. Was she implying…? That floored him. He came off as throwing his weight around sometimes, but he didn't like being taken for a jerk. "No, wait, you've got the wrong idea."

"Listen," she said frankly, tossing her hair. "I'm not accusing you of anything. But this has been one weird blind date so far. I like to keep my feet on the ground and my head out of the clouds. I think I'll just stick with you until you take me home."

"Ah. Better the devil you know, is that it?" He tried to act in his usual debonair fashion, but at the same time, he gazed at her uneasily. This was the woman he'd thought he was going to manipulate? Obviously, those plans were due for a rethink. But that would come later. Right now, he had other problems on his hands.

"This might not be pleasant," he warned her. "I'm not sure what we're facing here. So be prepared for anything."

She shrugged, wondering if he had noticed how her fingers were trembling. She was nowhere near as sure of herself as she tried to sound. When she'd said this date was weird, she'd been soft-pedaling the circumstances. She'd been bowled over at first by his presence, his confidence, his obvious savoir faire, and she'd been intimidated. But that was then.

Now, with the calls from the mother and the visits to slum neighborhoods, she had a bad feeling about this whole situation. He might be Mara's husband's cousin, but he was not your usual Texas boy. She'd have to keep this man in her sights and stay on her toes.

"If there's a problem, maybe I can help," she suggested. "I don't want to drag your assistant away when you need him most." She managed a stilted smile. "Don't worry, I won't get in the way. But I'll be in the background the whole time, ready to help if you need me. In the meantime, you won't even know I'm there."

His gaze was skeptical. "Right." He grimaced, but decided to play this one by ear. He ran a hand through his thick hair and sighed.

"Okay. If you're up for this, let's go on in and see what Tito has gotten me into now."

The building was dirty and smelled like day-old food. They found the apartment quickly enough. Max knocked and the door opened. A short, stocky man built like a fireplug greeted them nervously, nodding when Cari was introduced, his mind obviously on the business at hand and not on her.

"Let's see it," Max said, and Tito stood back to let them in.

Cari followed. She walked into the room totally unprepared for what she would find. The two men went quickly to the far end of the room, and at first she couldn't see where they were headed. When she caught sight of the baby crib, she froze.

No! Not a baby. Oh please, not a baby. Her breath caught and panic fluttered in her chest. Memories of her own four-month-old baby, Michelle, flooded her senses, hitting her unexpectedly. She wasn't prepared to deal with this. Cringing, she almost whimpered aloud.

It had been almost two years since the car accident that had taken the lives of her husband, Brian, and Michelle, their much-adored infant. Two years where she'd avoided every possibility of coming face-to-face with a real, live baby. She turned blindly, her impulse to rush out into the hallway and then away, as far away as she could get. Anything to escape the pain that seeing a baby like this represented.

Just as she hit the doorway, the baby began to cry. She stopped, unable to take another step. There were little gurgling sobs at first, then full-fledged piercing screams.

Turning, she looked back. A baby was crying. A baby needed comfort. Everything in her, every instinct, began to pull her back. Babies were tiny, helpless things with little waving arms and tiny kicking feet. They needed help. She was a woman, naturally equipped with the talent and emotions custom made for doing that. And yet…

She stood where she was, unable to take those steps that would bring her back to the baby's crib, unable to take steps out the door. Closing her eyes, she tried to catch her breath and still the wild beating of her heart. The look, the feel, the smell of her own lost baby filled her head. And the pain was almost too intense to bear.

Max's entire focus was on the baby. As he looked down at the dark-haired infant, his heart swelled with bittersweet anticipation. Was there a hint of Gino in that little face? Did the hands look like his brother's? Was this child all that was left of his brother's life? That was very possibly the situation. He would move heaven and earth to find out. And if it turned out to be the case, there was no way he would let this baby go.

"Boy or girl?" he asked the stalwart assistant standing beside him.

"Boy."

He supposed he should have known. The gown, the blanket, everything was blue. Despite the cluttered, messy condition of the room, things inside the crib looked clean enough.

"Name?"

"The babysitter says his name is Jamie."

"Babysitter?" For the first time since he'd come in the room, he raised his gaze from his study of the baby. "There's a babysitter?"

Tito nodded. "I told her to wait in the bedroom."

Max nodded back, then his eyes narrowed. "Where's Sheila?" he asked, naming his brother's girlfriend.

He'd only met her once. She was pretty, of course, and nice enough in her way, but her way tended to be a ditzy combination of brainless chatter and limitless desire for luxurious things. She and Gino were no longer an item when he was killed in the crash of a small plane. No one seemed to know what had happened to her. It was only months later that she began calling, claiming she'd had Gino's child, demanding money.

Tito's shrug was all encompassing. "The babysitter doesn't know. She says she was hired three days ago, and Sheila was supposed to be back in twenty-four hours. She has no contact number and Sheila hasn't called."

"Have you searched the place for phone numbers or addresses?"

"Of course. I haven't found anything relevant."

"Damn. Well, we can't just wait here."

"The babysitter said she was getting pretty scared herself. She was about on the point of calling the police when I got here."

"But she didn't?"

"No. At least, that's what she claims."

"Good." Max nodded again. "We'll get a local lawyer to handle this before we speak to the authorities."

Tito looked at him intently. "So you plan to take the baby?"

"Of course."

Tito nodded, but as if on cue, the baby began to fuss.

Max stared down at it. So did Tito. The fussing got more serious.

"It's crying," Tito said at last.

"Yes. So it seems." Max backed away a bit. Crying babies were not within his sphere of experience and he wasn't sure he wanted to know more.

Tito tried wiggling his fingers in front of the baby's face, but he only cried louder.

"It won't stop," he noted, beginning to look worried.

Max frowned, uneasy as well. "No." He looked at his assistant. "Was it crying before?"

Tito shook his head. "It's been asleep, I think. I know it wasn't making this kind of noise."

"It is now." Max winced as the decibel level increased.

"Well, what do you do when they cry?" Tito asked his boss, seemingly at a loss.

Max's frown grew fiercer. "How the hell should I know?"

The two men looked at each other, then back down at the baby. The mood was grim.

By now, Cari had managed to cross the room and was right behind them. She could just barely see the baby. He was crying as though his heart would break, holding nothing back. Her fear, her panic, was gone now. Her heart thumped in her chest, but she had things under a fair modicum of control. Taking a deep breath, she pushed her way between the men.

"Don't knock yourselves out looking for the off switch," she advised tartly. "They don't have one."

Max stepped back, seeming relieved as she reached the crib and curled her fingers around the bar. Steeling herself, she looked down, bracing for the sight. A mass of dark hair, fat cheeks red with crying, eyes squinted shut, two little fists waving in the air—this child looked nothing like hers. Relief flooded her and she closed her eyes for two seconds, then glanced down again and spoke to him.

"Hey little fellow," she crooned. "What's all this about? Don't you worry. You're going to be okay."

The sound of a feminine voice stopped the last cry in his throat and he opened his dark brown eyes and looked up at her. A remnant sob shook him, but he stared at her curiously as though she were something brand-new and possibly very interesting.

She smiled. He was adorable. Reaching down, she gathered him up and took him into her arms. And then she closed her eyes and let the feeling wash over her. She had a baby close against her. That special sort of enchantment had been her daily experience for such a short time before it was taken from her. And now, for the first time in two years, she could feel it again. Tears welled in her eyes.

"You can handle this, then?" the man who'd brought her here was saying.

She nodded without looking at him. She didn't want him to see that her eyes were wet.

Max stared at her. He wasn't always as sensitive as he should be to women's feelings, but he could tell something was going on here. He just wasn't quite sure what it was, and Tito beckoned from the door to the bedroom. He hesitated only a moment before he decided she was okay, and he turned and went into the side room to question the babysitter.

Cari held the baby gently and cooed, rocking the tiny body, until all whimpering quieted. The little eyes closed, long, dark lashes fluttering against rounded cheeks, and then he was still. She kissed his head and hummed softly. It seemed so natural. Her own baby had trained her well, though she didn't want to think about that. Blocking out the past was a part of accepting the present for her right now. She'd done a lot of time in her own personal agony and she couldn't live that way forever. But she'd spent much too long trying to avoid all contact with babies, hoping to avoid the pain memories brought with them. Now that she'd been thrust into this situation and forced to deal with it, she found she was in a special sort of heaven and she didn't even look up when the men came back into the room. She was floating on feelings and ignoring everything else.

When she heard the woman's voice she looked up in surprise, but hardly paid attention as the older lady left the room, Tito leaving close behind her. Vaguely, she was aware that this had been the babysitter and that Tito was driving the woman home, but it seemed to have nothing much to do with her enjoyment of this wonderful baby.

Max watched her for a moment, surprised to see how quickly she'd adapted to a style of nurturing he didn't remotely understand.

"So, what do you think of him?" he asked.

"He's a duck," she murmured, smiling wistfully as she hugged him close and rocked him. "A sweet little baby duck. I don't ever want to put him down."

He nodded. "He looks pretty good to me, too. As long as he's not crying."

She flashed a startled look at the tall man beside her. She'd had dealings with a man who was irrationally bothered by a baby crying. It wasn't a good thing. But she calmed down immediately. After all, what he'd said was probably a common complaint.

"Who is he?" she asked, stroking the hair on his little head. "What's the connection?"

He hesitated, then decided he might as well tell the truth. "He's my brother's child," he said. "At least, that's the assumption. We'll find out after DNA testing is done."

She drew back. Something didn't sit well with her. All the sense of well-being brought on by holding this baby seemed to melt away quickly.

"He's your brother's baby and you've never seen him before?" She frowned, searching his face for clues.

He shrugged. "I've been in Italy," he said, as though that explained everything.

She made a face. "Where's your brother? Or the baby's mother, for that matter?"

"Good question." He decided to ignore the part about his brother. "We don't know. She seems to have disappeared. The babysitter said she should have been back days ago."

She nodded, taking that in. "So I guess you're going to call the police?"

Without missing a beat, he said firmly, "No. Not yet."

"But…"

He moved impatiently. "Listen C.J., this is really none of your affair. I've been involved in the search for this baby for weeks now. We've finally found him and we'll do what we think necessary."

She shook her head, exasperated. "Why do you keep calling me that?" she asked. "My name is Cari. It's a fine name and it doesn't need shortening to C.J."

He raised a dark eyebrow. "A little formal, isn't it? You actually want me to call you Miss Kerry all the time?"

"No." He was such an annoying man. "Drop the 'miss'. I'm not a Southern belle."

He looked puzzled. "Let me get this straight. You want to be called by your last name?"

"Cari isn't my last name," she interjected quickly. "I don't know where you got that idea. It's my given name. Just plain Cari. And there's no *J* involved at all."

He shook his head, bewildered by that. "Your name is Celinia Jade Kerry, right?"

"No." She wrinkled her nose in distaste at the silly name he was trying to pin on her. "My name is Cari Christensen. That's been my name for quite some time now. In fact, it's official, and I've got proof. Want to see my driver's license?"

He stared into her clear blue eyes for a long moment. She certainly looked like a woman telling the absolute truth. The light began to dawn. Something had been a little off about this entire operation from the start. She hadn't fit the profile he was expecting. He should have trusted his instincts. And now—what the hell had he done? This was the wrong woman.

"Uh-oh," he said at last.

CHAPTER THREE

CARI sighed, impatience building ever higher as she hugged the baby to her chest. This date had been strange from the start, but it was getting stranger.

First this man had turned out to be so incredibly different from what she'd expected. Then there was the Italian element—not to mention the accent. The mother on the phone. Abandoned babies in dirty apartments. An assistant named Tito. If she hadn't known better, she might think she'd landed in the middle of a scene from a bad B movie and was caught up in some really crazy dialogue. Mara had not forewarned her of all of this.

"Listen, Randy," she began, eyes flashing as she prepared to read him the riot act.

His own eyes widened and his head went back. "Who the hell is Randy?" he demanded.

Shock jolted through her. This man wasn't Randy? This man wasn't the one she'd been waiting for, the one her friend had set her up with? This wasn't her blind date?

But of course he wasn't. Hadn't she suspected that

all along? The scales fell from her eyes—so to speak. This wasn't Mara's husband's cousin after all. And that just about explained everything.

"Aren't you Randy Jeffington?" she asked, though by now she knew darn well he wasn't.

He shook his head, looking like a man who expected all things in his path to snap into place and had been sorely disappointed once again—a man who was planning to make sure someone paid for this.

"Never heard of him," he growled at her.

"Uh-oh," she echoed softly, swaying and feeling just a bit unsteady on her feet.

Suddenly she had a clear and shining picture of a tall, sandy-haired man in glasses carrying a red rose. She'd seen him just as they were leaving the club and she now had an epiphany. That, no doubt, was Randy. Poor guy.

But something in the back of her mind had known all along, hadn't it? This handsome figure standing before her was just too good to be true. Or too bad, as the case might be.

And poor Randy Jeffington. Was he still wandering around the Longhorn Lounge looking for her? Her hand went to her mouth, her eyes huge.

"Omigosh. We've got to go back."

He nodded grimly. "You've got that right. We've got the wrong dates."

"There must be a woman named…whatever that weird name you said was…waiting for you back there."

"Holding a red rose."

"Oh, no." She grimaced tragically. "Too bad we all picked the same color, isn't it?"

He was still glowering at her. "Too bad we didn't get identities straight from the beginning," he said curtly.

She frowned, shifting the baby from one hip to the other and trying to remember how it had happened. "You called me Miss Cari. My name is Cari, with a *C*. I thought—"

"I called you Miss Kerry with a *K*."

"Oh. Well, it was hard to know that at the time."

"It was perfectly straightforward. You should have guessed."

"*I* should have guessed? What about *you?* You acted like you were sure I was the one. I sort of just... followed along—like a dummy." She frowned, remembering how she'd almost been in a trance. She could hardly believe that a man like this was the Randy she was waiting for. And it turned out she was right. She sighed plaintively.

"Oh, well. What's done is done. Now we have to do our best to undo it."

"Exactly." He glanced down at the sleeping baby in her arms, then around the simple room. "Let's get out of here."

She looked down at the baby. "Are we taking him with us?"

"Well, we're not going to leave him here."

"No, I suppose not." She bit her lip. This didn't seem right, but she didn't know what else they could do.

From the crib, she picked up a blanket and wrapped it around the baby while he picked up the diaper bag. Looking up, she sighed as her gaze traveled over the handsome man who'd brought her here. He was like a mythic figure, so tall and strong with matinee-idol looks. When something seemed too good to be true, you had to know it was likely to be so. Oh well, this had been interesting.

"So what is your name, anyway?" she asked as they looked around the apartment to make sure they weren't forgetting anything.

"Max," he said grimly. "Max Angeli."

"And I'm Cari Christensen."

He looked down at her and almost had to smile. She seemed to be able to maintain a sunny personality despite all odds against it. In contrast to what he was feeling himself, which was dour indeed. "You said that."

"I thought you might not have caught it in the heat of the moment."

He nodded, mouth twisting. "I wish you'd mentioned it while we were still at the club," he said. "There you were waving at me with that damn red rose."

"Oh!" She stopped and glared at him. "You're not going to blame this whole catastrophe on me."

He liked the fire in her eyes. She wasn't his type and he would never have picked her out of a crowd, but there was something appealing about her just the same. He liked the liveliness of her reactions and he couldn't resist teasing her a bit.

"Why not?" he said with a careless shrug. "If you'd been on your toes, this wouldn't have happened. You made me stand up the woman I was supposed to be with. You may have killed that relationship."

"And you messed up my date with Randy," she reminded him, though she was beginning to realize he wasn't really serious.

"Wasn't it a blind date?" he asked her as they headed out of the apartment. He turned back to make sure the door was locked. "And you know what they say about love."

"I know they say love is blind, but I think you have to give it a chance to grow before you can kill it."

"Murderess," he muttered, choking back a smile.

She sighed, glancing at him sideways. "You're not exactly the Lone Ranger, my friend," she chided, teasing him back now. "For all you know, you may have destroyed a great love affair."

He raised a skeptical eyebrow. "You and Randy?"

"Sure. Why not?" She made a face at him. "Romeo and Juliet. Anthony and Cleopatra. Debbie Reynolds and Eddie Fisher." She struck a pose. "The names Cari and Randy might have belonged right up there with them all."

"All doomed to tragedy," he noted helpfully. "If a great passion is meant to be it'll take more than a missed connection to destroy it."

"Perhaps." She flashed him a smile. "And yours, too."

His laugh was short and humorless. "C.J. and I aren't

meant for love," he said cynically. "But we are destined to make beautiful music together."

She looked at him with bewilderment. "How can you know that when you don't even know who she is?"

He knew enough about C.J. to know she was meant—unfortunately—to be very important in his life. He might not know what she looked like, but he had her number, just the same. His smile was bittersweet as he shrugged, pushing open the outer door to the building for her.

"Destiny is relentless."

"Destiny. Such a strong word."

But all that was forgotten as she looked at what they were heading into.

"It's starting to rain," she said with dismay, just as they stepped outside and the door clicked shut behind them.

"Yes," Max said, wondering what else could go wrong. Just another layer of bad luck he supposed. But this was getting monotonous.

"Where's the car?" she asked.

"The car?"

He looked where he'd parked it. The space was empty. His first thought was—did Tito take it? But no. He glanced at the driveway. Tito's rental car was gone. He looked back at the place where he'd left his newly minted beauty. Sure enough, it was gone, too. His heart sank. And now he knew what else could go wrong.

He swore coldly and obscenely, and she pulled the baby closer, frowning at him, even though the words were in Italian. Reaching into his pocket, he realized he'd left his mobile in the car, which had now been stolen. He swore again.

"Where's your phone?" he asked curtly.

She shook her head. "I forgot to bring it," she said.

He stared at her, unable to believe this string of bad luck wasn't over yet.

"My car's been stolen. You have no phone. I have no phone. We just locked ourselves out of the building and it's starting to rain."

She sighed, shoulders sagging. That was quite a litany of woes. "We're also stuck in the middle of a rather bad neighborhood," she reminded him, looking around at the menacing shadows.

"Not for long." He picked up the diaper bag and glanced down the street. The lights from downtown were visible in the sky. It was quite evident which way they needed to travel. "We're going to have to walk, at least until we can flag down a cab. Let's go. The sooner we start out, the sooner we'll get there."

Cari looked down at her three-inch heels. "Okay," she said sadly, trying to smile.

He looked down at them, too. "Those shoes aren't made for walking," he noted dryly.

That was certainly a fact, but her feet sure were cute in them, and what that angle did to her beautiful legs was beyond mentioning. He swallowed hard as the thought came and nestled into his senses. Raising his gaze to her clear blue eyes, he got another jolt of erotic sensation and he shook his head, trying to stave it off. This was no time to let his libido go wild.

"I could carry you," he said gruffly, still holding her gaze with his own. "But with the baby and all…"

"You will not!" she retorted, taking a step away from him. "I can walk. Believe me, I've done it for years." She started off down the street, just to prove it. "I'll carry the baby. You get the diaper bag. It's heavier."

They set off into the dark neighborhood, trying to ignore the drizzle. Most of the buildings seemed to be industrial and there was no sign of life coming from any that lined the street they were hurrying down. It was downright spooky.

Max pushed all thought about his beautiful Ferrari out of his mind. There was no point in mourning over a car when he had so many other things to worry about. An occasional driver went by, driving too fast to be flagged down, and there were no people out on the street—at least, none that made their presence known. But there was an eerie feeling, a sort of vague menace. This was not the sort of neighborhood either one of them would have wandered into voluntarily. Bad things tended to happen at night in areas like this.

Cari was feeling the creepiness as well, and instinctively she held the baby closer. Looking down, she felt a quick surge of tenderness for the child. Babies should be protected from harm and that was what adults where there for. But just as she had that thought, a flash of pain sliced through her. If only she'd been able to protect her own baby from harm. If only Brian had been more careful. If only…

No. She shook the regrets away. She'd been down that road so many times. Right after the accident that took her husband and her baby, she'd spent months almost drowning in recriminations, all the old "if only" cries of the heart. It had taken time and a bit of counseling to help her pull out of that downward spiral and she never wanted to take a plunge like that again. You could either immerse yourself in the past and die bit by bit, or reach out to the future and make a new life. Slowly, painfully, she was trying to do the latter.

But for now the past was useful in the training she'd had with her own baby. She seemed to bond naturally with this one, and that felt better than she had any right to expect.

So she looked over her shoulder, wishing they were in a better neighborhood.

"Do you have a weapon with you?" she asked Max, not really expecting him to answer in the affirmative, just expressing trepidation.

"Unfortunately, I forgot to bring my Glock," he quipped, but she noticed he took a quick look over his shoulder as well. "If only I'd known I'd need it."

"There you go," she said lightly. "I guess you were never a Boy Scout."

He gave her a long sideways look. "What would that have done for me?"

She shrugged her free shoulder and pulled the baby

more closely to the other one. "You'd have known about their motto. Be Prepared."

"Oh, I'm prepared."

"Still, you're not a real Texan, are you?" She sighed, pretending it was such a pity.

That was meant to get his goat and it did the job.

"I'm Italian," he said with quick native pride. "That's just as good, you know." He grunted. "On second thought, it's better."

"Is it?" She gave him a mockingly taunting look. "From what I hear, Italians are pretty emotional, compared to Texans. They talk real fast, yell a lot, say outlandish things."

"Sort of like Texans?" He got the joke, but he grinned and played along. "Why not? We enjoy life more than most people do. What's more, we're warm, loyal and generous to a fault." His voice dropped in a husky way that was meant to make her senses quiver. "And we're the most passionate lovers on earth."

She was glad the darkness hid how hot her cheeks suddenly became. The surge of warmth surprised her. She'd fallen for this guy's good looks and masculinity from the first, but in a reserved way, the way she dealt with most of life. She usually didn't let emotions— or even attractions—down into her inner core. Her heart was protected by a thick wall of experience, not much of it good. Had she actually allowed this handsome Italian to get to her? She couldn't let that happen.

"Well, good for you," she said as lightly as she could manage. "I guess Miss C. J. Kerry will be glad to hear it."

He frowned, not pleased to be reminded of the mess this evening had turned into. He wasn't happy that he'd done anything to put Celinia Jade Kerry in a hostile mood. He needed her happy and compliant. The woman might be short on cash, but to a female, a sense of having been overlooked and ignored for another could blot all that out. He was going to have to be very tactful with the lady—tactful and apologetic.

Still, the night wasn't a total loss at all. They had found Gino's baby. Just an hour before, he hadn't been sure there really was a baby. And now Jamie was in Cari's arms and on his way to a complete medical checkup and a DNA test.

The fact that baby Jamie's mother was missing disturbed him, and yet it made things easier in the short run. Eventually, he had no doubt they would find her. For just a moment he imagined what it would be like for his mother when he returned to Venice with Gino's baby in tow—and hopefully, the deed to her family ranch in hand. Maybe that would erase some of the sadness from her eyes and bring back just a touch of joy to her life. That had been his goal from the start of this adventure. His mother's happiness meant a lot to him.

Lost in thought, he didn't notice the small group of nasty neighborhood thugs until they stepped out in front of them, blocking their way. The effect on his danger radar was immediate, though. He stopped Cari and the baby with an outstretched arm, putting his body between her and the three gang-bangers.

"What do you want?" he barked at them.

"I don't know, man," one of them sneered. Tall and thin, he wore a red bandanna tied tightly around his head. "What you got?"

"Nothing that will do you any good," he said. "Let us pass."

The one who had spoken before gave an ugly laugh. "No way," he said, and suddenly there was the flash of a knife in his hand.

Max stared at the knife, knowing this was not good. What a night. This, on top of all the rest, just about did it for him. How much bad luck could one night bring? Fed up, he let his inner Italian take over. Moving toward the men in an aggressive rather than a defensive manner, he began to curse loud and long, in Italian, shouting at the men, shaking his fist at them for good measure. Instead of allowing himself to be the victim, *he* was threatening *them*.

Cari watched, her heart in her throat, fear sizzling through her. From every advice column she'd ever read, this seemed to be exactly the wrong way to go about this and she knew it. This could end very badly. But in the meantime, what could she do? Should she run? Not in these shoes. There was no chance. Everything in her wanted to protect the baby. But the way Max was acting, she was very much afraid she was going to see the knife slashing into his chest any moment.

And then what?

Still, it didn't seem to be playing out quite the way she'd expected. To her surprise, the shortest of the men was pulling on the arm of the one with the knife.

"Hold on," he was saying. "Just hold up, dude. Look at the guy."

"Hey, get a load of that suit," the third was saying nervously. "And listen to the way he talks. I think he's Mafia, dude. You don't want to screw with those guys."

"Mafia?" The three of them stared hard at Max who was still cursing. "Hey, they can mess you up bad."

"It's not worth it, dude," the one with the knife said at last, backing away. "Let's get out of here."

And they vanished as suddenly as they had appeared.

Max and Cari both stood very still, letting the adrenaline slow down, getting their breathing back to normal.

"Is that it?" she said at last.

"It seems to be," he responded. He turned and came back quickly, taking her by the shoulders and staring down into her eyes. "Are you okay?" he asked intensely.

She nodded, still too shaken to say much. Being almost mugged by thugs was enough to ruin a perfectly good evening walk, but watching Max explode like a smoldering volcano had been almost as shocking. She'd never seen a man do that before.

"Good." He let out a long breath. "We're lucky they gave up so easily."

She nodded, finally finding her voice. "Wow, I guess you don't need a weapon after all," she said, looking at him with reluctant admiration.

He brushed it off. He knew how to handle himself and he'd been pretty confident, even with three men opposing him, until he'd seen the knife. That could change everything. Luckily, they had weighed the odds and decided not to risk annoying the mob.

Though that made him want to smile. Some people thought anyone Italian had ties to gangsters. That was an ignorant assumption, but it had come in handy this time.

"Okay, let's go. We've got to get out of this neighborhood. Places like this seem to breed thugs like rats thriving in the shadows. Let's head for streets that are better lit. That way I think." He pointed down another street and they headed in that direction, moving quickly.

Her feet were aching, but she ignored it. She'd go barefoot if she had to. Anything to get out of this part of town.

"Hold tight to the baby," Max ordered suddenly, slinging the diaper bag up over his shoulder.

She looked up, startled, and the next thing she knew, he'd bent to slide support under her legs and was swinging her up into his arms, baby and all. She squeaked in protest, but he ignored her.

"You're going to trip in those shoes," he told her. "I can handle it. Just hold on."

She held on and somehow, it worked. He cradled them both in a warm, muscular embrace and walked firmly along the wet sidewalk. She clung to the space just above his chest and beneath his chin and closed her eyes, reveling in the sense of his masculine strength. His heart was beating against her shoulder. She let herself fall into a sort of daze, listening to the rhythm and soaking up the whole of him.

He moved quickly, wondering how he'd let himself get into this insane situation. She was light as a feather, despite the added weight of the baby, and she smelled like a garden in sunshine. Strands of her blond hair flew up and tickled his nose, which he found tantalizing rather than annoying. All in all, she was warm and soft and round and he felt like a Neanderthal. He wanted to take her home and keep her—preferably in his bed.

This wasn't right. She wasn't meant for him. In fact, he had other fish to fry, and he was late for the barbecue. But she seemed so small and vulnerable in his arms and he couldn't resist filling his head with her fresh, intoxicating scent.

A few steps more and they were around the corner, and suddenly cars were whizzing past and the streetlights actually lit up the street instead of just muddying the atmosphere.

"Civilization," Max muttered, lowering Cari to the ground carefully and looking up and down the road. "But still no cabs."

And more rain. Thunder rolled and the heavens opened up.

"This way, quickly," he shouted, pulling her and the baby along until he got them under the limited protection of an empty bus stop shelter. They dashed inside and quickly clung together, trying to stay out of the spray, as water poured off the rounded roof of the tiny kiosk, shooting all around them. After the first moment or two, Cari looked up and realized just how close they were standing. Her nose almost touched his chin.

"Oh," she said, thinking she should pull back. Being this close when she was being carried was one thing, but this was ridiculous.

"No." Reaching out, he held the two of them against his chest. "You'll just get wet."

"But…" She bit her lip, not sure what to say or where to look.

"Don't worry," he said, his voice so low she could hardly hear it over the rain. "I don't bite."

"Don't you?" She heard herself say the words and winced, knowing they sounded almost as though she were flirting. She hadn't meant to do that.

The way his mouth twisted in a half grin let her know he'd heard it that way, too. "I suppose I could be convinced," he said softly.

She gazed into his dark eyes and somehow couldn't look anywhere else. The sound of the rain, the momentary isolation, the way they were pressed so closely, all blended together to weave an enchantment around them. He was going to kiss her. She could see it in his eyes. And if she didn't watch out, she was going to end up kissing him back.

"No," she murmured, trying to dredge up the strength to resist.

"Yes," he countered, lowering his lips to hers.

"No," she said again, shaking her head.

"Why not?" he asked, so close to her.

"The baby…"

"The baby's asleep. He can't see a thing."

"This is all wrong." Looking up, she searched his eyes. "We're not even supposed to be on this date."

"This isn't a date," he said, his own eyes deep and smoky with something nameless that set her pulse pounding. "It's an encounter. A moment in time." He dropped a quick kiss on her lips. "A bit of magic. You'll forget all about it by morning."

"I don't think so," she said with a sigh. "You really shouldn't…"

"But I want to," he said huskily. "And you taste so good."

And then he took her mouth with his and kissed her like she'd never been kissed before.

CHAPTER FOUR

IN THE harsh and revealing sunlight of morning, it all looked a bit fantastical. Cari buried her face in her pillow and wished she'd done a better job pulling together the drapes on her tall windows before she'd gone to sleep. She wasn't ready to face reality yet. Did last night really happen? Impossible.

The phone rang, but she let the answering machine take it. Her heart thumped as she waited for the voice she knew was coming.

"Cari?"

Yes. It was Max. His deep baritone sent chills all through her system. She drew in a shuddering breath.

"Go away," she whispered into the empty air.

"Cari? Surely you are there. I wouldn't bother you so early, but I need a bit of advice. If you could pick up…"

She knew she shouldn't pick up. In her sleepy, morning state, she imagined herself standing at a fork in the road. Her life could go one way or the other, depending on what she did in the next few moments.

She knew what she should do. She should mark the whole experience from the night before as lessons learned and move on. She had to ignore him. Go back to real life and not fool around with fairy-tale princes who came breezing in from Italy with a knowing smile and a boatload of hunkiness. She shouldn't pick up. She knew better. She wasn't going to do it.

"Cari? Please?"

She writhed beneath her covers. Don't do it, Cari!

"Cari, it's about the baby."

The baby? Well, if it was about the baby…

"Cari?"

With a sigh she reached out and picked up.

"Hello," she said somewhat mournfully.

"Buongiorno," he responded.

There was a long pause while neither of them said anything. Cari wondered if he was as hesitant about this as she was. After all, last night it had been assumed they would probably never see each other again. Hadn't it?

He'd kissed her and she'd swooned. Yes, there was no way to deny it. She'd gone all gaga on him. Luckily a cab had come cruising up before she'd made a complete fool out of herself, and they'd piled in and raced back to the Longhorn Lounge where they'd found Tito waiting anxiously. The two dates they should have been with were long gone, of course. That was only natural. Tito then left for the hotel with the baby while Max headed for the police station to make a stolen car report. And

Cari had slipped into her own car and turned toward home, still tingling. Still swooning. Still out of her mind!

But pretty darn sure she would never see or hear from him again. After all, their little—what had he called it? Their encounter? Whatever it was, it had been illegitimate in the first place. Time to wipe it out of her life and her mind.

Only, here he was on the telephone.

"How did you find my number?" she asked at last.

"I have people on my staff who can find these things for me."

"Oh."

She supposed he meant Tito. Or were there others? Hmm. She wasn't sure she liked that.

"How is he?" she asked.

"Who? The baby?"

"Yes."

"Okay."

"Has his mother shown up?"

"No. I've got someone monitoring the apartment periodically, just in case."

"Good." She couldn't imagine what could have kept a mother away from that beautiful baby. "But you said there was some sort of problem?" she asked quickly. That was what she'd picked up for, after all.

"Not exactly a real problem," he said. "But…I've hired a live-in nanny."

"Oh. Well, good. You checked her references?"

"Of course."

She let out a long breath. She didn't let herself think a lot about the baby she'd held so closely the night before. That was all a part of that other fork in the road she wasn't going to take—even if she had picked up the phone.

"Okay, then."

She waited. He had something else to say, but he was having trouble getting it out. She could picture him looking thoughtful, brow furrowed, then she blinked that image away. If she kept doing that sort of thing, she would be swooning again.

"Max, what is it?"

"Nothing, really, it's just that…" He sighed. "Listen, I'm just not sure about this nanny thing. I did the regular vetting, but what the hell do I know about nannies? Or babies, for that matter. And you seem to know a lot. So I thought maybe you could come over and see if you think she knows what she's doing."

Wow. He needed her. That was almost enough to get those tingles started again. Everything in her wanted to say yes. She cared about the baby, but there was more. To see him again, be with him doing something important, wouldn't that be ideal? But no, that would be wrong—on so many levels. So she didn't say yes.

"No," she said instead. Then she waited for the rush of self-congratulations that would surely follow. Funny, but that didn't happen. "I'm sorry, Max," she went on, falling back on the honest truth. "I've got to go to work."

"Work? You work?"

It almost made her smile to realize how little they knew about each other. They'd shared a night of intense emotions and setbacks, more in one night than she'd had in months. She felt as if she'd glimpsed a clear picture of his character, his personality. And yet she didn't know much about him, what he'd done with his life, what he cared about, and he didn't know those things about her, either. But they were going to leave it that way for the most part. At least, she knew they should.

"Of course I work. What do you think I live on? Air?"

"What do you do?"

He sounded candidly surprised and interested. What the heck? Didn't he know any women who actually had real jobs? She licked her lips and stuck to the facts.

"I'm a waitress."

"At a supper club?"

"No. In a local coffee shop."

There. That ought to be guaranteed to turn him off. She was just a waitress. Not one of those high-falutin', jet-settin' fashion models he was surely used to.

She was also the assistant manager and studying for her real estate license, but he didn't need to know all that. After all, she wasn't trying to impress him. She was trying to get rid of him.

"Take a day off," he said bluntly.

"I can't do that. People are counting on me."

"And I'm counting on you, too."

"Yes, but you don't pay the bills."

"I could do that," he said, as though it was a new idea and he rather liked it. "That's it. I'll pay you a salary. I'll hire you."

"Nonsense." Her voice was quivering a bit and she bit down on her lip. No! She was not going to give in to that sort of crazy temptation.

"But it would be perfect."

"For you, not for me."

"No?"

"No."

"Consider it, at least."

"No." She was firm. And darn proud of herself, too. "You'll be fine with this nanny person."

He hesitated, then said skeptically, "I hope you're right."

There was another long pause.

"Everything is all right, then?" she prodded. "I mean, everything else?"

"Oh, yes. Going great. I had the baby checked out by a pediatrician first thing, and we've put in a request for a DNA test. I've arranged for the delivery of the relevant charts from Italy. It will all take time, but everything is moving along."

"Good."

Why was he still hanging on? She was torn, wanting him gone, yet enjoying this more than she ought to. "Well, have you gotten in touch with your date from last night yet?" she asked, suddenly remembering there was still that issue to be dealt with.

There was yet another hesitation, then he answered, "Not yet. How about you?"

She sighed. Apologizing to Randy wasn't something she was looking forward to. "No, not yet. But it's early. I wouldn't want to wake him up."

Something in the pause this time was electric, and finally he said softly, "Did I wake you?"

Warmth flooded her body. How did he manage to make one simple question imply a wealth of intimate contact? Something in his tone, the low, husky quality of his voice, conjured up a picture of the way he might awaken her, his hand sliding down beneath the sheets, his lips leaving a trail of hot kisses. She suppressed a gasp.

This was ridiculous. She wasn't a schoolgirl. She was a grown woman. She'd been married, for heaven's sake! She knew what it was like to have a man in her bed.

But not this man. Oh, my!

She wasn't going to answer his provocative question. She had to think of something else, quick. Something to break the mood and put an end to this.

"I've been up for hours," she lied shamelessly. "I've got a life, you know. Things to do. Places to go."

"And you'd like to get back to it," he said softly, taking the hint. He sighed. "All right, Cari. I'll let you go."

Her fingers were so tight on the receiver, they were beginning to ache. "Thanks."

"So that's it, then."

She blinked, suddenly feeling almost weepy. "It seems to be."

"It was nice knowing you, Cari."

"Yes. Same here." Now her eyes were definitely stinging. Ridiculous! "Goodbye."

"*Ciao.*"

She hung up, said a word she hardly ever said, and threw a stuffed animal against the wall.

Cari was just finishing up a bowl of morning cereal when Mara called.

"So," said Mara brightly. "How was it?"

"How was what?" Cari answered, her mind still stuck on mulling over her conversation with Max.

"The date with Randy."

"Oh. Uh…" She grimaced, putting her spoon into the bowl and pushing it away across the counter. "Well, actually, we didn't have it."

"What do you mean you didn't have it? Don't tell me you chickened out?"

Mara's voice was sharp with what was fast working into a sense of outrage. Cari tried to nip that in the bud.

"No, Mara, I did not chicken out. I was there with bells on. And I waited for quite some time. But then…" She sighed. This really wasn't all that easy to explain. "Well, I kind of went off with the wrong man."

"What?" There was still an edge to Mara's voice. "How did you do that, exactly?"

"Believe me, it was not that hard. Not when he came up carrying a red rose, just like you told *me* to do for Randy, and he seemed to call me by my name and…

and…" She sighed. "It's kind of hard to explain. Listen, I've got the lunch shift. I'll swing by on my way to work. We'll talk."

"I guess. Okay."

Mara sounded grumpy. Cari knew she was disappointed. She thought she'd planned the perfect date for a good friend and it had all gone wrong. Who wouldn't be disappointed? And Mara had been so excited. She groaned internally. But she would take care of things when she stopped by her friend's house. Face-to-face it might actually be possible to give her a better picture of exactly what had happened.

"In the meantime, uh, do you have Randy's number?"

She was tempted to put it off for a while, but she steeled herself and called the man. Once she had him on the phone and explained who she was, he reacted well. Instead of demanding an explanation, he was apologetic that he'd been a little late.

Which only made her feel more guilty. It was hard to explain why she'd dumped him for some suave Italian guy. There was no good excuse for it, actually. One look into Max's deep dark eyes had mesmerized her and she'd been ready to follow him anywhere. But how could she tell Randy that?

"Well, it was certainly an interesting evening," he said. "I haven't had many like that."

He sounded just as likable as Mara had said. She was impressed that he didn't seem at all disgruntled. She had a quick flashback to how her husband, Brian, would have reacted to what had happened, and the memory of his volatile temper made her cringe.

"Did you wait for long?"

"Only for an hour or so." He chuckled. "Actually, I met the woman who was supposed to be dating the man you ran off with."

"Ran off with" seemed a bit harsh, but she let it go. After all, the man deserved a little dig here and there, didn't he? He'd paid his dues.

"Oh. C.J.?"

"Celinia Jade. Do you know her?"

"No, I don't, but Max told me something about her."

"Well, she's somethin' else."

His voice conveyed a sense of awe. Cari tensed a bit.

"Is she?"

"Oh, yeah. She's dynamite."

For some reason, that didn't make her smile. She chewed on her lip and wondered if Max was going to be as impressed with the woman once they got together. But what did that matter, anyway? Grimacing, she avoided the impulse to slap herself.

"We were both wandering around with red roses," Randy went on. "So we started talking. It didn't take us long to figure out what must have happened. So we hung out for a while, sort of commiserated, so to speak." He chuckled again. "She had some funny stories to tell. That passed the time for a while. But when y'all didn't come back, we called it a night and headed home."

She nodded. It sounded like he'd enjoyed the evening

with C.J. as much as he might have with her. Maybe more. She frowned at the trend in her own thoughts.

"So it wasn't a total waste," she said quickly.

"Oh, no, not at all."

"Well, would you like to try it again tonight?" she said, knowing she pretty much had to suggest it. "I sort of promised Mara I would."

"I guess we both promised Mara, didn't we?"

"She can be persuasive."

"Oh, yes." He chuckled again. He seemed a happy sort. "Let's do it," he agreed. "Only this time, why don't I pick you up at your place? I'm not sure that red rose thing works very well."

She hesitated. The rationale for meeting at the club had been to avoid letting a strange man know where she lived. She was wary these days. She didn't want to risk any man getting the upper hand in a relationship. But he seemed so genuinely nice, she decided it wouldn't hurt to give him her address.

Maybe all would go great. Maybe she and Randy would get along so well, the crazy night with Max would be forgotten, a relic of history, a strange interlude in what she was hoping to turn into a sensible, placid life. Maybe.

Max was restless. He'd spent the afternoon hovering over the nanny, second-guessing everything she did. She'd snapped at him once, and he'd almost fired her. But he'd quickly realized that he had no replacement lined up. If she left, he would be on his own. And what he knew about taking care of babies could be blurted out in one quick epithet.

Tito was no help. Every time the baby cried, he stuffed cotton in his ears and went out on the hotel room balcony, plunked himself down into a plastic chair and tried to sleep. But Max couldn't sleep. His existence was caught up in this baby for now, and that was all he could think about.

That, and Cari Christensen. She was the one person he knew who could help solve a lot of his problems. But he had to forget about her.

He'd come to Dallas with two clear goals in mind. First, he'd wanted to find Sheila and discover if the baby she claimed she had was really Gino's. That was pretty much in the works. He had no idea where Sheila was, but when you came right down to it, that didn't matter. He had the baby. And he would soon know the truth about the baby's parentage.

He'd never been a baby person, never been around the little things. And he hadn't expected to feel much of anything for this one. Babies were nothing but potential people—little blobs of flesh and noise. Puppies had more personality.

But the funny thing was, he'd felt something of an instant connection when he'd seen baby Jamie. One look at that little face had torn a hole in his heart. He was as sure of this as anything—this baby was his brother's.

When word had come that Gino had died in the crash

of the plane he was testing out, Max had felt his world tilt on its axis. His big brother had been his guiding star all his life. For a long time, he'd thought he might never feel joy again.

But he'd had to suppress any overt mourning, because his mother's despair had been so deep and so complete it had taken all his effort to pull her out of what he was afraid could have developed into a suicidal impulse at any moment. And now, to think he might be able to bring her Gino's baby—the thought took his breath away. He couldn't allow himself to get too invested in this until the tests proved the connection. But he was pretty sure what the results would be.

His other goal had been to find a way to wrest the Triple M Ranch from the daughter of his mother's old rival. That wasn't going so well. But he hadn't really concentrated on it as yet, so there was plenty of time to figure out ways to succeed there, too. He'd contacted Celinia Jade, or C.J. as he preferred to call her—and she didn't seem to mind—who came across as something of an airhead at first. But in no time at all, he'd noticed a sharp turn of mind that sent up warning flags. The woman might talk like she had nothing in her mind but fluff, but underneath there was a steely sense of purpose. She knew what she wanted, and she wasn't going to be easy to snow. He might have more trouble there than he'd anticipated.

They had made plans to try to meet again tonight, same time, same place. This time he was going to make damn sure he had the right woman. No more screwups.

He was going to be pure Mediterranean charm and solicitude. The woman wouldn't know what hit her.

He knew what he was doing. His life for the past ten years had been immersed in real estate—big real estate, big deals. This was nothing. It should be a piece of cake. C.J. was in financial trouble and he planned to make a very nice offer for the ranch. He was prepared to be fair, generous, even. He wasn't out to cheat anyone. His mother seemed to think emotional ties would make it hard for her to sell, but he had his doubts. When faced with the facts, he was pretty sure he would be able to make her see the light.

If he could return to Italy with the deed to the ranch in one hand and Gino's baby in the other, some of the heartbreak that shadowed his mother's eyes might fade a bit. That was his hope.

The baby was crying again. He paced the floor for a few minutes, then gave in to the urge to go into the nursery they had rigged up in the smallest bedroom of this lavish hotel suite and see what was going on. Mrs. Turner, the nanny, was sitting in the rocking chair, reading a mystery novel. Meanwhile, Jamie was turning bright red as he cried his little heart out.

"The baby's crying," he pointed out sharply.

Mrs. Turner looked up and nodded, glaring at him. "It's good for him to cry. It develops his lungs."

He was nothing if not skeptical, but he hesitated. "Really?"

"Absolutely." She gave him the supercilious smirk he

was growing to hate. "Why else would they have that ability?"

He gritted his teeth. "I thought it was so they could let people know they needed help."

She smiled as though he were a poor fool who knew nothing about children. "That's only part of it. You can't baby them, you know. You mustn't spoil them, even at the infant stage. It's best to encourage them to grow and stretch themselves. You wouldn't want the poor dear to fall behind in development, now would you?"

He wanted to argue, but he had no ammunition. What did he know about this, anyway?

"I suppose you know best," he grumbled, turning away. But the picture of Jamie's little tragic face, all twisted with grief, staying in his mind.

Back out in the living room, he went to the folder where he was keeping his papers and pulled out the certificate that was meant to guarantee the expertise of the nanny. Maybe he should give the school that issued it a call. He frowned. Or maybe he should just call Cari and see what she thought.

His hand was already on the telephone receiver when he stopped himself. No, he couldn't do that. He had to break all ties with the woman. That was the only way he would ever get her out of his head. He couldn't let himself think about Cari and her sweet, pretty face. He'd set his sights on charming C.J. and that was where they had to stay. Swearing, he reached for the cotton to put in his ear and started out to join Tito on the balcony.

* * *

The Copper Penny where Cari worked was just off the interstate. A mix of locals and tourists patronized the trim little café. She liked the early afternoon when the hectic lunch crowd had dwindled down to a few house-wives lingering over coffee and the assorted cowboys who came in from riding fences at some of the nearby ranches. The easy camaraderie was what she liked best about her job. It was pretty much the same group of cowhands that came in every day. One by one, most had tried to hit on her, but in a relaxed, friendly way that never got serious. She could swat their propositions aside like a mama dog controlling her puppies. Few took offense, and those that did were easily joked out of it.

Today Cari wasn't doing any joking. Her mind was on other things and she poured coffee and took orders with a distracted air. The men she served were a blur to her. Her thoughts were full of Max.

"I've just got to think about him as much as I can now, so I can be done with him and get him out of my head," she told herself impatiently. It was a plan, but she wasn't at all sure it was a plan that was going to work.

She'd known from the moment he'd walked into the club that he was absolutely the wrong man for her. Too tall, too handsome, too arrogant, too sure of his right to command the attention of everyone there.

Her husband had been like that in a way. Well, not so tall, not so handsome, and not so full of self-confidence. But he'd had the arrogance down pat. Brian had mostly been frustrated in his attempts to take charge of the rest of the world. He'd had a bit more success in boxing her in with his small life and visions. And he'd managed to make her life miserable because of it.

The autocratic husband was the worst kind, as far as she was concerned. She wasn't sure she ever wanted another man in her life at all, but if she did decide to try another relationship, it sure wouldn't be with a man like Brian. Or Max, for that matter.

"That's why Randy is so perfect for you," Mara had pointed out when she'd stopped by to see her and try to explain how she'd ended up on a date with the wrong man. "You've really got to get to know him. You'll have to date him more than once to really give him a chance."

"Oh, Mara, I don't know. After what happened last night…"

"Listen, you owe it to him. The poor guy spent hours waiting for you at the club."

"No he didn't. Not from what he told me. And anyway, he should have left after half an hour or so. I would have."

"In fact, you did." Mara gave her an exasperated sigh. "He was so excited about meeting you, of course. And now he's got to be wondering what all that meant. You've got to be nice to him and really give him a chance."

Cari had to hold back a smile. Mara was pushing a little too hard for this. That meant she'd begun to doubt it was going to work out. Oh, well. Cari would give it a shot. That was all she could do.

A new customer had come in and was about to seat himself at the counter. When she turned and saw it was Max, she gasped and almost dropped the coffee urn she was carrying. He gave her a halfhearted grin and shrugged. She put down the coffee and caught her breath. She'd never imagined he might show up here.

He was wearing slacks that fit his muscular body like a glove, bulging in all the right places, and a silky white shirt open low at the neck. He hadn't shaved and his face looked stunningly sexy with a day's worth of dark beard.

"What are you doing here?" she demanded in a voice just above a whisper. She didn't bother to ask how he'd found out which of the city's hundreds of coffee shops she worked in. She knew his answer to that one. His people knew how to find these things out. Something told her he would always find her if he wanted to, and she wasn't sure if that was a promise or a threat.

Max looked at her in wonder. She had her thick blond hair tied back, but little curls were breaking free all around her face. She wore a stiff, starched uniform, baby-blue with white lacy trim and a white lacy apron, sensible white shoes and a perky little hat. She looked for all the world like an exceptionally adorable matron in a fantasy children's ward. He half expected to see friendly cartoon characters bouncing along behind her.

"I came because I need to talk to you," he said. "You're the only person I know who knows anything about babies."

"What's wrong?" she asked quickly, a tiny flare of alarm shivering through her. "Has something happened?"

"No, nothing. Jamie's fine. Just fine." Max hesitated. He knew he sounded defensive and that made him frown more fiercely.

"Then what's wrong?" She shook her head in bewilderment.

"Nothing. Well, something."

He shook his own head, trying to figure out how to express the discomfort he felt with the childcare he'd arranged without sounding like a candidate for a mental clinic. Maybe what he'd seen was normal. Maybe he was being a crank. But maybe, just maybe, Mrs. Turner was a lousy nanny. He just didn't know the answer.

He sank down into the stool at the counter and turned up the cup. She moved automatically, filling it with coffee.

"Explain," she demanded impatiently. "What are the symptoms?"

His beautiful hands with their long, tapered fingers curled around the cup. She watched him do it, fascinated. Everything about him seemed better, even the way he held a cup. But she didn't have time for any swooning this afternoon. This was all about the baby.

"Well?" she said.

"It's just…oh, hell." He looked up, appealing to her supposed expertise. "He's crying a lot."

Cari froze and looked at him quickly. Brian had hated it when their baby had cried. In fact, it seemed to drive him a bit crazy when it happened. Her heart beat a little faster, but she took a deep breath and forced herself to calm down. Max wasn't Brian. He hadn't said he couldn't stand it, just that it worried him.

Okay, start over again.

She nodded a little stiffly. A baby crying wasn't really unusual. But if it was happening to the point where Max was worried, she was going to delve into it a bit.

"No fever?"

"No, I don't think so."

"Gas?"

He made a face. "I don't know."

"Does the nanny hold him against her shoulder and pat or rub his back?"

He thought for a minute, then nodded. "I've seen her do that a time or two. But not for long." He frowned. "I don't trust the nanny. She's obsessed with making sure she doesn't spoil him. It's like she thinks we're raising a Spartan kid or something. She doesn't want to make him too comfortable, as if he'll get too soft if he's happy." He grimaced. "So she lets him cry."

Cari was sure he was exaggerating, so she didn't take him too seriously. She closed her eyes, thinking, then opened them again and shook her head.

"You know what it probably is? He misses his mom."

Max searched her eyes. To his relief, Cari was taking his worries seriously. She was frowning, thinking over her instant diagnosis. She looked down at him.

"Did you get in a good supply of formula?"

"Of course."

She nodded again, then her eyes widened. "Oh, maybe he was being breast fed. The formula might not agree with him. Maybe that's why he's crying."

He groaned, looking miserable. "But Cari, there's nothing I can do about that."

"Of course not. He'll just have to get used to the formula."

"How long will that take?"

She had a hard time holding back a smile. His face was a picture of tragic helplessness. He was a man of action. He wanted to do something to make everything better. But he was being told there was nothing he could do, and that was maddening to him.

"Of course, the best thing would be if the baby's mother came back. You haven't found her yet?" she asked, knowing it wouldn't be a welcome question at all.

He gave her a baleful look. "Why would I want to do that?"

She stared at him, hoping he was just being flip. "You know darn well you *have* to do that."

His sigh was impatient. "Yes, I know. I've got people looking into it. We'll find her."

She frowned. His "people" had been pretty good at finding out where she lived and worked, but she was pretty easy. A woman who went off without telling anyone where she was going was probably going to be a tougher case.

"I hope you really mean that. It's important. What if

she comes back and her baby's not in the apartment? Can you imagine how frightened she'll be?"

He looked at her as though she'd lost her bearings. "Cari, this is a mother who walked out and never looked back. What makes you think she'll care that much?"

"She's a mother. I know what that's like."

To think a woman could walk out on her baby was incomprehensible to her. She'd lost a baby once herself. It had almost destroyed her life. "You don't know why she disappeared. Maybe something happened." She shrugged, getting into her speculative mode.

"Maybe she was kidnapped. Maybe she's unconscious in some hospital somewhere. Maybe she bumped her head and has amnesia."

He grimaced, not buying a bit of it. "Or maybe she went on a hot date and forgot she had a baby waiting at home."

She swallowed hard, shocked he would say such a thing. The cynicism reminded her of some of the terrible things Brian would say, and she didn't want to think he might be anything like her husband.

"You don't have a very high opinion of women, do you?" she challenged.

He looked up as though surprised she was taking his offhanded remark seriously. "That's not the point. And yes, I have a very high opinion of women. Some women."

His mother. Whoopee. She was appalled.

"No matter what kept her away, when she comes back to her senses, she'll want to know where her baby is."

"That's probably true. For what it's worth." His wide

mouth tilted at the corners, but there was no humor in his dark eyes as he looked up at her. "You forget. I know Sheila. I never understood what Gino saw in her, and I was glad when they broke up. And I was the one who took her phone call when she tried to shake us down for money. I'm afraid that experience has made me a little cynical where Sheila is concerned."

There was certainly no point in arguing about this. He knew the woman. She didn't. But the baby needed to be protected. At the same moment she had that thought, so did he.

"Listen," he said, rising from the stool and moving toward her. "I can pay you double whatever you're making here. I could really use the help."

She shook her head with vigor. She couldn't even allow herself to imagine such a thing.

"No," she said firmly. "Never."

"Cari…" He took her hand in his and she stared down at those wonderful fingers. The nails were so even, so beautiful. He had hands like an artist. She could hardly breathe.

"Cari, listen. It wouldn't be for long. Just until the DNA testing is completed. Then I'll be taking him to Venice with me and I won't need you anymore."

Her gaze jerked up and met his. Did he have any idea what he'd just said? But she supposed he didn't look at it quite the way she did. She yanked her hand out of his and turned away.

I won't need you anymore.

Wasn't that just like a man? Oh!

"Max, you'd better leave. I've got work to do."

"Cari…"

"I'm serious. Go. I'm not going to work for you. Not ever."

"Not ever." He repeated it as though he couldn't believe she'd said that and turned to go, then looked back. "By the way, the police found my car. It was only a few blocks from where it was stolen and they didn't damage anything. So that's okay."

"I'm glad."

He nodded, then shrugged and turned to leave again.

"But Max."

He turned back, one eyebrow raised.

"Max, please take care of the baby. And find his mother. It's really important."

He was on the verge of pointing out that she could help make all that happen, but he bit his tongue, knowing it would be too much like begging.

"Okay, I'll take that under advisement."

"Good."

Their gazes caught and held. For a moment she was afraid he was going to come back and grab her and carry her out, just like he'd carried her the night before. But the moment passed and he gave a half shrug.

"I'd better go back and see what the nanny's up to," he said at last. "If she's trying to get Jamie to make his own bed, I'm throwing her out on her ear."

And then he turned and was gone.

CHAPTER FIVE

RANDY was the perfect match for Cari, just as Mara had insisted all along. He was good-looking in a salt-of-the-earth kind of way, tall with a slender build, friendly, with sandy hair neatly cut and combed, steady gray eyes, a nice smile and a warm attitude. Cari liked him and immediately found herself thinking of women she knew she could set him up with. Seemingly, he was perfect for a lot of people.

"Why didn't you say something when Max called you C.J.?" he asked, after she'd gone over exactly what had happened the night before.

"I had no idea what he was talking about. For all I knew, he was calling me Calamity Jane. That's pretty much what I felt like once I realized what we'd done."

He laughed. They had just been seated at a comfortable booth in the main dining room at the Longhorn Lounge. The atmosphere was pleasant, the servers attentive, and drinks were on the way. The scene was set for a lovely evening, and a lovely evening they would have. But that was all.

She'd gone on this date to make a friend happy, and that was as far as her commitment went. Shortly after the dinner was consumed, she would thank the man, shake his hand and go off into the sunset—alone. In the meantime, she was determined to be nice to Randy, if only to make up for the night before.

But she had to mentally kick herself to stop looking toward the door, hoping Max would make a sudden appearance. She'd already seen him once today, and that was one time too many.

"Well, it was all my fault," Randy was saying graciously. "When I got there I knew I was half an hour late. I was afraid you'd have gotten disgusted and left me flat. So when I saw a gal coming in with a red rose, I was thrilled. Only, I took one look and I just really couldn't believe it could be you."

Déjà vu all over again.

"Really? What was she like?"

"Gorgeous."

He said it like a man smitten, and she had to recoil, just a little. So he'd thought the woman he saw was too good to be true, had he? Funny. That was exactly what she'd thought when she saw Max for the first time. What a coincidence.

"Well, thank you very much," she said a bit tartly, pretending to take offense. He hurried, a bit clumsily, to reassure her.

"No, I mean, you're beautiful. Of course you're beautiful."

She knew she was actually looking pretty good tonight. She'd worn an electric-blue number with spaghetti straps and more cleavage showing than usual, and she'd topped it off with a cute little fake fur shrug that didn't cover much of anything. Then she'd let her hair tumble free around her shoulders. But from the look shining in Randy's eyes, she had a feeling her "pretty good" was nothing compared to C.J.'s "gorgeous."

"You're a lovely woman," he was saying. "But in a totally different way. This gal looked like one of those heiresses with the big hair and the fancy clothes and diamonds and all that. Like the Dallas of the old TV show rather than the Dallas I usually live in."

His gaze grew dreamy as he thought of her. Cari had to laugh, shaking her head.

"I must be quite a disappointment after all that," she noted dryly.

Randy was surely planning on coming back with more reassurances, but he didn't get the chance, as visitors were stopping by their table. Cari looked up right into Max's intense gaze. Her heart leaped and the room seemed to tilt, and for just a moment she wondered if she was imagining things.

I could get lost in those eyes, was the thought running through her mind. Lost and bewitched. Again.

At the same time, his gaze made a quick trip along the line of her low-cut dress, and he gave every indication of liking what he saw there. Suddenly she realized she'd worn it for just such a reaction from him. And only him. And that only made her more light-headed.

It took her a beat too long to realize there was someone with him. Someone with a head of sumptuous red hair and a rather annoyed look on her beautiful face.

"So I guess we got it right this time," Max was saying, nodding to Randy. "Max Angeli," he said shortly, shaking hands with the other man. "And this is C.J. Kerry."

"We've met," C.J. noted, making an exasperated face at Randy before she favored Cari with a slight smile. "So nice to meet you, date stealer," she said, making it obvious she was joking, but letting the edge to her tone shine through all the same. "I'm glad we've got things straightened out at last."

Flustered, Cari wasn't sure what she said in return. Before she knew what was happening, Max was sliding in to sit beside her in the well-padded booth.

"Listen, Cari, I need some advice," he said, looking serious. "Do you mind?"

"Oh." Cari knew this had to be about the baby. "No, of course not." She turned toward him feeling a bit anxious.

"Hey," C.J. complained, still standing in the aisle, one hand on her hip. With her flaming hair and the tiny shimmering dress that just barely covered up her generous assets, she had heads turning all over the restaurant.

"You can sit down, too," Max told her in an offhanded manner. He nodded toward the seat beside Randy, who grinned and moved over eagerly, his eyes shining.

"Come on," Randy said to C.J., noting her outraged face. "I'm not so bad."

"Hah," she harrumphed, flouncing the ruffles of her glittering skirt, but she joined him willingly enough.

Max ignored her and leaned toward Cari. He was back in his Italian silk suit with the white shirt open at the throat, looking very sleek and continental. He'd shaved, which was a shame, really. But he still looked lethally sexy.

"The nanny was trying to get him to drink his evening bottle just before I left," he began. "He wouldn't touch it, wouldn't even let it into his mouth."

Cari frowned, growing a bit concerned. "Was he crying?"

He hesitated. "Not really. Just sort of whimpering." He thought for a minute. "But he did cry a lot earlier in the afternoon. It was enough to set your teeth on edge."

"And you're sure he wasn't in pain?"

Max shook his head, looking tortured. "You know, that's really hard to say. Just looking at him, I would say no. I didn't see any sign of that. But it's kind of hard to be sure when you don't speak their language, you know?"

Cari bit her lip, nodding. She could remember many long nights walking the floor with Michelle, wondering whether or not to call the doctor. Barring overt signs of illness, injury or distress, that was always a wrenching decision, especially at two in the morning.

"So here's what I want to know," he went on, gazing hard into her eyes, taking up all her attention. "Should I fire the nanny?"

Cari stared back at him. A part of her knew he had no business asking her to give him this sort of advice. What was she to him? She had no responsibility, no ties to this child. Why would he ask her?

But another part wanted to make sure baby Jamie was safe just as much as he did. The thought of a baby left to the winds of chance horrified her any time she came across such a situation. Babies needed protection at all times.

"Do you have someone else you can call?" she asked.

He shook his head, his eyes never leaving hers.

She could see how much this was bothering him, and it completely surprised her. She never would have pegged him for the sensitive type. That was the good thing. But he sure couldn't seem to handle a crying child. That was the bad thing—a warning flag to her. Brian had been totally intolerant of baby noises. That had been exactly what had triggered what had happened the nightmare night of the accident.

But she couldn't think about that. This was completely different. Max wasn't Brian. And listening to babies cry could be very frustrating, especially when you didn't really know the child. But babies did cry. Sometimes it was nothing more than being unfamiliar with their new surroundings.

"Give it until morning," she suggested. "By then you'll have enough experience with the woman to know if you want her to stay or not."

He seemed to wince and looked away. It was obvious

he wanted to be told his instincts were right and he should fire the woman.

C.J. had been watching their exchange, her gaze going back and forth between them as though it were a Ping-Pong match. "So, let me get this straight. You two have a baby together?"

They both looked at her and cried in unison "No!"

"No, no, no," Max amplified, looking impatient with the interruption. "This is my brother's baby."

"Oh." C.J. looked surprised. "I didn't know Gino had a baby."

They stared at her.

"You knew Gino?" Max demanded.

"Sure." She smiled, looking pleased that the attention was back where—in her mind—it belonged. "I met him when he was here last year."

Max looked incredulous. "Gino was here? What for?"

She shrugged. "Pretty much the same thing you're here for," she noted, giving him a sly look. "He wanted to buy the ranch."

Max's head went back. This was news to him. He and his brother had been close in many ways, including the family real estate development business they had taken over from their father and ran together. Why would Gino have come to Texas without telling him? It didn't make a lot of sense. Unless he'd been as intent on doing something to make their mother happy as he was himself.

"You know that he recently died in a plane crash,

don't you?" he asked her, grimacing at the effort it took
to talk casually about him when the pain was still so raw.

"Yes, I know, and I'm so sorry about that." She
nodded her sympathy and actually looked as though she
meant it. "He seemed like a great guy. Though I didn't
care much for the woman he had with him."

"Sheila?" Max frowned.

"Yes, I think that was her name." C.J. made a face.
"Shifty looking." Then her face changed as though she'd
just remembered something. "Actually, funny thing. I
heard from her the other day. She was on my answering machine. I didn't call her back. She said she was
here in town, and I could tell she was going to be asking
for money."

"You were probably right. She's been doing a lot of
that lately." Max was staring at her hard, as though he
was seeing something new in her, something that gave
him pause. "So Gino couldn't talk you into selling," he
said softly.

"Of course not." Her chin came up and her huge
green eyes were glittering with resolve. "I'm not selling
the ranch. Ever. It's my heritage. It's all I've got now that
all my family is gone."

Max's dark eyes narrowed speculatively as he gazed
at the woman, but the server arrived with the drinks
before he could make a comment on what she'd said.

"We should go get ourselves a table, honey," C.J. said
to him, raising an eyebrow for emphasis.

He looked around as though surprised to find they

weren't where they belonged. Then he decided to do something about it. "There's plenty of room at this table," he said. "Let's eat here."

"What?" the other three cried, staring at him.

"Is there a problem?" he asked, looking from person to person. There was no sense of give to his attitude, and the others were the ones to back down. One by one, each reluctantly shook his or her head, as he looked at them.

"No. Of course not."

"Well, then." He shrugged and looked at the server. "I'll have a Scotch, neat. And you?" He nodded toward C.J.

C.J. ordered, but Cari wasn't listening any longer. This evening was turning out almost as surreal as the last one had been. If only Mara had left well enough alone in the first place, she would be home right now with some soft music playing and a nice novel in her hand. If only!

As they ordered their meals and the first course came, Randy and C.J. seemed to be doing all the talking. They were bantering back and forth about things they'd done the night before and what it was like to have been dumped by their respective blind dates. They'd started out using it as a way to tweak Cari and Max, but as things went along, they seemed to be wrapped up in their own little joke, leaving the other two behind.

Not that she cared. Her attention was full of the man beside her and didn't have much room left for the other two at the table. Max was quiet, almost morose, as though he were pondering life and all its unpleasant pitfalls and annoying blind alleys, and feeling glum about the prospects for happiness in general.

And Cari felt some sympathy for that point of view. She was wondering how she could have chosen the right path at her mythical fork in the road and yet have wound up on the wrong leg of the journey, anyway. Surely there had to be a shortcut to sanity somewhere. She had to get back where she belonged. But every minute she spent in the company of this man only made things worse. Just sitting here in his presence seemed to solidify the extraordinary attraction she felt for him. There was no getting around it—he was hot!

And that was bad. Sexual attraction was an illusion that clouded the mind and made you do stupid things. She had to guard against it. Experience suggested she was susceptible to the influence of strong men, and she had to fight the temptation to succumb. It wasn't easy.

Every time his gaze accidentally met hers, every time his hand brushed her arm, every time he spoke and his voice seemed to resonate in her soul, all she could think about was the way that full, luscious mouth had felt on hers the night before. This was making her nervous. It took all her control to keep from shaking like a leaf.

At one point, she almost knocked over her wineglass and Max reached out to steady it for her, leaning in close to do it. His crisp, clean scent filled her head, and the sense of his pure masculinity swept over her like a tantalizing breeze.

"Stop it," she thought to herself, feeling a bit desperate. "Just stop doing that."

"Stop what?" he murmured as he drew back, looking at her in that heavy-lidded way that caught at the breath in her throat. "I'm not doing anything."

She stared at him, aghast. She'd only thought the words, surely. How could he have heard her? Had she actually said them aloud—or was she going crazy?

Okay, the votes were in. She was going crazy. Here she was, sitting beside a man who could never be for her, but could ruin her for all the other men in the world if she didn't watch her step. And what was she doing? Gulping down wine like it was high noon in the Gobi Desert.

Smart, Cari, my dear. Very smart.

Ooops. She looked up quickly, wondering if she'd said *that* aloud, too. But no one was paying any attention to her. What a relief. Putting her head down, she began to eat automatically. If she cleaned her plate, maybe she would be allowed to go home to that book.

Max was pushing the food around on his own plate. Eating was the last thing he felt like doing right now. His usual calm sense of confidence seemed to be fraying a bit around the edges tonight. Things weren't going his way. In the first place he was disturbed by C.J.'s attitude. Her bony little feet seemed to be encased in concrete, where holding on to the ranch was concerned. He could tell she thought she was going to scam him. She was just as set on her path as he was on his. He hated to think what that might mean for his long-term prospects of success.

But most of all, he was worried about the baby. What did he know from babies? He was desperately determined to do right by this one, but doubts kept nagging at him. He looked at his watch, wondering how soon he would be able to bid C.J. adieu so he could go back and make sure Mrs. Turner hadn't fallen asleep in the comfortable chair, leaving Jamie to cry his little heart out.

He looked at Cari, wishing she'd agreed to let him hire her for the job. Instinctively he knew he could trust her with the baby. He'd already seen her in action on that score.

She was acting very jumpy at the moment. Every time he caught her eye, she looked away quickly, as though she was afraid he'd think she liked him or something. Hell, *he* didn't like anybody. He had a couple of things to accomplish and "liking" had nothing to do with either thing.

Still, he had to admit he was drawn to her in a way that was unusual for him. He kept thinking about her, even when she was across town working in that funny little café full of cowboys. But mostly he was sure that was because she could be the answer to some of his biggest problems if she would only agree to help him. Though maybe there was a bit more to it than that. After all, he was human, and for a woman who was not really his type, she looked darn appealing tonight. Her little blue dress revealed some very delectable skin that hadn't seen the light of day for a while. But he wasn't supposed to be thinking about that.

"You know what?" she said suddenly, leaning toward him and speaking quietly. "I've been thinking. If you want, I could come by after dinner, just for a few minutes, and sort of scope out the situation. See what I think of the nanny."

He stared at her. She was not only the most beautiful woman in the world, how was it he had never noticed that shiny gold halo that hovered over her head? Or those big gorgeous white wings fluttering off her back? There was actually a lump in his throat. He didn't trust his voice, and he nodded.

"Great," he managed at last, though it sounded creaky. "Great."

She must have seen the abject relief and gratitude in his eyes, because she looked startled and drew back as though she was already regretting the offer.

"Excuse me," she said, gathering her little purse and gesturing toward the way out. "I'm going to go powder my nose."

"Me too," said C.J., sliding out right behind her.

Max rose and let her out, amazed at the peace she'd given him with her suggestion to come by and take a look at the nanny. He hated having things hanging over his head this way. When there was a problem, he was used to dealing with it so it would go away. This nanny thing had been like a bad toothache gnawing away at him all day. And now he was going to be able to do something about it. Thanks to Cari.

Sliding back into his seat, he smiled at Randy. "Wonderful woman, isn't she?" he noted.

And Randy nodded. "Sure is," he said, though he wasn't really sure which woman they were talking about.

Cari had groaned inside the moment she realized C.J. was really going to accompany her to the restroom, but she didn't let it show. The last thing she wanted was company. That was exactly what she was trying to get away from. Nevertheless, C.J. came along, chatting incessantly as they moved through the dining room and headed into the ladies' lounge. Inside, huge mirrors lined the walls with low vanities and comfortable chairs facing them. Cari sank into one of the chairs and pretended to freshen her makeup. C.J. chattered on.

"That Randy is so funny," she said, draping herself across the neighboring chair and fluffing her brilliant hair as she watched herself in the mirror. "He keeps me in stitches."

"He said pretty much the same about you."

"Did he? Aw, that's sweet."

Cari looked into C.J.'s face. She'd already realized the woman was smarter than she seemed at first glance. So what was her purpose here? Surely she'd come along for a reason.

"So what do you do, C.J.?" Max had said something

about a ranch, but the woman didn't look like a working rancher. "For a living, I mean."

"Well, that's a question, isn't it?" C.J. flipped her hair back behind her ears and made a face at herself in the mirror. "I tried college. Didn't like it. Did some modeling. That was sooo boring. Worked for a while in my friend's boutique, but that didn't pay enough to keep a parakeet alive."

Turning, she leaned toward Cari, who tensed, pretty sure the point was about to be made.

"So I looked around to see what I could do to keep myself in high-fashion lingerie and late-model luxury cars, and I finally realized marrying a rich man seemed to be the best match for my talents."

"Oh." Cari almost laughed aloud. What incredible nerve the woman had! "It's a blessing to know yourself, I guess."

"It sure is. Saves a lot of unnecessary heartache." She slicked on some lipstick, pursed her lips, and then looked straight at Cari. "Which reminds me. Just to let you know. I consider Max my territory. I went and planted my little flag in his big ole chest and I mean to bring him in alive."

Cari choked, amazed at the woman's candor. She looked at her in wonder. "Does he have anything to say about this?"

C.J. shrugged, smiling smugly. "Not much. You see, I've got an ace in the hole."

"Do you?"

"Sure enough." She nodded. "It's no secret that his

mama is crazy to get her hands on my ranch. She's got sentimental ties and all that. I let it be known that I love that place like an armadillo loves the yellow line down the center of the road." She snapped her fingers. "The results are as good as in the bag."

Cari shook her head, appalled and amused at the same time. "Why are you telling me this? Aren't you afraid I might tell Max?"

"Tell him." She shrugged good-naturedly. "He knows. Facts are facts. I've got something he wants and there's just one way he's going to get it. We both know the score. I'm just warning you not to try poaching in my paddock."

Cari had no intention of doing any such thing, but the woman's attitude certainly rubbed her the wrong way and she was tempted to pretend she had her own designs on Max. It was on the tip of her tongue to blurt out, "Make me!" but that would be childish. Satisfying, but childish. So instead, she rose from her chair with dignity and turned to go.

"Well, we'll see what happens," she said calmly.

"You got that right," C.J. said, coming right behind her. "May the toughest gal win."

Cari turned on a dime and stared at C.J. "Wait a minute. I'm not trying to win. I don't want Max."

"Don't you?" C.J.'s smile reminded Cari of a Disney crocodile. "That's okay, then. I assume you'll be keeping your cute little hands off my man. So all will be well." She shrugged extravagantly. "Forget I said anything."

Cari was still fuming when they got back to the booth. Max rose to let her in and she threw him a dirty look as she squeezed past him, even though she knew he had no idea what C.J. had been saying. By the time she'd calmed down and was listening to the conversation again, they were back talking about nannies.

"You better watch out," Randy was saying. "You know, they've been catching some of these nannies on those Nannycams, just throwing the babies around like a bushel of old sticks."

Cari's heart leaped into her throat, and when she noticed Max's vaguely grim look, she said quickly, "That's very rare, as I understand it."

"Sure. But it happens."

"Well, it won't happen to Jamie. The nanny Max has hired comes very highly recommended. She may not be the right fit for what Max needs, but she certainly wouldn't do something like that."

The conversation moved on with C.J. and Randy talking animatedly, but Cari was staring down at her plate. All she could think about was Jamie being thrown about like a discarded package. Echoes of what had happened to her own baby that terrible night. That little neck. That little head. Suddenly she felt sick to her stomach. Glancing over, she saw that Max wasn't looking tip-top, either.

Their eyes met and she could read thoughts very similar to hers written plainly on his face.

"Maybe we should just go check right now," she said softly.

He nodded. Reaching under the table, she covered his hand with hers and gave it a quick squeeze before she could stop herself. Drawing back, she wondered if he would understand that the gesture of comfort had been about Jamie and nothing else. Maybe not. But she didn't have time or energy to repair that blunder right now. Later she might have to explain. She turned her attention back to the others.

"Listen, folks," Max began. "New game plan. I'm going back to my place so I can check out the nanny. Cari has agreed to come along and help me. Are the two of you with us?"

Cari had to admit the flash of fire in C.J.'s eyes as they met hers made the whole thing worth it. But she also knew there was no way the woman was going to let her go off to Max's unescorted. With a sigh, she resigned herself to a long, long evening.

CHAPTER SIX

THEY could hear Jamie crying the moment they stepped off the elevator. Max's face turned to stone and he strode quickly to the door of the suite, using his card to unlock it. He disappeared inside. By the time the rest of them made it down the hallway and entered the room, Mrs. Turner was already packing up her things and preparing to leave.

"Well, I never," she was saying indignantly.

"Just go, Mrs. Turner." Max was having a hard time remaining calm. "I'll contact the agency and have the rest of your things sent over in the morning."

Cari didn't waste any time with the woman. She went straight into the bedroom and crossed the floor to the crib. There was Jamie, crying his heart out. Reaching down, she picked him up.

"There, there," she crooned lovingly as she pressed him to her chest. "It's all right, darling. It's all right."

Jamie's sobs turned into a long, heartfelt sigh, interrupted by a very loud hiccup. And then he quieted.

There was a sense of relief in his last little whimpers, as though he recognized her and was saying, "Finally! Where've you been, anyway?"

She cuddled him close, breathed in his baby smell and felt a little bubble of joy burst in her heart. She'd missed this all day long. It made her wince to think she could have been here, could have been taking care of this child. She mustn't let all her personal rules and fears keep her away. For once, she had to follow her heart, no matter where it led her. At least for now.

"Oh, you little sweetheart," she whispered against the dark hair on his baby head. "How can you be so sweet?"

"Well, she's gone."

Cari looked up to see Max standing in the doorway. She tried to read his eyes. There was something she had to know. Jamie's crying had sent him over the edge. That had happened right there in front of them all. There was no denying it. But had it been because of his empathy for the baby? Or was it because he didn't think the nanny was doing a good job—and he couldn't tolerate shoddy work from those who worked for him? Or had it been her nightmare fear—was it because of anger at the noise? That was a question that would haunt her until she knew the answer for sure.

She could see he was upset, though he tried to hide it behind his stoic, emotionless mask. But did he feel for the baby? Or was he annoyed with him? He hadn't made a move to come to him, to comfort him or touch him in any way. What did that mean? She held Jamie closer and knew she couldn't just walk away this time.

"All well and good," C.J. was saying as she came into the room behind him. "But what happens now? You're just going to have to hire another one."

"I'll get a better one," he said stoutly. "I think I'm getting a better handle on this job now. I'll know what to ask in the interview. I'll ask questions about child care methods and philosophy. I'll set up some scenarios and ask the woman how she would deal with each situation." He turned to C.J. and Randy. "Did you see her? Sitting there eating a cupcake and yakking away on the phone while the baby was crying. That wasn't child care, that was child neglect."

C.J. shrugged as though it was all the same to her. Randy nodded sympathetically. And Max turned to Cari to see what she thought. But she wasn't giving anything away. Not yet.

He came closer and looked down at the child, who was now gurgling happily.

"Listen, you're going to have to teach me how to hold him," he said, favoring her with a slight smile. "I'm not up on this stuff."

She nodded. "All right," she responded, heartened that he wanted to learn, but still wary.

"Good. And you can fill me in on anything else I should know before I hire another nanny."

She nodded again, meeting his gaze and searching his eyes. They were clear and intelligent. She couldn't detect any lingering anger or uneasiness. In fact, he looked relieved. That was good. But could she trust it?

"And right from the start," Max went on, "I'm going to have one of those Nannycam cameras installed." He nodded, looking around at the corners of the room as though planning where the camera would be. "That will help."

Cari took a deep breath. She was about to take a step here, and she knew it was going to put her in emotional jeopardy. But she'd come this far and she couldn't back down now.

"Forget the cameras," she said, then pressed her lips together resolutely.

Max swung around and stared at her. "Why would I do that?"

Lifting her chin, she gazed steadily into his eyes. "I'm staying. I'll take care of him. At least for now."

"What?" He frowned as though he didn't trust her motives.

She felt a quick twinge of exasperation. He'd been trying to talk her into this all day, and now that she'd agreed, he looked as if he'd rather go back to talking instead.

"I can't disrupt your life that way," he said, shaking his head and frowning at her, his expression wary.

She threw him a look. "I think you already have."

"Wait a minute," C.J. was saying, unable to believe what she was hearing. "You can't do that."

Cari looked at her over Jamie's little head. "Sure I

can," she said calmly. "Why don't you stay, too, C.J.? I could use the help." She pretended to smile and made her eyes big and innocent. "We could share a bed, you and I."

C.J. recoiled. "Are you kidding?" She shuddered. "Anyway, babies give me the willies."

Cari turned away. They could go on bickering about anything they chose, she'd made her own choice. She was staying with the baby. There wasn't anyone else looking out for him.

Max seemed to have his best interests at heart, but she couldn't be sure. Some men couldn't be with babies. She knew that from experience. Someone had to be Jamie's champion in the world. At least until his mother showed up, she would be the one.

An hour later they were alone. Randy took a very annoyed C.J. back to her car. Cari taught Max how to hold the baby. He was quick to pick up the subtle nuances. All in all, she thought he was a pretty good student of on-the-fly child care.

"I wouldn't say you're a natural exactly," she teased him as he awkwardly patted the baby he held against his shoulder. "But you'll do for now."

Jamie chose that moment to spit up. Luckily, Cari had taught Max to throw a clean burp pad over his shoulder before picking up the baby, so his silk shirt was protected. Still, the sound of the very loud burp made Max cringe and made Cari laugh.

"We'll move on to bottle feeding tomorrow," she warned him. "Think you're up for it?"

"Why not?"

They put the baby down in his crib. Cari cooed to him as his big brown eyes drifted shut. Max watched her more than he watched the baby. There was something about her that just made him feel happy to be around. Very odd.

"Cari." He took her hands in his and gazed deeply into her eyes. "I am so grateful to you for doing this. I can't tell you how much I appreciate it."

It was true. He'd been going nuts ever since he'd brought Mrs. Turner in and she'd begun her tyrannical reign over his hotel suite. Well, he supposed it hadn't been that bad, really. But it had been bad enough. The dilemma had been whether to trust her or not when everything she did just seemed wrong to him.

With Cari it was different. Maybe they were on the same wavelength. Or maybe he just liked her better. It didn't matter. What did matter was that he was calm inside. There was no longer a battle raging between his heart and his head.

"Don't think of it as me doing something for you," she said pertly. "I'm doing this for Jamie."

He only half believed her. He knew there was a provocative buzz between the two of them. She couldn't deny it, though he could see she wanted to. As though to remind her, he smiled and dropped a quick kiss on her lips.

She drew back, eyes widening. "No, Max," she said quickly. "I didn't stay for that. Honestly, I didn't."

"I know. I'm sorry." But he didn't sound very convincing, even to himself.

She turned and began putting away toys and supplies. He watched her for a moment, then asked, "So tell me, Cari, where did you learn so much about babies?"

To his surprise she froze for a moment, then turned slowly and looked at him with huge, shadowed eyes.

"I had one," she said softly.

That surprised him. "You have a baby?"

She shook her head. "Not anymore. She died."

His breath caught in his throat in a way it had never done before. Shock knifed through him and he felt pain for her.

"Oh, Cari," he began, moving toward her.

She went ramrod stiff, holding him at bay. "I was married, you know," she said quickly.

He hesitated, fighting the urge to take her in his arms for comfort. "No, I didn't."

"My husband and my baby both died in a car accident. It was two years ago."

"Cari, I'm so sorry."

She shook her head, not quite meeting his gaze. "Now you know. Okay. I'd rather not talk about it."

"Of course."

He watched as she gathered things into piles to go through in the morning. Knowing that she'd been married, knowing about the tragedy in her past, answered a lot of questions for him. He'd known there was something disturbing her. Now he thought he knew what that was. No wonder she seemed to hold the world at arm's length. To have lost her baby and her husband at such a young age—horrible.

He wanted to hold her close and make it all go away, but he knew she would reject that. He would have to bide his time. Maybe once she knew him better, she would trust him. Oddly enough, he wanted that badly. In fact, he ached to do something for her—anything, and he wasn't sure why he felt that way.

Oh, he knew the mechanics. She'd had tragedy. He cared about her and wanted to do something to help her get over the agony of it. But why did he seem to have this deep, unfamiliar need to do that? He didn't remember ever having it before, not with anyone outside of his immediate family. Very strange.

Tito came in from visiting relatives in a local suburb. He was surprised to see Cari there, but welcoming enough. Still, he went off to his own room pretty quickly. And Cari knew it was time to get her sleeping arrangements settled.

She didn't want to stay in the room Mrs. Turner had used. The nanny's bags were still scattered across the floor, and her clothes were in the closet and dresser. So Max ordered up a rollaway and set up the bed in the baby's room. That was for the best. She wanted Jamie to have the feeling someone was always there for him. No gaps. No more being left to cry his heart out on his own.

"I actually understand the theory behind what Mrs. Turner meant to do with him," she told Max as they were arranging the room. "It doesn't do to let babies think they can manipulate you all the time. But Jamie's case is special. He's missing his mom and he needs extra love to make him feel secure right now, not discipline."

"I think you're probably right," Max told her, talking softly so as not to wake the baby. "I sure feel more comfortable with your methods than I did with the nanny's."

"Good." She smiled at him. Everything he said was reassuring her. Still, she knew the best of intentions could evaporate when one was under stress. She wanted to be there in case she was needed as a buffer. There was no substitute for hands-on child care.

"I'm going to need something to sleep in," she pointed out, looking down at the blue cocktail dress. It gave her a start to notice how low the neckline was. She'd forgotten. Her cheeks felt hot. Looking up, she saw that Max had been watching and was reading her mind. The awareness between them almost made her gasp. She turned away quickly and didn't look at him again until he left the room and came back with a large T-shirt for her to use as a nightgown.

He began to talk about random things and she realized he was trying to put her at ease again. She appreciated that, but she didn't feel comfortable. Despite the presence of Tito in the room on the other side of the suite, they were basically alone together. That made him a threat—to her peace of mind at least. He was too potent a force to ignore.

At one point, he made a comment about C.J. and she couldn't help but give her own take on things.

"She means to marry you, you know," she said, looking down into the crib at Jamie as he slept.

He didn't flinch. Coming up beside her, he smiled down at the drowsy baby. "Yes," he said casually. "I was hoping it wouldn't come to that. But I'm afraid you're right."

She turned to look at him in exasperation. "How can you be so calm about it? You hardly know her. I mean, you thought I was her last night."

"I wish I'd been right," he said dryly, and she gasped, but he was smiling. He turned and gazed at her as though her naiveté amused him. "This is not a love match, Cari. If there is anything to it, it's more like a business deal."

"That's exactly what she told me," she noted, nodding. "You marry her, your mother gets the ranch. Isn't that the way it goes?"

"Pretty much."

She shook her head. "It sounds crazy to me."

"Life can be crazy sometimes," he said vaguely, waving her objection away. "But it has its own special logic. People get married for all sorts of reasons. To do it as part of an exchange of goods is one of the most ancient methods in every culture."

"It seems way too medieval."

"Really? What will you marry again for, Cari? Love?"

His voice rang with sarcasm at the word, as though

he didn't believe in it. That put her back up a bit, and yet she couldn't really argue with him when she was going to deny the need to love in her own right.

"I won't marry again at all," she said instead. "I don't need a man in my life."

He stared at her for a moment, then threw back his head and laughed out loud. "You're priceless, Cari," he said. "But this is the way it is. I've been dating women for over fifteen years now. I've yet to find one I desperately want to spend the rest of my life with. Evidence suggests she's not going to come breaking out of the woodwork anytime soon. So why not use a marriage to get what I want?"

She snorted. His cynicism appalled her. "The question is, why do you want it?"

"To save my mother's life."

That shut her up. She couldn't help but feel it was a bit melodramatic. She supposed that was the Italian in him. But it left her speechless nonetheless. After all, what would she be willing to do for the people she loved best?

"Not that," she whispered to herself as he turned and left the room.

She watched him go, then followed him out into the living room, ready to ask him more about this, but he sandbagged her with a question of his own.

"So what did you think of your blind date?" he asked, sinking into the sleek yet comfortable couch.

"Who? Randy?" She flopped down into a chair

across from where he was sitting. Her chin rose. "Obviously, he's perfect for me," she said with only a tiny touch of sarcasm.

He caught her nuance. "Is he?" Amusement danced in his dark eyes.

"Of course." She shrugged. "Hand picked, in fact, by my best friend, Mara. And she was right. Can't you tell?"

He allowed himself a halfhearted grin. "Oh, yeah. Nice guy. Funny guy. I enjoyed him."

"Me, too." She punched a pillow. "He's exactly the sort of man I need."

"Ya think?"

"Yes." She faced him frankly. "He's very calm and very…" She drew in a long, deep breath. "Very ordinary."

"Ordinary." He frowned thoughtfully, then raised an eyebrow. He'd never thought of that quality as an attribute. "Is that a plus?"

She nodded. "I'm ordinary. What's wrong with ordinary?"

He gave her a look. Maybe the word didn't mean just what he thought it did. "Did I say anything was wrong with ordinary?"

"Ordinary can be okay," she said a bit defensively. "I come from ordinary people. My father was an accountant, my mother worked in a bank."

"Do they live in Dallas?"

She shook her head. "No. My mother died of cancer and my father died of a broken heart."

"Ah." He nodded. He understood that sort of thing.

"It's true you don't get the thrilling highs with ordinary," she went on. "But you don't get the bone-rattling lows, either." She winced, thinking of Brian. "Excitement can be scary when it goes bad," she added softly.

He noted the haunted look in her eyes as she spoke. There had been some scary excitement in her life, something that had gone badly. Of course, there were the deaths of her husband and child she'd told him about. Tragedies like that could have life-crippling effects on a person. But he had a feeling this was something more deeply rooted in the past, and maybe more specific to one person—for instance, her husband. What else could have made her so wary of a relationship?

It only made sense. When you lost a significant other who made you happy, you tended to be in a hurry to replicate that happiness as soon as the grieving period began to die down a bit. People with good relationships believed in good relationships. She was scared to connect. Something had gone wrong somewhere along the line.

He wanted to ask her about that, find out what was troubling her, but he held back. He didn't want to scare her off, and he knew she didn't want to talk about personal things. She had to be coaxed, cajoled and brought along casually. He would take his time.

"So what about me?" he said instead. "Would you call me an ordinary guy?"

"Hardly." Her sudden smile was like the sun coming

out from behind a cloud, fascinating him. "You're the sort mothers warn their daughters to stay away from, don't you think?"

"Me?" He was genuinely startled that she felt that way. Truth to tell, he didn't consider himself exactly ordinary, but he didn't relish the bad-boy role either. "So what's scary about me?"

"Nothing, I guess." She was still smiling that radiant smile. "You haven't scared me yet."

He noted the "yet."

"But you *are* a little larger than life," she added, just to be clear.

He frowned, not sure he was going to like this. "In what way?"

"Let's just put it this way—you're a little too exciting. Too good-looking. Too powerful. Too adventurous. Shall I go on?"

"No. That's plenty." His frown deepened. "And not really fair."

"Fair has nothing to do with it," she told him firmly. "Do you think it's fair that I'm definitely ordinary? I can't help it. I was born this way. And naturally, if I'm going to have a relationship again, I need an ordinary man."

There it was, the point this whole conversation seemed to be leading up to. She was giving him a message.

"Like Randy," he said softly.

She nodded, her eyes huge in the gloomy light. "Yes."

He gave her an incredulous look. Randy was all well

and good, but he wasn't right for Cari. She needed someone…well, someone more like Max himself. Someone with a little style and energy.

"You need excitement," he stated firmly.

She shook her head, challenging him with her bright gaze. "No. I need security."

He stared at her, mulling that over. What did she think she was, ready for retirement?

"Bull," he said at last. Rising from the couch, he erased the distance between them, reached out and took her hand and pulled her up to face him.

"What in hell makes you think you're ordinary?" he demanded, face-to-face. "You're careful. You're responsible. You're a good person. If you think that makes you ordinary, you have a higher definition of the term than I do." He looked deep into her eyes. "I think that makes you pretty special."

She was tingling. He made her tingle more and more lately. Was that a good thing? Probably not.

What if he was right? That was what scared her. The thing was, Randy was exactly the kind of man she had decided she could deal with, if the need came. Mara had said it best—Randy was perfect. But did her senses zing when he smiled at her? Did she feel faint when he touched her? Did her breathing stall when he whispered near her ear? Did she tingle?

Hardly. Things never worked out that way, did they?

"I think it's time to go to bed," she said, pulling away from him and backing toward the nursery.

"Alone?" he said, pretending a plaintive tone, but obviously just teasing.

"Alone." She smiled one last time, then turned, went into the nursery and closed the door.

CHAPTER SEVEN

IF MAX had been one to fantasize what mornings with a wife and child would be like, this would have been a part of that dream. He walked into the nursery with two mugs of coffee and there was Cari, standing in the sunlight streaming in through the window with a baby in her arms, singing a lullaby. She wore his big T-shirt and nothing else, and her bare legs looked golden and gorgeous in the morning light. She turned to greet him, her hair wild around her face, and she smiled that smile that could knock him dead, beaming happiness and welcome.

He stopped in his tracks and stared at her. *"Bella,"* he said softly. *"Bellissima."*

"I didn't think you'd be up this early," she said. Her gaze traveled appreciatively over him in a way that made his pulse quicken. He'd put on a pair of tight jeans and a shirt he hadn't buttoned yet out of expediency, but if she would like what she saw as much as she seemed to, he would do it more often.

"I brought coffee," he said.

"I see that," she replied.

"Here." He set the mugs down on the dresser and turned to her. "Let me hold him."

Her eyes widened. "You really want to?"

He nodded. "If all goes well, I'm planning to raise this child," he said simply. "I want to do it right."

"If all goes well," she echoed thoughtfully as she handed Jamie to him. "In other words, if Sheila lets you take him." And why would a mother do that without putting up a very fierce fight? Well, she had to admit, this mother didn't seem to be quite as interested in being a mother as one would hope. Max might very well be able to negotiate something with her for enough money. But that was only a part of the problem.

She frowned, then asked a question she knew would be unpopular. "What if the DNA comes back negative, Max? What if there is no biologic connection to your brother? What then?"

He shrugged dismissively, smiling down at Jamie all the while. "I don't think that will happen."

"But don't you think you ought to be prepared just in case? What do you plan to do with this baby if he isn't Gino's?"

His gaze rose and met hers. "I've already talked to a lawyer. They're setting up legal strategies for when the DNA results comes in. We'll play it by ear."

Cari felt chilled. "If Sheila isn't found and Jamie isn't Gino's, will you just go off and leave him?"

His face hardened. "Cari, I told you, I don't think that is something we will have to face. Drop it."

He was right. She had to drop it. If she didn't, she would be riling herself up over something she couldn't do anything about. It was best to let it be for now. Taking a deep breath, she steadied herself and tried to move on.

But the prospect of seeing Jamie abandoned wouldn't fade from her mind. She knew she couldn't let that happen. If it came to that, she would do something. It only bothered her that Max couldn't make that commitment himself right now. And that made her think she'd been right to come to stay with them. Someone had to protect the baby.

They played with Jamie for another ten minutes and then his eyelids began to droop. Max laid him down gently in the crib and Cari pulled his little blanket up over him.

"Isn't he adorable?" she said, smiling down at the shocking head of dark hair.

"He's okay," Max said gruffly. "He'll do."

She smiled to herself. He was more soft on Jamie than he would admit. It wouldn't be long before he wouldn't be able to turn his back on this baby no matter what.

Looking up, she found him watching her, and his intention was clear as a bell.

"Max," she said warningly, taking a step backward. He was looking very seductive in a very Italian way, and she was feeling particularly susceptible to Italians this morning. Danger!

Reaching out, he put a finger under her chin and

tilted her face up. "I'm sorry Cari, but you're too beautiful to resist this morning. I have to kiss you."

"Oh, Max, no."

"Just a simple good-morning kiss. Nothing more."

"Max…"

Somehow his name turned into a sigh, and then she was parting her lips to accept his mouth on hers. She shouldn't do this. She'd warned herself from the start not to let this happen. But now that he was here, so close, so male, so hard and insistent, she felt so soft, so female, so ready to mold herself to whatever his passion might suggest. His mouth was hot, his tongue provocative, and she sensed her own needs beginning to waken from a long, long slumber.

His shirt was still open and she ran her hands over his muscular chest, trembling as she felt the pounding of his heart beneath her fingers. He groaned, pulling her closer, and she melted like wax against his tall, hard frame. There was only the thin fabric of the T-shirt between them. He wanted her with a force that stunned him. This was something on a different level than he usually felt. This was new. This was sweeter and more overpowering than he was used to.

He sighed against her neck, murmuring her name as he dropped kisses and let his tongue caress her. She gasped as the heat from his body flooded her with sensation. She could sense his desire quickening and that gave her a taste of power she'd never known before. He was reacting to what her body did to him. That took her breath away.

She knew it was time to put a stop to this, but she couldn't quite muster the strength to do it yet. She was struggling to surface from a sea of pleasure, struggling to push her head back above water and breathe real air instead of this enchanted substance that felt so intoxicating, but was so dangerous. The truth was, she didn't want to stop.

And then there was a loud knocking at the door of the suite.

"Hey, y'all, here we are."

The voice was C.J.'s. The groan was Max's. He dropped his face into the curve of her neck and swore softly as he dropped a string of kisses on her skin.

"What time is it?" Cari murmured groggily as he began to pull back from her.

"Too early for visitors," Max grumbled.

But he unwrapped his arms from around her reluctantly and went to the door anyway, letting in C.J. and Randy. Cari watched him go, feeling cold all of a sudden. Max's simple morning kiss had proven to be pretty darn special. She could grow to like this. In fact, she might get addicted if she didn't watch out.

She pulled her arms in and hugged them close. But no matter how hard she held herself, she knew she would never come close to duplicating the magic of Max's embrace.

"We brought doughnuts," C.J. cried, waving the bag around as she entered the living room.

Cari slipped her fake fur shrug over the T-shirt and

looked at herself in the mirror. She looked ridiculous, but she didn't have much choice. It was either this or wrap herself in a bed sheet. So she came out, head held high and smiling.

And then she saw the doughnuts. Her downfall.

"Wow," she said as C.J. spilled them out onto a plate. "Those look great."

"Don't they? We got them at a bakery Randy deals with."

C.J. looked at her sharply, and she knew she was looking for signs of hanky-panky. The signs might very well be there. Cari was still reeling from Max's kisses and she didn't really care who knew it. C.J.'s gaze raked over the giant-size T-shirt with disdain, but Cari met her gaze unblinkingly. Whatever C.J. thought, she wasn't going to show her any embarrassment. Let her deal with *that*.

C.J. pursed her lips, but seemed to accept that there was nothing she could do about anything between Max and Cari at the moment, so she let it go.

"Did you know our boy Randy has a catering business?" she said, giving him a quick smile that served to include him in the group.

Cari blinked, looking at the jovial man. "I thought you were a stockbroker."

"That's my day job." He grinned at her and snagged the biggest doughnut.

"He hates it," C.J. announced to the world at large. "That's why he started up this little ole catering business on the side. He loves setting up parties."

"No kidding." Cari wondered if Mara knew about that side of her husband's cousin. He looked more like a stockbroker than a caterer, but then, what did a caterer look like?

"Yup. I'm getting him some clients. I know people who give huge parties."

Cari was impressed. It seemed C.J. had her uses after all. "Wow. Lucky Randy."

She looked at him. He was grinning happily. It was evident he did feel like a lucky man today. Cari had to laugh inside. She might think Randy a perfect match for herself, but it was pretty obvious he had other plans. C.J. looked just right to him. Poor guy.

But then, how was Randy any more of an object of pity than she was herself? She sighed, feeling ordinary, and turned to the kitchenette to make coffee for the guests.

They were sitting around the table sipping coffee and munching on delicious donuts when C.J. dropped her bombshell.

"Hey, I talked to your mama this morning, Max."

His head rose sharply and he stared at her in horror. "You did what?"

"I called her. Don't worry, I paid attention to the time difference. She sure is nice. I just love her." She darted a particularly smug look Cari's way. "We had a great talk and we put our heads together and figured out a few ideas for presents you could get her before you go back to Venice. So I'm takin' you shopping, you lucky boy. I know all the best department stores in Dallas and I'm going to introduce you to them, too. We'll have a great time."

"What?" Max sounded like a drowning man.

"Oh, come on, you old meanie," C.J. said, slapping him playfully on the shoulder. "You want to make your mama happy, don't you?"

He looked to Cari for help, but she shrugged. "I'm going to be taking care of Jamie all day," she said serenely. "He needs a bath and then I'm going to take him out in his stroller."

"You'll probably need some help," Max said hopefully.

"Who, me? I don't think so." She favored him with a devilish grin. "You'd better go with C.J. and Randy. They've obviously got their hearts set on making you come out to play."

"I'm only going," Max told her a few minutes later as he finished dressing and prepared to meet the other two in the lobby, "so that I can get a chance to work on C.J. about selling the ranch. I've got a new angle I'm going to try on her."

"Why not just marry the woman and be done with it?" she teased. "I thought this was just a business deal."

He turned to look at her. "The more time I spend with her the more I realize business like that is a perilous game," he told her. "But you're right. I may have to marry her. I'm just going to do everything I can think of to avoid that fate." He looked back at her seriously as he started out the door. "But bottom line, I've got to get control of that ranch."

Her smile evaporated as the door closed. She hadn't

discerned one little bit of give in C.J.'s position, but maybe Max could find something. She certainly hoped so—for his sake.

Cari called the Copper Penny later in the morning to let them know she was going to take a few days off. She felt guilty leaving them in the lurch, but this was an emergency, and she had some time off she could use. Tito drove her home to pack up some clothes, and on the way back, they stopped at a baby store. Max had given her a credit card and told her to get what she thought they needed. It was a virtual baby wonderland and she ordered an outlandish amount of baby equipment to be delivered to the hotel.

That put her in a great mood. Shopping trips often seemed to have that effect—and something told her she was having a lot more fun than Max was right now.

Taking care of Jamie was a breeze. He was such a sweetheart, so responsive and free with his baby smiles and gurgles, that being with him was a joy. And dressing him in his cute new outfits was fun, too. She was glad he was a boy and about a month older than Michelle had been, so the comparisons and memories, though they did come up and did bring a wave of sadness, didn't sting the way they might have.

The situation that worried her most right now was the status of this baby. What was going to happen if the DNA result was negative? If Sheila appeared and had a good explanation for where she'd been, she supposed

Jamie would go back to his mother and the rest of them would go on with their lives. But what if Sheila was on drugs or something else that made her impossible as a mother to this little angel? That would present its own problems. But there was no point thinking about that. Sheila claimed this was Gino's baby and there was, so far, no reason to doubt her.

So what if Sheila didn't return and the test did come back with the result Max was looking for? What would happen then? It was perfectly obvious. Max would pack Jamie up and take off for Venice. She would lose again. Another heartbreak.

No, now she was letting her emotions run rampant. She wasn't that attached to this child and she wouldn't let herself be. She was a caretaker, nothing more.

And she wasn't going to fall in love—with either one of them.

It was midafternoon and Max wasn't back yet. Jamie was napping peacefully. Cari decided to take a shower. A few minutes later she was luxuriating in the multiple-spray waterfall of the fancy bathroom when she thought she heard something. She turned off the water, listening intently.

There it was. Jamie was crying. Wouldn't you know her timing wouldn't work out? Sighing, she stepped out of the shower and grabbed a towel and that was when she heard Max at the bathroom door.

"Cari, the baby's crying. Why is he crying?"

"Well, pick him up and see what he needs," she called back, toweling fast. She hurried to blot her hair and put on her robe. As she emerged from the bathroom, she could hear Jamie down the hall.

"I'm coming, I'm coming," she called, pulling the robe more tightly around her as she rushed down the hallway. In the nursery, Max was standing at the side of the crib looking down at Jamie. Cari pushed right past him and picked the baby up, cooing and rocking him as he slowly quieted down. Glancing up, she saw from the look on Max's face that he was not happy.

"Why was he crying?" he demanded.

This entire scene was putting a knot in her stomach. "Relax," she said shortly. "Babies do cry."

His frown was ferocious. "But if it was bad when the nanny let him cry…"

A scene flashed in her mind. It had been very late and she'd been frantically trying to heat a bottle and get it back to Michelle before Brian completely exploded.

"Can't you shut her up?" Brian had yelled from the bedroom. "I've gotta get some sleep. I've got to work in the morning, you know."

"Just a minute."

"Cari, if you don't shut that baby up I'm leaving. I can't live like this."

"Brian, just give me a minute…"

A crash came from the bedroom where Brian had thrown the lamp against the wall.

Cari blinked away the memory. She looked up into Max's face.

"You left him alone," he said accusingly. "Why did you leave him alone?"

Cari took a deep breath and gathered all her resources. "Max, listen to me carefully. He was asleep when I went to take a shower. He was only alone for a couple of minutes." She gazed at him earnestly. Surely he was mature enough to understand.

But maybe not. Maybe he was going to be like Brian. Her heart sank. If so, what would she do? She wouldn't dare leave the baby here with him, and yet how could she stay?

"Max, this is not a major issue. Babies do cry. You don't leave them alone to cry for hours, but now and then it's going to happen."

Fascinated, she watched him visibly begin to relax. He looked down at the baby and ran a hand through his hair, then looked up at her again. "I'm sorry," he said gruffly. "You're right, of course. It's just, I came in and heard him crying and didn't know where you'd gone."

A surge of relief that developed quickly into affection rolled through her. She wanted to touch him. She wanted to reach out and run her hand down the side of his face. Instead she challenged him.

"Here's a question for you. Why does the crying bother you so much?"

He stopped as though that was a new one he hadn't thought about before. "I guess it's because I'm afraid something is wrong and I won't know what to do about it," he admitted at last.

She smiled, feeling such relief. He wasn't like Brian. That was becoming clear.

"Good answer," she murmured. "So it's not just that the noise drives you crazy?"

"Well, I can't say I love the noise," he said. "But I don't think it's driving me crazy, exactly."

"Good."

She hugged him. It was spontaneous and it was one-handed and it was quick. In fact, it was over before he realized it was happening. And then she was gone again and leading the way out into the living room with Jamie in her arms.

"What all have you got there?" she cried, surveying the piles of packages in exclusive department store bags and boxes.

"You wouldn't believe it," he said, coming out behind her. "What I've got is presents. Presents for my mother. Presents for the servants at my mother's house in Venice. Presents for all the people who work for me." He shook his head, looking at her in bewilderment. "Why the hell do women love presents so much?"

She shrugged and grinned at him. "You're the one buying them."

He snarled just a little. "C.J. made me."

"Of course." She laughed.

He looked at her sideways. "I wanted to buy you a present. But C.J. wasn't as enthused about that."

"No kidding." Cari laughed again. She shook her head of wet curls. "You don't have to buy me any presents," she told him. "Just being here, taking care of Jamie, is enough."

He smiled as though he enjoyed her laughter. "The whole time, I wanted to be back here with you," he said softly.

She rolled her eyes. "Right." She turned away, bouncing Jamie in her arms.

"No, really. You don't believe that?"

Looking back at him, she flushed. She could see his honesty in his eyes. Yes, she believed it. But still, she didn't trust it. She sighed, remembering the morning kiss. If she didn't take care, they would be right back there again. She could see it in his eyes.

"Max, we have to talk."

"About not getting involved?" he asked gruffly.

She looked at him, marveling. What—did he read her mind?

"Exactly." She shook her head. "Especially if you're going to be marrying C.J. for heaven's sake."

"Marrying C.J." Slumping down onto the couch, he groaned, his head in his hands. "It's not going to be as easy as it seemed from a distance."

"You don't seem to like her very much."

"You can tell, can you?" He looked up, adorably cha-grinned, with his beautiful black hair falling over his eyes. "It's not really fair to say I don't like her. She's okay. For someone." He chuckled suddenly. "Randy, for instance."

She agreed, smiling. "He does seem to have a major crush there."

"Oh, yeah. He can't take his eyes off her."

She threw a hand up in the air. "Then let *him* marry her."

"Good idea. One flaw. That doesn't get me the ranch."

She dropped down beside him on the couch, sitting with her feet up on the coffee table and Jamie propped by her legs. The baby laughed at them both and they played with him for a moment. Then she turned to Max.

"Are you seriously considering marrying her just for her ranch?" It did seem a bit of a stretch.

"Yes, I am."

That was like a knife through her heart, though she knew it shouldn't matter to her at all.

"Why?"

He looked at her, his eyes clear and determined. "For my mother's sake."

He'd said something along these lines before but she had a hard time buying it. "Your mother tells you whom to marry?"

"No." He shook his head. "You don't understand."

She shrugged. "You got that right."

"Okay. I will try to explain."

"Please do."

He sat very still for a moment. She waited, her heart beating just a bit faster, anticipating what he might tell her. She knew it would involve heartbreak. When reasons seemed irrational, heartbreak was usually lurking somewhere in the mix.

"My brother, Gino, the one who died recently, he was just the best."

Max moved restlessly and Cari could see that this wasn't going to be easy for him to get through. He leaned forward, his elbows on his knees and his head in his hands. She resisted the impulse to reach out and run her fingers through his thick, lustrous hair.

"Gino did everything right. He was a skiing champion and a world-class swimmer. He danced like Fred Astaire and sang like Caruso. He was smart and good at business. He turned a small pair of cafés he took over when my uncle died into a major chain with restaurants all over Europe. He was handsome and loving, the sort of man whose smile was always his first reaction." His voice cracked, but he went on. "He was flawless."

Her breath caught in her throat. She gazed at Max with a compassion that threatened to overwhelm her.

"It's so tragic that you lost him."

"Yes." Clearing his throat, he looked up at her, his eyes dark and troubled. "But for my mother, it was more than tragedy. It was the end of her life."

Cari shook her head, confused. "But she still has you."

He nodded, but there was something that looked like anguish in his face. "Yes. Of course. But you see, it was Gino that she…" His voice trailed off and he looked away. For a moment he couldn't say the words. "Gino was the oldest, and he and my mother had a special bond. Gino was her helper when she went through some very bad things. I was too young to understand at the time, too young to be of much help. Gino was her right arm. When my father left her, she always said she couldn't have survived without Gino."

Cari frowned. She didn't really understand this. He was implying that his mother loved his brother more than anyone or anything—even Max himself. And yet she couldn't detect a bit of bitterness in him. He seemed to accept it in a way she'd never seen before. She didn't get it.

"Are you telling me you didn't resent her attitude?"

He looked up, shocked. "Resent it? Not at all. I felt the same way about him that she did. He was my best friend. He was my idol, my mentor, my guiding star. I would have given my life to save his."

Cari was struck by a sense of admiration. She wasn't used to a man who could put others before himself quite this way.

Brian had lived on bitterness. He always thought everyone he dealt with was out to cheat him and he tried to cheat them first, just to protect himself from their schemes. It had been hard to try to get him to see that others weren't really against him, because every attempt she made to do that just cast her in the role of his enemy, and he would accuse her of doing it, too.

Poor Brian. Now, at this distance, she could pity him. At the time, understanding had been harder to come by.

"My brother died trying out an experimental small plane. He was considering investing in the company that made it. It was a tremendous blow to us all, but to my mother, it was the end of her world. I had to have her closest servants watch her night and day to make sure she didn't take her own life. My heart was already broken by the death of my brother, but every time I saw the tragedy in her face, my heart would break again. I resolved that I would do anything—anything I could think of, to bring back her smile."

"And you think getting the ranch will do that?"

"Yes." He straightened and looked her full in the face. "I know it will. You see, her family settled the area where the Triple M Ranch is located in the nineteenth century. Her great-grandfather cleared the land. Her grandfather started the first profitable herd. She grew up on that ranch." He shook his head and his voice turned a little bitter. "And it was her own father who gambled away the family fortune and sold the ranch to C.J.'s father to keep from going to prison."

"I see."

"From the time I was a little boy, I was raised on stories of the Triple M. It just tortured my mother to think it was in C.J.'s family's hands instead of where it belonged. C.J.'s mother, Betty Jean, was my mother's best friend, but when C.J.'s father took over the ranch and then married Betty Jean, they broke all ties. My mother went to Europe and met and married my father. But she never got over losing the ranch."

"I think I'm beginning to understand some of the intensity here," Cari said tentatively, watching Jamie fall asleep propped against her legs. "But it still seems a bit extreme. Maybe it's an Italian thing?"

"My mother is as much a Texan as she is anything," he said with a crooked grin. "Maybe it's really a Texas thing."

She nodded, giving him that one. "Could be. We can be intense in our love for the land," she admitted.

"Anyway, a few weeks ago, C.J. wrote to my mother. She wanted to come to Italy for a visit." He frowned, thinking that over. "Okay, now I get it. Gino coming here last year, hoping he could buy the ranch, must have been what led her to believe we might be willing to do almost anything to get it back in our hands. So she decided to use it to leverage herself a husband."

"A rich husband," Cari reminded him.

"Of course. What good would a poor husband do for someone like C.J.?"

Cari shook her head. "You have a point there."

"Anyway, I didn't want her in Italy bothering my mother. And that was soon after Sheila called to tell me she'd had Gino's baby."

"And what did *she* want?"

"Just money. But when I demanded proof the baby was Gino's, she disappeared. It was a few weeks before my people traced her to Dallas. And that gave me a reason to come here to take care of two things at once."

That explained a lot of things, but it didn't make anything seem easier. Max needed to get the baby situation settled, and he needed to get control of the ranch. Both were up in the air right now. That was one thing she had to keep in mind. No matter how much she cared for him, no matter what happened between them, Max Angeli was just passing through. In another few days, he'd be gone. And maybe her life—and her heart— could get back to normal.

"So now I know why you parachuted by mistake into my life," Cari said with a tiny smile.

"Fate," he said. "Fate can be a—"

"Don't say it in front of the baby," she warned, rising and getting Jamie and his things together for the walk back to the nursery.

"Cari, Cari," he drawled, leaning back and looking at her languorously. "How long has it been since a man has made hot, sexy love to you?"

She threw him a sideways glance. "It's been so long that I'm not sure I remember what those words even mean."

"We should rectify that situation." There was a smile in his voice, but a thread of interest, as well, and a hint of sensual urgency that made her pulse race.

She gave him a quick smile and turned to leave. "No, thank you," she said back over her shoulder.

Laughing softly, he rose and followed her. "I forgot to tell you. C.J. and Randy are coming here for dinner."

"Oh? Down in the dining room?"

She assumed they would want to be away from the baby so they could have a relaxing evening. No matter. She would just as soon be up here, taking care of Jamie. She really didn't need any company.

"No," he said, surprising her. "Actually, C.J. wants to show Randy that she can cook. So she's going to prepare something wonderful on the little stove in the kitchen-ette."

Cari turned and stared at him. "What?"

"So she says." He grinned. "But we do have room service as a last resort."

She shook her head ruefully. "Somehow I'm afraid we're probably going to need it."

CHAPTER EIGHT

But Cari was wrong. C.J. turned out to be a wonderful cook, to the surprise of at least two of the dinner participants. She threw together plates of finger food, which included bite-size pieces of filet mignon on toast, salmon and crème fraîche on rye crackers, a light-as-air pâté on sautéed slices of croissant, lobster tail on sourdough bread rounds, bruschetta on deep-fried parmesan toast, and a few other things, each more delicious than the last.

"Appetizers," Max said without enthusiasm when she first put out her spread. But once he'd started eating, the only sounds to be heard were sighs of ecstasy.

"You see," C.J. said to Randy, flouncing her apron as she sashayed past. "I can cook. And on little tiny good-for-nothing stoves, too."

It turned out her purpose was to convince him that she could help him cater one of his large parties. He didn't need much more persuading once he'd tasted her food.

"Hire her," Max proclaimed, his mouth full of lobster. "She's a genius at cooking. This is wonderful stuff."

"I'm not trying to get a job with him," C.J. said pertly. "I'm trying to hire on with *you*, and you know it."

Max looked at the two women, one after the other, and inwardly he groaned. C.J. was gorgeous in an exaggerated way, all red lips and aggressive breasts and swinging hips, with fire-engine-red hair as icing on the very tempting cake. She was vivacious, exciting.

But—what the hell? He'd been there, done that. She was just like every other woman he'd dated since he was seventeen. He was bored with it, bored with her.

Cari was something new to him—warm, sweet, principled. She had standards. Imagine that! Rules she used to guide her life. He'd thought such things went out with high-buttoned shoes, except for boring, shriveled people who wanted to stop anyone from having fun.

But what Cari had was something different from anything he'd ever known. She had integrity. Wow. What a difference it made. Loving her would make him a better person. He knew that intuitively. She would change his life. Too bad it was so impossible.

Still she had a special spark that attracted him in a way C.J. and her type never could. What was he going to do about that? Or did he really need to do anything at all?

"That was the best meal I've had in ages, C.J.," Cari told her when the men had gone down to the bar for an after-dinner drink and left the women behind.

"My one talent," C.J. said with a sigh. "You see why I need to marry Max."

They were lounging on the couch, and Cari was feeling almost friendly to the woman.

"Do you really need to marry him?" she asked hesitantly. "I mean, after all, I'm sure he's willing to pay you quite a bit for the ranch. Why not just sell it to him and invest the money you get out of the deal?"

C.J. shook her head fervently. "No can do."

"Why not? You could get a lot of money for it."

"'Money' per se, isn't what I want. Security is what I need. The kind that major wealth can bring. That's my goal." She settled into the corner of the couch, pulling her legs up under her. "Here's a lesson in life, Cari. Money is very nice, but just plain old money has a way of slipping through your fingers. I've learned that often over the years. Money evaporates." She nodded wisely. "The land is always there. It's the goose that lays the golden egg. You don't sell off that darn old goose. Not if you're smart."

"So the ranch is doing well?" Cari asked, wondering just who was managing it. C.J. didn't seem to be doing it and she never seemed to talk about it.

"As well as can be expected. But that's not where I count on to get my support. It doesn't matter how much money the ranch makes. As I said, money can disappear in an instant. All kinds of things can make money disappear. Life can soak it right up. I've seen that happen. The ranch is my leverage. It's something I can use to get the life I want. I'm just lucky I've got it."

"I see."

"You know what?" C.J. went on. "This may surprise

you, but I'm tired of being a party girl. It's getting hard to keep up that front. Once my looks go, it'll be over anyway. I've got to prepare for my future. I want kids and a family just like everybody else."

"You do?" Cari stared at her. "I thought babies gave you the willies."

"They do. You don't think I'd be caught dead taking care of my children, do you? That's what servants are for."

"Oh. Why didn't I think of that?"

"Because you don't think ahead the way I do. You really should start planning for your own future, honey. I'm a bit older than you. I've been around the block a few times. I can teach you a few things." She nodded wisely and Cari tried to smile, but was afraid she wasn't very convincing.

"But as for me," she went on, "here's the bottom line. I want it all, but I don't want to do it grubbing in poverty. Max is my only hope for the good life. And I mean to take advantage of that hope any way I can."

Cari had to admire her honesty, even if she didn't think much of her ethics. Later, when C.J. and Randy had left, she told Max about what the woman had said.

"How well does that ranch do?" she asked him.

He shrugged. "The ranch is mortgaged to the hilt, from what I've been able to ascertain. They tell me she can't come up with the monthly fees at this point."

"Isn't there some way you can just sort of squeeze her out?"

He grinned at her terminology. "It's complicated. If this was an ordinary project, I wouldn't hesitate. That's how you make the big deals. But in this case, my mother wouldn't stand for it. She wants everything aboveboard and by the rules. She has a certain compassion for C.J."

Cari could understand that. For Max's mother, C.J. was a part of the Texas she'd left behind and still seemed to yearn for.

"So you'll have to marry her?"

He merely shrugged and looked deep into her eyes without saying anything. Finally he just walked away.

A half hour later, he asked if she'd like to come out to the ranch with him the next day.

"I want to go out to see it. Every time I ask C.J. to take me out, she finds a way to avoid it. I want to go out on my own and find out what she's trying to hide."

"Sure. We'll go with you." She didn't go anywhere without Jamie anymore.

"Good. I've ordered a picnic basket from the kitchen. We'd better leave early, just in case C.J. and Randy get a yen to visit again."

She laughed. She thought it was funny that Randy seemed to have attached himself to C.J. so thoroughly at the same time the woman thought she was romancing Max—sort of.

She left Max to watch a little television, and she went to bed, glad she had her own nightgown instead of the T-shirt. She was exhausted. Taking care of a baby was tiring work, even when you loved every minute of it. She quickly went to sleep and slept like a log until the wee hours.

Something woke her. She opened her eyes and for just a few seconds, wasn't sure where she was. Turning toward the crib, she saw a shadowy figure standing there and she gasped.

"Relax." It was Max. "It's only me. Jamie was whimpering, so I came in to make sure he was okay."

She reached out and turned on the bedside light and there he was, holding Jamie in his arms, the picture of the perfect dad. Joy filled her heart and tears sprang to her eyes.

"Oh, Max," she said, blubbering a bit.

"What's the matter?" He was astonished. "Did I frighten you that much? Cari, I'm sorry."

"No, it's not that." Slipping out of bed, she pulled her robe on and went to him, kissing his cheek and then smiling at the baby. "I'm just so happy," she said, choking on her words and smiling at him tearfully. "I just… it's just that my husband…" She sniffed and shook her head. "Never mind."

Max looked concerned. He started to put Jamie down in the crib but the baby was having none of it and started to whimper for real.

"Uh-oh," she said, looking down at the baby lovingly. "It looks like it's going to be one of those nights."

"One of what nights?" Max said as he pulled him back up into his arms.

"We're going to have to walk him."

"What do you mean?"

She smiled at him. "You'll see. I'll take the first shift. You can watch and learn." She shrugged. "Or go ahead and go back to bed," she added, giving him an out. "Whatever."

She changed his diapers and put on a fresh shirt and they tried putting him down to sleep again, but, just as she'd feared, he was totally awake and ready to play.

"No hope," she said cheerfully. "He going to need some coaxing to get back to sleep."

She pulled Jamie's blanket around him and put him to her shoulder, then started out toward the living room. Max followed close behind, slumping onto the couch as she began to pace with the baby in her arms.

"They love this," she told him. "The longer you walk, the happier they get."

"But do they go to sleep?"

"Ah, that's the question. That's why we're doing this. But sleep can be long in coming." She held Jamie close and kissed the top of his head. "There were nights I spent hours walking Michelle. Luckily, I think Jamie is a better sleeper than she was. He ought to go out pretty quickly."

He watched for a few minutes, then said quietly, "You've never told me much about your marriage, Cari. What was your husband like?"

"Brian?" She bit her lip. This wasn't one of her favorite topics. "He was just a guy."

"There's something I've wondered about," he went on. Rising, he met her on one of her passes and took her hand in his, spreading her fingers. "No rings. Why is that? As a widow, I would think you would want to have that sort of memento of your marriage."

She stared at her own hand and nodded slowly.

"I used to have rings."

"What happened to them?"

She looked up into his face. "I sold them."

He narrowed his eyes, searching her face as though he wanted to understand. "You sold your rings?"

"Yes."

Jamie began to stir, and she pulled her hand away from Max so that she could start pacing again.

"I had a beautiful wedding set with a very pretty diamond," she went on as she walked. "But I sold them. They went to pay for me finishing college and starting on my real estate license." She smiled at the irony of it all. "Brian never knew that he financed my new start in life."

Max had a point about the rings. If she'd valued her marriage, she would have kept them, no matter how tight money got. But she couldn't really grieve for Brian, not the way she knew she should. By the time he'd died, she'd known she was going to have to leave him one way or another.

He'd made life with him impossible and had pretty much killed the love she'd once had for him. When she thought about it now she couldn't believe she'd stayed as long as she had. What had kept her with him once she'd known he was getting more and more irrational? The fear of admitting failure, she supposed.

"So you're getting a real estate license?" he noted, interested that she would have chosen a field so close to his. "Why? Residential real estate is dead as the proverbial doornail in most areas right now."

"I know. But real estate always comes back. And I want to be ready when that happens."

He nodded, glad for the evidence that she was an optimist. He liked that about her.

She smiled at him. "In the meantime, I don't mind working as a waitress. It's honest work and I can make a decent living as long as I only have myself to take care of."

Jamie chose that moment to begin happily making motorboat noises. They both laughed.

"It doesn't sound like he's falling asleep," Max said.

"Not yet," she replied. "It takes a while sometimes."

"Let me take my turn," he said, reaching for the baby. "You sit down and tell me about your marriage," he said.

She gazed into his eyes. "Why do you want to know?" she wondered.

He touched her cheek with the palm of his hand. "Because I care about you," he said simply. And as he said the words, he knew it was true. He'd never known a woman like Cari before, never had a relationship like this. He liked her. He wanted to talk to her. He wanted to know more about her. That had never happened with a woman before. But it felt right.

"Sit. And talk." He began to pace with Jamie cuddled nicely in his arms.

She sat. She usually hated to talk about the past. But tonight the words just started to flow out.

"I knew Brian for years. All through high school. I had no excuse." She sighed. Wasn't that the truth? It was amazing how one could delude oneself. "I knew what he was like. But I had the young girl's syndrome, thinking love would conquer all, marriage would change him, I would change him, my love would show him the way."

"Change him how?" Max asked.

"Change him from being a jerk, I suppose," she said with a short laugh. "Change him into a decent person and a good husband and father. It didn't happen, of course."

"It hardly ever does," he agreed.

She nodded. "Living with Brian was like living with a human geyser. You never knew what might set him off, but you knew he was going to blow. And it was over something different every time."

Max's tone was tense. "Was he violent with you?"

She hesitated. What was the point of going over all that? "Only a little."

She could see the veins in Max's neck cord and she hurried to add, "I knew where it all stemmed from. His father was an alcoholic and he had a very rough childhood. You always think that love and goodness will heal things like that. And they so seldom do. It's just not enough to overcome the damage that sort of childhood does."

It was funny. She'd never told anyone, even Mara, all these details. So why was she telling Max? Of all the people in the world, he was probably the one who least needed to know these things about her. But it was such a relief to tell someone about it.

"I don't want to make it sound like unrelieved agony. It wasn't like that at all. There were many good times. He could make me laugh. And he loved the baby." Her voice softened as she thought of her baby. "Michelle was a perfect baby, all pink and plump and smiling. He was so proud of her. And yet…" Her voice got a little rough.

"When she cried, he would go crazy. He couldn't stand it. It almost seemed as though he thought she was trying to get to him on purpose. He took it personally. I would do everything I could to keep her from crying." She choked as painful memories surged. "Sometimes he would smash things," she said, her voice barely above a whisper. "And then he would leave."

Max stopped in front of her, staring down. "But he didn't hurt you? Or the baby?"

"Not…not really." She was skimming over the truth a bit here, but she really didn't want to dredge all that up again. "I was afraid of that, though. He would just get so irrational. There was no telling what he would do eventually. That last night, he was so angry."

She closed her eyes as she remembered, and her voice became almost robotic.

"He grabbed Michelle and raced out to the car with her. I ran after him, pleading with him to leave her, but he threw her into the backseat and started the car up. She was screaming at the top of her lungs. I was frantic. I managed to get into the car before he had time to lock the doors. We took off down the street. I was trying to climb over the seat to get into the back to take care of Michelle when he…he…" She closed her eyes again, seeing it as though it were yesterday. "We crashed into a fence and then a tree."

She took a shuddering breath and looked up into his face. His beautiful eyes were filled with compassion and reflected her pain. Somehow that was so comforting.

"It could have been my fault," she hurried to add. "I'm just not sure. The way I was climbing over the seat, only thinking about getting to Michelle, not about how I might be interfering with his driving. I can't put all the blame on Brian."

Max snorted. "I can," he muttered, beginning to walk again.

"I was in the hospital for about a week. A couple of broken ribs and injuries to a few internal organs." She shrugged. "I got better. They didn't." She took a deep breath. "They didn't tell me that Brian and Michelle were dead at first. I kept asking for her."

Tears filled her eyes and she shook her head angrily. She didn't want to cry. She'd done enough crying to fill an ocean, and she'd thought she didn't have any more tears to give. But there were always more.

Max was leaving the room. She blinked after him.

"Where are you going?"

"He's asleep," he told her softly. "I'm putting him in his crib."

She nodded, rising to follow him. By the time she got to the nursery, he'd put Jamie down and covered him. He turned and took her in his arms, raining kisses on her face and muttering something in Italian.

She laughed with tears still filling her eyes. When he kissed her, she kissed him back, giving him her passion as well as her joy. But only for a moment.

"No," she said, pulling away from him. "Max, no."

He said something in Italian. She didn't understand the words, but she knew his meaning. She shook her head.

"No," she said again. "Max, you're going to marry C.J. You're going to belong to another woman. We can't."

This time the Italian was a curse word she fully understood, but he released her, only to grab her hand and hold it up.

"You should have rings," he said with Italian intensity. "You should have beautiful jewelry to match your beautiful eyes. You should be draped in diamonds."

She laughed aloud. What a concept!

"I don't need jewelry," she told him. "It just gets in the way."

He shook his head in disgust at her attitude, and then he kissed her again. Gently but firmly, she pushed him away and led him to the door of the room.

"Good night, Max," she told him, her growing affection for the man shining in her eyes. "Better get some sleep."

"Yes," he reluctantly agreed. "Don't forget. We're driving out to the ranch in the morning."

"I'll be up early," she promised.

He gave her a crooked grin. "So will I. We have no choice. We play by Jamie's rules these days, don't we?"

The drive to the ranch went through some beautiful Texas landscape. Max filled the time with stories his mother had told him over the years of adventures she'd had growing up in the Texas countryside, stories that made it sound like an ideal place for an old-fashioned upbringing. But the arrival, when it came, was anticlimactic.

"This can't be it," Max said, staring at the dilapidated buildings on a hill that appeared to stand at the end of the driveway leading up from the highway where the Triple M Ranch sign hung by one corner on a rusty archway.

There was a gate, but it gave easily to a little push from the nose of the car. They drove slowly up the long entry. Straggly trees lined the way, only a few of them still alive. The buildings were empty. It was pretty obvious no one had been living there for quite some time.

"I don't see any sign of cattle," Max said, shielding his eyes from the sun as he gazed out over the dusty plains surrounding the hill. "This doesn't even look like a working ranch." He shook his head. "And this certainly doesn't look like the ranch my mother told me about all my life. They've let it go to hell. It's a damn shame."

Cari could see how disappointed he was. "Maybe we came to the wrong side of the property," she suggested.

He shook his head. "No. This seems to be it. No wonder C.J. didn't want me coming out here."

"Well, we can have our picnic here at least," she said, beginning to unload the car and set up a shaded place for Jamie.

Max agreed, though he was grouchy about it. She felt sorry for him, but she couldn't help but wonder how this was going to impact his plans. If this made him look at things more realistically, maybe it was all for the best.

They spread out a ground cloth under a tree and opened up the picnic basket to find fried chicken and biscuits and corn on the cob.

"In February?" Max said, looking at the corn suspiciously.

"It's either imported or frozen," Cari agreed. "Not quite up to the quality you expect in the good old summertime, but it tastes pretty good."

They ate and chatted and played with Jamie, and gradually Max's mood improved. He got to the point where he could see some of the good things in the land around him, such as the wildflowers just beginning to poke up their heads, and the white, puffy clouds scudding by in a pure blue sky.

"You know, I have to admit, this place could have fit in with my mother's stories in better times. But beyond that, I had a different picture of the ranch in mind."

"Did you?"

"Yes. I realize now it wasn't even based on what she'd told me. I watched that TV show. What was the name of that ranch on it? Southfork? Well, that was sort of the picture I had in my mind. A big house. A big barn. Lots of big cars parked out front. A helicopter pad out back. Miles and miles of expensive fencing. Some cattle, maybe."

She smiled, nodding. "I've seen the show."

"Even though this might have been an impressive place in its day," he said, "it was never like Southfork. Still, it was probably a good working ranch. Too bad that time seems to be long past." He grimaced. "I'm glad my mother isn't here to see this. I hope no one ever tells her about it."

They drove back to the city, taking the long way and enjoying the scenery. Max's mobile chimed and he pulled over to take the call. He looked serious as he listened, but Cari was playing with Jamie and didn't pay too much attention. When he'd hung up, he turned to her.

"Bad news," he said shortly. "Sheila won't be coming back." His gaze flickered over Jamie and he winced slightly. "They found her body in the river. Seems to be drug related."

"Oh, Max!"

They both looked at the child who was happily playing with a ring of plastic keys, totally oblivious to the fate of his mother. Then they looked at each other and without a word, came together for a long embrace. This was a tragedy for a baby, but at least he was too young to understand what an earthshaking event had just contorted his life. Perhaps it was best that way.

Back in town, Max made some calls and came up with more news.

"The police haven't been able to find any relatives for Sheila, and neither have any of my people." He looked deeply into Cari's eyes. "Everything is going to ride on the DNA results."

She laced her fingers under her chin as she considered that. "And if they come back negative?"

He looked pained. "Cari, if that happens, it will be out of my hands. If I have no marriage or blood ties to Jamie, there is nothing I can do. I'll have no right to keep him here." He shook his head. "Even all those lawyers I pay so much money to won't be able to fix that one."

She shrunk back. "So he would go into the county system."

"I imagine so."

If that happened…

Oh, it couldn't happen. Blindly, she turned and hurried back to the nursery. Jamie was sound asleep, but she had to hold him. Hadn't there been a time she'd vowed not to fall in love? That time seemed very long ago.

CHAPTER NINE

"As I UNDERSTAND it, tomorrow is Valentine's Day."

Cari straightened as Max came into the nursery two days later. She gave him a mischievous smile.

"You are correct, sir," she replied.

He stood gazing down at her, a twinkle in his eyes.

"Is it true that this is a fairly important day to women in this country?" he asked.

She frowned, wondering what the catch was going to be. "Well, it can be."

"Good." He smiled like the proverbial cat. "I've made arrangements."

"Arrangements?" Did she really have to hear about the details? "Are you going to do something with C.J.?"

His dark gaze was like velvet. "No. I'm going to do something with you."

"Me." Her eyes widened. Why not C.J.? Wasn't that the woman he was supposedly going to marry? Maybe not. She knew he'd been working on that for the past few days.

"There's got to be a way to convince her to sell that

wreck of a ranch," he'd fumed more than once. "I'm willing to pay her twice what it's worth. And I want her to close on this as soon as possible. I want to begin renovating the place before my mother finds out what a mess it's in."

"She claims she'll never sell."

He'd stared at her with haunted eyes. "She has to sell," he'd said. "She'll do it. If I can just find the right approach." But he didn't sound very convincing.

And now he was talking about taking her to a romantic dinner instead of C.J.

"I can't go anywhere," she protested. "I've got to be here for Jamie."

He nodded. "We're going to bring him along."

She gazed at him suspiciously. "Where are we going?"

He raised an eyebrow. "Nowhere."

"What?"

He grinned, chucking her under the chin. "It's a surprise. You wait and see."

And then he was gone.

She sighed, half laughing. Anyone watching the two of them over the past few days would swear they were lovers. And in truth, she felt like his lover. The only things missing were commitment and some honest-to-goodness lovemaking. But neither of those things could happen with C.J. lurking in the wings.

And of course there was the constant awareness that this was a passing fancy, something meant to last for days, not years or a lifetime. But she was intrigued that he meant to celebrate Valentine's Day with her and not with C.J. And just what would C.J. have to say about that, she wondered?

The phone call came the next afternoon, just as Cari began getting ready for their Valentine's dinner. The DNA test results were in. Max was asked to meet with a panel of lab technicians and legal representatives, and he left right away. Cari stayed behind and worried.

They'd had a small memorial service for Sheila. C.J. and Randy had come. Cari had taken Jamie as well, just so someone could tell him in later years that he had been to a ceremony honoring his mother's life, even if he had no idea what it was all about at the time.

And now they were going to find out whether Jamie would be staying with Max, where Cari was completely sure he belonged, or not. It was nail-biting time. She went into the nursery and watched Jamie sleeping. If they had to give this adorable child up, surely she wouldn't be able to stand it.

She heard Max come in and she ran to the front room. One look at his face told her all she needed to know. The test had come in with a positive match. With a shriek of joy, she ran to him and he swung her up in the air, both of them laughing with happiness. Tears streamed down her face. It was the best moment she'd had in many years.

They went into the nursery and Max looked down at the little child who carried his brother's legacy. Finally he was free to let his heart fill with love for the boy without reservation. This was truly a special day.

"The first thing I need to do is call my mother," he noted.

"Not now," she protested. "The time difference."

He shook his head. "She won't care. Not when she hears what I'm calling about."

"Does she have any idea that there is a baby?"

"No. I didn't want to get her hopes up so I never told her about Sheila's claim." He grinned, shaking his head. "This is just incredible, isn't it? I can hardly believe it."

Cari nodded happily. She was bound and determined not to let herself think about the fact that this meant it was the beginning of the end for her and her connection to Max. She would think about that tomorrow. Tonight, they would just enjoy the news.

"Now we really have something to celebrate," Max said.

Two hours later he was leading her, with Jamie in the stroller, to the elevator.

"Did you talk to your mother?" she asked.

"No. It turns out she is staying with a friend. But I left a message for her to call me as soon as she gets my message."

"Good. Now tell me. Where are we going?"

He shook his head, eyeing her with thinly veiled affection. "My lips are sealed. I ought to put a blindfold on you. That way you might actually be surprised."

"No blindfolds," she said. "I promise to be as surprised as I need to be."

She'd assumed they would be eating somewhere in the hotel, but she hadn't realized it would be a private conference room. When he opened the double doors to let them enter, she gasped. Max had ordered up decorations, and the staff had filled the room with red and white balloons, with white lacy streamers hanging from the rafters and beautiful potted trees covered with white and red birds in each corner. A small table was set with delicate china and gleaming silver. In the corner, a guitarist was setting up his music and soon was playing soft, romantic melodies.

Cari was enchanted. She'd never seen anything more beautiful. She turned to Max, her eyes shining.

"Happy Valentine's Day," he said.

"Oh, Max, thank you. This is lovely."

He dropped a kiss on her lips and then escorted her to her place at the table and rolled the stroller up next to her. Luckily, Jamie had fallen asleep as soon as they had started on their journey through the hotel, so she would have some time to devote to Max and the wonderful dinner he'd ordered up. She tucked the blanket around the baby, then straightened and noticed a long, flat velvet box had been set in front of her.

"Max," she said warningly.

"Just a little Valentine's present," he said.

Her heart was beating in her throat as she pulled open the box, then drew her breath in sharply. She was

almost blinded by the flash of fire from diamonds—
more diamonds than she'd ever seen in one place before.

"What…?"

"Let me help you."

He came behind her to put on the necklace. It was
surprisingly light for something with so many diamonds. She looked at her own reflection in the mirror
on the other side of the room and she could hardly
breathe. She'd never seen anything so beautiful.

"And to go with the necklace…" He reached into the
pocket of his suit coat and pulled out a matching
bracelet. "One without the other would be incomplete,"
he said as he put it on her wrist.

"Oh, Max." She was stunned and overwhelmed. "Oh,
Max, I can't—"

"Yes, you can," he said firmly. Going down on one knee
so that he could look into her eyes, he was adamant. "Cari,
don't insult me by refusing my gift. I can well afford it.
You don't have to feel any special obligation or gratitude
or anything like that. It's just a gift. A token of my affection for you. And you know very well that's for real."

He kissed her gently, softly, and with a purity of
emotion she could hardly stand to accept. It was like
looking into the sun. It was almost too much to bear.

Looking at his face, she realized how much more
than handsome he was. There was honesty and integrity there, and an earnest desire to make her happy. Her
heart was full. Yet she was uncertain.

"But I don't need gifts to prove that," she protested.

"No, you don't need them. But it makes me happy to give you diamonds. Can you allow me that happiness?"

She looked at him in wonder, and then she laughed. "Oh, Max," she said. "Do you always get your way?"

"Of course."

Dinner was served, and it consisted of a wonderful Italian pork dish in a pinot noir reduction sauce along with a cheesy pasta to die for. There was also a lovely salad and the pièce de résistance—a heart-shaped baked Alaska. They ate with gusto and sipped red wine and talked and laughed, and when the meal was over, they danced to the music the guitarist played.

Diamonds glittered when she moved and the reflections of their light flashed against the walls of the room. It almost seemed a counterpart to the way Max's touch sizzled on her skin. It had been a magical evening, but she knew it was drawing to a close. If only there was some way to keep it going all night.

"This is the most perfect Valentine's Day I've ever had," she told him simply.

"Good." He dropped a kiss on her lips. "Not too ordinary?" he teased.

She shook her head. "Not a bit ordinary," she said. Reaching up, she touched his face with the flat of her hand. "Oh, Max," she began, feeling the need to express to him how she felt.

But she never got the chance. Before she could get another word out, C.J.'s voice was booming through the room.

"So this is what you're up to, is it? I should have known."

There she stood, hands on her hips, green eyes flashing angry fire.

"C.J." Max started toward her. "What are you doing here?"

"Looking for you. What else? It's Valentine's Day. But I see you know that." She glared at him. "Don't you think you should have been with me? I'm the one you're supposed to marry."

Max stopped dead and stared at her coldly. "C.J., I haven't made any sort of commitment to you and you know it."

"It's her, isn't it?" she cried, pointing at Cari. "It's because of her. You've fallen in love with her, haven't you?" Swinging around, she faced Cari. "If it wasn't for you, we could have this whole deal done by now." She took a step toward Cari, shaking her head as though she were beseeching her. "Look, I've stood back and I've been tolerant. I knew he went for you, not me. That was okay. I figured, if he wants to have some fun on the side, let him. That doesn't bother me at all. But I want the wedding ring on my finger, I want the marriage certificate in my hand. Then he can do whatever he wants."

"C.J., you're embarrassing yourself," Max told her quietly, controlling his temper with obvious effort.

"Oh, yeah?" She tossed her flaming hair back and glared. "Well, get this, mister. This is it. No more Ms.

Nice Guy. I want a wedding date and I want it now. Or you can forget about your mother getting back her beloved ranch."

Max looked pained. "Go home, C.J. You weren't invited here."

Her face reddened in outrage. "Be careful, Max. My patience is not infinite."

"Good. It shouldn't be. And in that vein, let me explain more explicitly." He stood before her, legs apart, arms at his sides. "I'm not going to marry you. Not ever. And if that means my mother will have to forgo having her ranch back, that is the price we will have to pay."

C.J.'s head went back, but her glare didn't dim.

He shook his head, exasperated with her. "But you know very well we aren't in love with each other. And even more important, we don't suit each other at all. We would both be miserable tied together by a wedding vow. Upon reflection, I've decided it would be a very bad move. So it's out. Sorry."

On a certain level, Cari felt sorry for the woman. She'd made her intentions clear from the beginning. It was too bad she hadn't noticed earlier that her plans were just not panning out. Cari was watching the scene carefully and she saw the anger in C.J.'s face. Anger and frustration. But no pain, no sadness. This failure had touched her spirit, but not her heart. That relieved Cari somewhat.

Randy appeared out of nowhere and was helping to get C.J. out of the room, though she was still railing at Max.

Valentine's Day was over. And just in time, Jamie woke up.

CHAPTER TEN

IT WAS a good hour later before they settled down and got Jamie back to sleep, in his bed this time. Cari was still trying to come to terms with what had happened. Max had pretty much rejected the plan to marry C.J. Did he mean it? And what did that mean for the prospects of getting his mother the ranch? She couldn't help but worry.

Max was taciturn and restless, sitting on the couch not watching the television which played in the background. She knew he was thinking over the ramifications of what he'd just done. She slid onto the couch beside him and took his hand in hers.

"Max, you always say that you came to Dallas with two big goals in mind. Number one was to find your brother's son and to find proof that he is Gino's. And you've done that. You've saved Jamie's life and you are going to have a beautiful baby who will carry on Gino's memory and be a part of your family forever. You're giving your mother a gift of love that can't be equaled.

Jamie will remind you and your family every day of what a wonderful brother you had."

Max inclined his head, acknowledging everything she'd said as his fingers curled around hers. "You had a part in it all," he mentioned, but she waved that away.

"Your second goal was to return the ownership of the family ranch to your mother because losing it had preyed on her mind for years and you thought it would make her happy to have control of it again, something to help heal the unhealable wound losing Gino had dealt her. This you haven't achieved as yet."

"True."

Now came the hard part. "You know you could achieve it by marrying C.J."

He nodded. "But that's not going to happen."

She frowned, shaking her head. "Then how are you going to get control of the ranch?"

He grimaced and shrugged. "I'll find another way."

That chilled her. What if desperation drove him to do something illegal, or even underhanded in some way? She knew that would eat away at him. She couldn't let something like that happen. But what could she do? When it came right down to it, this was none of her business. Why was she even delving into it?

Because she wanted to help him. Because she was worried about him. Because…and this was the bottom line…she was in love with him.

Yes, it was true, and she had to admit it to herself.

She'd fallen in love with the man she'd vowed to harden her heart to from the start. What a fool she was.

Turning, she looked at his handsome face, and some of her self-criticism faded. He was so gorgeous and so good and so lovable. How could she not fall for a man like this?

Especially now as he moved closer and he took her chin in his hand and he began to kiss her mouth with quick, hungry nips that made her gasp. Ordinarily she would pull away. Ordinarily she would protest. But he wasn't marrying C.J. anymore. So she was going to give in to temptation for just a few minutes. It just felt so good.

His hands held her head on either side now, and his kisses were growing deeper and more urgent. Reaching up, she dug her fingers into his thick hair and arched her breasts against him. He was so very male and she was so very female and they were caught up in a dance as old as life. Every part of her body began to relax, and then to tingle with pleasure. She wanted his hands on her breasts, and his lips, too. She wanted to feel him crush her to the couch with his hard body. She wanted all of him.

The phone rang. For a moment she thought he was going to ignore the sound of the phone and make love to her instead. That was what she wanted. That was what he wanted, too. But in the back of her mind she knew this had to be his mother. Gathering all her strength, she pushed back and startled him into noticing.

"It's going to be your mother," she panted, pulling her clothing together. "You'd better take it."

"I'll call her later," he muttered, kissing her again.

"No, Max. You'll hate yourself if you don't take this call."

It took another minute for him to come to his senses, but when he did, he rose and took the phone call. She sat on the couch and smiled as she listened to their conversation. It was in half in Italian, but she understood every word and every emotion. As Max explained about Jamie, the astonished joy on the other side of the Atlantic was easy to feel. It was a good night.

And a lucky phone call. If his mother hadn't interrupted, she might have made love with Max. Her willpower had eroded beyond usefulness for a moment there. She had it back now. She knew it would be crazy to make love with a man, no matter how much you loved him, without some sort of plan or commitment. And she had neither. So she was going to give him one last kiss and go off to her bed—alone. Sighing, she turned and prepared to do just that.

Cari was juggling baby bottles and Jamie the next morning when her phone rang. It was Mara.

"Did you have a nice Valentine's Day?" she asked hopefully.

Cari smiled into the phone. "It was wonderful."

"Good. I'm so glad we fixed that." Mara sighed happily. "So, where did you and Randy go last night?"

It had been a while since she'd talked to her friend. Her heart sank as she realized Mara didn't have a clue as to what had been going on. How was she going to tell her?

"Mara, I didn't go out with Randy."

There was a shocked pause, then Mara cried, "What? But I talked to him and he said…"

"If he said he was out for Valentine's, he must have been out with C.J."

"C.J.?" Her voice was rising. "Who is C.J.?"

Mara was sounding a bit tightly wound at this point. Cari tried to use a soothing tone.

"You remember about C.J. She's the other woman in the big mix-up."

"Oh. Ah. And so I imagine you were out with the other man?" She was back to being hopeful again.

"Yes. Max Angeli."

Mara laughed. "Okay, I can hear it in the way you say his name. You're in love, aren't you?"

She never gave up. Cari was halfway between laughter and outrage.

"No!"

Mara nagged at her for another twenty minutes but, Cari wouldn't break down and admit it, not even to her best friend—even though she was very much afraid it was true.

And if it was true, just what exactly was she going to do about it?

There wasn't really much she could do. Max had told C.J. he wouldn't marry her last night, but in the bright light of morning, she couldn't take that seriously.

She knew him well enough by now to know he would do anything he had to do to heal his mother's heart. And that was one of the things she loved about him.

She gave Jamie a bath and cleaned his room and put him in an adorable baby suit. But all the while, her mind was on the facts, and the facts were stubborn things.

She had to face them. She had to be realistic. Max had a lot of affection for her. He enjoyed being with her. And he definitely wanted her in his bed—he'd made that perfectly clear. But he'd never said one word about marrying her, had he? He hadn't even contemplated that as much as he had contemplated marrying C.J. Marriage of any sort did not seem to be on his horizon.

He'd made it clear from the beginning that he wasn't the marrying kind. And she'd told him much the same about herself. Too bad she'd changed her mind. He obviously hadn't.

And no, she couldn't see herself as a paid mistress, traveling to Venice with the family, being with Max as long as his interest lasted, then segueing into the role of nanny once he'd moved on to someone else.

Ugh. That picture didn't fit at all. There was no way she could live her life like that. Painful as it was, she was going to have to withdraw from the field. There was no other way.

But how could she leave Max? She knew now that she loved him. And how could she leave Jamie? She loved Jamie almost as much as she'd loved Michelle. Well, she'd survived losing her own baby. Now she would have to develop ways to live through losing Jamie—but with a broken heart that might never be repaired.

She tried to talk to Max about it the next day when he came home for lunch. He brought in burgers in a sack and they sat down at the dining-room table to eat out of cardboard containers. She mentioned a few things obliquely at first, venturing carefully into the subject, but he dismissed it out of hand.

"I'm not marrying C.J.," he stated firmly. "I'll find another way to get the ranch. And I want you here with Jamie. That's all there is to it."

She licked her lips and tried to think of a way to make him understand. "I think I should go. I have a feeling you would be better able to negotiate with C.J. if I was out of the picture."

He was astonished and not very happy to hear this theory. "I don't want you out of the picture. I need you in my life."

"Max, there's no room for me in your life. It's already too crowded in there. You've got too much going on as it is."

He dismissed that with a wave of his hand. "Cari, C.J. is irrational. She wants things that cannot be. Whether you are here or not, she is still going to want those things."

Cari shook her head, looking troubled. "I don't know. I think my being here puts her back up and makes her more rigid in her demands. If I were gone she might be more reasonable."

"Yes, but I wouldn't be," he noted dryly. "If you were gone, I'd be a bear to live with."

He was teasing and not really taking what she was saying seriously. She could understand that. He didn't want her to go, so he was rationalizing that it was for the best that she stay. But she felt she could see things a little more clearly. She had to go.

Max left for a meeting with the lawyers, and she called Mara and got the number of the person she used for babysitting. Calling her, she made arrangements for the woman to come right over and begin taking care of Jamie. Then she went into the nursery and pulled out the velvet box with the necklace and bracelet inside. She looked at it for a long moment, sliding her hand over the surface. Then she pressed it to her cheek and closed her eyes, remembering how it felt to dance with Max while a guitar played in the background. It had been a wonderful night she would never forget. But it was over. Bracing herself, she walked briskly into Max's room and left the velvet box on his dresser.

She spent an hour showing the babysitter where everything was and getting Jamie used to her. And then she packed all her belongings into one suitcase on wheels and took one last look around the hotel suite. She'd only lived there for a little over a week, but it had become home very quickly. She was going to miss it.

And the emotion she was going to feel when she left Jamie behind didn't bear thinking of. Her heart dropped every time she did think of it. But she had to do what she had to do. And finally, it was time.

She'd barely made it to the hallway when the elevator dinged. Tensing, she waited to see if Max was back. But it wasn't Max. An older woman got off the elevator and started her way.

Max's mother. It had to be.

Cari watched her for a moment. A tall, regal-looking woman, she seemed more European elite than Texas rancher. Where was the evidence of that wild young girl who had ridden bareback over the plains and hunted rattlesnakes with the boys?

"Hello," she said, her eyes friendly as she looked at Cari. "I'm looking for the suite that belongs to Max Angeli. Can you direct me?"

"Of course," she said. "Please come this way." She escorted her to the door and rang the bell. "Someone will let you in any moment," she said, and as the woman turned to face the door, she added, sotto voce, "I'm in love with your son."

"What is that, my dear?" she said, turning back to look at her curiously.

Cari shook her head and smiled. "Nothing," she said. "It was nice to meet you, Mrs. Angeli."

She walked away quickly, not waiting for a reply.

It was almost comforting to be back at work at the café—the same old routine, the same old people—she'd missed it all. It felt so nice and ordinary. There was that word again. That made her laugh, and then it made her tear up. Ordinary. That was exactly what she was.

All the diamonds and the luxury rooms and the fancy foods—that was for some other person, not for her. She belonged here in ordinaryland.

Mara was upset, of course. "Well, there's still Randy," she pointed out when Cari told her what had happened.

"Oh, Mara, please! He's head over heels in love with C.J. You should see him mooning after her."

"But if she goes off with Max—"

"No. That won't work. You see, the whole situation was never going to be Max and C.J. setting up housekeeping. She just wanted to be his wife for all the rights and privileges—and money—and wasn't expecting to fulfill any of the responsibilities. She made it perfectly plain that was never in the cards. I'll tell you, from what I've seen, I think she prefers Randy when you come right down to it. She can boss him around."

On the first day back at work, she kept looking at the entry doors, expecting to see Max come strolling through. But he didn't come. And he didn't come the next day, either. By the third day she had pretty much decided she must have dreamed the whole thing. Maybe there really wasn't such a person as Max Angeli. Maybe Jamie was a manifestation of her grief. Who knew?

She'd been so sure she would never love again. She'd been so sure that she was too wary to let another man steal her heart. But she'd thrown all that to the winds

and fallen for Max. Now she was back to square one,
but with a new crack down the center of her heart. Hopefully, she'd learned something. Why did lessons like this
have to hurt so much?

On the fourth day she was talking a cowboy into
having a piece of lemon meringue pie when a lovely
older woman entered the café. Cari didn't recognize
her at first, as she wouldn't have expected to see her
there in the café in a hundred years. But she knew right
away she'd seen her before, and for just a second, she
assumed it was a movie star or a TV performer. Then
she realized it was Max's mother.

Max's mother. Her first thought was something had
happened, something bad. But that fear died quickly.
The woman looked too calm, too sanguine.

She came up and took a seat at the counter.

"Hello," she said as her gaze met Cari's.

"Mrs. Angeli," Cari said a bit breathlessly, wiping her
hands on her apron and hoping her hair wasn't too wild.

"You recognize me." She smiled.

"Of course. I'm…"

"Cari Christensen. Yes, I know." She reached out and
shook Cari's hand. "I just felt I should come in and say
hello to you and thank you for all you did to help settle
my grandson into his new life."

"It was my pleasure. How is he?"

"Wonderful. Perfect. We couldn't be happier."

"I'm so glad." They smiled at each other.

"I'm sure he'd like to see you again."

Cari's smile faded. "I'd love to see him, too. But I don't think it would be a good idea."

"I understand. Breaking away is so hard."

"Yes."

She ordered a piece of chocolate cake and a glass of milk. Cari wondered if that was what she used to order as a girl whenever she came into town. But the café was filling up, and Cari was too busy to talk any longer. When she looked up a bit later, Mrs. Angeli was gone.

It was the next day that Max came in.

"Hi," he said, his gaze never leaving her face from the moment he entered the café.

"Hi."

He stood before her, his eyes luminous. "I've missed you."

She could hardly breathe. "Me, too."

Reaching out, he cupped her cheek with his hand.

"Max, don't," she whispered helplessly.

He shrugged and drew his hand back.

"Can I get you anything?" she asked.

"Sure," he said, sliding onto a seat at the counter. "How about a piece of apple pie?"

"Coming right up."

It was good to have something to do with her hands. They were shaking. She put a piece of pie on a plate and carried it over to where he was sitting.

"Thanks."

"You're welcome."

She stood watching him as he ate, her heart beating in her throat. Why was he here? And why hadn't he come looking for her sooner? But she knew the answer to that. He had other things on his mind. Like the ranch. Like C.J.

"I hear my mother came in to see you," he said suddenly, looking up.

"Yes, she did."

He had a slight smile. "She liked you."

Cari's smile was bigger. "That's nice. I liked her, too." She hesitated, then added, "She said Jamie was doing well."

"Oh, yeah. She adores him."

"Of course."

They smiled at each other, agreement about Jamie's wonderfulness warming the connection between them.

"He's going to be the most spoiled baby in Dallas."

"I'm sure of it."

"And the ranch? Has she been out there?"

He pushed the pie plate away. "See, here's the funny thing. I didn't want her to go. I was scared to death to have her see what a dump it was. But she insisted, so we packed up and went out there. C.J. even came along."

"And? Was she devastated?"

He shook his head. "Not at all. In fact, as far as she's concerned, it looks a lot like it looked when she lived there."

Cari's jaw dropped. "No!"

He grinned. "She was ecstatic. She went running around exploring every nook and cranny, remembering when she'd hidden under the front porch when trying to get out of chores or where she'd found an arrowhead near the well. She told C.J. stories about her mother she'd never known before, showed her where she and Betty Jean had snuck out to go to a dance in town when they weren't supposed to, things like that."

Cari was astounded. The place was such a dump. "How did C.J. like that?"

"She was very touched. She was crying half the time."

"C.J.?"

He nodded. "In fact, she's selling us the ranch."

A wave of emotion hit her hard and she was light-headed. "No kidding," she said breathlessly. This was huge. But what did it mean?

"She and Randy are going to use the money to fund an expansion of his catering business. They want to be the biggest caterer in Texas." He shrugged, looking up at her. "I think they'll get married."

Cari had to grip the edge of the counter to keep from falling over. "Wow. Well, more power to them." She blinked rapidly, wondering why he was torturing her this way. "And you? Are you going back to Venice soon?"

"Yes." His gaze was black as coal. "We're getting ready to go this weekend. Just for a few days, though. We'll be back."

"Oh," she said faintly.

He rose from his seat. "Well, I'd better get going. I've got a lot of packing to do. Jamie's got enough stuff to fill a plane on his own by now."

"I imagine." Her heart sank. He was going. So that was it, then. It really was over.

"Cari?"

"Hmm?" She looked up, feeling bereft.

He moved close to her. "Jamie loves you and misses you."

She shook her head, confused. "How do you know that?"

His mouth twisted at the corners. "Because we all love you and miss you."

"Oh." What? Maybe she wasn't hearing words right any longer. She didn't really get it. What was he saying?

"Where's my bill?" he asked.

"Don't worry about it." She waved a hand in the air. "I'll take care of it."

"Okay." He smiled. "Then I'll just leave you a tip."

He put a small box on the counter. She stared at it.

"It's not a snake," he told her. "Go ahead. Open it."

She turned to look at him, terrified. "Max, what is it?"

"Open it and find out."

Her heart was beating so hard she could hardly make out what he was saying. "I don't think I should."

"Come on, Cari. I dare you. Do it."

Her fingers were trembling so hard she could hardly hold the box, but she managed to open it. Inside, set against black velvet, was the most beautiful diamond engagement ring she'd ever seen.

"Max!"

She turned to find him on one knee.

"Cari Christensen, I love you with all my heart," he announced to her and to everyone else in the place. "I need you in my life. Jamie needs you, too. He's got a grandmother, but he needs a mom. So here's the deal. Will you marry us?"

"Oh, Max, get up off the floor."

"Not until you answer me."

"Of course I'll marry you," she said, pulling at his hand and laughing at the same time. "I can't believe it took you so long to get over here and ask me."

EPILOGUE

THEY started out planning a small, simple wedding, but naturally, that didn't last. In no time at all, it grew into something monstrous. So it was a good thing they knew a good caterer.

They decided to have the event out on the ranch. Cari wasn't so sure at first, but once she saw the changes Max was already making, she was convinced. The driveway was lined with newly planted trees. The main farmhouse was still being renovated, but the lower floor was usable and a couple of the outer buildings, including the bunkhouse, were looking sturdy with new repairs to their structures and a couple of coats of new paint that left them gleaming. The sweeping area that made up the yard was green with new sod, creating a lawn where there hadn't been one for decades. Tables were set up on it, and a radius of white chairs for the ceremony. White tablecloths and silver vases filled with tulips decorated each table. The scene was magical.

People from all around the area began streaming in

an hour early. The ceremony itself was short, but touching. Handkerchiefs were liberally in use all around. And then came the reception.

Max and Cari stood in a seemingly never-ending receiving line, greeting old friends and meeting new ones. Jamie was with them when he was awake, and everyone oohed and aahed over him, which was just what he deserved. He'd grown ever closer to Cari, and she to him. As far as she was concerned, he was her baby, and that was all there was to it.

Her dress was a simple, strapless gown embedded with seed pearls. Her hair was piled high and the diamond necklace adorned her neck.

"You're a gorgeous bride," most people who passed told her. She knew it was traditional to say exactly that, but something in the eyes of the people saying it was beginning to convince her it might be true.

The food was spectacular—at least, that's what everyone told Cari, though she didn't have time to try any for herself.

"Does it occur to you," she noted to C.J., who was responsible for most of it, "that you've found a new golden goose with your catering business, one that you are raising and nurturing yourself?"

"That's right, go ahead and rub it in," C.J. snapped. "You won. I lost." But she smiled to soften her words and added, "I can take it. I've been kicked in the teeth a lot over the years. I must say, this is better. It's nice to have a man who adores me."

Cari nodded, watching Randy checking on the wedding cake. "He does do that."

"Yeah. But then, you've got that, too, don't you?"

Cari had to agree. She smiled at Max. He was making faces and gesturing and trying to convey something to her, but she couldn't understand what he was trying to say. She looked at him questioningly, but his mother came up to say something to him, and he looked away, just as Mara appeared before her.

"Hey," she said, beaming at her friend.

"Do you realize you would never have met Max if it wasn't for me?" Mara demanded. "I think I deserve some recognition. A plaque would be nice." She grinned at Cari.

"So you have to admit it has all worked out for the best," Cari responded.

Mara nodded. "Although I'd rather have you in the family than that C.J.," she told her with a sigh.

"Oh, C.J.'s okay. And she sure can cook."

"My, yes. I would never dispute that."

Cari turned away. One of the neighborhood girls who had been hired to help serve was tugging on her satin dress.

"Excuse me, Mrs. Angeli," she said.

Cari thrilled to hearing her new name for the first time. "Yes?"

"There's something wrong in the bunkhouse. Something broke. I was asked to get you to come right away."

"Oh, dear."

The bunkhouse was where they were storing most of the supplies. She looked at the receiving line and couldn't find Max. Whatever it was, she would have to handle it on her own and she'd better do it quickly. Gathering her skirt, she dashed across the sod to the bunkhouse and hurried inside. As she did so, the door closed behind her, the lock snapped, and she was suddenly engulfed in gloom.

"What is it?" She turned quickly and found herself being dragged into the arms of her new husband. "Max!"

"I couldn't wait any longer," he told her, raining kisses on her upturned face. "You are the most beautiful bride I've ever seen. Ripe for ravishing, I'd say."

"Would you say that?" She laughed low in her throat as he began a slow, sexy seduction. "A quick ravishment sounds pretty good to me, too."

She kissed him back, then sighed. "But we really can't. We've got to cut the cake and lead the dance and…"

He said something in Italian and began to peel her dress away. Sighing, she gave in. The cake and the dance would have to wait. Right now, love had the right of way.

TIPPING THE WAITRESS WITH DIAMONDS

NINA HARRINGTON

Nina Harrington grew up in rural Northumberland and decided at the age of eleven that she was going to be a librarian—because then she could read *all* of the books in the public library whenever she wanted! Since then she has been a shop assistant, community pharmacist, technical writer, university lecturer, volcano walker and industrial scientist, before taking a career break to realise her dream of being a fiction writer. When she is not creating stories which make her readers smile, her hobbies are cooking, eating, enjoying good wine—and talking, for which she has had specialist training.

Special Recipe for the Perfect Romance:

Step 1
Take One Single Italian Girl
Step 2
Add One Handsome Chef in a Kilt
Step 3
Throw in Two Teaspoons of Shock and Uncertainty
Step 4
Whisk Everything Together in a Tiny Bistro
Step 5
Add a Couple of Big Decisions…
Step 6
A Valentine Wish…
Step 7
Two Sparkling Brown Eyes…
Step 8
And a Pair of Pink Pyjamas
Step 9
Sprinkle with Pink Flamingos
Step 10
Add Hot Pink Psychedelic Flowers
Step 11
And a Box of Warm Memories
Step 12
Add a Platter of Sweet Dreams

Step 13
And Three Wedding Cakes…
Step 14
Eight Spinning Designer Rainbow Pizzas…
Step 15
And Two Glasses of Red Wine
Step 16
Smother in Wild Mushroom and Cream Sauce
Step 17
Mix with Three Heaped Spoonfuls of Tears
Step 18
And Two Pink Cupcakes
Step 19
Add One American Chef Without a Kilt
Step 20
Beat Vigorously
Step 21
Finish with One Portion of Chocolate Tiramisu
Step 22
Keep the Mixture Warm Until Valentine's Day; Top with
a Red Rose Before Serving with a Kiss.

CHAPTER ONE

Step 1: Take One Single Italian Girl

ONCE UPON A time, Sienna Rossi thought as she sat back in a creaky staffroom chair, *restaurants were filled with wonderful guests who loved your food and drink and smiled sweetly to the waiting staff.*

Then she grimaced at the memory of the businessman who had snapped his fingers at her not once but *twice* within ten minutes, because first there had been too much ice in his drink and then his starter had arrived with a garnish of salad leaves which had clearly been added specifically to poison him. No leaves. *Those days were gone.*

I could have decorated the shoulders of his expensive business suit with the salad leaves and poured the dressing over his shiny head, Sienna thought.

But she wouldn't have done it, of course.

There was far too little dressing on the salad to do any serious damage. Also, successful head waiters did not do things like that in exclusive country house hotels—especially head waiters who wanted desperately to be promoted to restaurant managers.

Now, if he had ordered Chef André's signature Hollandaise sauce... That might have been a different story.

Sienna yawned widely before reaching down to pull off her

stylish high-heeled shoes and massaging her feet with a satisfied sigh of relief. She should be used to swollen hot feet and crushed toes after ten years in the restaurant trade but it never got easier—especially in luxury hotels which excelled in fine dining.

Greystone Manor had become famous for fabulous food and its glorious English country house setting, and business lunches were booked weeks in advance. She should be delighted that they had a full house every lunch and dinner service. Only it was *her* job, as head waiter and sommelier, to make sure that every single one of the sixty diners enjoyed some of the best food and wine in England, excellent service, and came away feeling that they had shared in the aristocratic lifestyle that living in a stately home could bring.

Unashamed award-winning luxury was tricky to pull off day after day.

It was like being an actress in a top London show, who had signed up to perform at both the matinee and the evening performances six days a week. In full make-up and tight costume, combined with even less comfortable shoes.

Singing and dancing on tables optional.

Sienna glanced at the huge antique wall clock as she rubbed the life back into her toes. Fifteen minutes to go. The new management team had called a special meeting to announce who they had decided to appoint to two crucial posts in their award-winning restaurant.

In a few minutes she would know the name of the new head chef. *And* find out who was going to be the restaurant manager who would be running front of house. That magical combination of wonderful food and excellent service which would take the Manor to the very top!

A shiver of anxiety ran across her shoulders and down her back, and she quickly checked that the staffroom was still empty. Of course she was nervous. But nobody else could know how scared she truly was.

Scared? Who was she kidding? Make that terrified.

On the glossy surface she was 'Miss Rossi'. The elegant and professional head waiter who was always immaculately turned out and who presented the perfect formal image the Manor aspired to in their fine-dining restaurant.

They would probably be horrified and totally amazed to know that the real Sienna Rossi was quaking inside the designer suit and shoes.

It had taken her four years of hard work to rebuild her shattered confidence to the point where she could even *think* about applying for the role of restaurant manager, in which she would be responsible for running her own projects and team.

This was going to be her dream job.

After so much sacrifice and hard work it was time to prove that she was capable of coming through heartbreak and rebuilding a career for herself.

A career in which she would never have to trust and rely on another person to make her dreams come true.

She *needed* this job so badly.

'You were a total star today. Did anyone tell you that? If I had an Oscar I would hand it over in an instant!'

Sienna blinked up from her reverie as her best friend Carla burst through the swing doors with a characteristic gush of black suited hotel receptionist elegance and single city-girl attitude.

'Thanks. You're cutting it fine today,' Sienna replied with a smile. 'I thought the staff meeting was at four.'

Carla grabbed what was left of Sienna's coffee and swigged it down in one gulp before sighing out loud as the espresso cup hit the saucer.

'It is. Two of the guests managed to get lost in the maze. I know, I know.' Carla waved both hands in the air. 'That is supposed to be the point of having a proper maze in the first place. But in February? I'm freezing! It has taken me twenty minutes, using cellphones and a whistle, but they are now sitting all comfy and warm by the fire with hot tea and crumpets. *Unlike* the rest of us.'

Carla shivered inside her smart suit and shoved her hands deep under her armpits as Sienna poured her a fresh hot coffee.

'"Chefs in Kilts"!' Carla suddenly squealed, reaching forward to snatch up the colour supplement of the *Hotel Catering* magazine. 'Why didn't you tell me? I've been waiting all week for this! Who have they got as Hunk of the Month this time? Maybe we'll be working with one of these hot young celebrity chefs in a few weeks. Wouldn't that be totally cool?'

Not if I have anything to do with it, we won't, Sienna thought in silence. *Never again! Been there and do not want to go back, even for a visit. And it would not be cool.*

Carla shook her head before passing Sienna her precious magazine. 'See you in five minutes. And best of luck with the job, sweetie—not that you need it. Every confidence!' And with a small finger wave she was gone.

Sienna chuckled and started gathering together the coffee cups, but as she did so the magazine flipped open and the breath froze in her lungs at the sight of a studio photograph of a tall, muscular man in a white T-shirt and tartan kilt.

Hunk of the Month: Brett Cameron.

In an instant she was transported back twelve years, to the cramped and crowded kitchen of Trattoria Rossi. And her first passing glimpse of Aunt Maria's new trainee chef.

She'd been sixteen and had wandered straight from school into the kitchen, where her father and older brother, Frankie, had been prepping for the evening service. Training places at Rossi's were fought over at the catering college, and only the best students made the grade.

Dominating the kitchen had been a skinny teenager with fire in his eyes who'd had the cheek to argue with her brother, Frankie, over the best way to divide fresh basil.

And she had been smitten.

Completely. Absolutely. Without hesitation or rational thought. *Smitten.*

Just one look. That was all it took.

She closed her eyes and revisited the vivid image that had been burnt into her memory all of those years ago.

Under a striped bandana, his long blond hair had been tied back in a ponytail which had highlighted the hard lines of a face so intense with suppressed fire and energy it that seemed to vibrate out and fill the air around him.

Every ounce of his concentration had been focused on the fresh green basil leaves in front of him, which he was tearing with long delicate fingers, while Frankie had shredded more fragrant leaves with a curved blade into thin strips.

Each of them had sprinkled sea salt and a little extra virgin olive oil onto their own stack of basil.

She had watched, entranced, as Frankie and then the blond had tasted each of the leaves in turn, with bread, then cheese and plum tomatoes, going back and forth between the two chopping boards until the blond had smiled up at Frankie and nodded.

Her brother had slapped the blond on the shoulder—which she had never seen him do to another chef in his life—and they'd turned around, smiling, to face her.

And for just one fraction of a second the skinny teenager had glanced up in her direction with such power and intense focus that it had felt as if a pair of pale blue lasers were boring holes through her skull.

Oh, boy...

Of course Frankie had broken off from the work to introduce his little sister to their new trainee, Brett, but by then she'd been a gibbering wreck.

No wonder he had responded to her squeaky hello with a low grunt. To Brett she must have seemed like just another idiot teenage girl—an interloper in this special world of edible sorcery where chefs were the magicians.

The fact that she'd been plump, awkward, clumsy and painfully shy when boys were around probably hadn't helped much, either.

For the next six weeks, which Brett had spent learning the trade in the Trattoria Rossi kitchen, it had been amazing how many excuses Sienna had found to be in the kitchen at the same time.

Desperate for the chance to be close to Brett for a few seconds. To smell him.

To feel the frisson of energy that seemed to spark in the very air around him as he worked feverishly. To hear his voice respond with 'Chef!' when her father passed an order for a salad or cold starter.

To run to the dining table on Sunday afternoons so that she could have the chair facing Brett at the family and crew communal meals.

No other boy at school or in her life had come close to the great Brett Cameron.

She had spent her schooldays in a dreamy daze, in anticipation of those precious few moments when she could see him again, in the evening and at weekends.

Even if she *had* been so shy back then that she'd been totally incapable of speaking to him. That would have been far too terrifying even to consider.

Brett Cameron had been her first crush.

For a fleeting second Sienna succumbed to a ripple of those same teenage fears and intense shyness. She wasn't the first schoolgirl who had ever felt like a total outsider and fraud, and no doubt she would not be the last, but merely thinking back to those sad days was enough to take her to a dark place.

She shook off the memory and blinked hard to clear her head.

They had both come a long way since then.

Sienna smiled down at the magazine article and chuckled to herself for the first time that day. Hunk of the Month, indeed! *He was still the best-looking chef she had ever seen!*

Back then, the nineteen-year-old Brett had been a tall,

skinny teenager with a total obsession for food. His only clothing had been chef's trousers and two identical off-white T-shirts that had become increasingly less fragrant as each week went on.

Now he looked as if a team of professional stylists had spent hours working on him. And it had been money well spent for one of the top chefs now taking the catering world by storm. Last time she had seen his name in the press he had been accepting an award for a hotel restaurant in Australia. That probably explained the suntan which made those blue eyes sparkle even brighter.

He certainly had filled out. The white shirt stretched out across wide shoulders below a firm neck and a solid jawline defined by expertly clipped short blond hair.

Two things had not changed.

His eyes were still winter-sea-blue. Smiling out at her.

Sharp. Intelligent. Focused.

Tiny white smile lines fanned out from the corners of his tanned face. Well, he certainly had plenty to smile about. He had come a long way from Maria Rossi's tiny trattoria in North London to headline in the Food and Drink Awards 'Top New Chef' list.

And then there were his hands. In this photograph they were splayed out on each hip. Those clever fingers, which had used to move so fast that she'd been afraid to blink in case she missed something crucial. Long narrow fingers. How many hours had she spent dreaming about those hands?

She had fallen for those hands. No doubt about it. The only other man who had come close to having hands like those was Angelo.

Oh, Brett. If you only knew the trouble you have caused me!

She blamed him entirely for giving her a chef addiction virus. That well known form of contagion and pestilence.

At college, Carla had given her the nickname of 'chef magnet'.

Any chef within a hundred-mile radius would somehow sense that Sienna was within range and hit on her.

The chiming of the clock snapped Sienna out of her dreamy thoughts, and she glanced at the photo for one last time before closing the magazine and squeezing her swollen feet back into her shoes.

Drat! She was going to be late!

One more thing to blame on Brett Cameron! Wherever in the world he might be!

She need not have rushed! Sienna had been sitting very impatiently with the rest of the hotel management team for almost ten minutes before Patrick breezed into the dining room with head chef André following a few steps behind.

Patrick was the stylish hotel manager for the company who owned the Manor and a small group of other luxury hotels in the most prestigious locations across Europe—hotels where Sienna had every intention of working as a top restaurant manager. *After* she'd persuaded them to give her the position of restaurant manager here at Greystone Manor, of course.

She wanted this job *so* badly. It was everything she had been working towards since the first time she'd put on a waitress uniform in the Rossi family restaurant back in London.

Little wonder that her heart was racing.

Patrick looked around the room and smiled as he tapped gently on a water glass with a table knife. A sense of anxious anticipation ran around the room as the nervous chatter fell away.

'Thank you all for coming at such short notice. As you know, our brilliant head chef André Michon will be retiring at the end of the month, after thirty-two years of amazing work at the Manor. I'm already looking forward to his retirement party, but in the meantime André's decision has given the management team a real headache. How can we possibly find another chef with the same passion for excellence and quality that has made the Manor so successful?'

Please just get on with it, Sienna thought, bristling with impatience. *Please tell me who I will be working with from next month!*

'I am delighted to tell you that we have interviewed some of the brightest young chefs in the world over these last few months, and after much deliberation there was one clear winner. Ladies and gentlemen, I am very pleased to announce that the new head chef at Greystone Manor will be…TV celebrity chef Angelo Peruzi! I know that you must all be thrilled as I am.'

Sienna clutched hold of the sides of her chair with both hands and sucked in several breaths to keep herself from falling over or running out of the room in horror.

No. No. No. Not Angelo.

No. Fate would not play tricks like that on her. It had to be some sort of mistake. She could not have just heard that name.

Sienna sat frozen, her brain stunned. Exploding in on itself with the implications. And the horror.

Her heart was racing so fast and hard that it frightened her, and she fought not to burst into tears or scream out loud.

Angelo! Of all the chefs in the entire world they had to choose the one man who she wanted nothing to do with again. Her ex-fiancé. The man who had abandoned her a month before their wedding to heartbreak and despair.

This could not be happening. Not now. Not to her. Not here. Not after four years.

No! Hot tears pricked the corners of her eyes, blinding her to what was going on around her.

It took a few seconds for her to acknowledge that Carla was prodding her in the arm and gesturing with her head towards the dais. Patrick was saying something about a new restaurant manager.

'Miss Sienna Rossi has already shown what she can achieve as head waiter. Welcome to the team and many congratulations, Miss Rossi. I know that you will make a terrific restaurant manager. Chef Peruzi simply can't wait to start working with you!'

CHAPTER TWO

Step 2: Add One Handsome Chef in a Kilt

BRETT CAMERON stood with both hands thrust deep inside the pockets of his cargo trousers and stared up at the rubble-strewn building site that was destined to become his first signature restaurant.

Just four days earlier he had been in sunny Adelaide, celebrating at his leaving party, turning steaks on a barbecue and looking forward to working in his own kitchen in central London.

The reality of a wet, grey February afternoon, with deafening London traffic on the other side of this gate, was not quite the warm and glamorous welcome he might have liked, but at that moment he was totally oblivious to the noise and heavy drizzle.

This was it. After years of dreaming and planning it was finally going to happen. And from all of the possible locations in the world he had to choose from there was only one city he wanted to come back to.

It had to be London.

This was the city where he had suffered the worst years of his life as an angry and frustrated teenager, coming to terms with what life had thrown at him.

Back then London had been just one more cold and unfriendly place, where his single mother had dragged him from one cheap rented apartment to another while she found two or sometimes three unskilled jobs in order to pay the rent and keep their heads above water.

Jobs in which you did not need to read or write very well to earn a wage.

The kind of jobs he had come to detest—and yet he had been clever enough to recognise them as the kind of work he would probably find himself doing from the moment he was old enough to leave school.

Who wanted to employ a boy who could barely write his name and address on an application form, even assuming that he could read the questions in the first place?

A boy whom every one of the ten or more schools he had attended had labelled as having 'behavioural difficulties'? No matter how hard he'd worked and worked it had made no difference to the stigma of being classified as slow or lazy. An academic failure.

If he was going to prove to the world just how very far that boy had come, and what he had achieved in the years since he'd last walked these streets, then he had to come back to London.

Brett inhaled the moist air.

No regrets. It wasn't all bad. His life as a chef had begun in this city.

It was hard to believe that Maria Rossi's restaurant and his old catering college were only a few miles down the road! Sometimes it felt like a lifetime ago. A lifetime of exhaustion, hard work and even harder experience.

Maria Rossi hadn't known for sure what she was taking on all those years ago, when she'd given him a chance.

She had taken a huge risk with a stranger, not knowing how he was going to turn out, but had faith enough to make the commitment anyway.

Just as he was doing here.

There might be banks and financiers willing enough to back his new restaurant, but this was still totally personal. His own kitchen.

In a world where even successful restaurants struggled to make a living, it was precisely the kind of crazy, exciting, thrilling project he couldn't wait to get started on.

Energy coursed through his veins. *This was the greatest adventure of his life!*

Even the physical reality of bricks and mortar was exhilarating. Until now this place had just been an idea. A dream he had talked about with his friend Chris over endless cups of coffee and glasses of wine in the two hectic years they had spent in Paris as students almost a decade ago.

And now he was looking at that dream brought to life.

He had barely slept on the long flight from Australia. His mind had been a buzz of menus and all the bewildering and complex combinations of who and what and where that went into creating a successful restaurant business.

'Where's your kilt today, old chap?' A powerful well-spoken English voice boomed out from the well-spoken, short, stout man who came striding up to Brett between stacks of bricks. 'Left it back in Oz?'

Brett grasped hold of his best friend's hand, then reached back and gave him a slap on the back.

'Don't you start!' Brett replied, in an accent tinged with an Australian twang. 'Brilliant publicity, as always, but you *do* know that I only spent the first two months of my life in Glasgow? I'm never going to live that down in the Cameron clan!'

'I'm sure they'll get over it when this palace of modern cuisine is opened! What do you think of the progress so far?' Chris nodded towards the building site just as a length of waste timber came flying out of a side window and crashed to the tarmac below, to join a mound of broken bricks and wood.

Brett grinned at the fragments of timber and nodded a few times with pursed lips before replying.

'It's good to see people with so much enthusiasm for their work! I'll answer that question after you've shown me the kitchen!' Brett rubbed both his hands together and his mouth lifted into a broad grin of delight. 'I have been looking forward to this for a long time.'

Chris straightened a little, lifted his head, and gritted his teeth together in a sharp hiss.

'Ah. About the kitchen. Slight delay, I'm afraid. Not *quite* ready for inspection yet.' As Brett turned to look at him, Chris gestured with his head towards a huge mound of tarpaulin-covered shapes just inside the main entrance.

Brett swallowed down hard in silence, took a breath, and strode into what would be the main reception area once the walls had been finished. His shoulders were high with tension.

He carefully and gingerly lifted up one of the tarpaulins and stared in silence at the huge packaging crates.

'Tell me that's not what I think it is!' Brett blurted out, his voice a mix of barely concealed horror and amazement.

'Afraid so,' Chris replied with a tilt of his head. 'The ovens were held up in transit. Apparently cargo ships don't like to go out in hurricane-force winds. Winter. Ocean. Big waves. Tricky things. Strange, that, isn't it?'

Brett stared awestruck at the huge pile of boxes and containers and raked his hands through his hair, before turning back to the only person who truly understood the sacrifices he had made to arrive at this point, when his restaurant was so close to becoming a reality.

Chris shrugged back at him. 'Can't do anything until the ovens are fitted and tested. You know that. Your dream kitchen is going to be full of brick dust and filth for at least a couple of days. You wanted the best and you're going to have the best. Only not this week. Maybe longer.'

Chris faltered and raised both hands in the air as Brett groaned in reply and closed his eyes.

'I know,' Chris acknowledged. 'I've already used up all of the slack we planned on the building work. It's going to be tough to make the deadline.'

'Make that *very* tough,' Brett answered with a nod. 'We only have a couple of weeks before the doors open to paying customers, and I still don't have menus or staff. This building needs to be finished as soon as we can, or we could be late on the first payment of the bank loan. And our credibility will suffer.'

His fingers worked through his hair behind each ear. 'Maybe it wasn't such a good idea to invite all the key London food critics and journalists to our opening night when we hadn't started the building work yet?'

'It was great idea!' Chris replied. 'This is why I've set up a meeting with the architects, so we can bring you up to date on the project plan. You're the only one who can decide what compromises you are willing to make to push the project through. They'll be expecting us in about an hour.'

'An hour?' Brett chortled and gave a shake of his head. 'In that case you had better start talking me though the plan. Let's start with the services and—' The sound of an Italian tenor rang out loud from Brett's cellphone. He glanced at the caller ID, and then looked at it more closely before nodding to Chris.

'Sorry, mate. Have to take this one. Be with you in a minute.'

'No problem. Let me get that snag list.'

Brett flicked open the phone as Chris strolled away through the debris, and grinned to himself before answering the call.

'Maria Rossi's galley slave, here. Ready to do your bidding, oh, great one!'

Only instead of Maria Rossi's, a man's voice bellowed down the line.

'Hello? Is that Brett? Brett Cameron?'

'Yes. This is Brett Cameron. Can you I help you?' he replied, holding the phone away from his ear to prevent damage to his hearing.

'Oh, good. This is Henry. You know—Maria Rossi's friend from the ballroom-dancing class. I'm calling from *Spain*. She asked me to call you.'

Henry? Had he ever met a Henry? Maria had so many friends it was hard to keep up.

'Hi, Henry. Is everything okay?'

'No. Sorry, but Maria's in the hospital. Oh, don't worry. She's going to be fine. Are you there? Brett?'

The smile fell from Brett's face and he inhaled sharply before replying.

'Yes—yes, I'm still here. What happened? Has there been an accident? Is she hurt?'

'No, no, nothing like that. Did Maria tell you that she was going on the dance club trip to Benidorm? That's here in Spain, you know.'

'She didn't mention it, but, yes, I understand. What's happened to Maria, Henry?'

'Well. I don't really know. She was on her way back from the banana boat race yesterday afternoon when the pain started. At first we blamed too much paella and sangria in the club last night, but a few hours later she slumped over in the Spanish dancing class. Right in the middle of the Paso Doble. They carted her off to the local hospital. The instructor carried her to the ambulance. It was very exciting.'

'Exciting? Right. Did they say what's wrong with her?'

'Appendicitis. Caught just in time. Nasty, that. That's why I'm phoning, see. To tell you that she *is* okay. Surgery was fine but she's going to be here for at least— Oh, here she is. I need to pretend to be injured now.'

There was a shuffle, and the sound of fierce whispering on the other end of the line before a familiar and surprisingly cheerful voice sounded in his ear.

'Hello, Chef Cameron. Are you back?'

Brett smiled gently. The irrepressible Maria Rossi! Not even major surgery could hold this lady back for long!

'I am, boss. But never mind about me. What's all this about you being in hospital? Charming the handsome young doctors in Spain?'

A faint female voice laughed in reply. 'I've been kidnapped! One small operation and they want to keep me tied to this bed for two weeks! They even tried to confiscate my cellphone! I've had to crawl out onto the fire escape while Henry distracts them for a few minutes with a paper cut on his thumb.'

'Well, resist the temptation to make your daring escape. You can't fool me, Maria Rossi. There are probably teams of medical staff waiting on your every need. Now for the really important questions: what's the food like, and how are you feeling? And do not try and fob me off. Appendicitis can be serious!'

'The operation went fine, no complications—and I've had worse meals. But I'm knackered. Woman in the next bed snored the whole night. Did not get a wink of sleep.' Maria took a breath before asking, 'Have you got a fast car?'

'I can find one. Want me to drive down to the Costa Brava and pick you up?'

'Don't tempt me with offers like that! Thanks, but I do need a favour. Would you mind heading over to my place to make sure Rossi's is still standing? Sienna won't be able to manage without someone to do the cooking for her.'

'Sienna? Is that the new trainee chef you're terrorising in my place?'

'Sienna Rossi. My *niece*. Frank's sister. You probably don't remember her. Anyway, the poor girl left me a couple of voice messages earlier to tell me she was on her way over to Rossi's to stay with me for a few days. She sounded distressed, but by the time I could call her back her phone was turned off. Sienna doesn't know I'm away. I don't like the idea of her turning up to find me gone and the place closed up.'

Then Maria chuckled to herself. 'I love that girl dearly, but there is no telling what she could get up to if she is left in charge of Rossi's for two weeks. She'll probably be running herself ragged trying to open up the place on her own.'

Brett snorted in reply. 'I wonder who that reminds me of?

Chip off the old block, there. Why don't you just close the place for an extra week or two?'

There was a long pause on the other end of the line.

'Maria? Still there? Or have the nurses dragged you back inside?'

'Oh, still here—but I can't talk for long. Look, Brett. I won't beat around the bush. Things are not going too well at the moment and I need the business. To be honest, I can't afford to close down for another two weeks. Be a good lad and promise me you'll lend a hand?' She paused. 'It would help put my mind at rest if I knew that you could keep the old place going, rake in some cash, and look after Sienna for me.'

'Okay. It's a promise. I'll head over there tonight.'

Maria sighed in relief. 'You're a star. I should warn you that— Oops! I've been spotted. Later.'

And with that she was gone, to the sound of shuffles and muffled voices, before the call clicked off, leaving a stunned Brett in the bustle of electric drills and workmen.

Maria was obviously recovering well, but there had been no mistaking the concern in her voice.

February was always a slow month in the restaurant trade. And many of her regular customers were elderly couples who had been going there for years. Cold winter evenings and tight budgets… Hmm, that could mean trouble for any small restaurant.

Small? Who was he kidding? Maria's dining room was about the same size as the new reception area in the building he was looking at now.

Brett flicked down the cover on his cellphone. He owed Maria Rossi everything. This remarkable woman had taken a chance with a troubled teenager whom the world had labelled an academic failure. Over the years he had made it his business to keep in touch with her. Let her know how he was doing.

It was Maria Rossi who had stood by his side at the Young Chef of the Year Awards.

Maria Rossi who had opened the door to the most prestigious restaurants in Paris, where he'd learnt the true meaning of fine cooking.

And Maria Rossi who had persuaded the catering college to run a test which proved that he was not slow, not stupid, and certainly not lazy.

He had dyslexia.

And now he was back in London for the first time in ten years with something to prove, and Maria wanted him to do her a favour.

Consider it done.

As for Sienna Rossi? Oh, he remembered Sienna Rossi. He remembered Miss Sienna Rossi very well indeed.

'Everything okay? You look very thoughtful!'

Brett looked around to find Chris staring at him in concern, a large bundle of papers scrunched under one arm.

The architects!

'Sorry, mate. Change of plan. I have to help out an old friend for a few days. You're going to have to take the meeting on your own. I know you can handle it. Call me whenever you need me, but I have to go.'

CHAPTER THREE

Step 3: Throw in Two Teaspoons of Shock and Uncertainty

IT WAS almost seven in the evening when Sienna stepped gingerly down from the red London bus and shrugged herself deeper into her raincoat. The drizzle had been replaced by light rain, and the air was moist and heavy with diesel fumes and the city smog of a dark winter evening.

For the first week in February there was still a definite snap of cold in the air, and Sienna regretted her decision to leave Greystone Manor without changing into winter shoes, but it all happened in such a rush!

It had been surprisingly easy to convince Patrick that she needed to take the two weeks' holiday she was owed before the new chef arrived and she started work on their 'exciting new project'!

Pity that she was still as confused and undecided as she had been a few hours earlier. The shakes might have eased off, but she knew better. Shock and awe did not even come close! The train journey from Greystone had been a nightmare: sharing a carriage with happy people on their way to enjoy an evening show in London when all she had wanted to do was curl up into a small ball and whimper.

At least her legs were a little steadier. She had almost fainted in the dining room when Patrick had announced Angelo's name. It was lucky for her that everyone had been too busy to hang around and chat about the announcement, and she'd been able to escape to the sanctuary of her bedroom on wobbly legs.

She sucked in a deep breath of cool night air and blinked hard to clear her head as hot burning tears again pricked her eyes and seared her dry throat.

No tears. You are not going to cry, she told herself sternly.

She had done more than enough crying over Angelo Peruzi!

And now he had come back to Britain. To her home. To her safe place.

Sienna sensed her fists clench and unclench, the knuckles white, as she took another deep breath. She was a professional. She was used to handling problems. She could handle this one just like the others.

Focus on the options.

Basically she had two choices. Stay. Or go.

She could stay and be professional and keep her home by agreeing to work with Angelo and take the restaurant to the next level. They would be colleagues. Professionals working together. Nothing more. This could be the chance she had been waiting for to show what she could do on the international scene and persuade the hotel chain to transfer her to another restaurant.

Or—and this second option was so terrible that she mentally braced herself even to think about it—she could leave and start again somewhere else.

She would have to give up the job she loved and…and do what? Ask for a transfer? That was a possibility. She could always find another job as a head waiter, but it would probably set her back a year or two while she rebuilt her team.

Or she could run back to the Rossi clan with her tail between her legs. Her parents might have retired, but her brother, Frankie, was running an Italian delicatessen with his young wife and family—maybe she could ask them for a job?

And throw away four years of very hard work in the process.

No. She couldn't bear to think about that.

One thing was certain. She had to think this through. And fast. Angelo would be at the Manor in less than a week. She needed her parents—except they had chosen the perfect time to take in a cruise. And she wasn't even sure that they could help her.

That left the only person she could rely on for advice. Her aunt Maria Rossi.

Rubbing her arms for warmth, Sienna turned the corner and was immediately struck by the illuminated signs from not one but two pizza and noodle shops flashing in the dusky gloom. A lot had changed in the six months since her last short visit to this part of London.

Sienna paused on the pavement so that she could look across the narrow street at Rossi's, as it had always been known. This was where her aunt had offered her refuge from the disaster that had been Angelo Peruzi. Ironic that the same man was driving her back here now. She needed a warm hug, a hot meal, and all the advice that Maria could give. *And she needed them desperately!*

Under the streetlights there was no escaping the fact that there were a few more things that had certainly changed over the winter months—and not for the better.

Maria had some serious competition here!

Trattoria Rossi stood in what had been a prime location, set back slightly from the main street with just enough space out front for two or three patio tables. Except this was February, and the rain had a definite touch of sleet in it.

The harsh fluorescent light seemed to highlight the fact that the paint was peeling badly from the hand-painted sign that had once proudly carried the words *TRATTORIA ROSSI*. Several letters had faded to the point where to a passing car the sign might seem to be spelling out *RATT…OS*.

But that was not the worst of it. As Sienna skipped across the road at the crossing, the first thing she saw as she approached the bistro was a large crack in the plate-glass front window. Cracks in one corner spread out like a spider's web, sideways into the glass.

Standing in front of the bistro at that moment, Sienna struggled to recall what it had looked like when she had last visited Maria in daylight—sparkling clean, bright and cheerful. A welcoming and friendly family bistro—an ideal place to spend a lunchtime. What she was looking at now was dismal and dark and the kind of place she would never choose to eat. Even if it was open.

Which it wasn't.

A handwritten sign said—as best as she could read in the dim light and poor handwriting—that the restaurant was closed due to staff holiday and would be open again for lunch next week. Only which week and when it had been written was not made clear.

Her family would have told her if Maria was on holiday. Wouldn't they?

Oh, Maria. Where are you when I need you?

Emotion flooded through Sienna. For a few seconds she allowed the stress of the day to overwhelm her, and she bent over from the waist and clasped hold of her knees with her eyes closed.

Please be here. Please! It was not much to ask! She simply needed someone to be here whom she could trust and take refuge in.

With a loud sniff, Sienna pushed herself back to her full height.

This was what falling for chefs did for you! Dratted Brett Cameron! Or Angelo. Or both!

Perhaps tonight was Maria's night out? The Nifty after Fifty dance club members were some of her best customers and Maria was no slouch when it came to showing her own skills in the ballroom.

Cupping her hands around her eyes and peering through the glass, Sienna was relieved to see that electric lights were on in the kitchen, and she could hear the thump-thump beat of pop music above the noise of the traffic which was whizzing past her.

Someone must be working there. Maria always had at least one trainee chef and a waitress working for her. Usually one of them lived with Maria in the cosy house connected to the trattoria. Only, the house was in complete darkness.

Sienna knocked hard on the front door of the trattoria just as the rain started to fall more heavily. She had planned to spend the night in Maria's house, and the keys were inside the bistro. It was time to either wake somebody up or start ringing door-bells along the street to find out if anyone else had a key. Maria was so trusting it would not surprise her if half the elderly neighbours had spares.

Except, of course, most of the ladies were probably with Maria at the their local ballroom-dancing class, while she stood there and stamped her feet to avoid being frozen to the spot.

After her third attempt at battering down the door, and then ringing the doorbell at Maria's house, Sienna decided that it was time to try plan B. The rear door to the kitchen.

It was at this point that the rain became a more intense sleet, which dripped from the tree branches and cascaded from the rooftops of the parade of shops onto the pavement below—and anyone who happened to be walking there, trying to find the gate behind the bistro. Stiff with rain and misuse, the old wooden gate stubbornly refused to open, and Sienna had to abandon her luggage to the wet yard which was slick with rain water and unknown slime, and use both hands to push hard and lift at the same time.

The gate gave way in a rush, so that she half fell, half stum-bled headfirst into the yard and almost lost her footing. Taking a moment to calm her breathing, Sienna sighed in relief. Her reward was that Maria's kitchen was still brightly lit and def-initely the source of the music.

Sliding her luggage forward, Sienna tiptoed as best she could between the rubbish bins, sodden cardboard boxes and discarded plastic trays towards the back door, trying to save her shoes from the puddles of rainwater which had filled the gaps between the broken cement slabs and mystery dark objects which blocked the path. Nothing scurried away, meowed or barked as she dodged the blockade, which was a real plus.

There was a vertical line of light beaming out from the back door—it was open!

Maria must be home!

Her shoulders relaxed in relief. Thank goodness.

There was no sign of anyone through the kitchen windows, but, undaunted, Sienna took a step closer to the gap in the heavy metal back door.

Only at that precise moment the door swung open wider. And in one flash of an eyelid Sienna Maria Rossi took in three startling facts.

Leaning forward in the doorway was a tall dark figure, whose face was in the shadow of the bright kitchen light.

Attached to one long forearm was a pink plastic bucket, in which something was sloshing loudly from side to side as the arm drew back.

The arm was bent back for a very good reason. The bucket was already moving forward in a graceful arc to be emptied into the backyard. Only she was in the way and there was nothing either of them could do about it.

Half a bucket of warm water hit Sienna straight in the legs, and she only just had enough time to squeeze her eyes shut before the deluge splashed up to her knees, narrowly missing the bottom of her suit skirt as the cascade flooded into the tops of both shoes, filling them with dirty water she did not even want to think about, as well as soaking her luggage.

There was a horrified gasp from the figure standing in the doorway followed by a rasp of deep male laughter.

Sienna squeezed her eyes tighter together. *This person—this man*—was actually laughing about the fact that he had just completely soaked her legs and ruined her best work shoes in the process. Goodness knew what state her luggage would be in.

This was a wretched end to a terrible, terrible day. *It could not possibly get any worse.*

She slowly, slowly opened her eyes and wiped away the rainwater with one hand, before lifting her head to face the enemy. Only she never got the chance—because before she knew what was happening a strong male arm had wrapped around her wet shoulders and half dragged, half supported her towards the door.

'Hi, Sienna. Sorry about that. It's great to see you again. Want to come inside and dry off?'

Sienna looked up, blinking against the bright kitchen light, and stared, open-mouthed in shock, into the face of the man who was lifting her bag from her sodden fingers. Then the blood rushed to her head so quickly that she felt dizzy and leaned back against the door frame to steady herself before she could trust her voice to say tremulously, *'Brett?'*

A tousle-haired blond with a wide smile touched two fingers to his brow in mock salute.

'Welcome back to Rossi's. It's going to be *just* like old times.'

And at that point the ever cool and in control Sienna Rossi burst into tears.

CHAPTER FOUR

Step 4: Whisk Everything Together in a Tiny Bistro

SILENT TEARS streamed down Sienna's face, blinding her to everything and everybody.

Shoulders heaving, she tried to control her sobs and snatch back some form of self-control in tiny breaths.

This was agony!

There was a lump in her throat the size of an egg, her eyes must be red and puffy, and goodness knows what her hair must look like! What a complete mess!

She had never felt so humiliated in her life!

This, of course, made her feel even more wretched!

There was no way she would ever be able to look Brett Cameron in the face again. Perhaps she could emigrate? To a distant planet?

Or perhaps she had simply imagined the whole thing and the rain and her tears had blurred her vision?

Then he spoke, in a low, caring voice, and her heart twisted.

'Here. Let me take that wet coat for you.'

Before she had time to argue the point Brett had moved behind her and was lifting her raincoat from her shoulders.

His fingertips gently grazed the sides of her throat for a fraction of a second, sending delicious shivers across her shoulders and down her arms. She immediately covered the shiver by rubbing the palms of her hands up and down the arms of the thin cashmere cardigan she had thrown over her silk blouse, as though it was the damp and cold that had made her body quiver rather than the simple touch of those clever fingers.

'You're freezing! Take this. I'm more than warm enough.'

A soft extra-large and very masculine fleece jacket was wrapped around her shoulders, and she sighed in delight and relief before shrugging her arms into the sleeves and pulling the zip high to the neck. She was practically sitting on the hem when she straightened her skirt and snuggled into the wonderful warm comfort. It was like wearing a quilt.

Heaven.

And it was infused with his own personal scent.

'Better?' he asked, looking into her face with concern, then rubbed his hands down the length of her arms, flushing her with glowing warmth—and not just from the soft fabric.

'Much,' she managed to reply with a brief nod, before noticing that he was now wearing only a cotton short-sleeved T-shirt. All the fight and bluff she had planned died on her quivering lips. 'Thank you.'

'How do you like your tea?' He reached behind him to the worktop and picked up a steaming hot drink. 'I take mine white with two sugars. Careful now.'

Brett hunkered down on the wet floor and pressed the hot beaker between her cold shaking fingers, waiting until her sobs subsided before helping her wrap her fingers tightly enough so that she would not spill it.

The look of concern and anxiety in those blue eyes almost started Sienna off again, so she swallowed down a large sip of hot tea, feeling the warmth spread from her throat, and then another sip, until she was holding the beaker on her own.

Only then did Brett push himself effortlessly back on his heels to his full height, his slender strong fingers slipping away from hers, breaking their tenuous connection.

Sienna swallowed down another swig of the welcome hot

tea. Strange that she usually hated sweet tea with milk but at that moment it was the only thing she wanted.

The room seemed to come more into focus. She was sitting on a tiny metal patio chair that not even the local scamps would have stolen from the pavement in front of the bistro—they had *some* standards. She took a breath, squeezed her eyes shut, flicked them open, and did a double-take.

The lights were still on. She had shaken most of the rain from her hair and eyes. And it was definitely Brett Cameron or an identical twin brother she knew nothing about.

There was no mistaking the piercing blue eyes, and they were certainly the same hands which had touched her skin for the very first time only a few minutes earlier.

Too handsome to be true Brett Cameron.

Obsessive, passionate, serious, eyes as blue as the sea Brett Cameron.

The same Brett Cameron who had either totally ignored her or at best acknowledged her presence with a grunt or a nod for six complete weeks when he'd worked as a trainee chef, and then every Saturday evening when she'd worked here as a waitress for her aunt.

The same Brett Cameron who had haunted her schoolgirl dreams and was nowadays being photographed for catering magazines.

That Brett Cameron was at that very moment taking up most of the space in her aunt's kitchen.

And she was wearing his fleece and drinking his tea.

How had that happened?

It was as though the last ten years of her life had been an absurd dream, and she was back to being a gawky, awkward and awestruck sixteen year old.

Then he stretched forward to hoist her bag onto a bar stool and turn down the lively jazz music, and she got the full benefit of the well-worn grey rock-star T-shirt stretched over a broad chest and powerful shoulders.

The over thin, scrawny teenage version of Brett had been replaced by a man who looked as though he had spent his time in Australia on the beach. Or surfing. Those Chefs in Kilts photos had definitely not needed fancy editing!

Shame that those same teenage hormones now flared hot in her veins as a full-colour vision of a topless and tanned Brett in board shorts flashed in panoramic full-colour detail across her mind. Perhaps she had not changed as much as she thought she had?

Oh, no. *Not now.* Not on top of the news about Angelo. Two men. Both chefs. *Doomed.*

Sienna groaned softly to herself. This was starting to feel like a conspiracy.

'Sorry about your nice shoes! I should have paid more attention to the front doorbell.'

Well, that was new! The teenage Brett had used to have trouble saying even a few words over the Rossi dinner table—and then only when her aunt Maria had forced the words out of him. Now he was noticing her shoes!

Who was this man? And at what point in the last few years had he started to notice women's *footwear?*

She stared down at her sodden feet and squelched her cold wet toes inside what had once been designer couture heels. Now the leather felt positively slimy, and destined for the nearest wastebin. And at precisely that moment she realised that she had not packed any spare shoes in her rush to leave Greystone as fast as Carla had been able to drive her to the railway station.

No spare shoes. Not even a pair of slippers.

Her eyes closed and she quivered on the edge of more tears. Self-pity this time.

This was what happened when you dropped everything for chefs!

You left work wearing high heels with soles the thickness of writing paper.

In the rain.

In February.

The sensible and totally in-control version of Sienna Rossi who would have packed a range of suitable footwear to choose from had clearly left the building!

Hearing the name Angelo Peruzi being announced, after seeing gorgeous Brett Cameron in that magazine had clearly puddled her poor brain beyond rational thought. That was the only possible explanation for it. She would have to just sit there in wet shoes for the rest of the evening. Until she could escape to the shops to buy new ones or—gulp—borrow some of Aunt Maria's shoes. She had clear memories of her aunt's more memorable shoes. Bows. Stripes. *Flowers!*

Sienna lifted one foot and then the other out of the standing water on the tiled floor and fixed her heels behind the lowest rung of the back of her patio chair as Brett moved a heavy bucket out of reach and swished an industrial sized absorbent sponge over the tiles below, where she had been standing.

'Thank you.' At this point the sensible part of her brain started to kick in with extra warmth. 'They *were* nice shoes.' She looked at the back of his tanned head and was distracted by the tight-cut dark blond layers above wide shoulders, strong biceps and toned forearm. 'I'm amazed to see you here, Brett! Last time I spoke to Maria you were in Australia! This has come as a bit of a surprise!'

He stopped mopping for a second and turned back towards her, flashing a killer smile she had imagined was the product of airbrushing for those magazine shots.

But this was the real thing. White, white teeth contrasted against tanned blond stubble around a wide mouth which turned up more on the right side than the left as he smiled.

To her absolute horror Sienna's treacherous stomach performed a full somersault and backflip that would have pleased an Olympic swimmer.

Oh, boy.

The Hunk of the Month photo did not come close to Brett Cameron up close and personal—even if he *was* wearing denims which had seen cleaner and dryer days.

How dared he be even more handsome than she remembered from of those years ago?

'You never did like surprises.' He smiled back at her. 'Some things clearly haven't changed.'

He leant back on the workbench and crossed his arms over his wide chest, dominating the space between them as though he owned the place and always had done. His focused gaze made Sienna want to squirm and deny the accusation, but she deflected it by raising her head higher and trying to look uninterested.

'Would you believe me if I told you that your aunt Maria offered me a job mopping up while she was away on holiday in Spain?' Brett continued. 'Hard to turn down an opportunity like that! How could I resist? Jumped on the first plane back to London!'

A muscle twitched in the right corner of his mouth to match the twinkle in his eyes.

He was teasing her.

She was soaked, cold, tired and miserable.

And her aunt Maria was away on holiday.

Suddenly she felt as though the whole world has deserted her. *Double doomed.*

And Brett Cameron was teasing her. Looking for a reaction. Well, she could play the game as well as he could. All she had to was persuade her brain to start working again while she ignored her damp, dirty legs and feet.

At least the kitchen was warm. Even though it was wet. Very wet. *Too* wet.

From her patio chair, the view over the tiny kitchen was of uniformly shiny and wet floor tiles, with deeper standing water in some of the corners.

Brett had not been cleaning the floor. He had been trying to soak up a major flood. At least that explained why he'd been emptying his bucket outside. And why his boots and trousers were dark and soaked through almost as far as the knees.

Strange how knowing that he was also enjoying the benefit of cold clothing against his legs made her feel a lot better. And now curiosity won the battle between her deciding to be indifferent to his suffering or finding out why one of the allegedly finest young chefs in the world was mopping kitchen floors.

'I can see how you wouldn't want to miss that kind of offer. As for the mopping up… Let me guess. Has there has been a flood? The chest freezer defrosted?'

Brett shifted position and tilted his head to one side. 'Close. According to the girl I found trying to cope, Maria doesn't have a big freezer any more. It sort of caught fire and was never replaced. In fact, you probably had to scramble over it to get to the back door. This—' and he gestured with his head to the far corner of the room where the water looked deeper '—was the dishwasher.'

Sienna looked at him for a second, wide eyed, before blowing out hard. Freezers did not catch fire at Greystone Manor.

'The big freezer caught fire? Right. Any idea what happened to the dishwasher? Was there a power failure?'

'I wish!' Brett replied with a snort. 'Oh, sorry. Actually, it's not funny. Apparently the ancient rust bucket had been leaking for weeks, but Maria never got around to having it fixed before her holiday. Julie came in to open up for you and there was water everywhere.'

'Julie?' Sienna nodded several times before adding in a low voice, 'Oh, yes, of course. That would be Maria's waitress.' Her twice broken heart twanged a little at the thought of Brett chatting up yet another young waitress when he had never wanted to talk to her, then twanged again. He was single. The waitress was probably single. None of her business. So why was it that she could not resist the temptation to tease *him* this time?

She lifted her head and made contact with those remarkable eyes, all thoughts of her wet feet forgotten. 'Well, *some* things seem to have changed! You actually *talk* to waitresses these days! I'm sure Julie was *very* informative!'

There was silence from the man standing only a few feet away from her across the wet cold tiles, and an electric spark of tension crackled through the air.

Then he dropped his head back, uncrossed his arms and let out a deep, rough belly laugh that echoed around the tiny space and vibrated through the floor and worktops. Her chair seemed to tremble with the force of it, and her toes clenched inside her moist shoes so that she would not tumble forward from her stool. Her soul, her heart and her mind filled with the joy of that deep, masculine chuckle.

It was the first time that she had ever heard him laugh, and at that moment she was seriously delighted that she had a worktop to hang onto. She tried to move back, away from him, but in this tiny kitchen there was nowhere for her to go. Her back was already hard against the patio chair.

She revelled in the sensation, her heart soaring, and for a second she was so, so, tempted to join him. She certainly needed a laugh after a day like she had just had.

The day she was still having, Sienna corrected herself. It was not over yet.

Deep smile lines creased the corners of his mouth, bringing his sparking blue eyes into startling contrast. It was intoxicating.

If she had ever thought that Brett could not be more attractive, he was doing his best to prove her wrong—without even realising he was doing it!

He leant forward until he was well and truly inside her personal space, and as he did so his hands came together so he could salute her with a slow clap. Once, then twice, before he moved back and ran his fingers through his short hair.

Then he looked across at her and broke into a wide grin. 'Relax, Sienna. The only girl who has me over a barrel is your aunt. She has me wrapped around her little finger and there is not one thing that I can do about it. I'd promise that woman anything. And she knows it.'

'What do you mean? Did she call you from Spain?'

'Actually, her friend Henry called, but I did have a chance to speak to the lady herself for a few minutes. The lovely Maria is way too busy chatting up the Spanish medics to spend time with me.'

Sienna blinked in surprise before clutching at her knees. 'Medics? What do you mean?' The remains of the tea sloshed onto the floor as she slipped the beaker onto the bench. 'Is Maria ill? Injured? How bad is it?'

Brett reached out and grabbed hold of her flailing hands.

'It was appendicitis. She was whipped into hospital straight away, has had the operation, and is now recovering among her friends from the dance club. She sounds *fine!* If anything she seems more concerned about you staying here alone than the fact that she has just had major surgery.'

'I did leave her several messages, but then the battery on my cellphone went flat. How is she? I mean, how did it happen?' Sienna asked, trying to slow her breathing and bring her heart-rate back to something close to normal.

Brett released her hands and leaned back on the worktop.

'Apparently she was on her way back from a banana boat race when the pain started. She slumped over in a Spanish dancing class and the instructor carried her to the ambulance. It was "*very* exciting", according to her friend Henry.'

'Banana boats? Exciting? Right. But that still doesn't ex-plain why *you* are mopping her kitchen floor.'

'Ah,' Brett replied, his smile fading. 'Did you see the window?'

Sienna nodded. 'And the sign. How long have you been here?'

'A couple of hours. Long enough to know that Maria is in serious financial trouble and needs Rossi's to stay up and run-ning while she's away—which could be a couple more weeks. She admitted as much just before her phone was confiscated. That's why she made me promise to do something for her.'

'Really? What was that?'

'Well, apparently you have many skills, Miss Rossi, but cooking is not one of them. Until Maria gets back, you're looking at her new chef!'

CHAPTER FIVE

Step 5: Add a Couple of Big Decisions…

SIENNA STARED in open-mouthed horror and astonishment as Brett gave her a jaunty salute and a cheeky wink before recrossing his arms and stretching out his long, long legs, only too aware that this snippet of news was going to take a while to sink in.

He was watching her now. Smiling. Totally confident and comfortable in his superiority. Just because he had announced that they were going to be trapped in this tiny kitchen together.

Trapped with Brett Cameron. Just the two of them. Together. *Alone.*

Her feet took a tighter grip on the chair inside her shoes. Making them squeak slightly.

He heard it and the smile widened.

How more infuriating and arrogant could this man get?

He had known that she was on her way here the whole time! Known it before she had even got here! He had been expecting her to turn up!

But he still threw that water out of the door without a care about whether she would be standing there or not!

Well, she could change that quite easily. She had no intention of going back to the Manor, so *he* would have to be the one who made the move to…to whatever seriously important opportunity he was working on next as a superstar chef.

The crushing reality of the difference between their options hit her hard. Then hit her again.

Brett was a star. *Destined for great things.* And she was… Well, she was still Sienna Rossi, and she would take control of her situation as best she could.

'Thank you for volunteering to cook,' she blustered, in as calm a voice as she could muster under such extreme provocation, 'but that will not be necessary. I know a few retired cooks who would be happy to step in and help out. I can easily make a call tomorrow morning and have someone here in a few hours. Don't worry, I'll find another chef to take over in the kitchen. I'm sure that Maria would understand how busy you must be.'

Brett merely smiled indulgently at her discomfort and pushed himself to his feet. For one exciting and terrifying moment she thought that he was going to move even closer, but instead he turned back to the worktop, where she could see an assortment of cooking utensils and knives were laid out on a surprisingly clean white tea towel next to cartons of dried goods.

He casually picked up a moist poly chopping board and began drying it carefully with a paper towel before replying, his hands working the towel back and forth as he spoke.

'Sorry, but you don't get rid of me that easily. I'm not going anywhere.'

Those magical hands stilled for a moment as Brett looked intently towards her.

'Maria asked me to help with the cooking and that's what I'm going to do. I made a promise and I have every intention of keeping it. Besides, you're starting to hurt my feelings. If I didn't know better, I would say that you didn't want me here for the next two weeks. I am genuinely pained!'

Sienna clenched her teeth together in frustration. *Why was he not taking her seriously*? What did she have to do to persuade him to pack his bags?

'I'm sure Maria would understand that you have important projects to be working on. Believe me. I can handle this.'

He acknowledged her words with a simple nod.

'I have no doubt that you can handle anything you set your mind to. And you're right. I flew in from Adelaide four days ago, and for the last three months a whole team of craftsmen have been tearing down a shell of a building and creating my first signature restaurant. The building work is behind schedule, and we're opening in six weeks. But from what I've seen, Maria Rossi needs help and she needs it now. I can afford to give Maria a few days out of my life to get this trattoria back on its feet. I owe her that. And I promised her I would do it. End of story.'

He turned sideways to face her and waved a packet of fusilli in front of her. 'Have you eaten this evening? Because I find it hard to think when I'm starving. Do you mind if I make something simple?'

Sienna bit down a quick reply. Lunch was a distant memory and she *was* hungry. And cold. And tired. And drained. At that moment pasta sounded pretty good. But she could *not* let him know how desperately she would love some hot food.

'I don't expect you to cook for me. And are you always so stubborn?'

'Always. And it is my pleasure. Oh, and, Sienna?'

The different tone of his voice was so startling that she flicked her head up towards him.

Too fast. The slight dizziness was back.

He winced at her before gesturing behind him with his head. 'One suggestion—and it is only a suggestion—before you make any decisions about taking on this bistro on your own, you might want to take a look into the dining room while I rummage around for something edible. That way we'll both be facing the horror of the situation.'

Brett swung open the refrigerator door and pretended to be

examining the jumbled contents of the small freezer compartment as Sienna gingerly stepped on tiptoe past him into the corridor.

He had to keep his distance.

Not because Sienna scared him—she never had.

Not even when she'd been the family princess in the royal Rossi family and he very much the visiting peasant. Or at least that was how he had seen it at the time—no matter how much the family had gone out of their way to make him feel welcome.

He had been a boy from the wrong side of the tracks and kind-hearted Maria had taken pity on him when the academic world had labelled him a failure and turned its back on him.

Maria would have been horrified to know that he'd felt that way at the time. She had made it clear that the only reason he was in her kitchen—this very kitchen he was standing in now— was because of his talent. A talent she had believed in from the very first meal he had made for her. He might not have been able to express how he was feeling in words or on paper—but he had through his passion for food.

No. When he was around Sienna Rossi, *awestruck* was a better description.

Brett pressed his back against the refrigerator door and looked around the kitchen where he had spent the best six weeks of his life. This was where he had eaten his first real Mediterranean food. Pasta which did not come ready cooked out of a tin. Tomato sauce made from fresh tomatoes and not from red plastic ketchup bottles.

For a teenage boy it had seemed as if a secret door had been opened into another world of endless delights and exciting new opportunities.

In that world he had found the potential to make something of his life without all of the labels he had managed to pick up over the years. Labels like 'difficult', 'sullen' and 'poor communicator'. 'Failure' and 'no future' had sometimes been added for good measure.

Apparently he had talent. All he had to do was prove it to others and convince them that he had potential. Face talking to trained chefs and persuade them to share their skills with him. Chefs like Frank Rossi and his family, who came from generations of skilled chefs and family cooks.

Frank and his sister, Sienna Rossi, had grown up with wonderful food and high expectations in a very different family from the one he was used to.

He had been so jealous of them back then it had been like a physical pain.

Little wonder that he had kept focused on what he'd had the power to control.

And yet here he was, back at Rossi's.

He turned back to the mini-freezer and his fingers closed over a plastic container with two large, brightly coloured dots stuck on the lid.

The air was sucked out of his lungs.

The red dot meant that this was a tomato pasta sauce, and the green dot told him that it was made using vegetables with herbs and spices. A basic sauce that could be used in a variety of recipes or served on pasta. No meat. No extras.

Unless she had changed her ideas, this was the same colour-code system that Maria has used all of those years ago, to hide the fact that she could not write or read well, and she was still using it now!

Brett carefully closed the freezer door and closed his eyes.

What was he doing here?

Chris needed him! The new business needed him! He should be working on his dream restaurant instead of mopping floors and defrosting pasta sauce!

What was he trying to prove by coming back to this kitchen where it all began? Maria wasn't here in person. And everywhere he looked in this tiny space caught him unawares.

Walking through that door tonight had brought it all back to him.

The uncertainty. The feelings of inadequacy he'd thought he had buried deep inside the outer persona he displayed to the world. It was all still there. Far closer to the surface that he had ever imagined.

And Sienna Rossi was partly responsible for making his world spin out of control.

He'd kept his distance from her tonight because of something he had not expected. Something which had hit him hard and hit him fast the moment he had swung open that back door and looked into her wide brown eyes.

Instant attraction.

Attraction which set his pulse racing and his heart thumping.

He had only ever felt that pull once before—the first time he had seen the most beautiful girl in Paris and been too terrified and stunned to even speak to her.

As usual he had covered up his true feelings with a cheeky smile and lively chatter—the happy-go-lucky attitude which had become his mask over the years to hide the vulnerable heart that he hid deep inside. Sometimes the mask fitted so well that it took a minor earthquake to make it slip a little.

And Sienna Rossi was certainly a seismic event as far as he was concerned.

The stunning woman in the fitted black skirt suit, designer shoes and tantalising smooth cream silk blouse was as far away from the plump, shy, teenage Sienna as he could have imagined. With her stunning good looks and elegant formality this Sienna was every inch the kind of head waiter that fine-dining restaurants would appreciate.

And that was the problem. He had just spent the last three hours fielding phone calls from Chris during his meeting with the architects, then cleaning up the mess in what had used to be a fine working kitchen—while all the time his brain had been in overdrive, conjuring up a vision of what a twenty-eight-year-old version of Sienna Rossi was going to look like.

Maria had told him that she was working as a head waiter and sommelier, but nothing could have prepared him for the woman who had been standing outside that kitchen door. Which for someone who took pride in their visual skills, he found deeply unsettling.

The suit, the uniform, the shoes. That was all surface gloss—designed to create the professional image fine-dining customers demanded when they were paying for the best. And Sienna certainly did it well.

Her long, straight, dark brown hair had always been tied back from a side parting, but from what he had seen of it tonight, even wet and unbrushed, she probably spent more to create that perfectly smooth, shiny, shoulder-length ponytail than he'd used to spend on clothes in a year at catering school.

She was stunning! Little wonder that his confidence had faltered. Perhaps he did not know who this version of Sienna truly was underneath that surface layer?

Except… It was her eyes that gave the game away.

He would have recognised those amazing deep caramel eyes anywhere—he had spent more than enough time staring at them over the dinner table at Rossi family meals, and then in the kitchen, where he'd never seemed to be able to escape her, no matter how hard he'd tried.

She had the most wonderful, gentle, feminine eyes.

He had certainly known plenty of women over the past ten years he had spent travelling the world—all wonderful, kind, generous and loving girls he had enjoyed spending time with as he worked hard to develop his skills.

But not one of them came close to having eyes like Sienna Rossi.

Eyes he could fall into and drown.

Those same eyes had been wide-open in shocked surprise

when he had opened the back door—and even wider when he had deposited her onto the patio chair.

Eyes filled with tears.

Tears which had torn into his heart like sharp Japanese sushi knives. Shredding his mask of cheerful bravado into ribbons of need and regret and loss.

Eyes which could throw him off track in an instant if he allowed them. Combined with tears and the fiery mature woman who now lived beneath the austere black suit.

Dynamite. Absolute explosive dynamite.

Those eyes and those tears had sucked him back to a place he had not expected. A place where his heart was still open and he did not have to protect it from the pain of loss and regret.

She unsettled him.

Perhaps it was time to find out what kind of woman Sienna had become?

Time to light the blue touch paper and watch the firework display.

CHAPTER SIX

Step 6: A Valentine Wish…

THERE HAD been something in Brett's voice which had told Sienna that all was not going to be well, but she wasn't prepared for what lay in front of her after she squelched down the hall carpet and flicked on the lights in the dining room of Trattoria Rossi.

Or tried to. Three out of the four lightbulbs in the room were broken, and the one remaining red wall light gave out a positively eerie and pathetic glow, casting the dark, depressing and gloomy room into shadows.

Cold, frigid, damp shadows.

Sienna shivered and huddled deeper into the warmth of Brett's jacket before running her fingers across the old radiator. Icy cold. Terrific!

The central heating had not been turned on, and the cold wet February evening had combined with the wide expanse of glass window to create a distinct chill in the air which no amount of hot soup was going to put right, should a paying customer wander in from the street by accident.

Even the stone walls of the wine cellar in Greystone Manor were warmer than this space.

The only bright thing in the whole room was a handwritten poster, shining white and red in the light beaming out from the kitchen like a beacon in the murk around her.

Rossi's Famous Valentine Day Special Menus.

Oh, Maria! Valentine's Day! Of course! That made it even worse. Rossi's had used to be *the* place to bring your date on Valentine's Day.

Generations of teenagers from the local high schools had brought their first dates to Rossi's over the years. Maria had used to be booked from Christmas! And now look at it!

Valentine's Day? More like Halloween.

If Sienna had needed any more information about how low the restaurant had sunk, this was it. Just when she'd thought this day could not get any worse, she had to see this sad room. It was enough to start her off crying again, but she was not going to let Brett see her so out of control.

She felt humiliated! It was going to be hard enough to face him after that pathetic display without more tears to add to her embarrassment.

But this was heartbreaking!

Maria should try and sell the restaurant and retire while she was still active enough to enjoy herself.

A shiver of cold and dread ran down her neck from a draught.

She was just about to slink back to her relatively warm kitchen chair when the telephone rang at the tiny table which served as reception desk.

Without thinking or hesitating Sienna switched back into head-waiter mode and took the call.

'Good evening, Trattoria Rossi. Sienna speaking. How may I help you?'

Her hand picked up the pen and flicked open the simple supermarket diary that was Maria's reservations book. Her hand stilled as she said, in as calm a manner as she could, 'Valentine's Day? Umm, let me just check for you.'

She took a breath, then another. Not because she wanted to keep the elderly gentleman on the other end of the telephone waiting by pretending that they were fully booked, but because of what she was looking at.

It was so remarkable that she actually held the book up into the light from the kitchen to check. She could hardly believe her eyes. But there was no doubt. Maria had not only taken bookings for Valentine's Day. She had taken *lots* of bookings. Easily enough to occupy three quarters of the tables.

'Oh, yes, I am still here. What's that? You've been celebrating Valentine's Day here for the last forty years? Well, yes, that is quite remarkable. Oh? You came to Rossi's on your very first date? That *is* lovely.'

Decision time.

Tell this nice gentleman that they were closed and likely to stay that way. *Or*… A totally crazy, outrageous and off-the-wall thought flicked into her mind.

She *could* do something remarkable. *She could stay.*

She could do this.

She could turn this dining room around. This *restaurant* around.

She had the skill, she had some time, and it would give her the boost to her confidence that she so badly needed.

There was a sudden clatter from the kitchen, followed by a smothered groan.

Of course she was going to need more than a little help with the food, and that would mean working with Brett Cameron.

On the one hand, he was obviously a wonderful chef, who was devoted to Maria—the food would be terrific, she had no doubt about that. And on the other he had clearly decided that he was going to be just as stubborn as she was!

She sighed out loud, and her shoulders slumped as the truth hit home.

In theory Brett Cameron and Sienna Rossi *could* be the best team Maria could possibly have hoped for.

They were both professionals with unique skills and talents. Two of a kind.

She owed it to Maria to make an effort and work with Brett. He had his own commitments, but was prepared to sacrifice them for Maria's sake. Surely she could find it in her to meet him halfway?

A smirking smile creased her mouth and she lifted the telephone closer. *Umm.*

Perhaps if she could succeed in working through a refurbishment plan with Brett then maybe, *just maybe*, she could work with Angelo or any other chef.

She would show Brett Cameron that she could put up with any challenge he threw at her.

And help sort out her decision making in the process.

Her head lifted and her voice suddenly sounded full of confidence. As though she was back in control, with a clear plan of what she wanted to do instead of being on the run. 'In that case I could not possibly let you down. Table for two. February fourteenth. Thank you, Mr Scott. I'll see you in…ten days' time. Have a lovely evening.'

Sienna gently replaced the handset and calmly added the reservation to the long list for February fourteenth.

She very carefully lowered the diary back onto the table, closing her eyes and trying to steady her nerves before going back into *that* kitchen.

Then the doubts started to creep back in. Threatening her resolve.

Things were happening far too fast for her liking.

First, she was on the run from Greystone and the mess that was the new chef, who might not have changed much from the arrogant *old* chef he'd used to be.

Second, the boy who had been her first crush was boiling water and reheating pasta sauce so they could have dinner together. And he was still the best-looking man she had ever met—anywhere.

She was stuck here in the wreck of what had used to be a stunning family bistro only a few short years ago. But it was either that or return to Greystone, while Brett struggled to cook and run her aunt's pride and joy on his own.

Sienna inhaled sharply and curled her toes inside her still moist shoes and stockings.

No way. Not going to happen.

She was here now and she had to make the best of it.

She could work with Brett and run the bistro for a week or two. Of course she could.

Time to get the team in place.

'*Brett?*' she called out as she squelched her way back through into the kitchen. 'What had you planned to do on Valentine's Day?'

'Come next week I'll be working like crazy on my new kitchen. Why do you ask? Looking for a date? You would be welcome in our spot in Notting Hill, only we are not *quite* ready to take guests at the moment.'

Sienna pushed her lips together and blew out hard. Notting Hill? That was where Angelo's had been. Her dream restaurant, in one of the most exclusive parts of London!

Of course Brett had been in Paris when all of that had happened. He couldn't know about that part of her life. Good. Best to leave it like that.

She hid her painful moment by turning it into a wide grin. 'Notting Hill? Congratulations. Maria never said a word, although I haven't spoken to her since Christmas. Work has been mad. Thanks for the invitation, but I plan to spend the day a little closer to Rossi's. In fact, I want to spend it right here. Serving paying customers.'

His half-second delay in responding gave Sienna just enough time to make her bold move.

'It's one of her biggest nights of the year. I'm sure that she wouldn't want to turn away the business. Not on Valentine's Day. I only worked here once on Valentine's Day, to help her out, but it was good fun then and we could make it fun again.'

Brett stopped stirring and slowly turned around to face her. He looked straight into her eyes before he spoke, startling her so much that she fell back to her old nervous habit of twiddling at the antique silver ring she wore on the fourth finger of her right hand.

'You want to open up that freezing cold dining room and serve food to paying customers? On Valentine's Day?' His voice was low. Challenging.

'Yes,' she replied with a smile, suddenly desperate to turn the conversation around. 'Do you remember what it used to be like here? On Valentine's Day?'

'Hard to forget.' Brett pressed both of his palms flat on the worktop and his upper lip curved slightly to one side in a lop-sided smile. 'Every one of my classmates was in here with his girlfriend, dressed in smart new clothes their mums had picked out for them. Pretending to be all sophisticated and mature while all of the time they were squirming and itching with their ties and starched collars.'

He returned his spoon to the saucepan and slowly stirred from side to side, releasing the most delicious herby fragrance into the room. 'I was too busy burning my arms on their lasagne dishes and pizzas to catch a lot of the conversation, but Maria was brilliant at making everyone feel at home and taking some of the nervousness out of their big day.'

Sienna watched Brett move between sink, worktop and hob. Fast. Slick. Practised. This was his life.

Pest. But a clever pest she needed to have on her side if she was going to pull this off. She was in control now; she would talk to him as though he was a colleague. That was all. A handsome, talented colleague who had the ability to make her dizzy.

'Exactly. That was what made Rossi's so special. Teenagers could come here for their first date and not feel intimidated. It might have been pasta and pizza, but it was served to them on a table with a tablecloth and napkins, in a real restaurant. I got the feeling that it was almost a rite of passage around here. Like buying your first car. That first date in Rossi's was something you would never forget—even if it did happen forty years ago.'

'Why, Sienna Rossi! I always *knew* there was a romantic streak in you! Where did *you* go for your first Valentine's Day date?'

'Sorry, I don't believe in romance any more,' she replied with a shake of the head and a dismissive sniff. 'And I think you can guess where I went. My dad wanted to keep a close eye on who, where and what was going on. I had no choice in the matter. And stop trying to distract me when I'm explaining why I couldn't say no to Mr Scott. Or any of the other couples who have booked for the evening. It's their special day. The fact that it is also good business is a bonus.'

'A-ha. Thought so. And I don't believe a word of it. Born romantic. Always have been. There is no use you trying to deny it. I do have one question. What will your current date think about you working on Valentine's Day?'

'My date? Oh. I'm between boyfriends at the moment. I always work through Valentines anyway. How about you?' Sienna asked, trying to sound casual. 'Do I need to keep a table for you and your lady friend?'

He smiled to himself. 'Not this year, thanks. Save the tables for gentlemen who want to show their ladies that they are special. *That* is what it is all about.'

'I agree with you. In fact…' Sienna ran her tongue over her lips before going on in a mad rush, desperate to get the words out before she lost her nerve. 'I was hoping that I could persuade you to be the guest chef for the evening. For Aunt Maria's sake. You *did* promise Maria that you would cook for her!' Sienna exclaimed in a louder voice than she'd intended to use.

Brett turned around to look at her, and tilted his head to one side before breaking into a wide smile.

'I did wonder where you were going on your trip down memory lane.'

He nodded once before turning back to the hob. 'Yes, I did make Maria a promise. And I keep my promises. The clock has already started ticking on my new venue. A few weeks from now there will be customers coming through the door. Not to mention top restaurant critics from around the world. I would only have a couple of days spare at most. Plus I have no kitchen, no menu and a massive loan to pay off. And do you know what?'

She held her breath. Waiting for him to come up with some totally credible and amazing reason why he could not possibly cook pasta and pizza for spotty teenagers and retired couples in a tiny bistro when he had a gourmet restaurant of his own to get ready.

He was Brett Cameron. Award-winning international chef. Not some catering student. Of *course* he wouldn't want to do the cooking himself. He probably had a whole brigade of minions at his beck and call.

What had she been thinking? Dreaming, more like.

She braced herself for the bad news. Why not one more thing to add to her disastrous day?

'Maria's sauce has been in the freezer since Christmas. It might have been delicious when it was made, but I've done the best I can to save it. Ready for some hot food? Then I'll tell you exactly how I plan to turn this place around in time for Valentine's.'

CHAPTER SEVEN

Step 7: Two Sparkling Brown Eyes...

BRETT PULLED OUT the ancient patio chair and patted it with one hand.

'Your table is ready, Your Highness. Sorry about the lack of fancy place setting, but I did disinfect the workbench while I was thinking up my master plan. It might not be up to fine-dining standards but it is clean. Providing, of course, you can lower yourself to eat at Maria's kitchen table? Just this once?'

One long, elegant tanned finger tapped the side of his nose, then he carefully folded the white tea towel over the crook of his arm like a silver-service waiter. 'It could be our little secret.'

'Funny. That's very funny,' Sienna replied, and squeezed her eyes together as she slid onto the chair. But he had already turned away to prepare their dinner.

A delicious aroma filled the space, and Sienna lifted her head in curiosity to see what he had managed to conjure up from the meagre contents of Maria's stores. And was stunned by a very nice view of Brett's broad shoulders and snug cargo pants.

He was cooking her hot food.

Maybe she could forgive him, *just a little*, for trying to drown her.

'Tell me more about this master plan for *you* to turn this place around!' she managed to squeak out into the uncomfortable silence, trying to keep her voice light and joking. 'Have I missed something in the time it took me to freeze my feet in the dining room?'

He clearly took no notice whatsoever of the implied sarcasm about his bid for power, and a low rough chuckle echoed back from the plain painted wall he was facing as he cooked.

'I would hardly call it a master plan, but the building work on my kitchen has cut back the little time I have to work on the recipes for my signature menu.'

He pointed his stirring spoon towards his own chest, narrowly missing adding a smear of tomato sauce to his shirt as he did so.

'I have ten key dishes which are going to define what I'm trying to achieve.'

He paused, then turned back to the bubbling saucepan as he added a colander of drained pasta and gently folded it into the sauce to give it the lightest of coatings.

'Most chefs have three of four. Not me. I want ten perfect recipes for that first night. No arguments. And right now I don't have a kitchen to work in.' He raised the spoon to his lips before hissing, 'And this *still* needs more basil.'

Sienna watched in silence as Brett grabbed a bunch of wilted-looking green leaves from the dehydrated plant barely surviving in a terracotta clay pot on the windowsill, before moving back to the workbench and tearing them into narrow strips with strong deft fingers. Intense focused concentration, energy, excitement. All in those few moments it took to shred some basil which was certainly past its best and stir it into the sauce.

In that instant Sienna recognised the same boy she had known at sixteen. Oh, he might look different on the outside, with all the self-confidence and self-belief that a career as a superstar chef in the top kitchens around the world could bring. But there was no mistaking that flash of passion even in this simple task. He had never lost it. If anything he seemed to have developed it even more!

Brett Cameron in action was mesmerising. And somehow, amazingly, touchingly, a little vulnerable.

She envied him that self confidence.

Confidence enough to be able to create something remarkable no matter where he was working, and with ingredients that might not be up to his usual standard.

Suddenly her brain started to defrost like her feet, and she was instantly aware that Brett was still talking. The diverting pest of a man could multitask. *Rats*!

A steaming bowl of soft multi-coloured pasta with the most amazing fragrance wafted past her nose and onto a huge white under-plate on the worktop.

Her tastebuds kicked in the microsecond they savoured the herby tomato tang with a twist of…something she could not quite place. She was used to the best from the best. How could she not recognise that subtle smell? It had to be a special herb or spice. But which one?

She slowly inhaled the aroma of the sauce and closed her eyes in delight. Any thought of holding back on her enthusiasm to make Brett suffer was instantly blown away.

Drat the man for knowing exactly how he could cut through the meagre defences she had built up! Perhaps it was this familiar and homely kitchen? Perhaps that was it? This was home.

'Basil, oregano, fresh rosemary. Garlic and onion with the tomato, and root vegetables and celery. But there is something else. I'm thinking dried chilli and marjoram?'

Brett was watching her with his fork poised to dive in. Waiting for her to try it first.

'I would recommend tasting some,' he said, with a satisfied smile in his low voice, and she took a breath. 'Or are you worried that you might like it too much?'

She opened her eyes, coated a single piece of pasta with the sauce and covered her lips around it.

'Wow,' she breathed, and chewed and swallowed with her eyes closed as pleasure flooded her senses. 'This. Is. Fantastic. Seriously good.'

Brett bowed slightly from his bar stool and dived into his own dinner, chewing through several mouthfuls in silence before gesturing towards her with his fork.

'I'm pleased you like it. Maria made the basic plum tomato paste, but the flavour was too bland for my taste, even with her choice of herbs, after a spell in the freezer. Hence the extras. Chilli flakes with a sprinkle of lemon zest. And fennel. Finely ground fennel seeds. No cheese.'

'Fennel seeds. That's it. That's the subtle richness. And I do like it. I like it a lot. Vegetarian dishes are always popular at the Manor.' Sienna chewed blissfully, aware that Brett was watching her as she ate. 'You could serve this sauce in so many ways. Very clever. And you're right. You don't need parmesan with this dish.'

'Absolutely. Of course it would have been better made with fresh ingredients. Wait until you try my three-mushroom cream sauce on fresh linguini. I'm still working on the best combination of dried and fresh mushrooms, but I'll get there. Or should I say *we'll* get there.'

He lowered his fork into his pasta bowl and leant forward, resting his elbows on his knees so that he could look into her face, his blue, blue eyes working their laser act on hers.

'I am a chef in need of a kitchen. Maria has a kitchen in need of a chef. It seems to me to point one way.'

The air crackled between them, and Sienna licked the sauce from her upper lip as her eyes locked onto his for one long, hot intense moment during which his eyes never left her face.

The heat from that gaze burnt away any lingering doubt she might have had that Brett Cameron had lost his ability to pull her from the real world and into the dizzy magical land where there was even the faintest chance that he might see her as someone he could care about.

'Go on,' she eventually managed to whisper.

'What if I agree to hire the bistro for the next ten days to work on my new recipes? It would mean closing the place to her regular customers, but I'll pay Maria the going rate for a commercial kitchen. Real money. Cash, if you like. What's more, I'll throw in a few extras to sweeten the deal.'

Sienna swallowed down her pasta.

'What kind of extras?'

'I owe Maria. And I can't work in a messy kitchen. Give me ten days and I promise you right here and now that I'll turn this place around. It's a winner. The lovely Maria gets a refurbished restaurant, publicity, and all the new kitchen equipment she wants. And our lovely girl can rest in her hospital bed knowing that her place is in good hands. What do you say? Do you think you can put up with me until Valentine's Day?'

Several hours later, Sienna sat on the edge of Maria Rossi's bed in the same shell-pink, first-floor bedroom which had become her safe refuge four years earlier, and ran the tip of her finger across the silver picture frame she had found on Maria's dressing table.

Laughing back at her from below the glass was a happy couple captured in time on one of the best days of her life. Sienna Rossi and Angelo Peruzi on the day they had opened their own London restaurant.

Angelo was so handsome in his chef's whites, with his dark curly hair and deep brown eyes. And that smile. That killer smile. How could she *not* have fallen for him?

They'd been young and in love and starting out on the greatest adventure of their lives together. Their own restaurant. Working together to create something amazing.

She had been so happy that day. So much to look forward to.

The Rossis had always loved their family photographs.

Perhaps that was why she hadn't been able to bring herself to destroy all of the other photos like this one, or lock them away out of sight in the special suitcase, along with the wonderful wedding plan and the lovely gilt-edged wedding invitations and the bridesmaid tiaras her future mother-in-law had sent from Los Angeles?

That special place where she had locked away her sensitive and loving heart.

Sienna dropped the photograph onto the bed and closed her eyes as the old familiar pain made her flinch. It was like a paper cut. Sharp. Deep. Only it could not be blinked away.

So what if she had survived the last four years by building tall, thick walls of prickly professionalism to protect her heart from that kind of pain? She needed those solid stone walls to give her some time to rebuild her confidence, so that she was capable and able to do her job without another control-freak chef.

Like Brett Cameron, for example.

Talking through his plans for the refurbishment work, she had come so close to dropping her guard that it scared her.

She was in serious danger of repeating all the mistakes in her life.

How could she fight the attraction to Brett and hope to win? He had all of the weapons he needed. Good looks, charisma, and a level of self-confidence that bordered on arrogance.

She was like a moth drawn to the light and heat of a fire. Destined to be consumed by the flames and fall to the earth and drown.

Only this time she didn't know if she had the strength to find her way back up to the surface for air.

She had to fight this attraction before things spun out of hand.

It had been four years since she had allowed anyone to take control, and look where that had taken her!

Maria had an awful lot to answer for! Even if this project *was* the distraction she needed.

All she had to do was survive the next ten days.

Then she would go back to Greystone Manor and face her past and her future. Alone.

CHAPTER EIGHT

Step 8: And a Pair of Pink Pyjamas

'TIME TO rise and shine!'

'Hmm. Who? What?'

Sienna pushed her nose out from below Aunt Maria's duvet and blinked several times before she focused on the wide shoulders of the tall, fair-haired man who was throwing back her curtains to let in the faint morning sunlight.

It was still raining.

'Oh, you have got to be joking…' she muttered, before pulling the duvet back over her head with a yawn. 'Why are you in my room? Go away!'

'And a very good morning to you too, sleepy-head.'

A long tanned finger hooked over the duvet cover, so that her eyes were just exposed, and she squinted up at the handsome, square-jawed blond who was grinning down at her.

He was shaved, his hair was still moist from the shower, and he smelt like every man should smell first thing in the morning. Fresh, clean, newly laundered, and radiating enough levels of testosterone and pheromones to make any half-drowsy girl want to drag him down under the covers with her.

If they could bottle that smell it would only be available on a medical prescription.

She inhaled another whiff. Free sample.

'I popped in earlier to check what you wanted for breakfast but you were still dreaming of Greystone Towers, so this is your first and only treat of the day. A lie-in.'

He pulled the duvet a little closer to his chest and leant forward, so that he could pretend to peer down under the cover.

'Lovely outfit, by the way. I can see that your fashion sense is still as stylish as ever.'

She instinctively reclaimed the duvet with both hands and pulled it tighter around her chest, to cover up the thick pink-and-white cotton pyjamas that she had found in Maria's wardrobe.

'It was freezing last night. Morning. Whenever I finally managed to get to bed. You might have noticed that the central heating is turned off.'

'Now I *am* offended. I am just across the hall, you know.' He gave her a saucy wink and a quick salute before sitting down uninvited at the bottom of her bed.

'Oh, please. Don't beg. It's embarrassing. And what are you doing, coming in here so early? Or is it very late?'

'Almost nine. I know.' He shook his head from side and side and tutted loudly in faked disgust. 'Hard to believe that anyone can sleep this late. You have special dispensation this morning, but don't think you can get away with this behaviour for the rest of the week. Lots to do, girl!'

'Get away with it? Hang on just a minute.' Sienna shuffled up higher against the headboard, but tugged the covers up over her chest, much to Brett's amusement. 'It was your idea to start working on the master plan straight after dinner! I left you at about one this morning with your head in the oven. Don't you ever sleep?'

'Not much.' He shrugged. 'A couple of hours are quite enough. Besides…' and he patted the bedcover twice for effect before grinning up at her '…I am totally jazzed by our little project. The phones have been buzzing since dawn. There are guys all over London loading vans with tools and catering equipment as we speak.'

'Guys? Equipment? I'm confused. I thought you had only just arrived back in London.'

He nodded in acknowledgement. 'See, I *knew* that you were secretly paying attention while you finished off that second bowl of pasta. My mate Chris is in charge of the building work at my new place. I think he calls himself the project manager, or some other fancy title, but Chris knows who to call when he needs tradesmen, and at this time of year there are usually a few guys who need the extra work or a small job. So I made a few calls. Just to get things moving. This place is going to be jumping with workmen in a few hours, and it might be better for them if you are wearing something less alluring.'

Her chest rose and fell as words failed to form inside her still sleepy head, and she faltered slightly before sitting back.

Sienna closed her eyes, took several deep breaths, and tried to steady her pulse which was racing as anger and frustration surged through her body.

She could feel stiffness building in her shoulders, and tried to clench her toes under the covers.

It has already started.

She should have known and trusted her instincts the night before.

He was already giving orders. Taking control and telling her how things were going to be.

How could she have been so stupid? Why hadn't she stuck to her guns and made him leave?

Stupid, stupid girl. Pulled in by a pair of wonderful blue eyes and Hunk of the Month sex appeal being wafted in front of her over a hot meal!

She should have known that Brett Cameron was too dangerous for her!

For a few hours she had allowed herself to let down her guard.

Well, that was last night. When she'd been cold and exhausted. Not now. Not today. Not any day. Maria was her aunt and she was going to sort out these problems on her own. She didn't need Brett Cameron telling her what to do and how to do it.

Sienna gulped down a huge lump of resentment and disappointment before daring to use her voice. Trying to keep calm. In control without being aggressive. That was the key.

Whatever signal she was giving out, Brett had dropped his grin and now sat in silence on her bed. Watching her with a smiling face designed to weaken her resolve.

'When we talked this through last night,' Sienna managed to say in a low, calm, matter-of-fact voice, 'I thought that we were going to work on this project *together*. Agree the plan of action *together*. You focus on the kitchen and I work the dining room—but we both make sure that the other person is involved in any final decisions. That was what we agreed.'

She paused and licked her dry lips before going on. 'Sorry, Brett, but this is not going to work out after all. There are other kitchens you can rent to test out your recipes, and I can hire another chef to finish the work here on my own. Thanks for your ideas, but I truly don't think we can work together.'

His face twisted into a frown for a few seconds before he replied in a low, intense voice. 'What's the problem? Don't you trust me to call a few contractors to come in and do the work? I might have been out of town for a few years but I trust Chris. His guys won't let us down.'

Sienna shuffled higher up the bed and leant forward, her eyes fixed on his. This infuriating man was still not getting the message! 'No. It's not that at all.'

Brett crossed his arms and tilted his head to one side. 'Then what *is* the problem? You were asleep, we have the clock working against us, and we need to get this ball rolling. Come on—spill. Because I am not leaving this room until I find out what the matter is. And you already know how stubborn I can be when I have a mind to do something. So start talking.'

The problem? The real problem was probably already on his

way back from California to take over as head chef at Greystone Manor, but she could not even *think* of Angelo right now!

'It's not you, Brett. It's how you work. I had a problem with another chef a few years ago, who let me down very badly. Since then I don't like being left out when big decisions are being made.'

She paused and gauged his reaction before going on.

'I don't like being sidelined. And I really don't like someone *telling me* how things are going to happen on a project I feel responsible for without asking me first. That is not what we agreed to do. I really cannot work this way. I'm sorry, but it might be better if I hired another chef.'

The muscles in Brett's arms flexed several times, and the thumping in Sienna's chest increased as the silence stretched out between them.

Maria *had* asked Brett to help—she believed him on that point. But the Brett she had asked to help was not the same Brett who had been a willing trainee years ago.

Far from it.

He was an intense, powerful man who was sitting on her bed.

That in itself would unsettle any female with a pulse.

His deep blue eyes were looking at her with intelligence and insight…and something else she could not put her finger on. Disbelief?

Her stomach clenched. Maybe she had overreacted, as he'd said. But it had taken her four years of hard work to build up her cool and controlled exterior. She couldn't allow Brett to knock away her carefully constructed barriers in only a few hours.

He was probably thinking that she was a spoilt brat who was too used to having her own way. And she had just presented him with a get-out clause—on a silver platter.

Brett Cameron perched on the end of Sienna's bed and watched her clutch the bedclothes tighter up around her chest.

She was trying to get rid of him.

Why? All he had done was get the work started while she slept!

What was she so afraid of? Losing her independence?

Or something more fundamental than that?

Why was she so worried that he had leapt ahead? What had this other chef done that was so terrible that she couldn't trust *him?*

He caught her eyes at that moment, and the reality of her fear shone through in a brief moment before she looked away, but too late. She had told him what he needed to know. She had been seriously let down by someone she had trusted—that much was obvious.

This was not the bossy self-centred, always right and very demanding princess talking; this was a frightened woman at the end of her tether.

Well, he could do something about that! If Sienna needed reassurance, that was what he would give her.

'You don't need to hire another chef.' He raised one hand and let it fall to the bedcover.

His next words took her breath away.

'We've all been let down by people at one time or another. You want to be part of the decision process. I can understand that. But I told you yesterday I am not going anywhere! So you're stuck with me...although I *have* been keeping things from you which you are going to find out one way or another.'

The side of his mouth crinkled up to match the creases beside his entrancing eyes, and the tension she had not even realised was between them cracked like a flash of lightning.

She could not help herself. The heated exchange was gone with his smile, and she brought her brows together in mock concern. 'It must be very serious.'

He snatched a breath and shook his head from side to side. 'Oh, it is. Sad case. Thing is...well, I know I can be very impulsive. I desperately need someone around who can point my idiot enthusiasm in the right direction. Think you can cope with that, Miss Rossi? Give me another chance to prove that we can work together?'

His eyes gave the game away, of course. Nobody with those blue, blue twinkling eyes could possibly be taking himself seriously. But Sienna raised her eyebrows slightly when he added, 'Or am I way too much for you to handle?'

'Oh, I think I can handle you quite well, Mr Cameron. Quite well indeed.'

'Good to hear it. Because—again—I am not going any-where. I made Maria a promise and I keep my promises. Especially to pretty ladies.'

He stretched out his long, denim-clad legs and eased off the bed in a smooth rustle of muscle and suppressed energy.

'I'm going to take my second breakfast in the bistro, so we can start work straight away.' And then he half turned back to smile at her with a cheeky grin. 'If that it is okay with you...boss?'

He dodged out of the way as Sienna's pillow came flying towards him.

CHAPTER NINE

Step 9: Sprinkle with Pink Flamingos

'YOU HAVE A checklist. I like it.'

He also liked her perfume, her flash of a smile and the way their bodies brushed up against one another as they manoeuvred their way around Maria's kitchen like ballet dancers, in some complex, unrehearsed choreography which only the two of them could come up with.

He really, really liked the way she looked in the morning, with her hair loose and messed up on the pillow, one arm flung out on top of the bedcover. Men had striven for years to paint women who looked so naturally beautiful. He had enjoyed a moment of guilty pleasure alone before she'd stirred and he tiptoed out of her room in stockinged feet to wake Chris up with an early morning telephone call, desperate not to disturb her.

Whatever demons had driven Sienna Rossi out onto the streets of London late on a wet, cold February evening would not go away after a few hours' sleep, but he wasn't the one who would drag them from her. If Sienna wanted to tell him why she had sought refuge at Rossi's out of the blue like that, that was fine, but he would not press her.

All he knew was that Sienna needed to be here, working, keeping herself busy to escape the inescapable—and he knew about that method. Only too well.

Besides, staying longer in that bedroom would have been seriously bad for his ability to keep his hands off her.

She'd been stunning then and was still stunning now, dressed in simple beige trousers and a light sweater the colour of ripe purple plums, with that lovely chestnut hair smoothed and sleek, pulled back behind her head and gathered inside a wide silver clip.

She looked up at him, her pen poised over the pink pad of writing paper she had found in the drawer in Maria's dressing table. Her pink pen had a jaunty pink flamingo made of bouncy rubber stuck on the end. He would have pulled it off the moment he laid eyes on it, but somehow the paper and pen were so perfectly matched it seemed a shame to spoil the set.

Oh, yes, he also liked the way she savoured and enjoyed every mouthful of food that passed her lips. Those slim hips must come from the most excellent of genes and a frantically busy life.

Time to think about something else, before he started cooking just to tantalise her with exciting new flavours and foods.

One thing was for sure. He was already looking forward to seeing this woman eat something extra special that he had made just for her. And soon.

'A girl needs a list,' she replied, before biting into a thick, crunchy piece of buttered toast made from a fresh loaf of unsliced granary bread he had bought from the local bakery at some silly hour of the morning. 'Where's *your* list? I need to know what you've been up to when I wasn't around to supervise.'

He tapped the side of his temple several times with his third finger.

'All in here. Shall I start while you eat? Great. Here are my top three priorities.'

He raised his left hand and started with his thumb.

'The cracked window needs to be replaced. My pal Chris is on the case. The glaziers we are using for my building work

will be around this afternoon to take the measurements and—
you are going to like this—they can etch the glass with
anything you like and have it fitted within forty-eight hours.'

His right hand swished through the air. '"Trattoria Rossi."'
Then he followed through with a sigh and a grin. 'Problem is that
I mentally tuned out the minute the glazier started talking about
fonts and layout. We need something classy, but simple. But also
fun and easy to read. Big letters.' He gave her a half smile before
confessing, 'That's the dyslexia for you. I have no clue.'

There was a sudden intake of breath and a stunned silence
from across the kitchen.

'Dyslexia? Are you serious?' Her voice was so full of gen-
uine surprise and concern that he turned to face her.

'Didn't Maria tell you?'

'Not a word. I am so sorry, Brett, I had no idea!'

He shrugged and slipped his toasted cinnamon-and-raisin
English muffin onto a plate, before sliding onto the stool on
the other side of the table from Sienna, who had stopped eating
and was watching him with wide-eyed interest and concern, her
toast halfway to her mouth.

He tried to dissipate the tension by taking a bite out of his
breakfast and waving the muffin around before answering.

This wasn't the time to tell her the truth about how hard it
was living day to day with dyslexia. And he certainly did not
want her pity.

So down came the mask as he made light of the whole sorry
mess that was pain and frustration, living in a world of words
and letters which made little sense to him. Normally he had
admin staff and Chris to take care of the paperwork side of the
business. Not here. Not at Rossi's.

*Here he was, back to being on his own. Without even Maria
to help him work through a raft of coping mechanisms.*

Unless Sienna helped him over the next few days he would
be floundering, just as he had been the first time he came to
work here.

And that made him feel even more inadequate than ever.

'It's no secret that I have dyslexia,' he replied in a casual voice. 'The Australian press caught hold of it a while back, and I was invited onto several TV shows. You know the sort of thing.' His hand came up and scribbled a title in the air. '"How I overcame my terrible disability and how it made me a better person."'

He sniffed dismissively and took a sip of coffee. 'I was amazed by how many people have some form of dyslexia and wanted me to talk to them about it. Luckily I had an excellent excuse. Work! So now you know. Making lists and sign painting are not among my special skills and will need to be assigned elsewhere.'

He lifted his head and pretended to look at her list, keen to change the topic. *Now*! His plan worked, as she flapped the paper at him before replying.

'Ah. Now you're trying to be modest. And failing miserably. I am even more staggered by how much you have achieved since the last time we met,' she teased in an amazed voice, before scribbling something on her pink paper, the rubber flamingo jiggling madly as she did so. 'Window-etching in the dining room. Got it. And thank you for your honesty. Now I know, it helps me to see which jobs I have to do.'

He grinned back in reply and seized upon the opportunity to change the subject. 'Teamwork. Right? You handle the window-etching, and in exchange I volunteer to help take out the old dishwasher and fit a replacement. The good news is that the dishwasher from the restaurant we are ripping apart is still on site, and it looks positively new compared to this baby. It should fit, so Maria gets it for free.'

Sienna smiled and waved her toast in his direction. 'Heavy equipment? All yours. Even better when it's a freebie. What's number three?'

He was so dazzled by her unexpected smile that it took a moment for him to reconnect.

'The other good news is that both the oven and hobs work, in their own fashion—they've been replaced some time in the past five years—and the fridge is fine. Except...'

Her last morsel of toast was being crunched noisily. 'Except?'

'Most of the ingredients in the fridge and storeroom are either out of date or I wouldn't want to use them. So I need to go food shopping today. More coffee?'

Sienna shook her head. 'I've already had more than I normally drink in a day. The caffeine rush is starting to kick in. Although I needed something to lift my mood after seeing the dining room in daylight.'

She winced and hunched her shoulders before giving an exaggerated shudder.

'Okay, those were my suggestions. Hit me with *your* top three,' he replied, before draining his own espresso.

Sienna tapped on her clipboard, and the flamingo looked as if it was trying to take off.

'Bad news first. The dining-room walls need to be repaired and repainted. They are *so* tired and in need of loving care and attention—but there are special chemicals to help lift the stains. That is my first job.'

She flicked up a glance towards Brett. 'I am going to need help emptying the room. This actually might be a bigger job than I expected. The carpet squidges and squelches when I walk on it. I don't want to even *think* of what has been spilt down there over the years. No more carpet. I would suggest hard flooring, but I'll get back to you with some options as soon as the carpet is gone.'

Her hand paused before the flamingo had time to rest, and her bright, open-eyed face looked up at him.

His heart thumped at how her face and personality beamed back at him for that microsecond, before the serious professional Sienna he had met the previous evening got back to the task.

'Most of the chairs can go out with the carpet! There are only about four I would trust with my weight. The rest are only fit for firewood. Discount warehouses should have what we need. And forget the tablecloths and napkins. Burnt, stained or torn. Darning is not one of Maria's finer skills.' Sienna shuddered before going on. 'I've already thrown them out.'

Brett groaned. 'So basically we don't even have a dining room. Wonderful. Is there any good news? At all?'

She thought for a second before nodding. Once. 'The tables are basically sound. I think Maria inherited them when my parents sold their restaurant a few years ago. I can use them. And I called Frankie at the deli—he says hi, by the way—and apparently there are boxes of old stuff from the restaurant which Dad kept as spares still stashed in my parents' basement. They have been there for ages and he is happy for us to salvage what we can since it is for Aunt Maria. I think that could be a good place to start.'

'Aha. You see? You *do* need me after all.'

She sighed dramatically before replying, instantly taking the wind out of his sails.

'Sorry, but Frankie is busy in the deli and the boxes will need to be lugged up narrow stairs. I need someone who is not frightened by either mutant spiders or heavy boxes, and you're the closest I have to a lugger type. So I'll have to make do.'

'Faint praise, which I accept none the less. So. When do you want to go back to your parents' house?'

CHAPTER TEN

Step 10: Add Hot Pink Psychedelic Flowers

'WELL, THIS is going to be weird. I haven't been back to the Rossi family house in years. Pity your folks are on holiday. I would have liked to say hello!'

'Caribbean cruise. A late Christmas present from the family. According to Frankie they are putting up with fancy cocktails and evening dress in glorious sunshine. Mum is having a wonderful time.'

Brett stared out at the lashing rain between the swish of the car windscreen wipers, and sighed as he turned into the small drive outside the Rossi house. He sat back, drumming his fingers on the steering wheel to the beat of the music playing on the car stereo and the rhythm of the wipers.

'Glorious sunshine! Don't remind me. Adelaide is lovely in February. But, hey, I'm going to be around for the long term. I'll make sure that their names are on the guest list.'

He glanced sideways just as she half turned to him with a distant smile and distractedly replied, 'Mmm. They would love that. Especially if some of the dishes are based on Italian classics. My dad would enjoy telling you how to cook them properly.'

Then she realised what she had just said, and fidgeted even more in the slippery leather passenger seat so that she could sit a little taller.

'Sorry. That came out in completely the wrong way. If the rest of your Italian dishes are anything like that amazing pasta sauce you concocted last night, they will be totally thrilled. Did you know that your name actually came up during Christmas lunch? One of my cousins was in Adelaide and ate in your restaurant. He went so far as to say that the food was excellent. Maria was very proud.'

Brett felt a blush of heat at the base of his neck and shuffled awkwardly. 'She never told me that.'

Sienna faced forward, staring at the house, oblivious to his discomfort as she twiddled her silver ring. 'Well, it would be awful if you developed a swollen head.'

He acknowledged the possibility with a low chuckle, and undid his seat belt so he could focus on the lady by his side, who had remained silent for most of the journey from Maria's.

Between Trattoria Rossi and her old home her get up and go had got up and gone. No sparkle. No fizz. Nothing.

Sienna stayed where she was.

Then, conscious that he was looking at her, she lifted her head and straightened her back, as though she was preparing to go for a job interview instead of visiting the house she had grown up in and called home for most of her life. She glanced up at the front door through the rain and bit her bottom lip. Her bravado faded with her smile.

Some part of Brett reminded him that Sienna's private demons were none of his business. But the girl who had burst into tears when he had soaked her lovely shoes last night was right back in the car with him now. Frozen in her seat.

She was scared! Well, he knew just what that felt like. She needed help and he was right there. As he had told her, he wasn't going anywhere.

'I hate to criticise any lady's footwear, but those are so *not* you.'

Sienna blinked several times at him, and then stared hard at her feet. Maria Rossi's short Wellington boots stared back at her. They were purple, with psychedelic white and hot pink flowers. The only vaguely waterproof item of footwear in Maria's extensive shoe collection. She might fit the same size of shoes as her aunt, but style was another matter completely.

'I would have gone for the yellow daisy sandals I found on top of the refrigerator and put up with wet feet—but, hey, that's who I am,' Brett added, in as casual a voice as he could muster, and shrugged.

She looked up from her boots and stared into his face. Those deep brown eyes that he had admired for so long locked onto his and would not let him go.

Sienna Rossi was holding onto his strength and positive energy every bit as much as if he had been physically holding her in his arms.

And the unsettling feeling swelled into something much bigger.

The only sound in the car was the swish swish of the wipers and the low beat of a Latin dance band for a few long seconds before she gave a weak, fragile smile.

'I did leave some shoes in my old bedroom. And a change of clothes. I should go and get them.'

'Absolutely. Stay right there for a moment, and we'll get ready to make a run for it!'

Sienna watched Brett shrug into his jacket, grab a golf umbrella from the backseat and fling open the car door before dashing out into the lashing rain with a shout. She barely had time to release her seat belt and grab her bag before Brett was opening the door and reaching inside for her to join him.

She let out a long, calming breath and swung her legs out of the car—into the largest puddle she had ever seen in her life. Brett was already beside her, his hand on the small of her back, drawing her closer to his warm body under the shelter of the huge umbrella.

Without thinking or hesitating, she wrapped her right arm around the waist of his jacket and huddled closer, so they could run for the shelter of the wide porch which covered the entrance to the front door.

Yelping and laughing like children, they dodged the puddles and the wet bushes which blew against their legs in the brisk wind. At last they reached the shelter of the stone arch and Sienna immediately started shaking the rain from her hair, grateful to be out of the downpour but reluctant to leave the safe embrace of the man whose hand was still on her back as he closed the brolly one-handed.

His life and passion and energy were exactly what she needed.

Coming back home shouldn't be a big deal, but it was. A *very* big deal. And she was grateful that he was there with her.

'Made it,' Brett joked. 'Maybe those boots were a success after all!'

His warm body was still pressed against her side, and he did not appear to be in any hurry to separate, so she had to twist inside his arms to look at his face, her raincoat sliding smoothly against his padded jacket. His hand drew her closer, so that when the palms of her hands came up to press against the front of his jacket there was nowhere else to look but into his face.

Close up and in daylight it was like seeing a stunning landscape at close range.

The tiny thin white scar that cut his heavy blond left eyebrow.

The slight twist on the bridge of his nose which told her that it had been broken at least once.

And his eyes. The blue was not one solid colour but a mosaic of different shades and variations, from almost white through cobalt, to dark navy and everything in between, each tiny dot subtly different from the others. And they were all looking at her with an intensity and strength and yet a vulnerability that told her far more about the real Brett Cameron than he probably would have liked.

Playing with fire could get you burnt. *And that look was incendiary.*

Her hands pressed a little harder before lifting away. Half of her already missed the warmth and intimacy of being so close to a man like Brett, while the other part shook its head in disgust and reminded her that she had been down this road before with a chef. And look where *that* had got her!

Chef magnet. She hated it when Carla was right.

How many times had the sixteen-year-old version of herself dreamt of being held by Brett Cameron? And here she was, snuggled up with only a few layers of clothing between them. Back home. Back where she'd started. Apparently none the wiser for twelve more years of life.

Time warp.

She was in danger of losing control just when she needed all of the discipline she could muster.

Brett could never know how this house she had once loved with such a passion had become a virtual prison. Her old childhood bedroom a place of nightmares, where she'd spent so many dark and depressed days wallowing in defeat and despondency after Angelo had abandoned her, taking her hopes and dreams and confidence with him. If Maria had not offered her an escape route, she would probably still be living here!

'Basement. Do you remember where it is?' she finally managed to ask, in a voice which sounded horribly squeaky against the rattle of the sleety rain.

Brett practically snorted in curt reply. 'Shall we try downstairs?' he said, but slid in beside her as she turned her key in the lock. 'Your dad had me running up and down those stairs for days when I first started. I remember every moment I spent in this house. They were some of the best weeks in my life. Allow me to lead the way.'

CHAPTER ELEVEN

Step 11: And a Box of Warm Memories

'AND WHO is this again?' Brett asked, holding up a very battered black-and-white print of a handsome dark-haired young man in a starched white apron with his arms folded across his chest. 'I'm starting to lose track.'

'Great-Uncle Louis. He was one of the original Rossis who came over from Tuscany to open the very first ice cream parlour in this part of London.'

'Fine moustache. What was the ice cream like?'

'He was horribly proud of that moustache and used to wax it every day.' She shuffled with her bottom along the step, and looked around conspiratorially before leaning in to whisper in Brett's ear. 'The hair wax tasted better than the ice cream. In fact, I think it was the same recipe. But you can't tell a soul.'

'My lips are sealed.' He smiled. His left side was squeezed tight against her from hip to shoulder, but he made no attempt to move to a more comfortable position on the narrow wooden stairs leading down to the Rossis' basement. 'Good old Great-Uncle Louis is still going to look wonderful in the Rossi gallery. Maria is going to love it. Great idea.'

Sienna bit her lip to hide her pleasure, and tried to deflect the attention away from herself. 'The Rossi restaurants have always had family photographs on the walls. I know it seems a bit kitsch now, but as far as Dad was concerned the restaurant was an extension of his own private dining room, and that meant you had your family around you. You know that Frankie has even more boxes of photographs at his place?'

Brett looked around the jumble of boxes and crates in amazement. 'There are more?'

She laughed and waved the folder of photographs they had selected together. 'I think twenty is enough for what we want. Modern picture frames and plain cream walls are going to make these pop. Wait and see.' She smiled up at Brett, only his attention had been taken with a large colour print which he seemed to be examining in great detail. 'Who's that photo of?' And then she caught a glimpse. 'Oh, no. I thought I had destroyed all the remaining copies. Pass it over!'

She made to grab at the offending item, only he swiftly passed the photograph to his other hand and held it at arm's length, high in the air.

'My, my, Miss Rossi. You *do* make a pretty bridesmaid. Is this Frank's wedding?'

She groaned and sat back, with her head in her hands.

'I was shanghaied, kidnapped and sold down the river. Pale green is not my colour. I don't think it is *anyone's* colour, but my future sister-in-law loved it. No choice in the matter.'

'Oh, I don't know…the ruffles are *very* fetching. Perhaps you should wear them more often?' he replied, with a waggle of his eyebrows.

'Oh, please. Like *you* are a fashion guru. I'd like to see your old family photos one of these days. Or do you keep them under lock and key in some bank vault where they can't be used for blackmail?'

His laughter came straight from the gut, and echoed around the long, narrow basement and through the stairs until she could feel the vibration of sound through every bone in her body.

'Sorry to disappoint you, but if there ever were any photos, they are long gone. My mother and I were never much for family gatherings. She was too busy moving from one rented place to another to keep in touch with any relatives we might have had in Scotland, and I certainly can't remember any photos on the walls.'

He glanced sideways at her over his shoulder, with that lopsided smile he did so well. 'When you are living out of a suitcase, you soon learn to carry only what you need.'

The fluorescent strip lighting overhead in the basement created harsh shadows and dark corners where Sienna knew monster mutant spiders liked to lurk. But looking into Brett's eyes she saw only the type of honesty and frankness that made the breath catch in her throat.

He was telling her the truth and he did not expect her to feel sorry for him. Just the opposite! The way he spoke was so matter-of-fact it was as though he told perfect strangers about his difficult past every day of the week!

It must be wonderful to be so confident and open to the world.

How did Brett do it?

How did he open his life up to such scrutiny?

And how, of all of the people on this planet, was he the only person *she* wanted to open up to? She *wanted* to tell him the truth about Angelo. Not the half-truths that her friends and family had passed around to cover up the whole sordid mess!

Even scarier, she *needed* him to know the truth. The poisonous secrets she kept within her hung like a thick security screen between them, just as they had with every other man she had come close to in the past four years. Except Brett was in another league. The boy who had been her first crush had dropped into her life less than a day earlier, and she already felt as though she had known him as a friend for years. The friend she'd never had.

Maybe that was it? Maybe she wanted to have a second chance to be friends with Brett? She had been too scared and intimidated the first time around to make the move to start a conversation, and he had been so withdrawn and obsessive back then.

Was it possible that she could take a risk and form a real friendship in the few days they would be working together at Maria's? It was probably the only chance she would ever have. One way or another they would soon be heading back to their real lives and jobs, where they would be destined to meet up on rare social events, if at all, when they would be surrounded by other people.

'I don't like it when you go quiet on me. Tell me what you are thinking,' Brett asked.

Not on your life.

'I was just wondering what it felt like to be dropped into the madness of the Rossi household when you took the job here. It must have caused you permanent psychological damage! We do tend to be a little exuberant when a few of us get together!'

He looked at her. Really looked at her. With an intense focus that made her fight the temptation to squirm away on the hard step and sit on her hands.

'I've carried your family with me every second since the day I left this house and the Rossi restaurant. They taught me everything I needed to know about what a family should be like, and I'll never forget it. They were great! Best six weeks of my life. I lived for that kitchen and those family meals on Sunday afternoons.'

Sienna stared at Brett open mouthed, and collapsed back against the step.

'You *lived* for them? The family meals that turned into yelling matches—or even fights when all my uncles were in town? You actually *liked* all of that? Most of my pals from school ran away, screaming!'

She squeezed her eyes tight shut and took herself back to those huge family Sunday get-togethers, when all the relatives and distant cousins, plus visitors, plus catering crew, would be assembled around one huge extended dining table for several hours.

'The noise! How could you forget the uproar and the arguments? You *cannot* have loved the noise of ten kids and a dozen adults all competing in decibels and speed to get attention! We were all exhausted, deafened and hoarse by Sunday evening. It was manic.'

'You've forgotten to mention the food.'

'Okay, the food was fantastic—but it was still manic!'

'The food wasn't just fantastic. The food was *amazing*. The best. I worked in those kitchens all week, but nothing came close to the wonderful meals your dad made for his family on Sundays. I never expected to be invited to join in, but, *wow,* I was so grateful for the experience. It took me weeks to work out what made it taste so delicious.'

'He always invited the kitchen crew to be part of our Sunday meals. But what do you mean about the food tasting different? Did he try out different recipes on us?'

'No, nothing like that.' He sat back against the wall and hitched one of his legs up, so that he was facing Sienna with his leg down one side of the step and his arm wrapped around his knee.

'It was the love. Every single dish your dad served was made with such love for the people around his table you could almost taste the pleasure he'd had making wonderful meals for his family to enjoy. Didn't you sense that?'

'I suppose it was what I was used to,' Sienna answered, shocked by the emotional depth of what Brett was saying to her. She could hear the passion and fire in his voice, as though he was reconnecting to those Sunday afternoons.

'Exactly. You have to remember that until I started working for Maria my only experience of eating hot meals someone else had cooked were takeaway pizzas and school dinners. And—' he gestured to his chest with one hand '—I am an only child. Put those things together and being dropped into the Rossi family table was like jumping onto a moving roller coaster at a fun fair.'

She tried to imagine how her family must have appeared to someone who had not grown up with them and failed. Miserably.

'It must have been totally bewildering.'

'It was.' He chuckled. 'For the first two minutes sitting at the table. Then Maria pushed a huge plate of antipasti in front of me, and slapped me on the shoulder, Frankie started talking about football, which caused an argument with one of your cousins who supported another team, and suddenly the foccacia was flying everywhere and your parents were laughing their heads off.'

Brett paused and picked up the photo of Frank's wedding, so that Sienna's attention was diverted away from his face when he spoke again in a soft voice tinged with feeling.

'I felt like I had come home. Even though I had never experienced a big family home it was what I had always imagined it would be like. I was completely and absolutely at home.'

Sienna sat in stunned silence. Brett had found his home within her family. While she hadn't been able to wait to leave it when the going got tough.

How had that happened?

Brett tapped the photo twice with his fingernail. 'Frank invited me to his wedding, you know. But I had just started a new job in Paris and couldn't get away. Shame that I missed it. I would have liked to see you in that dress.'

'Me? Do you even remember me from back then?'

'Of course. I remember you very well indeed.'

'I don't understand. You never said a word to me. Not one word. In the whole six weeks you worked as a catering student. I thought you didn't like me. Couldn't bear to have me around. I was far too shy to talk to you when I worked for Maria, but you could barely manage to say hello and even that was forced out of you. I was so crushed.'

His chest rose and fell, his lips parted, and without warning Brett stretched out his hand and took Sienna's fingers in his, lifted them towards him.

She tried to snatch her hand back. 'Hey! My hands are filthy from working in those boxes.'

'So are mine,' he replied lightly, not giving way. Stubborn. She stared in silence as he gently turned her hand over, stretching out her fingers in the wide palm of his left hand, stroking the life line with the fingertip of his right.

The feel of that fingertip was instant, and so electric that she gasped out loud. It was probably the silliest thing she could have done.

Hot sensation hit her deep inside. Warmth and welcoming sensations she'd thought she had left behind for good on the day she'd stood at the departure gate and watched Angelo board his flight for California, knowing in her heart of hearts that she had lost him. The kind of heat that was addictive in small doses and killed you in larger ones.

No man had ever done this to her before with one touch of his hand, and she tugged to release herself before he could throw her life and her careful plans even more off balance.

'You see this beautiful hand? It's soft and warm. There are no cuts or burn marks or rough skin from scraping tons of vegetables and fish scales in freezing water.'

His fingertip moved further up her longest finger, stroking the whirls in gentle circles and prolonging the delicious torture she was totally helpless to resist or fight.

'I can see your fingerprint. The skin is so smooth it could be a child's. It is so lovely no man could possibly resist it. Including me.'

He lifted her hand closer to his face, and she sucked in a breath and closed her eyes as he kissed her palm.

'This is the hand…' his mouth moved over the bump at the base of her wrist with gentle pressure '…of a princess.' Then those lips pressed gently onto her pulse-point, the lightest of pressure. It made her quiver under his mouth, but if he felt it, he did nothing. He was far too busy kissing her wrist.

'I think Maria knew that I felt like an outsider from the wrong side of the tracks, but I was made welcome all the same. I envied you so much. You were born into a wonderful family and you seemed to take it all for granted. Have you any idea how angry that made me feel? How frustrated?'

His eyes locked onto hers.

'That's why I didn't speak to you, Sienna. I was jealous, angry and bitter. And I never once felt good enough.'

Heart racing, she swallowed down the apprehension and found her throat had somehow become completely dry.

So when her cellphone started to ring in her handbag it took only a few milliseconds for her to make the decision not to answer it. Especially when her bag was on the floor of the basement and it would mean breaking her contact with Brett to jog down the few steps and pick it up.

For the first time in a very long time she decided that some things were more important than answering her phone.

Brett shot her a grin, folded her fingers one by one over the spot where he had kissed the palm, and carefully lowered her hand to the floor—as though it was the most fragile, precious object in the world and any breakage would be on his bill.

The wooden planks felt cold and rough compared to the warmth of his fingers, and she shuddered with regret.

'The window guys will be wondering where we've got to.' He smiled at her with eyes that spread the warmth of those fingers all over her body. 'Ready to go?'

Nowhere near. There was music. She was hearing music when she looked at him.

No, she wasn't. It was the ringtone of *his* cellphone.

An operatic tenor was singing in Italian.

'That's probably them now. Excuse me.'

Both legs swung out, and in an instant he had flicked open the cover.

'Hi, Chris. Yeah. Great to speak to you, mate. Yes, we…er… found what we were looking for. It's a *real* treasure trove down here.'

He raised his eyebrows towards Sienna at that moment, and she instantly felt the heat from her blush send fire up the back of her neck.

'Tablecloths, napkins and loads of old family photos. The

works. Sienna is really pleased. How are you getting on with that window?'

The smile on Brett's face faltered. 'Tell me you are kidding.'

The tense wire that had bound them together in the silence and intensity of the moment twanged. And snapped.

There was just enough of a pause for Sienna to blink hard, sit up and clasp hold of Brett's arm.

'You're not kidding. Sorry to hear that. Well, here's an idea. We can't let a measly thing like a flood prevent a little girl from having her birthday party, can we? Why don't you have it at Rossi's? I'll trade you one birthday party complete with balloons and entertainment, for one replacement window. Providing you can get the work done in time, of course, otherwise it might be a bit draughty. What do you say?'

The implications of what he was saying slapped Sienna in the last sensible part of her brain, and her fingers bit into his arm as she mouthed the word 'No' and sliced her right hand through the air in a vigorous cutting motion.

He ignored both. 'It's a deal. Thursday. Four o'clock. Looking forward to it. See you in three days. No problem, mate. No problem at all.'

CHAPTER TWELVE

Step 12: Add a Platter of Sweet Dreams

'IS IT safe to come in yet?'

'No. You are still in disgrace.' Sienna fluttered her hands in front of her face to wave him away. 'Go talk to the boys who are loading the skip with rancid carpet and broken furniture while the rain holds off.'

'I did explain on the way back that Jess is Chris's only daughter. How could I let Jess down when her party venue was flooded out? You only have a sixth birthday once in your life. That's special!'

'You are wasting your time looking at me with those pleading eyes,' Sienna said as she pressed tape onto the back of a picture frame.

She raised the scissors and waved the pointy ends at him before he had a chance to reply.

'*How could you do this to me?* How could you promise a little girl a fabulous birthday party when we don't even have a room to eat in? Three days, Brett. Two for the paint to be dry. There is so much to do it is making my head spin!'

The scissors were put to use on the tape and she added the framed photograph to the stack by her side. 'I am onto your cunning plan now,' she added with a shake of the head. 'You have those male-model good looks and the kind of winning smile that makes girls go dizzy, and then you go and spoil it all by agreeing to things without asking me first.'

Brett grinned at her and leant both of his elbows on the table, so that he could stare into her face with an innocent look. 'Do I make *you* go dizzy?'

Sienna picked up the next photograph and moved the mounting card around until she had the best frame for her Great-Uncle Louis. She fought down the temptation to groan out loud when the memory of the magical ten minutes she had spent with Brett on the basement steps tingled through her body. Dizzy did not come close.

'You did for a few seconds before you went crazy and started making promises without knowing all of the facts,' she replied, when photo and card were lined up. Then her hands stilled. She *was* talking about Brett now, wasn't she? *Not Angelo?*

She shrugged off the idea and carried on.

'Now I can put the dizziness down to low blood sugar and lack of sleep. Could happen to anyone. Lucky for me that Henry's niece is running his fish-and-chip shop while he and my aunt are sunning themselves in Spain. I popped in to say hello and catch up with the gossip on the way back from the flooring shop. Maria is on the mend, Henry is thinking of opening a café on the beach in Benidorm, and I think his niece has succumbed to your dizziness because she offered me free chips if I sent you in… What?'

Brett had started groaning and dropped his head forward to his chest.

'Maria!' He sighed. 'I *knew* there was something I had forgotten to do this morning. Call Maria and let her know how things were going. I know that woman. She will be driving the nurses mad if she is out of the loop and can't control everything, and—'

His head came up, and whatever he was thinking hit Brett so fast and so hard it was like a blow which knocked him backwards and ended up with him slapping the palm of his hand flat on Maria's dining-room table.

'Oh, that is *brilliant*!' he said, shaking his head from side to side.

'An undeniable truth, but what have I just missed?'

His answer was to casually stroll over, take hold of both her upper arms and physically take her weight while he pressed warm full lips to her cheek.

The intense scent of Brett filled Sienna's senses with delight, and cooking, and Brett.

Blue eyes focused intently on hers and his voice was calm, determined, with only the glint in his eyes giving the game away.

'You are a beautiful, clever woman—and I am sorry that I did not ask you first before I offered Chris the use of the bistro. I am an idiot. Maria Rossi is a genius. You are a princess. I am begging you to give me a *second* second chance. Won't happen again.'

Then he let go of her arms, so that she dropped back a couple of inches onto her low heels in a stunned daze.

'You're doing it again with the dizzy thing. Please explain what strange thoughts are going through that head of yours.'

'I've simply remembered something Maria said to me on the phone the other day. About you being a typical Rossi. Chip off the old block. There is a lot more of Maria in you than you care to admit. Right down to being a bit of a control freak! That's all. Give me another chance. You know that you want to.' And he flashed her the cheekiest wink she had ever seen.

'Do I indeed? Maybe I should have eaten those free chips after all? Because that makes no sense whatsoever. You have to be the world's best at making my poor brain spin. Take a paper prize. And, yes, okay—one more chance. *One*. Third time and you are out on your ear.'

He laughed. 'Thank you. I love prizes. And here's one for you. I actually came in to tell you that Chris will be here with the gang, bright and early tomorrow morning, to start taking out the big window. Those boys will need some real food in exchange for all of the work I have lined up, and chips are not on the menu. Not in our kitchen.'

Her head came up. '*Our* kitchen? Umm. *Much better*. In that case, Chef Cameron, I should warn you that any minute now two hunky blokes will be laying a new wooden floor, once the horrible smelly carpet has been ripped out.'

'Two-timing me already,' he muttered with much tutting as he planted both hands on his hips. 'No other way you could persuade tradesmen to turn up at such short notice.'

She couldn't help it. She had to press her lips together hard to stop herself grinning.

'Simple. I told them it was for Maria. They were round like a shot, offered me a big discount on a lovely new oak floor and agreed to fit it today. Apparently the boards click together like a jigsaw puzzle. Very clever. Our dining room is going to look superb.'

'*Our* dining room? Like the sound of that. Umm. *Much better*, Miss Rossi.'

And just like that the invisible cord that tied them together was pulled so taut she was frightened it was going to knock her over onto the table and into his arms if she didn't lean backwards slightly.

His eyes softened, the pupils wide and alert. He was feeling it too, and her poor broken heart missed a beat.

This time it was not the sound of music which snapped the cord, but doorbells. And hammering.

'Front door. Flooring,' she said, without breaking eye contact.

'Back door. Dishwasher,' he replied, with the kind of infectious grin that made it impossible for her not to surrender to the smile that had been bursting to come out since he'd planted that kiss on her cheek. 'Later.'

And he turned and was gone.

Sienna stared in silence at the space where he had just been standing. It was impossible to stay annoyed with this man! Drat him for having the most infectious grin! When in the past twelve years had he picked up *that* unique skill? And talk about stubborn!

Strange how much she was coming to like it.

CHAPTER THIRTEEN

Step 13: And Three Wedding Cakes…

'BIRTHDAY cake. Has to be pink, of course. Jess is totally into pink at the moment. Even her pencil case and school bag have to be pink. Apparently it's driving her nanny around the bend.'

'Pink ice cream. Pink jelly. Pink cake. Got it. Do we have pink birthday cake candles?'

'Absolutely. I have already told Chris that pink pizza is out—it's do-able, but you wouldn't want to eat it. Too much food colouring.'

Sienna paused in taking notes long enough to shudder. 'Yuk. Her mother is going to freak. Can you imagine eight little girls high on sugar and artificial colours? Do you have to check the ingredients with her first?'

'Her mother? Ah. Of course. You wouldn't know about Lili,' Brett whispered.

He leant further inside their replacement dishwasher and scrubbed the stainless steel as though there was some form of pestilence living there, and as if he had not already cleaned every surface until it shone, inside and out.

'Lili? Is that Jessica's mum?'

A quick intake of breath.

'Was. Lili died of cancer when Jess was four. Chris has been on his own since then.'

Sienna put down her pen and paper and her shoulders slumped. 'Oh, that's tragic. How terrible. Did you know her well?'

There was just enough of a pause for Sienna to stretch to one side, so that she could see the rear end of Brett as he moved on the dishwasher. Several years of frustrated hormones and deliberate celibacy counted for nothing when she had *that* view to look at. Could those denims *be* any tighter?

He was dirty, scraped with rust and rainwater from manhandling two dishwashers in and out of the kitchen in the dusk of a winter evening, and the hem of his T-shirt was soaked with washing water—but he was still the best-looking man she had seen in a very long time.

And he had been working harder than any head chef she had ever worked with—including her own dad. Angelo had never cleaned and scrubbed in his life. There had always been someone lower down the food chain to do it for him. Not Brett. She admired him for that—and he had stuck to his word. Their new dishwasher was a huge improvement.

Then that fine rear shuffled back, and he stretched up to his full height, rolling his shoulders back to release the tension and restore some flexibility, and giving her the benefit of a flash of exposed skin above his belt as the T-shirt rose higher, stretching taut across his chest.

She swung back in an instant, heat flashing at her throat.

'Sorry—did you ask me a question just then? The rack got stuck.'

I'll say!

'I was just wondering how you came to know Chris and his family,' she replied, trying to keep a casual tone in her voice now that he was within touching distance.

The salty tang of masculine sweat, antiperspirant and cleaning spray filled the space. No expensive perfume could have been so enticing. She lifted her chin and smiled.

'Curiosity. Being nosy. You can tell me to mind my own business if you like.'

Brett wandered over towards her and dried his hands, before collapsing down on a bar stool with a bottle of water.

'Not at all. But I have a question for you first. Do you have a best friend? Someone you can talk to any time, day or night, about anything?'

Sienna tried not to stare at the gleam of sweat on his throat as he swallowed down the cold water, or the wet curls of dark blond hair that extended down inside the shirt.

'As a matter of fact I do,' she gushed. 'Carla is the head receptionist at Greystone. We met on our first day at college. She is a real character! Why do you ask?'

Brett nodded and drained the water. 'Ten years ago I hit Paris, with the address of a restaurant I had never seen in my life on a scrap of paper, about four words of French, and no social skills whatsoever. But I had a fire in my belly and I was prepared to put up with the ribbing from the French guys to make my way.'

He held up one hand. 'There was one other English guy in the whole place. Chris. Oh, I do beg your pardon. The Honourable Christopher Donald Hampton Fraser.'

Brett stood to attention and bowed towards the dishwasher.

'Chris had come straight out of a fancy business school, had several degrees under his belt, and was being fast-tracked to great things with a hotel chain who owned the kitchen. A big one. Some wag at the restaurant decided it would be fun to cram the scruffy, sullen galley slave into the same tiny flat with the elegant smooth guy who spoke perfect French and watch the fireworks.'

Brett grinned and pressed two fingers to his forehead in a silent salute.

'Best two years of our lives. I never worked so hard in my life—or had so much fun.'

Sienna caught his infectious grin and smiled back at him.

'So you didn't kill each other after all?'

'Oh, I wanted to. Especially after he binned all my clothes and then cut my ponytail off when I was asleep.'

Her mouth fell forward with a gasp. 'He did not!'

'A Cameron and a Fraser in the same room! Both born in Scotland! Bound to be trouble—for all of five minutes.'

He leant forward to rest his elbows on his knees, hands cradling the empty water bottle, at just enough of an angle so that Sienna could see further down the front of his moistened T-shirt.

'Chris grabbed me on my first night off, when all I wanted to do was sleep, and forced me to share several bottles of very good wine. Hours later we decided that I was a young, scruffy and ignorant poor mess, he was an older, wiser and richer mess, and together we were going to conquer the world.'

Brett raised his bottle of water in a toast. 'Watch out, world! Here we come!'

They laughed out loud at the same time, Sienna shaking her shoulders in delight at the image.

'So what happened after you pledged world domination. Was there a master scheme?'

'Oh, yes. I was going to become a charismatic celebrity chef who would woo the customers, while good old Chris would run the business side and count the cash. It was brilliant. Except for one tiny, tiny detail.'

She looked up and raised her eyebrows with a little shake of the head, as if to say *carry on*.

'I wasn't charismatic. I was quiet, withdrawn, bitter and angry at the world, and I had zero confidence in myself and my talent. And I had dyslexia. Apart from those small problems we couldn't lose!'

'What changed? How did you do it? I mean, Chef in a Kilt? Excuse me for being so bold, but that is *not* the persona of a galley slave without an ounce of confidence!'

Brett winced and bared his teeth. 'Saw that, did you? Did I mention that Chris is also my manager and publicist? He's the only man alive who could persuade me to don the Cameron tartan!'

'Manager... Publicist...' Sienna nodded sagely. 'Aha. I think my point is proven. Hunk of the Month was a *very* popular feature at Greystone Manor.'

There was a gruff clearing of the throat from the man in the chair. 'Is that really what they called me?'

She nodded slowly, just once, and took delicious pleasure in seeing Brett groan, blink hard, and squirm in embarrassment before she smiled and took the edge off his pain.

'You're a lot braver than I am. Should I be asking Chris to give me some tips on how best to win friends and influence people?'

'Easy. The same way that I persuaded him into investing his hard-earned savings in a joint venture. Namely that special restaurant that we dreamt up in Paris all those years ago, as some kind of crazy wine-fuelled dream. Well, that dream will be opening in a few weeks. One thing was for sure. When I got tired of working as head chef for other people, Chris wasn't the *first* person I called. He was the *only* person I called.'

'Trust. There's a lot of trust there.'

'Both ways,' he admitted with a wink. 'I've sold everything I had in Adelaide to make my investment in the site. He's a single parent who's backing his shirt on this new place. We're both taking a huge risk.'

'But you still haven't answered my question. How did you go from galley slave in Paris—' and she waved her arm towards the darkness outside the kitchen window '—to Hunk of the Month who's about to open his own place?'

Brett leant forward to rest his elbows on his knees and prop his chin up with his hands, and for a moment he had all of the vulnerability of the teenage Brett that she remembered. Her heart leaped.

'I was in Paris. I was single. And I was doing the job I loved to the exclusion of everything else in my life. I didn't go out. I worked twenty-hour shifts. It was mad, but it was all I knew. Chris was the one who introduced me to the wonderful city and a world outside the kitchen that I had no idea existed. He made me talk to people. Talk to *girls!*'

Brett screwed up his face into a look of mock terror and shuddered, which made them both smile.

'I found out who I was in Paris, and eventually I was ready to take the final step and actually ask a specific girl for a date.'

He paused and gave Sienna a poignant smile. Not a full-mouthed grin but something quite different.

Something deeply personal.

He was going to tell her something it would cost him to admit.

Something worth her silence.

He leant back for a moment, to select a perfect strawberry from the bowl on the worktop.

'Lili was a Parisian girl, right down to her manicure and perfect skin. She was clever, polished, elegant, and so beautiful it took your breath way. The kind of girl that every other woman envies and every man wants to have on his arm.'

Sienna's eyes never left his face as Brett held the strawberry by its stalk and took a delicate bite from the juicy fruit. The tang and sweetness of the berry hit her nose with sensory overload.

But she stayed silent.

This was a story that only Brett could tell, and he swallowed down the fruit, his gaze still fixed on the remains of the berry as he spoke.

'I had waited eighteen months to ask her out for a drink on a double date with Chris and his girlfriend. I had hoped and dreamt that she would say yes. But it still came as a shock when she agreed. For a few hours I was the happiest man in Paris. Until the moment Lili laid eyes on my pal Chris. Love at first sight for both of them. Poor fool didn't know what had hit him.'

Brett popped the rest of the strawberry into his mouth and pulled out the stalk and hull in one piece.

'Four months later I stood next to Chris as his best man when he married Lili.'

The blunt statement was made without a hint of hesitation, but Sienna was close enough and focused enough to see the telltale twitch at the side of his mouth. His eyes narrowed and flinched so quickly that anyone else would have missed the signs which shouted out distress before he recovered and forced a light voice and a joky smile.

'I had to make three wedding cakes. *Three*. Five layers of light-as-a-feather sponge with fondant orchids for the British contingent. A tower of fresh profiteroles filled with Chantilly cream served with warm chocolate sauce for her French family and the kids. And of course a low-carb pink champagne jelly with fresh fruit for the fashion models who—'

He never got the final words out, because Sienna couldn't bear to tolerate the deep, deep pain in his voice any longer. and before he could finish the sentence she crossed the few feet that separated them, leant in, and covered his lips with hers.

She tasted the salty tang of his sweat, and the sweet strawberry juice in the heat of his mouth, and he froze for a moment. Then he kissed her back, sweet, welcoming, insistent, blanking out any coherent thought that might have lingered in her brain.

Eyes closed, she felt the soft warmth and taste and scent of his kiss wash over her like a warm blanket, drowning her in the sensation of being held in the circle of his arms, so that when he finally pulled away, her head fell forward onto his chest.

Heat. His unique body fragrance. The background of light jazz music playing on the radio. Her senses reeled with the intensity of the moment.

She was going to capture this in her memory. Savour every second.

Instantly his hand moved to the back of her head, and she became aware of the vague pressure of his lips on the top of her hair as he held her closer.

Her hands pressed hard on his damp chest, the thumping heat of his heartbeat resonated though her fingers, telling her everything she needed to know about the man. Her instincts were right, even if she was not ready to open her eyes and look at him.

No. She wasn't ready for that. Not yet.

His hand caressed the back of her head, and the heat of his

forehead pressed against her hair, made her tremble. His voice was low, and so close to her ear that it was more of a whisper. 'What did I do to deserve that?'

'Does there have to be a reason?' she answered, her words muffled into his chest.

His hand slid down her back from her hairline, and she could almost feel the mental and physical barriers coming down between them as he pulled back and lifted her chin so that he could look at her.

The look brought tears to her eyes. Intensity. Confusion. Pain. It was all there.

'No pity. Lili chose the better man.'

Don't say that. Don't ever say that. You deserve better than to feel that way!

She swallowed down the fast response and stroked the line of his jaw with one finger, still not ready to look into those laser blue eyes where she knew she would instantly be lost.

Whatever happened between them going forward, the very *last* thing she wanted was for Brett to think that she had kissed him out of some sense of pity!

Yes, she did feel sorry for him.

Brett had been in love with Lili. Who had married his best friend.

He had lost the woman he had loved not just once, but twice.

First to his best friend and then to disease. But *her* feelings for him were *way* more complicated than that, and they both deserved better.

If Brett believed that he was a lesser man than Chris, then perhaps she could do something creative to redress that balance.

Starting right now.

'Then how about understanding? I *am* sorry for your loss. And,' she replied with a warm smile, 'little Jess is going to have the best birthday party *ever!*'

The tension eased from his shoulders and his chest dropped a few inches under her hands.

'Okay…' Then a second small smile of mutual understanding crept over his face before he repeated, 'Okay…' But this time it was in a stronger voice as he fought to regain control.

His arms moved away from her waist and rubbed up and down her arms for a few seconds as his breathing slowed.

She gave him one long smile, and then slapped the palms of her hands twice against his T-shirt before stepping out of the circle of his arms and casually picking up her clipboard.

'Pink balloons. Let's make that thirty. A girl can never have too many pink balloons, and each of the guests can have one to take home.'

She risked a faint smile in his direction, and was rewarded with a grin and a tip of the head.

'Absolutely! In the meantime I'm heading for the shower. Then how about we pay a visit to the local pizza shop? Check out the competition! Especially when you still have to practise your singing and pizza-making skills.'

'You're on. Except I can't cook and I don't sing. Apart from those two tiny details, I'm starving! Then we need to get seriously busy to make that room ready for a *real* little princess. I'm only a pretend one, after all.'

The scent of strawberry still lingered and wrapped around her senses as he strolled out of the kitchen, so casually it was hard to believe that he had just turned her world upside down.

Time to turn up the heat.

She had meant what she said.

Lili's daughter was going to celebrate her birthday in a lovely room—even if she had to work all night to finish the paintwork.

Except she had the strange feeling that she would be doing it more for Brett than the little girl whose mother had broken his heart.

Brett was a better man than he knew. And she was the one who was going to show him just how special he truly was. Even if it meant kissing him again to prove it!

CHAPTER FOURTEEN

Step 14: Eight Spinning Designer Rainbow Pizzas...

BRETT STOOD in the middle of the dining room, pushed his hands deep into his trouser pockets and gave a low whistle.

This was his first official viewing of the redecorated room. And it took his breath away.

Sienna had chosen a warm natural oak wood flooring which worked brilliantly against the fresh cream paintwork. The table-cloths, napkins, curtains and lampshades were plain forest green or pastel pink, with a faint check in the same colours as a border.

Even on a cool February afternoon light flooded into the room through the pristine window glass, increasing the sense of space and relaxed comfort.

All in all, the overall impression was modern, chic, clean—but also comfortable and welcoming.

This was not Maria Rossi's trattoria any more. This was Sienna Rossi's bistro.

Everything about this room screamed Sienna. Her personal style shone through in all the details his trained eye picked up around the room.

The family photos were in plain oak picture frames which perfectly matched the floorboards and the chair backs. But it was the arrangement that was so clever.

Sienna had collected them into groups of four, all hung on one wall—the far wall—so that they would be the first thing the customers saw when they came into the dining room from the street. The eye was immediately drawn to the smiling faces of the Rossi family who had gone before, in order for her to be in this world.

But it was the long, plain dining-room wall which was so amazing that he could only stand and smile at what she had achieved.

The words *Trattoria Rossi* had been painted in forest green in large letters along the whole of the middle section, using the same type of script Sienna had chosen for their new plate-glass window. He would never have thought of using the same stencil that had been used by the glaziers on the outside inside the room. The same name, inside and outside. Fresh green inside, acid etch outside.

It was inspired.

Put that together with sparkling glassware and simple but elegant cutlery, and he was looking at the idealised perfect yet informal dining area he had searched for all of his life.

He had never told Sienna what his dream was, never described it or even mentioned it. Yet this amazing, wonderful, special woman had created the dining room he had been talking to Chris about ever since Paris.

There were already *way* too many formal restaurants, where starchy people in smart uncomfortable clothes were served wonderful, spectacular showpiece dishes made by master craftsmen at the top of their game. Meals were usually eaten in silence, or with classical music played in hushed tones in the background, and children were considered an unnecessary nuisance to be tolerated.

He had worked in hotels and restaurants all over the world that specialised in providing an exclusive experience to the privileged few who could afford the cost of total luxury.

Of course they were brilliant! And he had loved working for those masters of their craft. But that was not what he wanted for his own restaurant. Far from it.

His dream was to serve fantastic food cooked with love in precisely the same type of warm, open, friendly and informal surroundings he had seen in the Rossi family home all those years ago and experienced for himself in family restaurants across Europe.

Whichever country he had visited, for work or holiday, he had made it his business to ask the local people where *they* would recommend for a family meal. Friendly, open and welcoming dining rooms, where whole generations of families could come together to celebrate good food.

He had sought out dining rooms where guests of all ages, all sizes and all shapes were equally welcome. Where they could relax and be comfortable. Free to laugh and argue and sing and dance if they wanted.

All the time searching for his ideal version of a family restaurant, where children would be welcome and the whole family could eat wonderful food at the same table.

That was why Chris had searched all over London to find the perfect location where there would be enough space to accommodate children, laughter and music while he created the food to match.

The irony was that he had found it in the very place where he had started his career all those years ago!

There were footsteps on the hard oak floorboards.

Sienna came to stand next to him, and he could sense her anxiety seeping out of every pore of her skin. A quick glance sideways told him what he needed. She was chewing the corner of her mouth with her top teeth.

The great Sienna Rossi, princess of the Rossi clan, was nervous in case he hated the room she had worked so hard to create, and wanted it turned back to terracotta dark walls and gloomy spider lairs before Jess arrived for her party.

Without thinking or hesitating, he reached out and took her hand in his, meshing their fingers together so that they stood in silence together and looked around the space.

It smelt of fresh paint and wood varnish.

And as far as he was concerned it was magical.

'I only had time for one more coat of paint last night, but it is dry. Jessica and her friends will be fine today, and then I'll clear the walls and finish off over the weekend.'

'You don't need to change a thing. It's perfect.'

'Really?'

'*Really* really. It's everything I could wish for. And more. Maria is going to be delighted.'

He lifted his chin a little and focused on the brass rail holding up the bistro curtain as he squeezed her fingers.

'I love it.' *I love you.*

He was conscious of his breathing speeding up to match hers, and the gentle pressure of her fingertips as they pressed against his in return.

For a few precious minutes they were not Brett Cameron and Sienna Rossi, with all the baggage those names carried with them, but two people who wanted to be with one another and had worked their whole lives so that they could stand side by side in *this* room at *this* moment in time.

He would not have missed it for the world.

Brett glanced at her from the corner of his eye and his stomach clenched. She was exasperating, stubborn and awkward—and absolutely gorgeous.

Words formed in his mouth, and he was just about to tell her how pretty she looked that morning when there was a bustle of activity and balloons from the hallway and Sienna dropped his hand as though it was burning.

'Did someone place an order for pink balloons?' Chris asked, his fingers clamped around enough balloons for him to be grateful that he carried his own gravity around with him.

Like a guilty teenager caught in a clinch, Brett shuffled as far from Sienna as he could without being insulting, and pretended to be testing that the wall lights worked.

As nonchalantly as he could manage, Brett turned to his

friend just in time to see Sienna fling her arms around Chris's neck and kiss him heartily on the cheek.

'Chris. You are a genius. Thank you, thank you, and thank you. You've done an amazing job. The window is fantastic!'

Considering that she had only met Chris once before, when he'd introduced the glaziers, this was a little over the top!

'Hey! I'm right here,' Brett intervened, pointing to his chest. 'And I seem to remember *I* was the one who has fed and watererd six workmen every hour on the hour for most of the day. Don't I get a hug?'

'Chance would be a fine thing.'

She turned back to Chris, who was looking at Brett with thinly veiled superiority and amusement.

'It's so sad when he grovels,' she said. 'Are you bringing Jess later? I can't wait to meet her!'

'My slave driver of a business partner needs me to work on this signature restaurant of his—' he scowled at Brett, who simply shrugged his shoulders '—but I'll be here for the cake bit, and to pick her up.' His eye caught Brett's with a wink. 'Something tells me that my little girl is going to have a whale of a time with you two around.'

'Is there anyone here who likes pizza?'

Every single girl in the room put her hand up. Including three of the nannies and Sienna.

'Excellent. Well, in that case, today we are making…*pizza!*'

Sienna smiled as the room exploded with cheers and waving, and even a pirouette from the twins in identical ballet shoes and pink tutus.

'But not just any old pizza. Oh, no. Today we are making Jessica's special rainbow pizza. *And…*each person gets to choose their very own, special, unique, personal and only for them rainbow, which only they get to eat!'

'*Pizza!*' Jess called out, and waved her pink sparkly wand

in the air while jumping up and down in her very pretty matching outfit, pink from hair to slippers.

'Rainbow pizza. Rainbow pizza!' they all called out, waving their fairy wands so vigorously that Brett had to reach forward and straighten Jess's tiara, which had fallen forward onto her face.

He stretched up onto the toes of his training shoes and put the flat of his hand to the front of his forehead like a cap, eyes screwed up in concentration as he turned from side to side from the waist.

'Where *did* I put those big pizza plates? Has anyone seen the big pizza plates? We can't make pizzas without pizza plates.'

There were giggles from behind the wands as Brett put both hands on his hips in his best sea captain impression and pointed directly at Sienna, who shuffled from side to side, whistling and looking at the ceiling—which was a big mistake, because hiding behind the light shade was a damp patch she had not noticed before—pretending to hide a stack of metal pizza plates behind her back.

'There they are. Aunty Sienna is hiding them! Aren't you, Aunty Sienna? *Naughty* Aunty Sienna.'

Brett wiggled his eyebrows at her and grinned.

He had every right to look victorious. There was no other man in the world who could have persuaded her to wear one of her aunt Maria's girly-pink flouncy dresses, cinched around the waist with a huge pink ribbon tied in a big bow at the side.

Especially when Maria was a good four inches shorter, which made for a lot more exposure of her legs above the knee than she was used to. A *lot* more.

No wonder he was enjoying the view.

'Now, dig your fingers in there. That's it. Stretch it out nice and round. Push into the corners, just like that—see what I'm doing?'

'Katie, sweetie, that's looking a bit square. Stretch it out. Like this—there you go. No, it doesn't matter if your nail varnish goes into it.'

'Wait. What's that music? Can you hear that music? What does the music tell us to do? *Mambo*!'

The kids all bellowed out the tune, since this was the twentieth time they had heard it, swaying and dancing from side to side, and Sienna could not resist joining in with the chorus, which made Brett look up and smile.

'Hey, I knew you had a lovely singing voice inside there! Let's all sing like Aunty Sienna. That's it, Jess, mambo.'

'Now we have to do the dance. Are you all ready? Let's spin that pizza to the music!'

Brett wiggled his bottom from side to side and made his shoulders do a little dance as he turned the dough round and pushed, then turned it again before looking up and dramatically staring around the table.

'Oh, *look* at these fantastic pizzas! One more dance, and then all they need are the magic words!'

Brushing the flour from his hands, he went around the table from child to child, whispering something secret in each ear which made the girls squirm and giggle.

'How does the magic work, Uncle Brett?'

Brett stepped back and looked hard at Jess.

'You mean, you've never seen it?'

She shook her head and looked around at her pals, and they shook their heads and shrugged.

'Well, that is just terrible. Does anyone else want to see the magic?'

Frantic nodding ensued.

'Okay. Here we go. Have to get ready first. Loosen up the old fingers.'

Brett stretched his hands out and wiggled his fingertips up and down on both hands, sprinkling flour everywhere as he did so. Eight little girls did the same, waving their hands in the air, some still clutching the pink plastic wands which Sienna noticed had lost a lot of their glitter. Probably into the pizza dough.

'Oh, that *is* better. You need both hands for this job. Ready everyone? I can feel that magic. Here it comes!'

Before they could answer, Brett flipped up his own piece of pizza dough and twirled it into the air, spinning it into a circle before passing it to his other hand so quickly that it was a blur.

Sienna watched the children stare open mouthed as Brett flicked his wrist and the circle of pizza lifted up into the air again, spun slightly, and fell back into his upraised hands. He slapped it down on the floured board.

'*Wooow*! That was so cool. Do it again, Uncle Brett. Do it again.'

'Yes, do it again, Uncle Brett.' Sienna smiled across at him in between helping the nannies—who were all ogling Brett—with refastening aprons and picking up fairy wings and wands which had lost their charm compared to Uncle Brett. Not that she blamed them. He was…wonderful.

The love shone through every time he looked at the children. He *adored* them. Being with them, talking to them, sharing their fun. He was one of them.

'For the pretty lady—anything!' He smiled back. 'You see, there are some advantages from starting your catering career in a takeaway pizza parlour on an industrial estate. I could spin sixty a night before I turned sixteen.'

Sienna nodded at the children, who were still entranced by his hands as he draped the dough and then spun it higher and higher, before catching it one-handed and slapping it back to the table.

'Yay! Do it again, Uncle Brett—do it again!'

She nodded more fiercely this time, and he got the message. 'Of course university is much better. But you can always do this for fun at weekends! What do you say? Are you all ready to make magic spinning pizzas?'

'Yes!'

As each of the children lifted and flung their dough shapes around the room, Brett bent down to Jess and lifted her up into his arms, twirling her from side to side to the music, sharing in her childish laughter before she threw her arms around his neck and kissed him on the cheek.

A lightbulb switched on inside Sienna's head.

And her heart broke.

Jess was all Brett had left of the woman he had loved in Paris. She was so pretty, so delicate and dainty and happily un-spoilt. Her mother, Lili, must have been a remarkable woman.

All she could do was watch them as they danced and sang together.

The tall, god-handsome blond man, who had always owned her heart from the moment she had seen him as a teenager, and the little girl in a pink tutu.

If ever there was a man who wanted his own family, she was looking at him now.

He had let down his guard, and the loving, caring and oh-so-vulnerable side of the real Brett shone through. And pulled her closer to him than she'd ever thought possible.

He had so many special gifts! She already knew that he could be tender and compassionate. The thought of him going through life alone was so terrible that hot tears pricked the back of her eyes, startling her with their intensity.

Was it possible that Brett could ever open his generous and warm heart to take a chance on love again? With her?

She was falling in love with Brett Cameron all over again, and there was not one thing she could do about it except run away before they broke each other's hearts.

She needed to get back to Greystone Manor. Back to the stone walls and safe places where she would only have to cope with awkward diners—not a handsome and loving blond man who adored children and would make a wonderful father.

CHAPTER FIFTEEN

Step 15: And Two Glasses of Red Wine

THREE HOURS later, the dining room was remarkably quiet and almost calm. The party was over and the clean-up crew had swung into action.

That was to say Brett had worked his magic with their new dishwasher, and Sienna was repairing the damage to her newly painted room. Her frilly dress was gone, replaced with comfy trousers, a waterproof apron and a pair of loafers she'd last worn when she was at college.

Every child had been stuffed to bursting with pizza topped with ingredients they had chosen themselves—she was the only person who had noticed that Brett had discreetly picked off several pieces of banana before dramatically sliding them into the oven with a great flourish.

He was a natural showman. No doubt about it. And he certainly had a way with the girls. But the pizzas had looked and smelled delicious when he'd slowly drawn them out, golden and bubbling, to the accompaniment of 'oohs' and 'aahs' from their designers.

She had rarely seen food enjoyed with so much delight and enthusiasm. The pizzas had gone down even faster than the ice cream, raspberry sauce and gorgeous fruit jelly.

The young ladies and more than a few nannies had then been

served pink fizzy lemonade in plastic champagne glasses to wash down the heavenly light pink birthday cake. And Brett had been called into service to hold Jess up while she blew out the birthday candles with her father Chris by her side.

Overall it had been a fabulous party. And well worth all the effort.

Shame that there was always pain associated with gain.

Sienna stretched up on tiptoe to wipe away two tiny pieces of pizza dough which had stuck to the dining-room ceiling after the extra-vigorous tossing practice.

'You wouldn't think that a six year old would have so much strength in her wrist. Watch out, world. Here they come. I'm frightened already. I wonder if I was so precocious at that age.'

Brett replied with a snort, then wiped his hands on the kitchen towel around his waist and carefully pulled the cork on one of the bottles of wine that Chris had deposited in exchange for a carload of squealing young ladies in sparkly pink sandals, clutching goody bags and balloons.

'Jess is a total sweetheart. I can see how she twists all the men in her life around her little finger. Especially her uncle Brett. She's a little diva in the making. No doubt about it.' She stretched higher, but still could not reach the floury patch.

'Here. Let me do that for you.'

Brett stood behind her and pressed his front into her back as he reached up with a wet sponge to wipe away a smear of sticky dough—only then he found another, and another. Any excuse for their bodies to be in contact for as long as possible.

She turned around and gave him a look. 'Thank you, but I think we are done. Time to call it a day.'

Her response was met with a chuckle, but he did concede and sat down at one of the dining-room tables. 'Amen to that. Ready for some supper? I have a very nice platter of antipasti from Frank's Deli, and a vintage Sangiovese from that grower near Pisa that Chris seems to like. And there's always more birthday cake if you need the sugar!'

Sienna groaned and pressed her hand to her stomach as she put away her cleaning materials and untied her apron. 'Thank you, but I'll stick to the antipasti. I was the one who had to share in six table picnics! It's so embarrassing when you can't manage to eat the same amount of pink cake as a six year old.'

Brett very carefully poured a tasting sample of the wine into two large wineglasses.

'Well, I hope this wine goes some way to saying thank you. Chris would like to add it to our wine list in the new restaurant. You're the expert. I would welcome your opinion.'

'Modesty prevents me from bragging, but I do love matching food with wine.'

Brett sat back in the new dining-room chair, legs stretched out under the table, and watched Sienna as she swirled the wine in the glass, her nose deep inside the wide bowl, sighing in appreciation before taking a tiny sip.

Delicate fingers selected a choice sliver of salty Parma ham and popped it into her mouth with pleasure, and a brief moan of delight that had fireworks lighting all over his body.

'That's good with the ham. Actually, I would go so far as to say that it's *very* good.' She lifted the glass towards him for a refill.

'Well, you certainly surprised me today, Miss Rossi.'

'Me, Chef Cameron?'

'You were brilliant! Truly! I always knew that head waiters went beyond the call of duty for their guests, but running a puppet show was a great idea.'

'Oh, it's amazing what you can do with paper napkins and a marker pen! You should try it some time—especially if you intend to run a family restaurant.'

'Which I do! Plus, someone who looked remarkably like you was singing. And for a moment you were actually making pizza with the kids. So tell me what else you don't do.'

'What do you mean?'

'Well, you told me that you don't sing and you can't cook.

I was hoping that you would tell me that you never, ever go out with pizza chefs.'

Sienna put down her glass and leant slightly forward before saying, in a clear, low voice, 'I never, ever go out with chefs. Pizza or otherwise.'

There was just enough emotion in her voice for Brett to hold her gaze.

'I take it you have tried it and been burnt?'

'That's right.'

Brett opened his mouth to say something and then shook his head.

'Not André Michon from Greystone Manor? I mean, he's brilliant, and I wouldn't blame you, but...'

Sienna laughed out loud.

'No. I adore him—and so does his lovely wife. No. Definitely not André.'

Brett picked up the extra tension in the room when she was the first to break eye contact and focus instead on the glass of red wine which she was holding onto with both hands.

'I'm surprised that Maria didn't keep you up to date with the gossip on my past love-life.' Her eyes flicked up and saw his confusion. 'Obviously not. The truth is that I was engaged to a chef a few years ago and it ended badly. So that's another reason for me to stay *out* of the kitchen and never, ever go out with pizza chefs.' She raised her glass and toasted Brett with a smile.

'He must have been quite someone. Would I know him?'

She faltered for a few seconds before replying as casually as she could, with a slight nod. 'You might do. It's no secret, and someone is bound to tell you. Does the name Angelo Peruzi ring any bells?'

There was a stunned silence for a few seconds before he replied in a low voice, 'You were engaged to *Angelo Peruzi?*'

'And he was engaged to me. Only he seemed to forget that fact when he moved back to Los Angeles.'

Brett blew out hard and raised his glass towards her. 'Peruzi. I met him at an award ceremony in Milan. Like I say, you are certainly full of surprises. He's a lucky man. I'm sorry it didn't work out.'

She popped a stuffed olive into her mouth and played with some bread for far longer than necessary before answering.

'So am I. And, yes, he *was* a lucky man. Long gone. Or should I say he *was* long gone? The wine is brilliant with the bread but a disaster with the olives. Sorry.'

Brett took a sip of the wine and winced.

'Right again. The wine stays. The olives are out. And you are changing the subject. Do you mean that Peruzi is back in London? I haven't heard anything about that.'

'Then here is a piece of juicy gossip hot off the press. You already know that André Michon is retiring at the end of the month. Well, come March Angelo Peruzi is going to be the new head chef at Greystone Manor. He is definitely back! It was officially announced yesterday, so I think I have a few days' grace before my friends start calling to find out what's going on.'

Brett pursed his lips together. 'How do you feel about working with him again? Isn't that going to be a little awkward? Or do you think you will get back together again?'

'Back with Angelo? No. Never,' Sienna replied in a dark voice, with a firm shake of her head. 'And *awkward* does not come close. But the truth is I don't have many options. I *have* to go back to Greystone.'

She looked around the room before turning back to him with a smile. 'This has been fun, and I want to help Maria as much as I can, but I have responsibilities. People are relying on me. I have worked so hard to be promoted to restaurant manager; I really can't afford to miss the opportunity.'

Brett reached out and wrapped his long fingers around her hand so tenderly that the touch of his fingertips on the back of her hand took her by surprise.

'Congratulations on your promotion. But there are always options. Other jobs.' His head lifted. 'Here is an idea. Why don't you come and work for me? I don't have a head waiter or a sommelier. Actually, I don't have *any* staff at the minute! You can start with a clean slate. The entire Rossi family can visit and party any time they like—there's plenty of space. It would be great!'

He gave her one of those smiles designed to melt the heart of any woman within a hundred paces. And for a moment she was tempted. Very, very tempted. Except of course it would change nothing. She would spend the rest of her life waiting to be let down.

She reluctantly slid her hand away from his grasp as she gave him a thin smile.

'Thanks for the offer. And I really mean that. But it won't work. Why should I run away because my ex boyfriend is back in town? No, Brett. I can do my job. I lost my home and my career to Angelo once before. I'm not losing it again. I know it won't be easy, but I can do it. I won't let any man run my life for me again.'

Sienna turned away from him and gazed out through the new window towards the rooftops, where the light was already fading to dusk in the low winter sun.

Sienna straightened her back, suddenly conscious of the fact that she had said more about her personal life in the last few hours than in the past year. This was the first time she had actually said the words out loud.

But even scarier was the fact that Brett Cameron was sitting across the table from her. Watching her. Studying her.

'Would you mind if we change the subject? That's next week's challenge. Right now I just want to get through Valentine's Day! Here's a question for you. How did the young Brett Cameron come to meet my aunt Maria in the first place? I'm far more interested in hearing *that* story.'

Brett dropped his head back and howled with laughter.

'You mean, she didn't tell you?'

He stretched out his arms on the table as Sienna shook her head.

'I ate all her food! When I was nineteen, Maria came to my catering college to do a demonstration about yeast and pizza dough. Different shapes and sizes and what you can serve with them. That sort of thing. I was in trouble for fighting, and my punishment was to clear up after the cookery class.'

'Hold it there. You were *fighting*?' Her face screwed up in disbelief. 'I find that hard to believe.'

'Oh, believe it,' he replied with a nod. 'I had only been there two months, and every one in my class took it in turns to come up with new insults for the stupid new guy who couldn't even read or write.'

He sighed out loud and grimaced. 'I won't repeat them. Just use your imagination. Believe me, it is no fun when you can't read. I was angry. Angry at my mum for moving—again! Perhaps if we'd stayed in one place someone might have spotted the problem and done something about it, instead of jumping to the easy conclusion that I was stupid, or lazy, and destined to follow my mum as a transient. Most of the time I think they were glad to see the back of me.'

'That must have been so hard. I'm sorry.'

'More frustrating than hard. I was angry at myself because I just couldn't work out what I was missing that the others found so easy! Angry at the teachers who were too stressed to ask why. And then one day a bully pushed me too far and I pushed back.'

She meshed the fingers of one hand between his and was rewarded with a smile.

He leant forward toward her. 'The thing Maria didn't know was that I had been working in the evenings at a pizza shop— my famous pizza spinning lessons—so when everyone had cleared out I picked up the leftover dough and ingredients and started making things with them. After half an hour I had a pretty decent foccacia on the table, and a couple of mini pizzas. My plan was to take them home for dinner, but I was so hungry that I started to eat them. Just as Maria came back.'

'Oh, no. What did she say?'

Brett grinned and shook his head. 'She said a lot. I ate. She asked questions. It didn't take her long to realise that I had memorised the recipes and had some talent. She offered me a job as a kitchen slave six nights a week and every weekend. Right here.'

He paused and looked around.

'Have you ever noticed that there are no cookbooks in your aunt's kitchen? Not one. There are some in the house, but they are for show. Maria recognised that we shared something more than talent and a love of great food. She knew she had dyslexia, and had come up with her own ways of coping. She recognised the symptoms in me, and thought there was a good chance that I had dyslexia too.'

'Wow. My dad told me that she had dyslexia a few years ago, but I didn't really give it any thought. She's my aunt Maria and that's the only thing that matters.'

His fingers moved slowly over the surface of her hand, pressing out her fingers as he spoke with such devastating intensity that speech was not possible.

'She is also an amazingly stubborn lady. It took Maria three months to persuade me to be tested at a special unit. I didn't want to go and have more assessments! More tests and exams that I was bound to get wrong because I couldn't read. I was tired of being pigeonholed as an academic failure who was simply lazy and had to try harder. What a joke that was. As far as I was concerned it was one more way for the system to hang a label around my neck with the word *loser* on it.'

The pressure of his thumb on her knuckles had increased so much that Sienna almost cried out for fear of being bruised, but something stilled in his face as he looked into her eyes, and he released her with a brief smile.

'In the end it was the best thing that ever happened to me. Do you know I had never even heard the word *dyslexia* until the assessor told me what the tests were about? These tests were different. Patterns. Shapes. And logic. Not just words and sentences.'

Brett reached out for his wineglass and took a long sip before going on.

'I remember I was sitting outside the test room with Maria when the assessor came out and said that my scores were some of the highest he had ever seen. I was clever and visually gifted. Artistic and creative. And I had dyslexia. Not a severe case compared to some people, but enough to make a difference in most parts of my life where letters were concerned.'

He glanced up at her. 'Of course the first thing I thought was—oh, great, now the bullies get to call me mentally handicapped. Brilliant! But Maria made me sit and listen to what they could do to help make things easier at college. Like reading the recipes out before class. Using video and tapes. I could even record the lessons. Suddenly I saw I had a chance.' He chuckled. 'It was still tough. Especially at exam time. But Chris helped in Paris. And I have a better memory than most people. The rest, as they say, is history. So now you know. That's how I found out that I have dyslexia.'

He sat back now, and his shoulders seemed to drop a little.

'But, to look on the bright side, my lack of ability with printed words might have held back my academic studies, but it always felt so natural to cook, to create—I would have missed out on all that with a traditional education.'

Brett lifted his glass and smiled.

'Can I suggest a toast to the lovely Maria? Who taught me that sometimes it pays to be stubborn even when the rest of the world thinks you are worthless.'

'No. I'm going to raise my glass to both of you. You should be proud of what you have achieved. Thank you for being so honest. It means a lot.'

'You're welcome. To Maria!'

'Maria and Brett! Two of the most remarkable people I have ever met.'

She hadn't meant to say that. It had just come out. From the shocked look in Brett's eyes he'd been expecting it even less, and it took him a few seconds to recover.

'Thank you. And you're not so bad yourself. Restaurant Manager Rossi.'

With a sudden burst of energy, Brett stood up from the table and reached across to the worktop for birthday cake.

'Speaking of which, if I am so remarkable, perhaps I can persuade you to change your mind about my earlier offer?'

'Birthday cake?'

'If you like. Or working for me? Take your pick. Come on.' He bent down to her eye level and wafted the cake in front of her. 'You like Chris and Jess. We seem to get on all right. Come and work with me instead of at stuffy old Greystone Manor. You won't regret it.'

Sienna put down her glass very gently and stood up.

'Thanks, but no. To cake, *and* your job offer.'

Sienna stood in silence and watched one of the few men she had ever come this close to push his hands into his jean pockets, shoulders high to his neck with stress, his disappointment lingering like a bitter taste on the air.

He was so gentle and tender. So understanding.

She wanted to run to him. Hug him. Tell him that she would love to spend time with him in this enchanted place.

But that would mean trusting him with her happiness. Even for a few short days. Until he went one way and she another. And she couldn't do that. To either of them.

Because she could never trust another lover to also be her business partner. She knew now that love demanded absolute truth. In business, that same trust could kill you if the going got tough.

There was no future for her here, or in working with Brett. Not now. Not ever.

CHAPTER SIXTEEN

Step 16: Smother in Wild Mushroom and Cream Sauce

SIENNA TURNED over and pulled the duvet a little closer around her shoulders as she snuggled down into the pillow and gave a little sigh of contentment.

Mmm. She was almost annoyed that she was being woken from such a sweet dream, in which Brett had carried her in his arms and laid her on a thick, warm bed.

Lovely.

She felt safe. This was such a comfy bed. Ultra-soft feather pillow. She could lie here all day.

Someone was knocking on her door, but she could afford to snuggle just a *little* longer. Birthday parties could be such hard work!

Her eyes creaked open. Just a little. Just to check the time. Strange that her alarm had not gone off. She stretched out her arm towards the bedside cabinet.

The alarm had not gone off because it was two thirty in the morning.

She pulled her arm back under the warm duvet and closed her eyes. For one complete millisecond. Before snapping them open and sitting up in the bed.

She collapsed back down again onto the pillows with a groan, and pulled the duvet over her head.

This was Maria's house, and something had woken her up in the middle of the night.

And the knocking had not gone away.

'Are you decent in there? I have coffee.'

She glanced down at her clothing before answering Brett. She was wearing her aunt's thick pink pajamas.

Yes, she was decent.

'Coffee would be good,' was her feeble reply, as she pushed herself up the bed and drew the covers up to cover her chest. *Pathetic. This was what happened when you agreed to work with chefs who assumed that you would be available twenty-four hours a day!*

'Have you any idea what time it is? It's the middle of the night! What are you doing knocking on my bedroom door at two in the morning? I should warn you that I have one of Maria's stiletto shoes and my brother's phone number if you try anything.'

Brett stopped pacing her bedroom for a few seconds to stare at her as though the problem was so obvious that she should have been able to work it out for herself.

'The three-mushroom sauce. It's not working. I've made it four times and it is still not working. I am going crazy.' He leant closer, so that their noses were almost touching. 'See these grey hairs? Crazy.'

'Mushroom sauce? Oh, thank goodness. Is that all?' Sienna replied as she collapsed back on the pillows.

'All? Oh, no, no. You don't understand. That is not *all*. Without the mushroom sauce I don't have wild-mushroom pasta, and we don't have anything to finish the braised organic chicken breast. Seriously, that chicken needs this sauce, and I am not going to bed until my recipe is perfect.'

Brett was pacing back and forward so rapidly that Sienna feared for the bedroom carpet. His own coffee was untouched, which was probably a good thing considering how much adrenaline must be rushing around his system.

He was obsessing about a sauce recipe.

Chefs. You either loved them or tolerated them, but either way you had to learn to live with them.

She covered her wide yawn with her hand before nodding between half closed eyes.

'Okay, I understand. Mushroom sauce. Got it. What can I do to help?'

'Thought you'd never ask. I need to borrow those amazing tastebuds of yours, because after four hours of this mine are fried. Tell me what you are about to eat. I want the fragrance of this sauce to tantalise your senses way before it hits, and then…'

'Then the flavour. I know. I can't guarantee that my taste-buds will be very responsive at this time of the morning, but I'll do what I can. Talk to me about the dish. What are the base notes?'

'Not this time. Tonight I want this sauce to do the talking for me. When those lovers taste this baby they will be putty in their partners' hands. So get ready to be blown away.'

'I'll be down in five minutes.'

Sienna sat down opposite Brett in the tiny kitchen and watched him fuss, stepping and reaching from pan to pan, dipping his tasting spoon into one then the other. Then grinding more black pepper and tasting again.

'Oh. Big talk from the big guy. So actually you are doing this for the boys, not the ladies? Is that right? Let me take a look in those pans. I'll soon tell you what I would be prepared to eat. *If* you can take the pressure?'

'Sorry. I want those girls looking at their dates, not the food.'

He reached forward and slid his bandana over Sienna's head, so that it rested on her forehead. 'Perfect. This test we are going to do blindfold.'

She lifted one hand to pull off the bandana, but he wafted her away with his fingertips.

'What? You don't want me to see what the food looks like?'

'It's the only way. I'll bring the pan over and feed you tiny spoonfuls so you can savour it. Then tell me the first thing that comes into your head. Okay?'

'Well, this is certainly going to be a first, but all right. I can tell you what my impressions are.'

'Excellent. But first you need to focus. All your concentration has to be on the dish. Don't mind me as I potter around. Just speak your mind. Ready?'

Sienna watched as Brett drew a tiny saucepan from the heat and left it to cool slightly on one side. She could sense her heart racing as he stepped in front of her. So close that his T-shirt was touching her dressing gown. He smelt of so many savoury odours she could almost have told him the ingredients he had been working with right there and then.

But where would the fun be in that? And, more importantly, what had he left out from the final recipe?

Her breathing sped up to match her heart as Brett hunkered down a little and flashed her one of his special killer grins as his hands moved either side of her head.

'Ready to be blown away?'

'Promises, promises. Let's go. Some of us need our beauty sleep!'

'I do wish you wouldn't talk about me like that! But you're right. Busy day tomorrow. Here we go.'

The bandana slid over her brow and rested on her nose. The last thing she saw was the burn marks on the underside of his arm as he slid the cloth lower. Her heart went out to him. He truly had suffered to get where he was.

The roof faded into a very dim glow, with only the electric lights as spots she could recognise.

'That works. Can't see a thing.'

'Excellent. I could be cooking topless and you wouldn't know.'

Oh, you are so wrong about that, she thought.

Through the faint sound of the radio in the background she

could hear him rubbing the work-rough palms of his hands together as he dried them on the towel tucked into the waistband
of his apron. Her whole body seemed to tune out the background noise from the electrical equipment, the hum of the refrigerator and extractor fans, and the gentle patter of the rain
as it fell against the glass of the kitchen window.

And the sound of her breath as she waited for Brett to serve
her something totally, totally delectable and delicious.

*I want this to be the most delicious thing this amazing woman
has ever tasted. Anywhere. And it's the worst mushroom sauce
I have ever made in my life. What is wrong with me? I have
made this in frantic, mad and busy kitchens in Hong Kong, New
York and Adelaide and it was fantastic. Then I come to Rossi's
and something is completely off.*

He turned around just as Sienna shifted her position on what
had to be the most uncomfortable chair in the city.

*Then I drag this woman out of her bed in the middle of the
night. In her pyjamas.*

He stepped to one side and took in the view, confident that
he was unlikely to be swiped around the head with something
solid since she was wearing his bandana over her eyes.

Pink check pyjama bottoms which ended just below her
knees. Maria's. Had to be Maria's. That probably meant that
she was wearing the matching jacket under Maria's housecoat,
which had certainly seen better days.

And probably nothing underneath. The only thing that separated Sienna Rossi from Brett and the outside world were two
thin layers of flannelette and a wicked smile.

The metal soup ladle in Brett's hand developed a mind of
its own and clattered onto the hard floor, making her jump.

'Sorry. Be with you in a moment. The temperature has to
be perfect. Get ready. Three. Two. One'

He leant against the worktop, dipped a new spoon into a
small bowl of the best sauce and wiped it on the edge of the

saucer before lifting it carefully the few inches towards Sienna and wafting it gently in front of her nose.

Her full, luscious lips opened a little as she inhaled the aroma, and Brett carefully fed her a small spoonful of the sauce between her lips, touching the upper lip so that her tongue came out and licked the thick creamy sauce away.

It was the most erotic thing he had seen in a very, very long time.

Until now he had been totally mesmerised by her eyes. Not now. Not any longer. Her mouth was so enticing it should probably be licensed, or covered up during the daytime to prevent exposure to the unprepared.

She had the power to hold him spellbound, and the warm bowl of sauce was cooling in his hands as he stared, transfixed, at Sienna. Strange how he could not force himself to look away from that amazing mouth.

Her tongue flicked out and wiped across her lower lip, leaving a moist and succulent impression like dew on a ripe peach.

Intoxicating.

'I'm getting white wine, celery, finely chopped shallots, a touch of garlic and a sweet herb. Tarragon, and I think lemon thyme and parsley with a touch of garlic. Am I right?'

'Uh-huh. Now the mushrooms. Tell me about the mushrooms.'

He speared a few choice segments and raised them towards Sienna, whose lips were slightly apart, displaying perfect teeth, just waiting for the next delicious treat.

He paused for a second and swallowed down too many months of celibacy and many years of loneliness, then brought the spoon close enough for her to savour the aroma with a pleasing *mmm* of pleasure before he popped the mushrooms between her lips.

She chewed slowly, as though savouring every possible experience.

'This is amazing. I'm getting at least three different textures. There is a meaty earthiness in one of the mushrooms—I think it has to be dried porcini or a wild mushroom—but then I find a smooth taste which is so silky with that creamy sauce. The last one is a chestnut. I'd recognise that texture anywhere, but I have never tasted anything like this combination. It's brilliant.'

'One more,' he whispered. 'There is one extra ingredient that's going to make all the difference.'

'More? There's more? I don't know how you're going to top those mushrooms.'

Brett dipped his spoon into the second pan and tasted a mouthful of the strips of caramelised sweet onions and fresh field mushrooms with aged balsamic vinegar he was planning to use as a garnish for the chicken dish.

It was sweet, yet intensely savoury and special. And the perfect temperature.

'This is the final touch. Ready?'

She nodded once and her lips parted.

Brett wet his lips on the spoon.

Leant in. And kissed her.

She kissed him back. Sweet. Soft. Warm. Melting. Tender. Everything he had been expecting, wanting, desiring for so very long since *she* had kissed *him*.

Her hands came up and slid the blindfold away, so that her eyes were totally fixed on his. Unblinking, intense, her mouth still partly open.

'Balsamic vinegar reduction,' she whispered, her mouth only an inch from his as he held his stance with his arms stretched out on the table. 'You're right. It's the perfect final touch. And so much better than from a spoon. Can I have some more?'

This time she was the one who leant forward, so that he could kiss her more deeply, prolonging the contact between them. They broke off forehead to forehead, her breathing keeping pace with his racing heart rate as he rolled his forehead to the other side so that he could slide his unshaven chin up against her temple and back down to her mouth, the friction acting like wood to the fire.

Her eyes stayed closed as he kissed her again, one hand pressed against the back of her head, drawing her deeper into his kiss. Deeper, and with an intensity that left them both ragged and out of breath when they broke off long enough for Sienna to lift from the chair and slide around the table, so that she could hold Brett's face and then work her sensitive fingers through his hair.

It was driving him mad.

His kisses moved over her chin, down her neck, then across to the other side, and as she tilted her head back with a sigh, she whispered, 'Promise me something?'

'Anything,' he managed to get out, before his mouth got busy on the sensitive skin on her temple.

'You will never make that exact recipe for anyone else.'

'I made it just for you. It's always been just for you.'

'In that case…what were you planning to serve for dessert?'

'Dessert? You want dessert?'

Brett froze in astonishment for a few seconds, before dropping back his head and laughing out loud with warm, joyous laughter that came from deep in his body. Wild, fun, natural and totally happy laughter that was so infectious Sienna could not resist laughing back in return, with a gentle thump on his chest.

'What's so funny?'

'You are.' He wiped away a tear of laughter with the back of a knuckle before shaking his head and lifting away a stray strand of her bed hair.

'Have you always been so demanding of your chefs, Miss Rossi?'

'Oh, this is nothing,' she replied in a mock serious voice. 'I can be much bossier when the occasion demands. Although it will be quite a challenge for you to come up with something to beat that sauce.'

She tilted her head and smiled into his face.

'I am thinking chocolate. Coffee. Cream, of course. The rest I shall leave to you.'

'Well, thank you. I'm sure I can think of something which will hit the spot!' His eyebrows lifted in a cheeky grin and she tutted in response.

'Please. I presume you are planning to serve desserts in this fabulous new restaurant of yours?'

He nodded in agreement and moved back a little. 'Speaking of which, I told you the other evening that I never break a promise—especially to a pretty lady… Well I have to break one tomorrow. But it is entirely your fault…'

'My fault?' she protested innocently. 'How can this possibly be?'

'I need to see Chris and the architects about some final decisions on the layout. That means heading across to my new kitchen. And I promised that I was all yours for a few days. On the other hand you could always come with me and cast your trained eye over my new building. Are you busy tomorrow morning?'

She closed her eyes and turned her head, so that his stubbly chin would have better access to her throat, trying to remember what day of the week it was and other unimportant things, like her name and what precisely she was doing here.

She had always known deep in her heart that Brett would be an amazing kisser, but nothing had prepared her for the depth of sensation his mouth on her throat would generate.

'Do you mean today tomorrow, or tomorrow tomorrow?'

'Today tomorrow. I'd love to show you where Chris has been spending his time these last few months.'

He moved forward to face her, his hands moving through her long loose hair and lifting it from her shoulders as it fell through his fingers—then he smoothed it down her forehead.

'You want me to visit your new restaurant?'

'Think of it as a special outing after the amazing job you did yesterday.'

He moved forward with feather-light kisses on her forehead, and she closed her eyes as his lips slid gently down to her temple, heating up the blood which was already pumping hot and fast through her body.

'*We* did a good job, Chef Cameron. Are you looking for an interior designer?'

'No. But I can always use an expert opinion.'

'You make it very hard for a girl to say no.'

'Then don't. I'll make it easy. Just repeat after me— Yes, Brett, I'd like to see the kitchen where your dream will come true.'

'Well, when you put it like that… Yes, Brett, I'd *love* to see the kitchen where your dream will come true.'

'Then we have a date in about—' and he glanced over her shoulder at his wristwatch, since his hand was still busy stroking her hair '—seven hours from now. Do you think you can be ready to face the outside world by then, sleepy-head? Because I do have one suggestion—you might want to rethink your footwear before we hit the building site.'

She reluctantly forced her eyes to leave Brett's long enough to glance at her feet. Then blinked and stared hard. Her left foot was inside a brown loafer. Only the toes of her right foot were poking daintily out from an open toed bright yellow sandal decorated with huge white daisies—Maria's summer specials.

'Oh. You see—this is what happens when I am woken up in the middle of the night by chefs looking for a food-taster.'

'In that case I shall have to do this more often.'

Sienna looked up into those hot bright eyes. There was no doubt whatsoever that he was referring to a lot more than comparing the flavour of sauce recipes.

Electrical energy crackled in the air between them—hot enough to burn paper—and her resolve crisped into white ash in the intense heat of his gaze.

She should be angry with Brett for showing her just how very wrong she had been—about so many things. But as his fingertips stroked her forehead and his lips found pleasure in the place between her jaw and throat it was impossible.

Brett Cameron had shown her that she was a woman a man like Brett could, would, *was able to* find desirable. He had even told her that she was beautiful! Every one of his touches gave her a glimpse of hope that another man *could* come to care about her.

She sucked in a breath as he found a particularly sensitive spot in the hollow behind her ear, and was rewarded with a low sigh.

Was it possible that she could fall in love again? And be loved in return?

Or was she in danger of making precisely the same mistake she had made before?

Chef-magnet.

This was all happening too fast. Too hot. And way, way, too intense for her poor brain to process what had just happened and make sense of it all.

'This has been a long day, Brett. Like I said, a girl needs her beauty sleep. And, no, that wasn't a cue for compliments.'

'You're going?'

She glanced across at the saucepans before smiling up at him. 'Maria made the right choice when she asked you to help with the cooking. I can't wait for that dessert. See you at breakfast.'

His hands moved over her shoulders and down her upper arms before he stepped back.

'Sleep well. Unless, of course, you want me to pop in and wake you up in the morning?'

She swallowed down hard at that prospect!

'Thank you, but I have my alarm clock. Goodnight, Brett. Goodnight.'

CHAPTER SEVENTEEN

Step 17: Mix with Three Heaped Spoonfuls of Tears

'I CAN hear your brain ticking from here! What's the hot topic today? Shoes? Dresses? Or let me guess. Which wine are you going to recommend for the chicken in mushroom sauce?'

Sienna half turned in the passenger seat of the Jaguar and stared at Brett in disbelief.

'I knew that you could multi-task. Nothing about mind-reading! How did you work that one out?'

He flashed a quick smile, which made Sienna grateful that she was already sitting down. 'You couldn't wait to scribble down my crazy ideas for the Valentine's Day menu this morning. Perhaps it was a mistake to talk about my seven-hour braised lamb at breakfast time?'

A puff of dismissal came from the passenger seat. 'I think you selected those dishes just to test me. I mean, ravioli with spinach *and* blue cheese after garlic mushrooms?'

'I prefer to think of it as a challenge to a sommelier of your talents. Guinea fowl with polenta? That has to be straightforward.'

'It would be—if you took out the parmesan and onion crisp garnish. And I really think you ought to reconsider the flavouring on the gnocchi. I'm just not sure the local high school boys are ready for that mushroom sauce.'

'Ah, but it's not for the boys, is it? That sauce is definitely one for the laydees!'

She slapped his knee with a light touch of her notebook.

'A medium red. Black cherry and plum, with some time in oak to offset the earthy mushroom flavours, but not too dry.'

'I can inhale it from here. Fantastic. What about a white?'

'Still thinking about that one,' she hissed. 'Pest.' She tapped the end of her pen against her chin. This pen was in a boring plain colour, and Brett was already missing the pink rubber flamingo.

'You must do this all the time as Head Waiter? Matching food and wine? That's quite a skill.'

'One of my favourite parts of the job. André and I can chat for hours comparing several bottles of the same grape variety from different parts of the world. I love it.'

'I can hear that in your voice. Greystone is lucky to have you. In fact, that gives me an idea. Chris has been interviewing for a sommelier for weeks. I'm going to be working flat out. Is there any chance you could sit in on the interviews and help him get though the shortlist? I need someone I can work with, who knows what they are doing! Unless of course…' He paused for a moment to focus on the road ahead, where there were multiple lanes of traffic.

'Unless?' she asked, when they were safely on a straight road.

'Unless I can steal you away from Angelo Peruzi!' he replied in a jaunty voice, completely unaware of how that simple statement ripped her apart. 'Come to work with me as my restaurant manager. Take a risk for once. Surprise yourself.'

Too late for that! She had spent most of the night after leaving the hot, hot kitchen dreaming about the life she could have with Brett by her side as her lover, if not her business partner. Working through the options. Trying to decide if she could trust this remarkable man to be her friend.

'You really don't know when to give up, do you?' Sienna replied, trying to keep her voice casual and jokey. 'I am deeply flattered, Brett. I truly am. But I know what it is like to open a new restaurant. That sort of pressure can destroy a friendship. I don't want that to happen.'

He quickly squeezed her leg in reply. 'Can't blame me for trying. I agree. Good friends are hard to come by.'

Suddenly distracted by a car horn, Brett turned back to his driving, and Sienna took a breath and looked out across the bustling London traffic to the lovely shops and art galleries they were shuffling past.

They were almost there. The narrow lanes around Notting Hill were just a few streets away.

Sienna shivered inside her coat. There was one thing that she had not told Brett when they set out that morning.

This was the first time she had been back to Notting Hill in four years. Former friends and old colleagues who lived in the area had invited her to their homes many times and she had always refused. The pain and the loss had still been too fresh.

Each street they were driving down linked her back to powerful and emotional memories which only seemed to intensify as they came closer to the site of Angelo's restaurant.

Protective instincts raised their ugly heads, poking fun at her apparent self-control, and the old anxieties rose inside her, low enough for her to master, but nagging away loud enough for her to be aware of them.

Heart racing, she turned for reassurance and support to the only person she knew would understand. Brett's face was full of all of the excitement and happy anticipation of a child on Christmas morning. It was all there for the world to see.

He started to hum along to an old song on the radio, and her heart listened and slowed a little. Tears pricked Sienna's eyes, threatening, but she blinked them away with logic.

It was only natural that she should feel a little sentimental, coming back to these streets that she'd used to know so well.

But one thing was certain: she was not going to allow her foolish anxiety to spoil Brett's day. This new restaurant was *his* dream, and he had asked her to share with him the special moment when he explored what was going to become his very own kitchen.

He had worked so hard to be driving here today. He deserved this.

Suddenly Sienna found herself joining in with Brett, happy to drink in the enthusiasm and positive energy that emanated from this finger-tapping, song-humming *tour de force*.

Without Brett she would probably never have found the strength to come back here. And with Brett? With Brett by her side she could do anything!

No tears. No trauma. Angelo's was part of her past, not her future!

She grabbed hold of that excuse for putting aside her own lingering doubts about her future role and grinned across at Brett. Friend or lover. She could still share this moment with him.

'Did you know that our restaurant used to be in Notting Hill? You've chosen a great location! And, from what Chris told me, the building work is almost complete. You must be very excited. Tell me about your plans.'

'It's a *fantastic* location! I had mixed feelings about coming back to London, but now the plans are coming together it is starting to feel as though I was meant to be here.'

He turned into a street lined by market shops and gestured from side to side. 'In fact, standing in the kitchen last night, I was thinking about my very first day at Trattoria Rossi.'

Brett laughed and slapped his hands down on the steering wheel as Sienna stared at his face, which had been transformed by such an expression of joy and pleasure it seemed as though every crease in that hard-working face was smiling.

'Maria set me to work paring and chopping vegetables for hours.' He shot her a glance. 'I'll never forget it. I was so nervous about getting it wrong I think I dropped my peeler on the floor a dozen times. I ended up spending more time washing up than actually cooking.'

They both laughed out loud, the sound of their shared laughter echoing around the confined space, warming her more than the bright sunshine.

'After a few days I progressed to actually frying onions and shallots and garlic, and by the end of my first week I was making minestrone soup.'

'Minestrone! You must have been doing something right!'

'I had a great time. Your aunt Maria gave me a chance, Sienna. Without her I would have spent a lot longer getting started in this crazy world.'

'But you would have got here in the end. Wouldn't you?'

He bowed slightly. 'Maybe, but I know that she made the difference. And of course without Maria I would never have met you!'

Sienna's heart was thumping so loudly she was sure Brett must be able to feel the vibration through the driver's seat. 'Would that have been a loss or a bonus?'

A wry smile creased one corner of his mouth, but he kept his gaze firmly on the road ahead. 'Loss. No doubt. Especially since my satellite navigation system has failed and we are now lost. Do your skills extend to navigating around Notting Hill?'

'I travelled down this road every day for eighteen months,' she replied with a dismissive snort. 'What's the address?'

Brett recited the house number and street that he had dreamt about, researched on the Internet, and planned and schemed about so often that it had become ingrained into his brain. New destination. New start. His dream come true.

'Take the next right turn,' she replied, in a faint voice tinged with anxiety. A few minutes later he pulled into the car park of the building site which was destined to be his new home, screeched to a halt and cut the engine.

He turned to look at Sienna and tried to rub some life back into her cold fingers. Winter sunshine, bright and clear, pierced the clouds and highlighted the pain in her tight-lipped face.

'What is it? Tell me what's going on.'

She seemed to come out of her trance for a moment and

looked down at his hands, tracing her fingers along the scars she had never commented on before. White, pink, old and new. The scars of a working chef who had served his time.

'Look at all these cuts. Burn marks.' She lifted her head and faced him on. 'Some of us have our scars on the inside.'

He steadied himself for the hard news that was coming next. She forced herself to smile. That simple twist of her mouth and glistening eyes melted his heart.

'Please ignore me. My own restaurant was down this road. I had no idea that it would be so hard to come back. Too many memories. That's all.'

She shuffled out of her seat to stand next to him, sniffing gently, and stared past him towards the building which, to Brett's eyes, was a lot more like a restaurant than it had been a few days earlier.

'I'm okay. Really. I'm fine now.' She seemed to give herself a mental shake, looped her arm through his and grinned. 'I want to see everything.'

A short, plump, pink-faced, dark-haired man in a warm jacket and yellow safety helmet was striding up to Sienna, and before Brett could intervene Chris thumped Brett hard on the shoulder and nodded towards Sienna with a huge grin.

'Well, I thought you would change her mind eventually. Welcome to the team, Sienna!' He stretched out his hand towards her.

She simply smiled and shook her head. 'Hello, Chris. What team? Have I missed something?'

'Our new restaurant manager, of course. I knew my boy Brett here would use his charm to win you around in the end. You have to admit his interview technique gets results with the ladies!'

Sienna stared at Chris's hand as if it was toxic waste for a second before turning to stare at Brett, who was groaning and glaring at Chris at the same time.

'Interviewing? So *that* is what you have been doing these last few days. Charming me to come and work with you. Have I understood that correctly?'

'Sienna, please.' Brett stepped in front of her, his face anxious. 'Of course I would love it if you could come and work with us, but I know you already have a great promotion. You don't understand…'

'Oh, on the contrary. I understand very well indeed. Nice meeting you again, Mr Fraser. Good luck finding someone willing to work with this idiot! In the meantime, I'll take the bus back.'

And with that she turned and walked away from them, back towards the road, one hand pressed firmly against her mouth, preventing them from seeing her bitter tears.

Only she never reached it. With a slight stagger, she leant against the wall for support, her legs unsteady and threatening to give way beneath her.

Brett stood there, frozen, watching Sienna retreat inside herself to a place where he could not go. He barely recognised the woman who had leapt into his car with a spring in her step that morning.

Ignoring the fact that Chris and other members of his design team were coming up to greet him, Brett wound his way around the front of his car, looped his arm around Sienna's waist and half carried her as far as the passenger door, where she had some hope of catching her breath, or at least passing out with some dignity.

She faltered on the icy path, and as he held her tighter around the waist, taking her weight, he felt her heart beating under her sweater in the cold air. He knew his fate was sealed as he lowered her into the passenger seat.

She looked up at him in surprise, and then, as though recognising something in him she could trust until her dying day, she stared, white faced, into his concerned eyes.

'Do not say a word. Not one word. Simply get me out of here, Brett.'

'You got it.'

Brett grabbed his padded jacket and wrapped it around her

shoulders, but he knew it would take more than a coat to stop this precious woman from shivering.

Doomed.

He was completely in love with Sienna Rossi.

No going back. This was it. He was going to find out who and what had broken this remarkable woman's heart and not stop until he had put those fractured pieces back together again.

Sienna squirmed against the sofa cushions and half opened her eyes, blinking in the glare from a single table light. She was leaning on something soft and pale blue.

She had fallen sideways, and her head was pressed into Brett's shoulder.

Horrified, she slid back to a sitting position and squeezed her eyes shut again as she yawned widely with both hands over her mouth.

When she opened them, Brett was scratching his scalp. It was a gesture she had seen him perform dozens of times before. Right hand, right side of his head, just above the ear. It was a wonder he was not bald in that spot.

'Looking for inspiration?'

He went pink around the neck, but stayed focused on the clever photos of perfect dishes on the pages of a book with a photo of a TV chef on the cover.

'I was hoping that this pastime would make me look more intellectual. On second thoughts, don't answer that. Not many girls fall asleep on me. This could be a bad sign.'

Sienna rubbed the back of her neck, turning her head from side to side.

'Sorry about using you for a pillow. Most embarrassing. Of course I blame you completely, for forcing me to drink hot chocolate on an empty stomach. Always knocks me sideways. How long was I out?'

'Over two hours. And you're welcome to cuddle up to me any time you like.'

He broke the tension then, by raising his eyebrows up and down a few times.

'Oh, slick. Very slick,' Sienna said, and grinned at him as she slid her feet to the carpet and stretched forward to take both of Brett's hands as he helped her stand.

He smiled back before replying in a soft voice, 'That's better. You always did have the cutest smile, Rossi. Even if you *are* dressed as a polar explorer.'

She stuck out the arms of her thick sweater and plucked at the cuffs. 'I work in air-conditioned restaurants and stone buildings all year round, but when I see real weather outside. Brrrr…'

She lifted away one corner of Maria's living-room curtains to demonstrate her point. And stared out. Open mouthed.

'It's snowing,' she eventually managed to pronounce, in a low, intense whisper.

Sienna almost pressed her nose to the glass, ignoring the vibration and engine noise of the cars whizzing past on the busy road on the other side of the pavement.

It *was* snowing. It was truly snowing. She could actually see the flakes against the darkness of the evening sky as they reflected back the light from the headlamps of passing cars and streetlights.

It was one of the most magical things she had ever seen.

'Brett! Look!' Without hesitation or thinking she grabbed his hand and hugged him tight against her so that he could see out of the window.

A wide grin spread out across his face, and she laughed out loud as he grabbed her by the waist and pulled her closer, so that the white flakes appeared to come straight at them through the layers of glass.

At that moment a large truck trundled past, momentarily blocking out the light, and the glass surface was instantly transformed into a mirror. Sienna found herself looking at two happy faces reflected in the glass.

Cameron and Rossi. Best team she had ever worked in.

Her head was pressed into Brett's neck, and he pressed his body along one side of hers so that he could share the first sight of snowflakes.

He was grinning, open-mouthed. So was she.

They were two happy people.

Then his smile faded—as did hers.

The reflection in the mirror window changed as Brett turned a few inches, so that she was close enough to feel his fast breath on her cheeks. She had nowhere to look but into his eyes.

His deep, intense, smiling eyes.

Laser probes burrowed into her skull and turned the sensible girl into mush.

His hand was still at her waist. The other meshed his fingers between hers and squeezed tightly as he spoke, his eyes never leaving hers.

'It's lovely.' *You are lovely*. 'Chris made a mistake this afternoon. I respect your choices.'

'I know. Going back to that street was just all too much for me. I feel quite foolish.'

He took a breath and his eyes scanned her face, as though checking that she was real. It was a millisecond before her neck was burning and her breathing had speeded up to match his.

'Not foolish at all,' he said, and smiled at her. 'But I do think it is time you told me exactly why you can't trust chefs. Stay right there!'

Suddenly he released her and slipped out of the room, leaving her staring ahead at the space he had occupied, while her heart rate struggled to return to normal. And failed.

Something inside her clicked into gear.

He deserved the truth. Even if it meant going back to a place she thought she had left behind.

CHAPTER EIGHTEEN

Step 18: And Two Pink Cupcakes

BRETT BREEZED back into the room, carrying a tray with two steaming beakers and a paper bag with pink glittery stars glued on it, which he opened and presented to her. He collapsed down on the sofa, completely unfazed by the fact that she was still standing at the window, staring out at the snowflakes with childlike fascination.

'Chris came round when you were having your nap. He says sorry for the misunderstanding about the job, and a big hi and thank you from Jess. You are now officially one of the princess gang, and I am commanded to present Your Royal Highness with these fine examples of baked goods as a token of their esteem. Apparently the nanny made them from a packet mix.'

He held up two pink cupcakes, each with a single pink cake candle sticking out from the centre, held in place by a thick blob of white icing.

Sienna and Brett both stared at the candles for a second in silence.

'Jess does have style. Decaf?'

All Sienna could manage was a single nod, and it took her several delicious sips of the hot, bittersweet drink before she was ready to speak.

'Brett?'

'Mmm?' he replied, between mouthfuls.

'Sorry about being so upset earlier. I'm…embarrassed about—well, what I must have looked like, and how my reaction was completely over the top. I had no right to be annoyed with you. Sorry.'

He shook his head and pursed his lips. 'You're not the one who should feel sorry. I should have made it clear to Chris that you had to make your own mind up and that I'd respect your decision either way. My mistake.'

He brushed crumbs into the paper bag, before sliding to the edge of the sofa. 'Now, I am under strict instructions that you have to eat one whole cupcake, or you are not an official princess.'

Sienna looked at the cake and swallowed hard. 'I don't think I can.'

'One whole cake. I promised Jess. And nobody goes hungry in this house.'

He slid the tray closer towards her.

'Slave driver,' she replied, but, since he was staring at her so intently, started peeling off the paper and broke the cake into two.

'That's better,' he said, reaching for his second.

'Hey!'

He brushed more crumbs from his fingers onto the tray. 'Okay. I'm ready to hear the whole story. We have coffee. We have something close to cake. Start talking. You can skip the bit about how his Hollywood charm made you swoon and get straight to the bit where you were working together at Angelo's restaurant. What really happened? What went wrong? And why did Frank not break his nose for you? Because I cannot believe for one minute that Angelo Peruzi dumped you. He's not *that* much of an idiot.'

'Yes, he is.' She found something very fascinating in the paper case. 'It's quite simple, really. Angelo Peruzi fell out of love with me, ran our business into the ground, and ran back home to California. He broke my heart and walked out on me. But in the end I was the one who broke up with him.' She paused.

'About a month before our wedding, I started taking calls from suppliers asking when their bills were going to be paid. Angelo insisted on taking care of all of the financial side of the restaurant, so I mentioned it to him straight away. He said it must be a mistake at the bank and he would sort it out and not to bother him again.' She lowered her head and shrugged. 'He hated to be challenged. About anything. Angelo had worked with his father in their restaurant all his life, and his food was amazing. He had the looks and the talent, and as far as he and his family were concerned he was the golden boy who could do no wrong.'

She smiled apologetically. 'I was not the only one who was dazzled by him. My family adored him. Until…the cracks started to appear. It was hard for him to admit that he couldn't handle the business side of things *and* run the kitchen and do promotional work and the thousand and one things he wanted to achieve. All at once.'

Brett rubbed the back of Sienna's neck—her strain was only too apparent.

'I was organising the wedding. He was in denial and refused to admit that he couldn't cope. Call it pride, arrogance— whatever. The end result was the same. We had a brilliant kitchen brigade and full tables every night. I had no idea that there was a problem with finance.'

Tiny fragments of cupcake icing had found their way onto her jumper, and she slowly picked them off, one by one, as Brett held her in silence.

'I remember the day I had to say goodbye to the staff—the tears, the hugs, the hours I spent sobbing alone that night after I'd closed the door for the last time.'

'Alone? You mean, he didn't even come back to thank his team? He left you here to handle the mess on your own?'

'He claimed that it would be too expensive to fly back for a few days, but I knew it was going to be too painful for him. Too traumatic.'

She shook her head from side to side. 'I still trusted him and believed in him. Even then. Angelo kept telling me that once the London restaurant was sold he would be able to pay off all of his debts and I would be free to move to Los Angeles and make our new home together in California.'

The muscles in Brett's neck clenched at the tension in her voice, and the anger rose in his soul as he suspected what was coming next.

'You know what really hurt?' she continued in a low voice. 'It wasn't the money, or that we had to sell the business. That was nothing compared to the fact that Angelo did not *tell* me there was a problem. I would have understood in a heartbeat. We were supposed to be partners! He knew that I would do anything for him—and that I trusted him without question.'

'He didn't know you,' Brett whispered.

'You're right. And I didn't know him, either. Perhaps that why it was such a surprise when he packed his bags and told me that he needed to go home for a few weeks. On his own. I thought *I* was his home.'

She gave a sarcastic laugh, but the tears still pricked her eyes as Brett asked her the question which had puzzled him from the start.

'I'm still confused about one thing. Why did you tell people that he had dumped you and headed back home? The truth was bound to come out eventually.'

'I didn't tell people anything. The family knew why I had broken off my engagement, but everyone else came to their own conclusions when Angelo did not come back. As for the truth? The Rossi family closed ranks and came to the conclusion that being duped once was humiliating enough for me, but being duped twice? That would make me a laughing stock. So no. The truth never came out. The suppliers were paid. And he got away with it. What a lucky escape. Eh?'

She had wrapped her arms around her body, as though trying

to warm herself and block out the bone-penetrating icy wind and the snowflakes on the other side of the window glass.

Brett waited for her to go on, but her voice had grown gradually quieter and more choked as she spoke. Her last words were so full of pain that he felt a shiver of cold run across her shoulders and down her back.

He zipped open his own padded fleece jacket and stepped behind her, pressing his shirtfront against her back, his arms circling her waist, so that she was totally enclosed inside his warm embrace.

Neither of them spoke for a few minutes as Brett followed her gaze out to the snowflakes, his head pressed against her shoulder.

Her head fell forward. 'I should have known. It took him a total of three days after we sold the business to build up the courage to make the telephone call telling me that he thought we should take a break before I flew out to join him. It took me all of ten seconds to realise that he didn't want me. I had ceased to be useful. He was far too cowardly to admit that he did not love me any more, so I did the only thing I could do. I told him it was over. Not the best way for a relationship to end.'

'What did you do?'

A snort and a chuckle. 'I packed up the few possessions I had left and went home to my old bedroom in the Rossi house. I was exhausted, lonely, vulnerable, more than a little depressed, and very, very angry. At everyone! The family persuaded me not to get on a plane to California and confront him face to face, and it was my aunt Maria who gave me sanctuary until I was ready to start work again. I owe her just as much as you do—so thank you for helping me find a way to repay her.'

She glanced up at him over her right shoulder, and the pain in those limpid brown eyes was only too apparent through the faint smile.

Brett looked deep into those eyes and his heart melted.

After all she had been through, she still had the capacity for happiness.

She was remarkable!

He closed his eyes. He was holding Sienna Rossi in his arms, and it felt so right. So very right. How had he doubted that this was what he wanted? What he needed?

There was no way he could allow her to walk away from him.

Slowly, slowly, he dropped his hands to her waist and started to turn her around to face him.

As though awakening from a dream, Sienna realised that she was not alone, and her head twisted towards him inside the huge jacket. As her body turned slowly his hands shifted, so that when her chin was pressed against the front of his shirt his arms were around her back, pressing her forward.

In silence, his eyes closed, and he listened to her breathing, her head buried into the corner of his neck and throat.

Her arms, which had been trapped inside his fleece, moved to circle around his waist, so that she could hold him closer.

A faint smile cracked Brett's face. She was hugging him back. Taking his warmth and devotion.

He dared not risk taking it any further. Dared not break that taste of trust she was offering him.

But Brett edged closer, hugging her tighter, and dropped his face a little so that his lips were in the vicinity of her forehead.

Sienna responded immediately, and looked up as he moved back just far enough so that their eyes locked.

For that single moment everything that had gone before meant nothing. They were a man and a woman who cared for one another very deeply, holding each other.

It seemed the most natural thing in the world for Brett to run his lips across her upturned forehead, then her closed eyes. He felt her mouth move against his neck. Stunned with the shock of the sensation, he almost jerked away, but then paused and pressed his face closer to hers, his arms tight on her back, willing his love to pass through his open hands, through the clothing to her core of her body.

Warming her. Begging her to trust him. But not daring to say the words that might break the spell.

This was unreal.

A single beam of light streamed out from a passing car on the road and caught on Sienna's face, like a spotlight. The golden light warmed her skin. They were both cold, but there was no way Brett would break this precious moment when the barriers were down and he could express what words would fail to convey.

His hands slid up and down her back. His mouth moved across her cheek and he felt her lift her chin. Waiting for his kiss.

Adrenaline surged through his body, all his senses alive to the stunning woman he was holding in his arms. His heart was racing, and he could feel her breath warm as they looked into each other's eyes, both of them open-mouthed. Nose almost touching nose. His head tilted. Ready.

For the kiss that never came.

It was Sienna who stepped away, sliding out of his arms.

'I felt so worthless. When Angelo left, he took every bit of confidence and self-esteem I ever had with him. It's taken me four years to piece together what was left of my shattered life, one day at a time, and rebuild a future for myself. I promised myself that I was never going to rely on someone else to make my dreams come true ever again. And I've kept that promise. I *have* to make my own way in the world. You understand what that is like better than anyone I have ever met. Don't you?'

He tucked her hair behind her ear and gently smoothed the strands away from her brow before replying in a slow whisper. Intimate and soft, and so loving it hurt to hear it.

'Yes. I do. Which leaves one final question. You may not *need* a man in your life, but is there any room in this plan for a man who cares about you and wants to be with you?'

She swallowed down a breath of understanding and replied with a quivering lower lip. She had seen through him yet again.

'I don't know, Brett. I truly don't know. This job at Greystone has been my only goal for so long I never thought about what came next.'

There was so much confusion and anxiety in her face that Brett took the initiative. He would have to work through the next steps more slowly than he wanted if he had any chance of convincing Sienna to make him part of her life. Biting down frustration and disappointment, he managed a smile before rubbing her arms for one last time this evening.

'I don't know about you, but this has been a very long day and we have the excitement of restocking the kitchen cabinets tomorrow. Come prepared to be grilled about this amazing new job of yours. How does that sound?'

A faint smile creased her pale and exhausted-looking face, but she slowly stepped away.

'Well, that *is* something to look forward to. Goodnight, Brett. Sleep well.'

'Goodnight, sweetheart.'

She faltered slightly, stopped in the doorway, and glanced back at him over one shoulder.

Her glance only lasted a few seconds, but something unravelled inside him.

It was as though a door which had been locked tight shut for too many years had been opened up. Rusty. Hesitant. Resisting. A large, heavy door, with a huge lock and chain across it, and a sign saying: 'Worthless. Unworthy of the love of an amazing woman.' Only now the chain had been lifted away and the door had swung open.

This was the same locked door that had made it impossible for him to tell Lili that he loved her. The lock had turned tighter each time he saw how happy she'd been with Chris. The extra chain had come the day his mother had died of a stroke, walking home from her night office cleaning job only a few months before he won his promotion to head chef. She had never had the chance to stand next to him at an awards ceremony, or see his name in the newspapers. He had wanted that more than anything else in his life.

He had created that lock and chain to protect his sensitive and tender emotions from the searing, traumatic pain of loss. To keep them safe and carefully hidden away.

As he looked at Sienna in that fraction of a second each instinct from his broken childhood should have screamed for him to turn the key in the lock and slam that door tight shut again. But instead they were blown away by the force of a hot wind so powerful that he had to physically stand taller to brace himself against the force of it.

He stood in silence, the breath catching in his throat as she tried to smile and failed. The pain in her lovely shining brown eyes shone out and hit him hard.

It was all there in her face. Her lips were parted and her cheeks flushed as if they had just spent the night together.

A warm soft feeling of tenderness and love enveloped Brett and he moved forward to hold her tight against him, but she gasped and shook her head, started to say something, thought better of it, bit her lower lip, turned in his arms and slipped away out of the room.

Leaving him standing there.

His head spinning at the turmoil going on inside his heart.

He had survived childhood by deliberately not making any connections and refusing to love anyone enough to make a difference.

The feelings he had for Sienna were terrifying, exhilarating— and challenged him more than he wanted to admit.

Only a few days earlier he had imagined that opening his new restaurant was going to be the biggest adventure of his life. Well, he had been wrong. Winning over the whirlwind that was Sienna Rossi meant more.

* * *

Telling her how much he loved her was going to be one of the biggest risks he had ever taken—he knew that she cared about him. Now all he had to do was prove that he was worth taking the risk on.

The door was open and passion and determination flooded out creating an echoing empty space where love was meant to dwell.

He had already lost Lili.

No matter how long it took or how creative he was going to have to become, he was going to be the man to show Sienna Rossi that she was loved.

He was not going to lose Sienna. Not now. Not ever.

He had to think, and think fast.

Sienna had made it clear that she did not need or want any man telling her how to run her life. Now he understood why!

Only she thought that she had a few limited options to choose from, where she could be free to make that possible. Perhaps she was mistaken about that? After all, he had seen her transform Trattoria Rossi into a perfect small local diner. Any family would be happy to eat there….

The perfect family diner…was it possible?

Flicking open his cellphone, Brett quickly found the number for his best friend.

'Chris, mate. How are you doing? Yes, I told Sienna. She was okay. Listen. Is there any chance you could come over here tonight? I would like to talk through a crazy business idea you might be interested in.'

CHAPTER NINETEEN

Step 19: Add One American Chef Without a Kilt

'HI, CARLA. Yes, I'm fine. How are things at the Manor? Yes. I'm sorry that I had to leave so suddenly. What's the best time for me to avoid…? He's what? Any idea when?'

Sienna pinched the brow of her nose tight enough to be painful. 'No. Of course I understand. Patrick is still the boss. Thank you for letting me know. I'll talk to you later.'

She flung the phone down before Carla could answer.

'That interfering—!'

Sienna pressed both hands down firmly onto the hall table to steady herself and closed her eyes to block out the nausea.

'Unbelievable!'

There was a rustle of plastic wrapping from the sitting room, where Brett had been unpacking some of his personal saucepans, and the man himself appeared in the doorway.

She looked up at his smiling face and marvelled at his ability to calm her and reassure her in one single glance.

'Did I hear shouting? Where is the fire?'

Sienna raised one hand and waved it in Brett's direction, before pressing it to the back of her head as she started to pace up and down the hallway in the mid-morning light streaming through the glass panel over Maria's front door.

'Patrick. The general manager at Greystone. He has

arranged a planning meeting for the design team for the new restaurant. Apparently Angelo is only in town for a few days, and they want to go through the first ideas before he heads back to California. They didn't even think about calling me until the very last minute! If Carla hadn't reminded Patrick he probably would have completely forgotten to invite me.'

She was gesticulating now, using both hands to strangle imaginary demons in the air, her mind buzzing with excitement and enthusiasm. 'As the new restaurant manager I *need* to be there. I have so many ideas, Brett, but this meeting has come completely out of the blue. I don't even have time to put together a formal presentation to the team!'

Her enthusiasm was infectious, and he smiled right at her before replying in a calm voice, 'This sounds like the ideal chance for you to make a difference as the new manager. When is the meeting?'

Her voice trembled with frustration. 'That's why I'm jumping.' She glanced at her wristwatch, totally absorbed in the momentum of the news. 'Carla has been told to expect them in about four hours. Four hours—*today*, Brett! I need to be there before they arrive, and then start work straight way on a detailed plan. There are so many things to get sorted out before Angelo takes over that I hardly know where to start.'

Brett took one look at her dancing eyes and knew that her mind certainly wasn't on helping him clean out the kitchen units—or any other excuse he could come up with to be in the same room as her. He had never seen her so animated.

This was how it should be. The scared woman he had soaked with a bucket of water was gone for good. Replaced with a professional manager who was at the top of her game.

The Sienna Rossi he was looking at now sounded confident, self assured and assertive about her new role. Just as he knew she could be.

He wondered how she would react if she knew that he had spent most of the night talking about her to Chris, while they thrashed out an idea for a new business where *she* could be the star. If she wanted it! But it was far too early to tell her about that option. There were still a lot of questions which had to be answered before the deal was final.

Pity that something just did not sound right about her situation at Greystone. He had the most horrible feeling that this amazing woman was about to have her dream trampled to dust under her feet. And that was not fair.

'Are you sure that they actually *want* you to be there for this meeting, Sienna?'

She stopped pacing and looked at him with a slight frown. 'What do you mean? I'm the person who is going to have to make the new dining room work after the paint has dried! Of *course* they want me there. Patrick simply forgot that I was on holiday. That's all.'

'So Patrick and Angelo just have to snap their fingers and you come running? Is that right?'

'Brett! I thought you would be happy for me.' There was such pain and disappointment in her voice that he walked swiftly up to her and took hold of one of her hands in his, meshing his fingers between hers so that she could not escape.

She was so shocked at this that she flashed open her eyes and stared at the offending appendage as though it did not belong to her at all.

'I am happy for you. I simply think you're forgetting something very important. You are an amazing, beautiful and talented woman, and any man would be honoured to have you in his life or on his management team. I have a few concerns.'

'Go on. I'm listening. But make it fast.'

'The way I see it, you have two ways to handle this meeting.' He looked hard into her face, his voice low and serious.

Sienna was about to give her opinion about people who defined *her* choices, when Brett reached out with a not so clean forefinger and pressed it to her lips.

'First choice. Angelo Peruzi pulls up at the hotel with his

fancy team of architects and designers. You graciously welcome him in, the two of you make small talk about the weather and the state of the restaurant business and then you start work on the design of your new award-winning dining room. *Together.* As a team. No past history, just focused on the job.'

He moved his hand from left to right. 'He talks, you listen politely, then accept or decline his suggestions in a ladylike dignified and professional fashion and wave at the door as he drives away.' There was a pause. 'Or maybe not so professional, depending on what he has to say. You are totally in charge of the situation and he knows it.'

Sienna started squirming again but Brett continued. 'Stop that. There are pluses to this plan. Best-case scenario: he falls at your feet, begs your forgiveness and tells you that it will be an honour and a privilege to work with you and he has total respect for you in your new role. You both go off into the sunset, or whatever, hand in hand and destined for greatness.'

'Have you been sniffing the icing sugar again?' Sienna replied with a frown.

He ignored her snipe with a brief narrowing of his eyes. 'Worst case: you have to suffer your ex for an hour or so over a conference table. But then the deed is done, the ice is broken, and you can get on with your life and start work on creating something amazing. Worst part over. You've done your duty to Patrick and the team, and maybe Peruzi has an apology for you. It could happen.'

He squeezed her hand once before releasing it. 'But you always have to have a back-up plan. So, onto your second choice… You go back to the Manor, take one look at what this team are proposing, give it up as a lost cause and look for another job somewhere else.'

Sienna gasped and slapped him on the chest.

'Have you not been listening to *anything* I have been telling you these last few days? All I am asking for is the chance to show them what I am capable of achieving. This job will give me that chance, and I am *not* taking no for an answer.'

Her brow furrowed into a deep frown of concern and anxiety.

'You don't know how hard it is has been for me to rebuild my confidence. This is what I want. It's what I've always wanted, and I've worked too long to let this chance slip away from me. I *have* to prove that I can do this work.'

'Prove it to Angelo? Or prove it to yourself?'

Brett's free hand touched her arm, thrilling her with the heat and warmth of his support. 'You're Sienna Rossi. The unconquerable! Have you not just designed, decorated and refurbished one complete dining room on your own? You can *do* this job—but you don't have to. You've already shown what you are capable of. Right here. At Rossi's. You don't need to go back to Greystone Manor and settle for what they have to offer you just because it is comfortable. There are other hotels and restaurants who would love to have you work for them.'

Sienna wriggled and pulled and tugged to free herself—then suddenly she stopped fighting him and sagged down with a resigned sigh.

'Wait a minute. Does that list include Brett Cameron of Notting Hill?'

He sucked in a breath. 'Yes. It does. The job is yours if you want it. But there are others. You have more choices than you know.'

The last few days flashed though her brain. The shared meals, the laughter and the pizza party with the kids. The jokes and glimpses of their pasts. Could she walk away from all that?

Slipping her fingers out from between his, Sienna broke away and stepped back to look at Brett, well aware of the fierce intensity in his eyes.

'You truly don't understand. I could *never* work for you.'

'You can't mean that.'

'It's not you, and I know that the job would be fantastic! I totally admire and respect what you are trying to achieve there. No, Brett. It's me.'

She cupped the palms of both of her hands against his cheeks, her fingers tingling from contact with the blond stubble, and looked deep into his eyes. Pleading for his understanding.

'This is my dream. The dream I created for myself when things were very dark in my life. That means that I am the only person who can see it through to the end. Not Angelo. Not Patrick… And not you. I can only rely on myself.'

'Maybe once. But you must know that I am here for you,' he butted in. 'You don't have to do this on your own.'

She nodded and sniffed. 'I'm sorry if that sounds hard, but it is the truth—and I always tell my close friends the truth. And I hope we *are* friends. I really do. Because people who care about me are in pretty short supply in my life.'

Brett sighed loudly, and before she could go anywhere pulled her towards him, gathered her into his arms and pressed his lips to her forehead.

'You're not coming back to Rossi's. Are you?'

Her answer was a brief shake of the head.

'So that's it? You're just going to walk out on me? On us?'

Her cheek rested flat against his shirt before she found the strength to speak, not trusting her resolve if she saw his face.

'In a few days from now you are going to be working flat out in your new kitchen. Seven days a week. Catching a few hours' sleep when you can.'

'Have you been talking to Chris?' His voice rumbled below the fabric she was leaning on.

'I've been there once before. Remember? Oh, Brett.' She moved back so that her fingers stroked his shirt in gentle circles. 'We're both going to be working harder than we have ever worked in our lives. I don't want either of us to resent the time we steal to be together. That's not fair. On anyone. These last few days have been so unexpected. Thank you for that. But, no. I won't be coming back.'

He ran his fingers through her hair one last time, kissed her gently on the forehead, and then on the lips with the sweetest kiss of her life, and finally he wrapped her tight against him until he was ready to whisper a few words.

'I can't let you go. Not like this. There's so much I haven't told you. So much I want to say—' But his words were silenced.

'Shh. It's okay. It's okay. I am going to leave now, while we still have hope. It's better this way for both of us than facing heartbreak down the line. We both know what that feels like…and I'm not sure I could come back if I had my heart broken again this time.' Her fingers stroked his face as he released his grip. 'You have to let me go. That way we can both hold onto something special. Because you are so very special. Never forget that.'

A deep shudder racked Brett's body, but she felt his heartbeat slow down just a little under her fingers.

The sensation of his hands sliding away from her back was so painful she almost cried out with the loss. He was letting her go. And she was already missing his touch.

'I'm going to miss having someone around to remind me of that. If you have to do this, do it now—before I change my mind. I'll give you a lift to the station.'

Sienna stood, rock-steady now, her back pressed hard against the door.

Brett took hold of both of her arms and looked into her eyes, his love and devotion so open and exposed it was like a whirlwind of confusion and suppressed energy.

'Sienna? You already know how stubborn I can be. This isn't the end. Whatever options you choose, I'll be right here if you need me. *You* never forget *that*.'

He watched as she took a breath, looked him straight in the

eyes, gave a sharp nod and then ran up the stairs to get ready to leave, the sound of her footsteps echoing back into the hallway.

'We still have a date here on Valentine's Day—and I'm making your favourite dessert, just the way you like it.'

'You don't know my favourite dessert!' came a distant voice, before the bedroom door closed shut.

Oh, yes, he did. He knew everything he needed to know about the woman he had fallen in love with. Just when he'd thought that his poor guarded heart would never be open to love again.

Brett could feel his throat closing with emotion, and struggled to pull the shattered fragments of his willpower together.

Even the thought of not being with Sienna twisted his heart tight enough to make him gasp. Suddenly the rosy future he had been looking forward to so desperately seemed dark and grey if Sienna was not part of it.

He had two choices. Tell her that he loved her. Or let her go in the full knowledge that the hectic lives they led would make a relationship so difficult it might destroy them with the guilt of all the missed birthdays and special occasions normal couples could hope to enjoy.

She was right about that.

But it would be worth it for every single second of time they spent together.

No. He could not be so selfish. Not with Sienna. Not with the woman he loved.

If he told her how he felt about her…how she had come to dominate his thoughts and his dreams…how he longed to see her, hold her, simply be with her…there was a chance that she might stay for the sake of their relationship—at the cost of her own ambitions at Greystone Manor.

Telling her that he loved her now would only make it worse for both of them. Once said, the words could never be unsaid. And then what? What kind of pressure would that create?

This was Sienna's dream!

He had waited ten long exhausting years to make his own dream come true.

How could he deny this amazing woman the chance to do the same?

He had to let this tender, funny, clever woman walk away and make her own dreams a reality before he could come to her on equal terms and build something where they could both achieve their goals.

He had never thought of himself as noble, but if there was ever a time for sacrifice, this was it.

Even if it did rip his heart out.

CHAPTER TWENTY

Step 20: Beat Vigorously

SIENNA STOOD in front of the full-length mirror in the stone-walled tower room of Greystone Manor, which had been her safe refuge for the last four years, and ran both hands down over her fine cashmere knee-length skirt to smooth away any creases.

She had spent time and money choosing the perfect black skirt suit and glossy designer shoes. It was easy to make the excuse that fine-dining customers expected a certain level of formality in the waiting staff, but the truth was harder to accept.

The last few days had shown her how much she missed working with wine and flavours and colour. Creating something amazing and unique which she knew in her heart that Maria's customers would love.

This suit was part of the armour she wore every day to convince everyone that she was totally in control and in charge as head waiter.

It was pathetic. *She* was pathetic.

Brett was right.

She was a coward. A brave woman hiding behind a façade she had made for herself.

She had needed these tall, solid walls to give her time to re-build her confidence that she was capable and able to do her job without a controlling man telling her what to do.

When would she ever get the chance to do that again?

Sienna strolled over to her window that overlooked the stunning grounds of the hotel and let the tears fall in silence down her cheeks, ruining her make-up.

She had looked at this view for four long years, but the hotel had never felt like home. A safe place? Yes. But not home. Closing her eyes, she could still see the view from the spare bedroom in Maria's house, of the busy London street, and longed to be back there.

The vibration of her cellphone broke the spell with a simple text message from Carla.

The design team had arrived. It was time to get this over with once and for all.

Carla was hidden behind a large contingent of men in suits carrying art portfolios and packaging tubes, who were being greeted by senior hotel management from across Europe.

Sienna sucked in a breath and lifted her chin, stretching herself to her full height and fixing a professional smile firmly in place.

In the centre of the laughing, happy group gathered in the reception area of Greystone Manor was the man she had last seen at the departure gate before his flight to Los Angeles.

Angelo Peruzi.

On that fateful day she had watched in silence as he had walked through passport control and out of view. He had not looked back at her. Not once. He had not spared one backward glance at the woman he had asked to be his wife only a few months earlier.

Today Angelo Peruzi was wearing almost the same clothing he had worn that day—a navy blazer, white pressed shirt and designer denims. And dark sunglasses.

In February.

Indoors, in a country house hotel.

She had forgotten how very handsome he was. The years had filled out his face, and there was a certain softness about his body, but life in California had served Angelo well. Every inch of his designer clothing screamed success and wealth.

He looked as though one of the photographer's stylists had spent a couple of hours working on him with false tan and teeth whitener to impress TV viewers. He probably had no idea how strange and out of place they made him look in this elegant, dignified house.

Sienna locked eyes with Angelo across the room. For a fleeting second she felt as though they were the only people present.

His brow creased slightly in recognition, before he flashed her one of his special smiles and made his way through the group of men in smart suits to stand in front of her. He stretched out his hand.

'Sienna. It's so good to see you again. You look wonderful. Perhaps we can catch up next week?'

'Of course,' she managed to reply through a closed throat, and was saved by Patrick, who had never left Angelo's side.

'Ah, Miss Rossi. Thank you for coming in at such short notice. I apologise for breaking into your holiday, but we only have a tiny window for a meeting with Chef Peruzi, and I know that you want to hear our exciting plans for the new dining room! Please join us. I know that you are going to be totally thrilled with the proposal.'

Thirty minutes later two things had suddenly become very clear.

She was not thrilled with the new proposals. *At all.*

The hotel management had brought in a top team of slick restaurant designers who had taken one look at the lovely antique wooden panels on the walls and the intricate ceiling work in the original hall and tutted. Loudly. This was *not* the space they had planned for the new Peruzi restaurant.

She had twice tried to make a suggestion. And twice been dismissed and talked down. Neither Patrick nor Angelo had spoken up for her, or given her the slightest hint of support and encouragement when she had argued against the obliteration of the very architectural features which made the Manor so unique.

The design team were not interested in anything she had to say—which was hard to believe, considering the outlandish ideas they were proposing.

Californian fusion? *At Greystone?*

Patrick she could understand—his bosses had paid this team of so-called experts to create a 'unique vision' for the new restaurant. He could hardly tell them they were crazy!

The second fact was even harder to accept.

Sienna took a long, hard look at Angelo, who was looking disdainfully around the beautiful oak panelled room, and wondered how they had both come to change so very much in so short a time.

He had walked out of her town, her family and her life, and now he had just waltzed into the hotel as though he was the cavalry who was going to save them all from disaster.

As though she ought to be grateful that he had taken the time out of his busy schedule to lower himself to say hello. No apology. No explanation. Not even an excuse for what had happened to the restaurant he had abandoned, leaving her to sort out the mess he had left behind.

At least he had not tried to kiss her. Simply shaken her hand.

This was what she wanted. Wasn't it?

For Angelo to treat her as simply one of his colleagues?

She looked across at the slight sneer on Angelo's mouth and in that second the reality of the man hit her hard and fast. This was not the Angelo she remembered!

That Angelo had been some fictitious, imaginary ideal. A mirage. A version she had put together from her own imagination. She had been infatuated with an idealised clone of a man who had never truly existed.

Whatever relationship they might have had once was long gone. That part of her life was finished.

There was a very good chance that he would destroy everything André Michon had built up. And she wanted no part of it. In fact, the more she thought about it, the more she realised that it would have been a horrible mistake for her to come back and try and work with Angelo under *any* circumstances.

Brett Cameron had shown her what it could be like to work with someone she trusted and who respected her opinion. Valued her. Cared for her. Maybe more than just cared for her.

Which made her the biggest fool in the world.

A wave of nausea and dizziness hit Sienna, forcing her to lean against the table for support. The coffee. She should have eaten breakfast. Now just the thought of food made her dizzier than ever, and she fought to get air into her lungs.

Sienna tried to control her breathing, and lifted her chin just as Patrick caught her eye and waved his empty coffee cup from side to side, gesturing towards the door.

Yes. It *was* time to leave the room. Only it wouldn't be to make more coffee. It would be to start packing.

CHAPTER TWENTY-ONE

Step 21: Finish with One Portion of Chocolate Tiramisu

SIENNA BENT down from the waist onto the pristine white dining-room tablecloth with her arms flopped down each side of her body, and bobbed her head down twice onto the hard surface before resting her forehead on the cloth.

'I think Patrick got the message in the end,' Carla said as she gathered together the glassware in the now empty dining room at the end of evening service. 'Apparently he has never had anyone resign from a management job before. It's a new experience for him.'

Sienna did not even attempt to raise her head to reply, so the words that did emerge were muffled by a lot of blubbering and a tang of self-pity.

'Perhaps you shouldn't have asked him for a reference? That might have been a bit cheeky? Anyway—stay right there. I'll be back in a moment with dessert, and you can tell me all the lovely details.'

A loud groan followed by a whimper coincided with the sound of her forehead thunking down again on the table.

Her eyes might have been tight shut, but Sienna could still hear the sound of a chair being drawn out and a china bowl sliding across the tabletop. The most delicious smell of cocoa, coffee, sweet liqueur and rich mascarpone wafted into her

nostrils, making them twitch, and her mouth watered in anticipation of the smooth lusciousness of her favourite dessert.

'That was fast! Oh, Carla. I've really done it now, haven't
I? Career over. Finished. Kaput. Perhaps I can ask my brother
for a job?'

'Well, you could do that, but I have a better idea.'

Sienna flung herself backwards in the chair with shock at
the sound of her favourite male voice, and almost toppled the
chair over.

'Brett?'

He was wearing a superbly tailored dark suit with a beautiful pale pink check shirt and a tie the exact same shade of blue
as his eyes. Her heart soared and screamed a halleluiah in joy.

She had missed him so much that just the sight of him sitting
there, with his elbows on the tablecloth, smiling across at her,
made her world suddenly bright.

This was why she had been so miserable for the few hours
since they had been parted.

'Hello,' she whispered, trying to be brave and not embarrass herself by leaping into his arms with joy and kissing the
life out of the man.

'Hello, yourself. Medals for courage under fire are in short
supply at the moment, so I rescued some of my special
tiramisu. I thought you might need the encouragement. It seems
I need not have worried after all. Congratulations.'

'I don't deserve a medal,' she replied, lifting her head
slightly to look at the bowl, heaped with delicious creamy
dessert, a gold spoon leaning on the rim.

Her head lifted a little higher.

Enticing curls of dark and milk chocolate were scattered
across the top of the creamy stuff in the bowl.

'Resigning from this job was a totally reckless thing to do,'
she added with a sniff.

His finger slipped under her chin and lifted it higher, so that
when he bent down to her level he could make direct eye contact.

'Not reckless. Right. How did you feel when you told them that you didn't want the restaurant manager's job after all?'

'It felt so good!' She managed a thin smile and pushed out her lower lip before lifting her head a little more. 'Actually, it felt wonderful!' She sat bolt upright and nodded at Brett. 'You're right! It was the right thing to do! I deserve better!'

Then she remembered the flipside of that statement and groaned. 'I have been a total idiot!' She almost slumped down again, except Brett had seen it coming and propped her up by lifting up the dessert bowl and wafting it higher and higher.

'Not another word until you have given me your expert opinion on the dessert. I'm still not sure about the chocolate curls, and you know that it has to be perfect before Valentine's Day or I won't be happy.'

She reached forward and took a heaped spoonful of smooth, creamy-chocolate flavoured mascarpone and soft, soaked sponge, and the wonderful aroma hit her senses only a few seconds before she tasted the amazing dessert. Her eyes flickered in delight and sensual pleasure as each of the ingredients was savoured in turn.

'Wonderful. Absolutely wonderful. Just don't tell Chef André. He would be terribly upset.'

She replaced the spoon, before she embarrassed herself even more by scoffing the entire bowl, and felt her shoulders drop down by at least four inches.

Brett was sitting opposite her, elbows on the table and both hands under his chin. Watching her. Simply watching her. And delighting in doing so.

'Feel better?'

'Much. Thank you.' She reached out and took the hand that he was holding out to her.

'Oh, Brett. I am so disgusted with myself. I've wasted four years of my life grieving over some idealised version of a man who probably never existed in the first place. I thought all chefs were the same—you've shown me how wrong I was. When I think of all of that pain…'

She shook her head in disbelief and gave in to the tears which had formed in the corners of her eyes, swallowing down her fears and regrets.

The long, sensitive fingers tenderly smoothed the hair back from her forehead, his blue eyes flicking longingly over her face.

She sniffed before smiling back at him in thanks. 'I missed you.'

'I missed you too. You've only been gone a few hours and Rossi's is simply not the same without you.'

She took a few calming breaths, eyes closed, before daring to look at Brett. One look. And her anger crisped, burnt, and was blown away in one sweep under the heat of that smile.

'Oh, Brett! I've made such a mess of things!'

He pretended to ignore her flushed face and puffy eyes, released her hair and took both of her hands in his before saying in a quiet and controlled voice, 'Not necessarily. Last night we talked about making choices. Well, now I have one more to offer you. What if you were in charge of *your own* business? Would that make a difference to your options?'

'What do you mean?' Sienna replied, intrigued.

'After you went to bed last night I started talking with Chris about a new idea which goes way beyond my signature restaurant. A long way!'

Brett squeezed her fingers in excitement as his eyes locked onto hers. Shining eyes, brimmed full of energy and enthusiasm.

'We want to open a chain of family restaurants. Imagine an informal but clean and well-run bistro a teenager could bring his high-school sweetheart to on their first big date. We'll run them as a franchise, based on the recipes that I come up with in my own kitchen, and with the same basic design of dining room you created this last week for Maria.'

He grinned at her with such love and fire and passion that the breath caught in her throat.

'Young couples all over Britain will have the chance to create their own version of Trattoria Rossi in their town. Good food. Informal and friendly. And not just for Valentine's Night but every other night as their family grows up. I think it would work. How about you?'

Her mouth formed a perfect oval for all of two seconds before she flung her head back and bellowed in laughter, slapping her fingers against Brett's in delight.

'It is a wonderful idea! I love it! I can't tell you how totally brilliant, brilliant and brilliant it is.'

She leant forward and kissed him, hard and quick on the lips.

'You clever man. No wonder you are excited!'

'I am. Except Chris and I have a major problem which could seriously hold the project back.'

She shrugged and pulled one hand away from his clutches to wave it in front of her face.

'Nothing that you can't handle. You're Brett Cameron! Superstar! Superhero! Tiramisu maker extraordinaire!'

'Thank you for that, but even superstars can't be in two places at the same time. I have worked all my life to open a dream restaurant in Notting Hill—and you know how that feels. It needs my total focus and dedication.'

He paused and gave her one of his special smiles before blurting out, 'I need a business partner to run our chain of family trattoria. Chris will be able to raise funding for the first year, and your aunt Maria has agreed to let me lease Rossi's from her at a special rate so that we can develop our first trattoria there, to be used as a model for the franchise—but we don't have a manager.'

Brett let that sink in for a few seconds before rushing on with his pitch. 'The ideal person would have to be used to dealing with very discerning customers, capable of running the whole business, and it would be a big help if they liked my food. And I have to be able to trust them. Completely. Know any likely candidates who might fit that description?'

Sienna froze. The smile faded on her lips.

'Are you serious? You're offering me the job?'

'No. I'm offering you a partnership in the business. You would be running *your very own* chain of family trattoria. *With* me. Not *for* me. This would be your project, using the amazing talent I've seen over these last few days. You can do this. I have no doubt about that whatsoever. You are the only person I could trust.'

'You trust me that much? You are willing to relinquish absolute control and let me make decisions without trying to interfere all the time?'

'With all my heart.'

'Wow, you know how to take the wind out of a girl's sails. I don't understand. This is *so* exciting. Why didn't you mention it before now?'

'Ah. I only came up with the idea after you had gone to bed last night, and I had to be absolutely certain of something very important before I even mentioned it. And there's the fact that you seem to like my food, of course.'

'Of course. Now talk to me. What could be that important?'

'I had to find out if you were willing to sacrifice everything to make your new job here at Greystone a success. Or not.'

Sienna sucked in a breath and stared hard at the wonderful man who had just offered her the chance to realise her dream, and something clicked into place which she had never even thought of before—and yet suddenly it made so much sense.

'Before I answer that, I do have one question for you. And it is equally important. I trust you to tell me the truth.'

She picked up the bowl of tiramisu and licked the chocolate from the spoon.

'This tiramisu wasn't just a lucky guess. Was it?'

He gave a brief shake of the head and a closed-mouth smile.

'You remembered. It was twelve years ago. But you remembered that tiramisu is my favourite dessert.'

His answer was to lift up the hand he was holding and kiss the back of her knuckles.

'Oh, Brett.'

'I was the poor boy from the wrong side of the tracks who was never going to be good enough to ask the Rossi princess out on a date. So I locked up my heart and hid the key so that it would be safe.'

His fingertip traced the curve of her eyebrow. So tenderly and lovingly it almost brought Sienna to the brink of tears again.

'So beautiful. Clever. Destined for great things. I might not have been good enough, but I paid attention.' He smiled as Sienna shook her head in disbelief. 'Your aunt Maria noticed, but kept quiet. Your dad just thought I was clumsy. I was so envious of the wonderful start in life you and Frank had. You had the family. The restaurant. You were living the kind of family life I had only dreamt about.'

Sienna groaned and pressed two fingertips to his lips.

'This might not be the best time to tell you that there was a very good reason why I stalked your every working day. Crush. I had a total girly crush on you. Only I was too shy to tell you.'

Silence.

'Not possible. If you saying that to make me feel better, I appreciate the sentiment but…'

She shrugged. 'Nope. You have the honour of having been my first crush, Brett Cameron.'

Then she grinned. 'Do you remember the other day, when I asked you to stay in the basement at the Rossi house when I went up to my old bedroom to hunt for shoes? I was *terrified* that you would come across my diary. Which includes the daily detailed itinerary of when I saw you, what you were wearing, what you said, what I did… Need I go on?'

'You…had a crush on me?'

She nodded several times, biting her lower lip, then gave up completely and started giggling, then stopped, then giggled again, then carried on giggling until he was forced to give in and roar with laughter.

'Could we have been more pathetic? You were in the kitchen, frightened to speak to me when I came in the room, while I was miserable when I wasn't in the same room as you. Both of us too shy or too scared to talk to each other. How ironic is that?'

'Crazy. I wish I'd known.'

'Me too. I do have one more question. And it's totally personal.'

'After that little bombshell I'm almost frightened to hear it, but fire away. I can handle it.'

'In that case I need to know if you are still in love with Lili. Or not.'

He stopped laughing and turned his attention to her jawline, his fingertips moving in gentle circles, then curving so that her face was being held in his hands.

'I'll never forget her, but I'm only capable of loving one woman at a time, and I'm looking at the woman I'm in love with today, and will go on loving for the rest of my life.'

Sienna looked into the depths of those amazing eyes, and what she saw there made her heart sing. Her words gushed out in joy. 'Then you will be pleased to hear that my answer is…not. A great big definite *not*.'

Brett never broke eye contact with her as he reached into his jacket pocket and pulled out a small velvet box.

Her heart was thumping so loudly in her chest that breathing and thinking and listening at the same time suddenly became a major challenge.

With the ease that suggested someone who had been practising, Brett flicked open the lid and pressed the open box into the palm of her hand.

Sienna looked down on a pink, heart-shaped solitaire diamond on an elegant platinum band, and pressed her free hand to her chest.

It was the most beautiful thing she had ever seen in her life, and she told him so.

'You're an amazing woman, Sienna Rossi. I never thought

you could surprise me any more, but you have done. Any man would want to have you in his life. Want you in his bed. Make you the last thing he sees at night. The woman he wakes up with every morning.'

She knew he was smiling by the creases at the corners of his mouth.

'I was a boy who thought that he would never be good enough for someone as beautiful and clever as you. Will you give me a chance to prove that I have become a better man, who is finally worthy of you?'

'I like the man he became quite a lot. I trust him with my life—and my heart. And my dreams.'

The smile faded, his eyes darkening.

'I'm also the man who wants to hold you in his arms and have you by his side every day. I want to spend the rest of my life showing you how much I need you. How much you mean to me.'

He swept both hands down from her forehead, smoothing her hair down, over and over, building the strength to say the words. His eyes focused on hers, and his voice was broken and ragged with intensity.

'I love you, Sienna. I walked into that kitchen a lonely young man in a frightening place, terrified that he would make a mistake and mess things up, and be back on the streets. Then you turned to me and gave me a tiny shy smile.'

Her eyes glistened as he stroked her face.

'And I knew that everything was going to be okay.'

His voice broke and he could only draw her up to her full height, so that his hands could wrap around her back, pressing his body closer to hers, his head into her neck. She could sense his heaving chest as they both fought back years of suppressed desires and hopes.

She could feel the pressure of his lips on her skin, but everything was suddenly a blur. If only the fireworks would stop going off in her head. Rockets seemed to be exploding in huge ribbons of light and colour.

Brett loved her. Brett Cameron. *Loved*. Her.

With all the strength she'd thought she had lost, Sienna slid her hands from his waist up the front of his chest, resisting the temptation to rip his shirt off, and felt this man's heart thumping wildly under the cloth. His shirt was sweaty, and she could feel the moist hair under her fingers as his pulse rang out under her touch.

She forced her head back from his body, inches away from this remarkable, precious man who had exposed his deepest dreams to her.

'It broke my heart when you left for Paris. Since then I've looked everywhere for the missing part, but nobody was able to mend it. How could they, when you were simply holding it safe for me? I was just so scared that you would break it all over again. So scared.'

Her hand came up to stroke Brett's face as he looked at her in silence, his chest heaving as he forced air into his lungs. She could still hear the pounding of his heart as he spoke.

His voice was full of excitement and energy, the desire burning in every word.

'Come and work with me. Run your own business. Sleep in my arms every night.'

His eyes scanned across her face, trying to gauge her reaction.

'Will you come and live with me? Will you be my partner, my lover, and the mother of my children? Can you do that? Can you take a chance at happiness with me?'

She gasped in a breath as the tears streamed down her face, knowing that he was saying the words she had waited a lifetime to hear.

'Yes.'

He looked back at her and his mouth dropped open in shock. 'Yes?'

'Yes!' She laughed, 'Yes, yes, yes. Oh, Brett. I love you so much.'

She had barely got the words out of her mouth before she was silenced by the pressure of a pair of hot lips, which would have knocked her backwards if not for the strong arms that pressed her body to his. Eyes closed, she revelled in the glorious sensation of his mouth, lips, skin and firm body. Lights were going on in parts of her where she had not known switches existed. She felt as if she was floating on air.

Her eyes flicked open to find that she *was* floating in air. Brett had hoisted her up by the waist, was twirling her around and around, two grown up people hooting with joy, oblivious to the tableware. A kaleidoscope of happiness, colour and light.

Sienna slid back down his body, her extended arms caressed lovingly by strong hands, looked into Brett's smiling face, stunned by the joy she had brought to this precious man, and grinned.

'Take me home, Brett. Take me home.'

CHAPTER TWENTY-TWO

***Step 22: Keep Mixture Warm until Valentine's Day; Top
with a Red Rose Before Serving with a Kiss***

PINK FAIRY lights still twinkled and sparkled in the branches
of the ornamental bay trees inside the refurbished dining room
of Trattoria Rossi.

The last few days since Sienna had left Greystone Manor
had passed in a blur of excitement, joy, and a lot of very hard
work—but the Trattoria had finally been ready to welcome
their guests on a very special Valentine's Day.

It had not only been her first Valentine's Day as the new
owner of Trattoria Rossi—but the perfect engagement party,
with everyone she loved around her. Even Carla had managed
to escape Greystone that evening!

The last of the paying customers had gone home, after what
many had told her was the best meal of their lives. There had
been Valentine kisses, holding hands under the table, and a lot
of laughter and chatter. But best of all, Maria Rossi had been
there in person, to help Sienna say goodbye to one part of her
life and prepare to start a new one.

Sienna smiled and shook her head. The irrepressible Maria
had escaped her hospital bed by promising to take it easy and
recover slowly, but there was no way that lady had been going

to miss her final Valentine's Day before handing the place over to Sienna and Brett.

The tables were now pushed together to create one long central eating area, with enough space around the chairs for Frankie's children to run around, laughing and playing with Jess and her new very best friends—Henry's granddaughters, who both lived in the area.

For now the room belonged to the family. *Her family.* Old and new.

It was as though every precious, warm feeling she had ever associated with her Rossi family meals had come together in one place. Now she understood how Brett had felt all those years ago.

Carla had already found a seat next to Chris, and was chatting away about the chain of Italian trattoria style bistros he was going to run for the future Mr and Mrs Cameron, while Maria took centre stage with the Rossi horde, talking of her plans to run a beach café with Henry under the Spanish sunshine.

Trattoria Rossi was still Trattoria Rossi. Only now it was Sienna's very own place. Not in competition with Brett's Notting Hill restaurant, but her own space, where she could serve wonderful food in a warm and welcoming cosy room.

This was the family restaurant she had known as a child, only better—because Brett was here. The man she loved was sitting next to her brother, Frankie, the two men flicking through one of the photo albums her mother had kept all her life, laughing as they pointed to one image then another.

Albums in which photos of her own children would be given a place one day.

Her heart expanded to take in her joy and happiness.

Palms sweaty, she gawped at the best-looking man in the room. He was wearing a chef's apron over a crisp white shirt, open at the neck, designed to highlight his deep tan and the brightness of his smile and eyes. Absolutely gorgeous.

Brett glanced over his shoulder at that moment, and her breath caught in her throat as he returned her smile and reached out for her with a grin that made her melt and her heart soar with happiness.

Sienna bent over and kissed Brett, before leaning back and smiling at the man who had brought such joy into her life.

A single perfect red rose lay across a crystal tulip dish filled with his special recipe chocolate tiramisu.

'Happy Valentine's Day,' he whispered, his voice so full of love it took her breath away.

Today marked the end of one part of her life and the start of a lifetime of perfect Valentine's Days. With a man who knew the perfect recipe for her happiness.

THE BRIDESMAID AND
THE BILLIONAIRE

SHIRLEY JUMP

New York Times bestselling author **Shirley Jump** didn't have the will-power to diet, nor the talent to master under-eye concealer, so she bowed out of a career in television and opted instead for a career where she could be paid to eat at her desk—writing. At first, seeking revenge on her children for their grocery store tantrums, she sold embarrassing essays about them to anthologies. However, it wasn't enough to feed her growing addiction to writing funny. So she turned to the world of romance novels, where messes are (usually) cleaned up before The End. In the worlds Shirley gets to create and control, the children listen to their parents, the husbands always remember holidays, and the housework is magically done by elves. Though she's thrilled to see her books in stores around the world, Shirley mostly writes because it gives her an excuse to avoid cleaning the toilets and helps feed her shoe habit. To learn more, visit her website at www.shirleyjump.com.

For Sherri,
my own maid of honor and best friend, even though
she got the part of the narrator in the fourth grade
play. The best part about having her as a best friend
is we're never too grown up to have fun.

CHAPTER ONE

KANE Lennox's bare feet sank into the new spring grass, his toes disappearing between the thick green blades like shy mice. He'd slept on mattresses that cost as much as a small sedan, walked on carpet that had been hand loomed in the Orient, and worn shoes made to order specifically for his feet by a cobbler in Italy. But those experiences paled in comparison to this one. Comfort slid through his veins, washing over him in a wave, lapping at the stress that normally constricted his heart, easing the emotion's death grip on his arteries.

He halted midstep, tossing the conundrum around in his mind. How could something so simple, so basic, as walking barefoot on grass, feel so wonderful?

"What on earth do you think you're doing?"

Kane whirled around at the sound of the woman's voice. Tall and thin, her blond hair hanging in a long straight curtain to her waist, she stood with tight fists propped on her hips. Her features were delicate, classic, with wide green eyes and lush dark pink lips, but right now her face had been transformed by a mask of confusion and annoyance. In one hand she held a cell phone, her thumb over the send button, 9-1-1 just a push away.

Not that he could blame her. Even he had to admit what he was doing looked…odd. Out of place. Kane put up both hands. The "See, I'm okay, not carrying any lethal weapons" posture. "There's a perfectly logical explanation for my behavior," he said. "And my presence."

She raised a dubious brow, but looked a bit worried, even apprehensive. "A total stranger. Barefoot. On my sister's lawn. In the middle of the day. Uh-huh. I'm sure there's a logical explanation for *that*." She turned, casting a hand over her eyes, shading them from the sun. "Either there's some cameraman waiting to jump out of the shrubbery with a 'Surprise, you're on *Candid Camera*' announcement, or you're here on some loony-bin field trip."

He laughed. "I assure you, I'm not crazy."

Though the last few weeks had driven him nearly to insanity. Which had pushed him to this point. To the small town of Chapel Ridge, in the middle of Indiana. To—

Being barefoot on, as she had said, her sister's lawn in the middle of a bright April day. Okay, so it was mildly crazy.

"That leaves the *Candid Camera* option, which I'm definitely not in the mood for, or…trespassing." She held up the phone like a barrier against a vampire. "Either way, I'm calling the cops."

"Wait." He took a step forward, thought better of it and backed up. As his gaze swept over her a second time, he realized she looked familiar, and now knew why. "You must be…" He racked his brain. Usually he was so good at names. But this time, he couldn't come up with hers. "The sister of the bride. Jackie's sister."

"I get it. You're a detective who does his best thinking in his bare feet, is that it?" She gave him a sardonic grin. "Must have been tough, putting all the puzzle pieces together, what with the Congratulations Jackie and Paul sign out front, the paper wedding bells hanging on the mailbox. Oh, and the happiness emanating from the house like cheap perfume." She paused midtirade. "Wait. How do you know who *I* am?"

Kane gave her an assessing glance, avoiding the question. "What's made you so disagreeable?"

She sighed and lowered the phone. "I've had a rough day. A rough life and—" She cut herself off again. "How do you *do* that? I'm not telling you a single thing about me."

"Listen, I'll just get out of here and leave you to your day. I've clearly come at a bad time." He bent over, picked up his designer Italian leather dress shoes and started to leave.

"Wait." She let out a gust.

He turned back and for a second, Kane swore he heard a spark of himself—of the last few months, the days that had driven him to this town, to this crazy idea—in that sound. Then, just as quickly, it was gone, and the spark of distrust had returned.

"You still haven't told me why you're barefoot on the lawn in the middle of the day."

Kane's jaw hardened. "We're back to that again?"

"When did we ever leave that topic?" She parked her fists back on her hips, the cell phone dangling between two fingers.

Telling her why he was here, and what he was doing, involved getting into far too many personal details. If he started opening up about his problems, he'd have all of Chapel Ridge—all 4,910 residents, as it were—knowing his identity, and there'd go his plan to enjoy some much-needed R & R.

He had no intentions of telling anyone anything. Particularly Jackie's sister.

Susannah Wilson. That was her name. Suzie-Q, Paul called her, like the packaged dessert.

Before she could question him further, he headed over to his little blue rental car, a cheap American model, light-years away from the silver convertible Bentley Azure he usually drove. The rental was nondescript, plain. Like something anyone else in the world would be driving. And perfect.

Susannah followed him. Not one to give up easily, that was clear. "You still didn't answer my question. Who are you? And why are you here?"

"That's two questions. And I don't have to tell you anything, either. It's a free country."

He could almost hear her internal scream of frustration. Oh, this was going to be fun.

She scowled. "Trespassing is a crime, you know."

He grinned. When he'd booked this trip, he'd had no idea there'd be a fringe benefit of this little fireball. "Only if you're not invited. And *I* was invited." He paused a beat, watching her eyes widen in surprise at the word *invited,* waiting to deliver the last punch of surprise. "I'm the best man, after all."

"You have the worst taste in friends."

Paul Hurst, Jackie's fiancé, laughed. "Suzie-Q, you need to give Kane the benefit of the doubt. He's not so bad. And he had his reasons for what he was doing, I'm sure."

"Where did you meet him anyway? Prison?"

"College. He had the room next door to mine, and we had a few classes together. And he's—" Paul cut himself off. "He's a good guy. Just trust me on that."

Susannah got to her feet, gathering the mess of dishes on the coffee table. The collection of plates and glasses had grown over the day, multiplying like bunnies in her absence. Jackie and Paul didn't move from their positions in the living room of the old Victorian-style house. Paul had his feet up on the scarred maple coffee table—a garage sale find of Susannah's from last summer—and Jackie was curled up beside him, the remote control in her hands. Across the room, a detective show played on the big-screen TV, an early wedding gift from Susannah and the bridesmaids, who had chipped in on the electronic extravagance.

"The last time I trusted you, you stole my sister's heart."

Paul laughed. He wrapped an arm around Jackie and drew her to him. The leather sofa, a replacement for the plaid one that had sat in this room for nearly twenty years, creaked beneath his weight. "Just think of it as gaining a brother."

Jackie leaned into the brown-haired man she had dated for the better part of three years and gave him a kiss on the cheek. "A very handsome brother."

Susannah grinned. "Santa must not have heard me when I said I wanted a *pony*."

She headed out of the room, the dishes in her hands, and loaded them into the sink. She ran hot water over them, added dish soap, then started washing. She had stood at this sink for nearly all her life, looked out this same window at the same yard, washing dishes ever since she'd been old enough to stand on the small wooden stepstool and reach into the deep-bottomed stainless steel sink. Back then, she'd washed while her mother dried, the two of them falling into a natural rhythm, working along with the radio in the background, and the sunny yellow kitchen seemed to beam back the sunshine in her mother's voice.

But those days were gone, the radio had broken years ago, and the kitchen's paint had faded. And now the dishes had become a chore.

"You don't have to do that," Jackie said. She leaned against the refrigerator, filing her nails with an emery board. "If you let them sit—"

"They won't break," Jackie cut in. "Leave the dishes for later. Or even better, don't do them at all."

If Susannah didn't do them, they'd never get done. Neither Jackie nor Paul was much for housework, despite their protests to the contrary. In exchange for living with the two of them for a nominal rent to help pay down the mortgage, Susannah had agreed to do the majority of the housework and even though the deal had worked out so that she ended up doing all the chores, most days the arrangement suited her just fine. It helped her save money, which went to her ultimate goal.

Freedom.

One week. Just one more week, and she'd be out of here. Out of this house. Out of this town. On her way to the life she had dreamed of for so long it seemed like she had been born with the dream. Susannah's gaze drifted to the stained-glass Eiffel Tower hanging in the kitchen window. Gold and orange glints bounced off the countertops as the sun's afternoon's rays streamed through the tiny glass shards.

I've never been here, her mother had said, that last Christmas when she'd given Susannah the small reproduction of Paris's famous landmark, *but I hope someday you can go, sweet Susannah. See the world I never got to see.*

Susannah would. No matter what it took.

"I'll just get these few before I go to work," Susannah said.

"But you just got home. I thought you were done for the day."

"I had a couple late appointments. Every appointment is another dollar, you know." She gave Jackie a smile.

"You work too hard." Jackie held her hands out, checked all ten fingers, deemed them perfect and tucked the file into her back pocket.

"All for the ultimate goal, sis. All for the ultimate goal."

"A discreet way of saying you hate living with us." Jackie laughed, showing Susannah no offense was taken, then gave her sister a quick hug. "Oh, when you go out, do you mind doing me a favor?"

"Sure."

"Can you stop by and pick up the centerpieces? I have a fitting tonight and then…"

"The party."

The bachelorette party. The same one that Susannah had planned, as maid of honor, but wasn't attending. She'd never known Jackie's friends very well, and as the date had approached, felt herself less and less inclined to spend the evening with the other bridesmaids. Women who had always been Jackie's friends and included Susannah only as an afterthought, like adding one more fern to an already perfect floral arrangement.

"You can still come. You are one of the bridesmaids, after all. The bachelorette party is one of the perks." Jackie grinned.

"I'm cool, Jackie. Really." She ran the sponge over a plate, scrubbing at the center until the stoneware gleamed. "I'm not much for parties anyway."

"You're just avoiding, like you always do."

"No, I'm not. I have to work."

Jackie sighed but let the subject drop. She placed a hand on Susannah's shoulder. "I appreciate you picking the centerpieces up. You're really saving me. Again."

Not that Susannah had the time. She had three dogs to bathe tonight, and a million errands of her own. "What about Paul?"

"Nothing against my future husband, but I don't think he'd know a centerpiece from a centrifuge." She laughed.

Susannah increased the water temperature, filling a casserole dish that had been used for nachos or cheese dip, or something equally hardened and stubborn about giving up its baked-on grip. "When were you planning on assembling them?"

"Assembling them?" Jackie paused, then smacked her temples. "Damn. I totally forgot about that part. Maybe tomorrow afternoon." She thought a second. "No, wait. That's the meeting with the minister to go over the rest of the ceremony details. Umm…tomorrow night? No, not then, either. Paul and I have plans with the Fitzgeralds. Remember them? They used to be Mom and Dad's friends. I don't know how long we'll be at their house. You know how they can talk. And then on Thursday night we have the reh—"

"Basically, you have a million other things to do," Susannah finished.

As usual. Jackie's list was filled with social engagements and outings and very few responsibilities. At twenty-six, Susannah was four years older than Jackie and had always run her life down the opposite track. She bit back a breath of annoyance. Soon Jackie would be married, and she'd *have* to be responsible. Because Susannah wouldn't be here anymore to carry the load.

"It's a wonder I have time to go to work with all that, huh?" Jackie said, laughing. "Believe me, if Paul and I didn't need the money, I'd be calling in sick every day. Gosh, how on earth am I ever going to find time to do everything for the wedding? It's like the clock is running out. Jerry said we could set up early at the hotel, because they have nothing else scheduled there this weekend, but I don't even have time to…"

Her voice trailed off and then that hopeful smile took over her face. The one Susannah knew as well as she knew every square inch of this house. Jackie leaned against the counter and met Susannah's gaze. "Hey, what are *you* doing tonight, sis?"

Susannah pulled the drain on the sink. "No way, Jackie. I've got—"

"Please, Suzie-Q. Please?" Jackie put her hands together, and gave Susannah a pleading-puppy-dog look. "Just this one more favor, and then, I swear, I'll never ask for another. I swear."

And Susannah said yes. Just like always.

CHAPTER TWO

KANE could run a multi-billion-dollar, fourth-generation, international gem import company. Negotiate million-dollar deals. Understand the most complicated of financial reports. Surely he could do something as simple as light a fire. The flame on the match met the log, sputtered briefly, then poof, disappeared.

Apparently not.

He'd rented the cabin on the outskirts of town, ordered a quarter-cord of wood, picked up some matches at the store downtown, and thought the whole process would be as simple as striking a match to a box, then holding it against a stick.

Uh…not exactly.

Kane let out a curse as his sixth attempt fizzled and died, then stalked outside. He drew in several deep breaths of fresh, country air. An hour ago, he'd been loving the whole experience. Now he was ready to call his chauffeur, have him hurry the hell out here with the limo and drive him straight to the private Lennox Gem Corporation jet.

No. He'd do this. He *needed* to do this.

He stepped back and appraised the situation with logic, thinking back over movies he'd seen and the books about camping he'd skimmed on the plane when he'd taken this impromptu escape from reality. Too many large, thick logs. Not enough skinny sticks. What he needed was more kindling. Not more thinking.

Kane headed outside, blew some warm air on his cold hands, then started picking up sticks from the ground. As he did, his hands brushed against the bare dirt, pushing soil under his nails when he dug into the earth to loosen a stubborn piece. He pulled his hand back and marveled at the sight of the dirt.

Such a simple thing, and yet, he'd never done this. Never had soil beneath his nails. Never cleaned mud from his uncalloused palms. Kane kneeled down and pressed both hands into the soft dark brown earth, squeezing the thick clumps. A burst of rich, earthy scent filled his nostrils. Then the dirt broke apart, slipping through his fingers and hitting the ground again with a soft patter, like fat raindrops.

Kane chuckled. Imagine that. One of the richest men in the world, amused at something so basic as communing with Mother Nature.

Something shivered the bushes beside him. Kane jerked to attention, grabbing his kindling as he did. He thrust his right hand forward, then realized his sapling ammunition made him about as dangerous as a sunflower. "Who's there?"

Or rather, *what* was there?

When he'd made the decision two days ago to come here for more than just Paul's wedding, he'd done a quick research overview of the location, right down to the last lack of amenities, but hadn't thought to look up "wild indigenous animals." For God's sake, the thing rustling around five feet from him could be a bear.

The rustling grew louder, the leaves shaking like can-can dancers. Kane took a step back. Should he head for the cabin? Stand his ground? He could just see the headline now: Idiot CEO Billionaire Dies: Money No Match For Bear In Woods.

The press would have a field day with that one. He'd be the butt of jokes for generations to come.

Then, out of the woods, a bundle of fur came bounding right for him, and Kane started to turn and run back inside, until he realized the bundle was—

A dog.

The mutt, a small barrel of brown-and-white fur and floppy ears, barked at him, then leapt at his legs, tongue lolling, tail wagging. Oh, God, it was *on* him now. Shedding. Kane had no experience with pets. Not unless he counted the one week his mother thought it would be cute to have a pocket pooch, then changed her mind once she realized live dogs actually peed and pooped—and gave the dog to the maid.

This thing was as friendly as a second-place politician desperate for every last vote. Kane took a step back, hands up, his sticks like finger extensions. "Whoa, there, buddy. Get down. Please."

Undaunted, the dog kept coming, launching himself at Kane in another greeting. Kane reached out a tentative hand, and gave the dog an awkward pat on the head. "There you go. Now go on home."

The dog barked, plopped his butt on the ground and swished a semicircle into the ground with his tail.

"Go home."

The dog's tail widened the dirt semicircle, creating a tiny cloud of dust. He barked disagreement. Stubborn.

"Well, if you won't, I will." Kane pivoted, and headed into the cabin. Before he could shut the door—hands impeded by the load of kindling—the dog was there.

Inside.

With him.

"Oh, no, you don't. Shoo." Kane waved out the door. The dog stayed put, staring at him. Expectant. "Go home."

The dog barked some more. This time it sounded like a feed-me bark. Not that Kane would know, of course, but the way the dog was looking at him, he seemed kind of hungry.

"I don't have any dog food. In fact—"

He didn't have any people food, either. For a man who lived his life by a schedule and a plan, he'd done a pretty lousy job of planning this one.

It was that woman. She'd gotten him all turned around this morning. Set him off-kilter. If he hadn't met her, he wouldn't have forgotten to buy food. Or thoroughly check out his surroundings. Or gather kindling. And then he wouldn't have this…this creature staring at him.

A creature he needed to get rid of. Kane opened the door, but the dog stayed put. Clearly, reasoning with the animal wasn't going to work. The dog wore no collar, so Kane couldn't call his owner. And he certainly couldn't keep the thing here. So he did the only other thing he knew to do—delegate.

He fished his cell phone out of his pocket and punched in the number for the woman who had rented him the cabin. "Mrs. Maxwell, do you own a dog?"

Angela Maxwell, an older woman with gray hair and a friendly smile, and most of all, a tendency not to ask any questions once she had a valid credit-card number in hand, laughed on the other end of the phone. "No, dear, I don't. But there are lots of stray dogs around the cabins. Sometimes they get separated from their owners who are on vacation. And we don't have much of a leash law 'round here. People kind of just let their dogs go, it being a small town and all. Most everybody knows most everybody else's dogs."

"Do you know this one? It's brown and white. Short. Stubborn." Kane glared at the dog. It swished its tail and, he swore, grinned at him.

"Well, no, can't say that I do, but I know who would know. You take that pooch on down to The Sudsy Dog. The owner there, she runs a sort of pet rescue thing. She'll help you out."

"The Sudsy Dog?"

"It's a hot dog wash." Mrs. Maxwell laughed at the pun. "Just off of Main Street. You can't miss it. On the sign you'll see—"

"Let me guess. A hot dog in a tub?"

"You got it. Except, he's really a dachshund. It's the cutest dang sign ever. My Orin painted it himself." Then she hung up.

Kane groaned. He looked down at the dog, who looked back up at him, still wagging. "Looks like we're going for a ride."

That got the dog off his feet. He popped to all fours, tail beating a drum of anticipation against Kane's leg. Kane headed out to his rental car, trying not to cringe at the thought of dog hair all over the leather interior, then opened the door. Before he could say "Lay down on the floor," the dog was sitting right beside the driver's seat.

Looked like he was going to have a new best friend for the next few minutes.

Whether he liked it or not.

Susannah latched the wire crate holding Mrs. Prudhomme's standard poodle, then took off her apron and brushed the bangs off her forehead. "You're looking gorgeous after your beauty treatment, Fancy Pants. Which is more than I can say for me."

The white dog let out a woof, then settled down in the cage to wait for her owner to pick her up. Fancy Pants was in here once every two weeks, and though she barely tolerated the manicures, she enjoyed the grooming process.

Susannah glanced at the Arc de Triomphe poster on her wall. Nine hundred dogs. Three hundred cats. And now she was there—she finally had enough money saved to take that trip. To finally experience a life outside this little town. To put all those years of French classes into practice. To dust off her never-used passport. And see the world.

She traced her finger down the two-dimensional image of the intricate carving of the *Departure of Volunteers on the Arc,* imagining herself in a world so much more glamorous than this one. Heck, working almost anywhere would be more glamorous than doing what she did for a living.

The bell over the door jingled and Susannah let out a sigh. Back to work. And back to reality.

"Take this…this *thing* off my hands. Please."

Susannah turned around and found first, an adorable brown-and-white dog at her feet. Then, a fuming best man behind him. The same man from the morning, only this time he was wearing shoes—and a frown. "You again."

"I could say the same thing. *You* work *here?*"

She nodded, not bothering to correct him and tell him she owned the business. Susannah bent down to scratch the dog behind the ears. He let out a happy groan and pressed himself against her legs, his tail wagging. "Is this your dog?"

"God, no. He's some stray who can't seem to get the hint."

She arched a brow. "Seems to be a lot of those in town lately."

Kane leaned an elbow on the cabinet and gave her a

smirk. When he did, the facial gestured transformed him, taking Kane from ordinary to...

Well, extraordinarily handsome, almost playboy handsome, like something out of a magazine. A quiver ran through Susannah's gut, but she ignored it.

"You aren't talking about me, are you?" he said.

"Not at all." Susannah's voice raised into high and innocent ranges. She straightened, the dog remaining by her side. "So whose dog is this? He looks like a Brittany spaniel, or a Brit mix."

"You tell me. He just showed up at my cabin." Kane thumbed toward the door, in an easterly direction. "I'm staying in one of the Lake Everett cabins."

He was renting one of the rustic cabins? Sure, he was wearing jeans and a T-shirt, but the shirt was as clean as one straight out of the package. And his shoes—

Now that he was wearing them, she noticed he had on expensive dress shoes. Not the kind anyone would wear in the woods, especially not that kind of leather, which looked as soft as kid gloves. A high gloss bounced light off the finish, which sported fine, delicate stitching.

He was too...perfect to be the typical renter who came into town in the summer, stayed a week or two for the fishing, then went back to his normal life. Kane Lennox could have passed for a cover model, one of those men clad in a three-piece suit, hawking expensive cologne or designer watches. Except...

Except for his eyes. His eyes held a summer storm, the dark blues of passing thunderclouds, the depths of unplumbed mysteries. Behind his cobalt gaze, Susannah wondered, was the real Kane Lennox the man in a suit, or the barefoot man she'd met this morning?

"Well, I don't recognize this little guy," she said, bending down to stroke the dog's silky ears, distancing herself from thoughts of his temporary owner, "but I'll put up a notice in my shop."

"Good. I appreciate you doing so." Kane turned on his heel.

"Wait. You're not leaving him here, are you?"

He stopped in the doorway. "Of course. I couldn't possibly be responsible for the caretaking of a dog."

"Why not? Are you allergic?"

"I don't believe so."

That right there. The way he talked. That, too, didn't fit with the image of a cabin renter. Some weekend fisherman, or an avid hunter on a few days' break from the daily grind. Every one of Paul's friends was the typical guy-next-door, the kind that sat at the bar and knocked back a couple of beers, told a bawdy joke or two. This guy...not at all that type. How on earth did he ever become Paul's friend, and not just friend, but *best* friend?

"Do you have two hands?" Susannah asked.

"Yes." He gave her a dubious look.

"Two legs?"

The dubious look narrowed. "Yes."

"Then that, along with this," Susannah grabbed a five-pound bag of dry dog food from the shelf and thrust it into his arms, "is all you need for now. Even though we take great care of our shelter animals here, we first try to find foster families for them."

"Foster families. For dogs."

"Yep. And since this little guy is already attached to you, it should be no sweat for you to take him home. He'll do much better emotionally with you, at your house, than he would stuck in a kennel all day anyway. And really, all you have to do is feed him, walk him and wait until his owner claims him."

He stared at her. "Are you *completely* insane? I am not a dog person."

Again, he had that air about him. Not just out of town, but completely out of her world. Out of her social stratosphere. Clearly, the man came from some money. He had to, given the way he dressed and talked. Why would someone like that want to stay in Chapel Ridge, Indiana, any longer than he had to?

While they'd been debating, the dog had left Susannah's side and was now plopped down beside Kane, his little snout turned up expectantly. "Apparently he disagrees."

"He's a dog, he doesn't know any better." Kane waved in her direction. "*You* are the hot dog wash person. *You* take him."

"No can do. I'm too busy with the wedding plans."

"Last I checked, you weren't the bride."

No, she wasn't. And Susannah had no intentions of becoming a bride anytime soon, that was for sure. A relationship, especially a serious one, would only derail the dream she'd worked so hard to fulfill.

"Let's just say that being a bridesmaid doesn't lessen my level of responsibility," Susannah said with a little laugh.

Kane eyed her with a visual question mark, but didn't press the issue. "He's just a dog. Surely—"

"You can handle it as easily as I." Susannah ran a hand through her hair. She didn't need one more thing on her to-do list. Couldn't the man see that? He may be handsome, but he had an obstinate streak as long as the Mississippi River.

She grabbed a leash and collar from the shelf and handed those to him, too, adding them to the top of the dog food. "You might want to put the leash to use right now."

"What are you talking about?"

"Rover there has some needs to attend to." She pointed at the dog, who was sniffing at the room like a drug addict.

"He can wait."

"Only if you don't mind him messing up your car later."

It took Kane a second, then he made the connection. His face wrinkled in disgust. "Absolutely not." He waved at her. "Well, tell him to go do what he needs to do then."

Susannah laughed. "I can't tell a dog to do anything, at least when it comes to that particular bodily function. But you could try walking him."

"Why? He has four paws of his own."

Susannah rolled her eyes, then took the leash and collar out of Kane's hand, fitted them onto the dog, then handed the other end back to Kane. "Walking the dog is when *you* move your two legs. The dog will get the idea, believe me."

He stared at her, seeming horrified by the entire idea. "What about you?"

"I have other things to do, like my job." She started to walk away.

"Wait!"

Susannah pivoted back. And nearly laughed out loud. Tall, muscular Kane looked lost. "It's a pretty simple concept, Mr. Lennox. Put one foot in front of the other. Rover will follow. And if you go near some grass, his natural instincts will take over." Before he could protest or ask her to do it, she pointed toward the back door of the shop. "There's some grass right in the back parking lot. It'll take five minutes, I swear."

Kane scowled, but did as she said, walking stiffly out the door, with Rover following behind, pausing every half second to sniff. Susannah watched through the window, biting her lip, trying not to laugh. Too loudly.

A few minutes later, Rover was feeling much better and Kane had returned to the shop. "*Now* will you take him?"

"Why? You're doing great. And besides, you're on vacation, right? Staying at a cabin in the woods? Think of him as…a roommate."

Kane scowled. "I don't want, nor do I need, a roommate."

The dog had plastered himself to Kane's leg. Susannah gave him a grin. An SUV pulled into the parking lot, a familiar golden furball in the passenger's seat. Her next appointment. "Seems like you have one, like it or not. Now, unless you want to help me bathe a golden retriever, and deck her out with some bows in her hair, you might want to head on home with your new best friend."

An incredulous look filled Kane's eyes. "Bows? On a dog?"

"She's a girl. She likes to look pretty. Even if doing so leaves me looking like a sopping wet disaster afterwards," Susannah added, brushing a clump of dog hair off her T-shirt. God, she was a mess. She looked about as good as her canine charges—before their baths.

Not that she cared, of course, what Kane Lennox thought about her appearance. It was simply that this man had her feeling off center. She didn't care at all if he found her unappealing because she'd just finished giving a poodle a bath.

Except a part of her did care. And that part was annoyed that she worried whether she had any lipstick left on her mouth. Whether her bangs were askew. Whether she reeked of eau de puppy.

"What if…" He hesitated. "What if I help you with your work? Will you take this—" he shifted his weight to the opposite foot "—this thing off my hands then?"

"*You're* going to help me give a golden retriever a bath?"

He dropped the bag of dog food onto the counter. The spaniel watched the kibble transfer and heaved a sigh of disappointment. "Why are you so surprised by my offer?"

"You don't strike me as the dog-bathing type. Especially considering the way you're reacting to your new best friend here."

Kane's stance straightened, consciously, or maybe unconsciously, putting some distance between himself and the small dog. "I'm simply making a business proposition. Quid pro quo."

Susannah considered the neatly pressed Kane again. She doubted he had any experience with pets. Nary a shred of shampooing or grooming background. Yet, she'd give about anything to see this stiff, uppity stranger covered in soapy bubbles and dog slobber.

She thrust out her hand and when he took hers, a spark traveled up her arm, taking Susannah completely by surprise. Attracted? To him?

She couldn't be. He was not her type. At all. For one, he had that air of uppercrust about him. For another, he was too vague about who he was, where he was from. She liked the men she dated to be open, friendly.

Sort of like a good golden retriever, come to think of it. This man was more of a Lhasa apso, too pretty to be a workhorse. But if Kane was willing to take a little of the burden off her shoulders, who was she to turn him down?

"You've got a deal, Mr. Lennox," Susannah said, attributing her reaction to him as being too tired, too overworked. "I just hope you can keep up your end of the bargain."

A slow grin stole across his face. "If there's one thing I always do, Miss Wilson, it's make sure that the deal is a win-win for me, too."

And as that smile widened, Susannah had to wonder whether she'd just been outwitted—and whether she'd be the real loser in this proposition.

CHAPTER THREE

INSANE.

Kane Lennox never made spur-of-the-moment offers. Every move in his life had an intention, a purpose, a plan behind it. He operated like a Mercedes with a well-tuned engine and a navigational system. No breakdowns, no detours and no surprises.

Then what on earth had made him open up his mouth and actually *volunteer* to bathe a canine? He didn't even like dogs. Or at least, he didn't think he did. He had no experience with canines, so therefore, no opinion one way or another, except he knew he had no time for that stray, and no room in his life for a spaniel. And yet, here he was, elbow-deep in soapy water beside a way-too-friendly golden retriever.

He glanced over at Susannah Wilson, who was cooing to the dog as she sudsed the animal's head, and knew exactly what had possessed him to throw that sentence out there. Her. She'd distracted him nearly from the minute he'd met her. Combined with the day he'd had, the dog and his discomfort at being in a strange town, out of his normal element—

Oh, hell, it was really all the pretty woman. The way she had half her blond locks tucked behind her ear, the other half drifting along her cheek in damp waves. And the way she stared at him like he was some kind of weird stalker come to invade her town with a highly viral disease.

The combination—attraction mixed with distrust—sparked amusement in him, and raised his interest in her to a level unlike anything he'd felt in a long time.

Kane had met hundreds of women over the course of his life. Dated dozens of them. But in the circles he traveled, the women were too perfect, too pampered. Susannah Wilson, on the other hand, had a less finished edge to her, like a diamond that had yet to be cut and polished. She was...

Unique.

Intriguing. Very intriguing.

"Hey, I thought you were here to help. That means holding her steady," Susannah said.

"Easier said than done," Kane grumbled. "This dog is as slippery as an eel in an oil vat."

Susannah chuckled, then tightened the rainbow paw-printed lead attached from the top of the deep stainless steel tub to the dog's neck, which shortened the dog's roaming room. "Didn't you ever have a pet?"

"No, never."

"Not so much as a gerbil?"

"No." Kane snorted. "Let's just say rodents wouldn't have gone with my mother's décor."

Susannah gave him a curious look and Kane cursed himself for that slip. He should have lied and told her he'd had half a dozen pets. But he was no better at lying than he was at starting a fire, so his best bet was to keep his mouth shut altogether. Except Susannah—when she didn't have that look on her face that said she thought he was either crazy or criminal—had the kind of personality that begged friendliness. Openness.

She had a wide smile, a deep, contagious laugh and luminous green eyes filled with curiosity. They drew him in, making Kane forget his cover story, his life in New York, and had him instead longing for a little of that magic she seemed to possess. The same magic she used to calm dogs, as easily as if she were a human warm blanket and bowl of puppy food.

Perhaps, Kane thought, studying Susannah's bent head, then letting his gaze slip along her lithe form, he could add a little female R & R to his holiday? After all, he was the best man, and she was the maid of honor. They'd have to be together for the wedding. Wasn't it almost expected that they end up sharing a little more than a dance or two?

The golden retriever squirmed under his inattention, sending a river of water down Kane's arm. "You better hold on there," Susannah said with a laugh and a tease in her eyes. "Or I might end up grooming *you* by accident."

"You wouldn't."

She held up the huge water sprayer. "Accidents do happen, you know, all the time in the workplace."

He laughed. "What is this, revenge for this morning?"

"What revenge?" She gave him a look of pure innocence. "I'm just saying—" her finger slipped a teeny bit on the button, sending a quick dribble of water his way "—I'm the one in control of the water here and you better stay on my best side."

The woman didn't seem to have a bad side, at least in the beauty department. From her bright smile to her deep green eyes, to the shapely curves that begged his gaze to slide down her form, everything about Susannah Wilson drew his attention over and over again. Even in jeans and a T-shirt, she looked as beautiful as the runway models he'd known in New York. Maybe even more so, because there was a natural rawness to her looks that set off his libido and had him craving everything about her.

"You're in control, huh?" he said, grinning. Then he stepped to the right, fast, ripping the sprayer from her grip before she even saw him coming. He gave her a quick blast on the belly, and she let out a shriek.

"Hey! No fair."

"All's fair in war and business, didn't you know that?"

Susannah squirmed around in his grip, which brought her directly beneath him, and made Kane very, very aware of their close quarters. Of her parted lips. Of how all it would take would be a breath of a movement, and he could be holding her, having her in his arms, and even more, kissing her.

"Give that back," she said.

"Make me."

She reached for the sprayer. He feinted to the right. She dodged to the left. They collided, closer. Then again, closer still, and both of them froze.

A second ticked by on the clock above. Another. Susannah swallowed. Kane leaned forward, the game forgotten, the sprayer falling into the tub, his hands moving to brace on either side of the stainless steel, when the dog, apparently sensing the distraction of the humans in the room, gave a quick shake, bathing all of them in soapy bubbles.

Kane jerked back. Susannah spun back around and soothed the dog. "We should, ah, get back to work."

"Yeah, we should."

But he knew—and knew she knew—that as much as they might be pretending to return to all business, there'd been a shift between them from just acquaintances to something a little more.

"What made you decide to do this for a living?" he asked,

changing the subject. *Get your mind in the game, Lennox.* Or he'd end up covered in dog and suds, possibly ticking off Susannah—which would mean she'd send him home with that spaniel. Definitely not a win-win. "It's not like dog washing is on the guidance counselor list of career paths."

She bristled slightly. Damn. He'd offended her.

"I'm sorry. I didn't mean—"

"No, it's okay. This is only a temporary gig anyway. I started walking dogs in high school for extra money, and one thing led to another. Before I knew it, I had a business."

"You own The Sudsy Dog?"

She grinned. "All mine, soap bubbles and all."

Yet another surprise. His esteem for her raised several notches. "I'm impressed. Seems like you're doing really well. A one-woman shop and everything. That's not easy to accomplish."

She shrugged. "It's not much."

He reached out, placing a hand on hers, intending only to get her attention, but when his touch slipped against hers because of the soapy water, a zing went up his arm. The charge detonated in his brain, reigniting the sparks from earlier. When was the last time he'd felt that way?

Seven years ago. Rebecca Nichols, a woman Kane had met in his business-ethics class. Rebecca hadn't come from old money or new money, or anything other than a normal apple-pie-eating American family. They'd dated for six months—six fast and furious, amazing months. She'd been the first woman he'd dated who hadn't been handpicked by his father. And Kane had hoped in some crazy way that Elliott would approve. That his father would see his son's choice in a woman as bold. Unique. Carving out his own path. Exactly the qualities Elliott always preached about to his employees—then seemed to do his best to squash in his son.

Kane and Rebecca's relationship had been fun, exciting and perfect—until Elliott Lennox found out his son was dating an "unacceptable" woman and paid Rebecca's family enough money to convince them their daughter would find a better education abroad.

Kane had gotten the message. His father didn't see his son as bold or determined. Simply headstrong and foolish, particularly when it came to women. Stepping out of line with the family plan would cost him. Dearly. The business and the family image came above everything, even personal happiness.

Kane had been allowed to stay at Northwestern, but only after agreeing to tightly toe the Lennox family line. And the price Kane had to pay? His father sent him a new roommate—to make sure Kane stayed in line.

Now, here he was, for the first time in forever, feeling a powerful surge of attraction again. Real, honest desire. For a real, honest woman, not the kind who put on social airs. Damn, it felt good. Real good. Kane caught Susannah's gaze. Had she been affected, like he?

But no. She gave him a look as blank as a clean slate, waiting for him to speak. Kane tried to refocus, to remind himself he was here for a short vacation, a work reprieve, not a major life departure. He cleared his throat. "It's a lot, believe me. Up to fifty percent of all new businesses fail within the first five years. You should be proud."

Now her gaze narrowed. "How do you know so much about business?"

Damn. He had yet to learn the keys to a good cover story. Keep your mouth shut and know your lines.

He couldn't very well rattle off his real résumé. Kane

Lennox: fourth-generation CEO of the largest gem importing company in the world. Kane Lennox, one of *the* Lennoxes, the family that had been listed in the *Forbes 500* issue for as many years as the magazine had been printed. Kane Lennox: the man with enough personal fortune to buy this town ten times over and still have change left over to line the streets with thousand-dollar bills.

If he told her any of that, she'd look at him just like everyone else did. With awe. With reverence. She'd step back and stop seeing him as just Kane. And for the first time in his life, he wanted to just be—

Kane.

Ordinary man. In ordinary clothes. Doing ordinary things. With no butlers. No limos. No expectations.

"I, ah, just like to read business magazines," he said finally. "When I'm not at work. You know, in the spirit of getting ahead."

"That I can understand." A soft smile of empathy stole across her face. "Working hard for what you want, right?"

"Exactly."

"That's my personal philosophy, too." She shot him a grin. "Who'd have thought I would have anything in common with a guy I met on my sister's lawn?"

He echoed her grin. "A barefoot guy at that."

She laughed. "And here I usually go for the kind who wear shoes."

"I'll keep that in—" The dog wriggled then, shaking off the soapy water, spraying the room, Susannah and Kane with a fine sheen of bubbles. Kane backed up, warding off the foamy onslaught, cursing under his breath. But that only seemed to encourage the golden dog, who shook even more vigorously, her tail becoming a soap-spraying fan.

"What is *wrong* with that animal?"

Susannah laughed. "If you held on to her, she won't do that."

"What do you think I was doing? She's not cooperating."

Susannah arched a brow.

"Hey, if you think you can do a better job holding—" Kane said, backing up and waving at the dog.

"Fine. I'll do your job and you can do mine."

"What are you talking about?"

"You can wash." She tossed a bottle of shampoo at him and moved away from the dog's head.

"No. No, I didn't mean I'd…" Kane stared at the bottle, then the animal, then Susannah, then the dog again. "There is absolutely no way I can wash this animal."

"A deal's a deal, isn't it? You said you'd help. You haven't been much help so far." She gave him a grin that was more of a challenge. And again, his libido roared to life. "Besides, Dakota here isn't so bad. Trust me. She's one of the easier clients I have."

"Easier?" Kane snorted disagreement. He looked at the dog again. The dog looked at him, her wide soulful brown eyes seeming to say, "Oh, no, not him." Kane took in a deep breath, squirted a little shampoo into his hands, then rubbed them together. "Uh, where do I…?"

"Her back. Just scrub it in, using your nails to really get in good under the coat. Think of it like a doggie massage."

Kane made a face. He'd rather massage a person than a dog any day. Specifically the female person beside him. He imagined his touch running down her body, over those luscious curves, followed by his lips, lingering along her long neck—

Definitely not thoughts he should be having when he should be helping her at work. He couldn't help it. Susannah

Wilson had intrigued him—even if she had put him to work on the least fun end of the dog. "Doggie massage?"

"Hey, dogs like TLC, too."

Kane didn't want to do anything resembling a doggie massage, but he also didn't want that stray hanging around his cabin, so he'd suck it up and do what Susannah asked. He leaned forward, splayed his fingers and sunk them into the dog's deep fur. The dog wriggled against his touch, and seemed to almost…smile.

Beneath his fingers, the retriever's fur was thick and heavy, but it parted easily, allowing him access to the animal's skin. He gave Susannah a dubious glance; she offered him an encouraging smile, and he dug in, doing his best to offer—

A soapy doggie massage, as insane as that sounded.

Yet his thoughts kept returning to the blond human beside him. Susannah started humming snippets of an old sixties tune, her hips swaying with the rhythm, her hair catching the dance, as if her whole body was part of the concert. So natural, so uninhibited. So different from anyone he'd ever met.

"I hear people find TLC rewarding, as well," Kane said.

"Mmm-hmm." Susannah stopped humming and stroked the dog behind the ears instead. "That's a good girl, Dakota. Just a few more minutes, pup."

But Kane wasn't thinking about the canine at all. His thoughts were entirely focused on Susannah. In a few days, the two of them would be at a wedding together, which meant he'd be escorting her down the aisle, then dancing with her at the reception. Holding her in his arms. The anticipation drummed in his veins.

Maybe…he didn't need to wait that long. He could ask her out and—

His cell phone began to chirp, its annoying ring cutting through the room like a bullhorn.

"Do you want me to get that for you?" Susannah asked.

"Ignore it. I'm on vacation. Apparently not everyone got the memo." His assistant was supposed to redirect all calls, but a few must have gotten past her eagle eyes. Either that, or his father was already noting his absence. Regardless, Kane refused to be reattached to the business umbilical already.

He had more important things to attend to right this second. Things like Susannah Wilson.

"Speaking of people TLC…do you know a place in this town that has good food? For people, not dogs." He gave her a grin. "I think I have the dog menu all covered."

"You can get great takeout at the Corner Kitchen over on Main and Newberry. The owner makes homemade everything, from strawberry jam to mashed potatoes. It's nothing gourmet, but—"

Kane chuckled. "To me, that'll be exotic, trust me."

She gave him a curious look. "How can mashed potatoes and strawberry jam be exotic?"

He directed his attention to the dog again, using the overhead sprayer to rinse out the shampoo, and to avoid looking at Susannah. Damn. Good thing he'd never gone into the CIA. His cover could have been blown by a three-year-old. "I, ah, eat out a lot. You know, all that nonhomemade food. The Corner Kitchen will be a real treat. I haven't had food like that since I was a little kid." Actually, he'd never had any of that kind of food, but at least saying "since I was a little kid" sounded plausible.

"Did you have an aunt or something who liked to cook?"

"Something like that." A maid. Who'd fixed gourmet meals at his parents' beck and call. And after that, a host of restaurants that served five-star meals, none of which had strawberry jam or sweet-potato pies on the menu.

"What about you? Do you have dinner plans?"

"I'm busy tonight, sorry."

The brush-off came as fast as a bucket of ice water. Something new for him—a woman turning him down so quickly. That must come with the incognito territory.

And instead of depressing Kane, the words invigorated him. Issued a challenge, of sorts. He had finally met a woman who didn't know who he was, had no interest in his money—because she didn't even know it existed. How many women had he met, who had looked at him with dollar signs in their eyes? They saw his money first, and him last, if at all.

All his life he'd wanted to meet a woman—meet people in general—who connected with him for *him*, not for his fortune. Not for his name. He'd thought he'd done that back in college, until his father had yanked the relationship away, with that all-powerful dollar. All Kane had ever wanted from his father was a relationship, but he'd only received criticism and money. Even now, his father was back in New York, probably in the Lennox Gem Corporation boardroom, raising a holy fit over the fact that he had no idea where his son was right now. Not because he cared, but because he'd lost control of the reins.

Which left Kane free to pursue Susannah Wilson, if he wanted to. If she did date him, even only for the few days he'd be here, it wouldn't be because he was Kane Lennox. Or because she hoped to be draped in diamonds by the end of the week. Not because of anything other than she truly liked him.

A curl of desire ran through Kane, a feeling so new, it was

almost foreign. It awakened a hunger he hadn't felt in so long, he thought he might have imagined it all those years ago.

Beside his feet, the stray dog, which Susannah had started calling Rover, raised his snout and let out a little bark. "I think someone else wants a bath, now that Dakota's about done," Susannah said. "We could always do a two-for-one today."

"Sorry. One dog's my limit."

"You did a good job," Susannah said a minute later, thankfully taking Kane's place and allowing him back into doing leash-holding duty. "Dakota's nice and clean. Maybe I'll offer you a job."

"I have one, thank you."

"What do you do?"

"I'm, ah, in the jewelry business." He left it at that. No telling her he imported billions of dollars worth of diamonds and precious gems.

"Really? Do you work in a shop, too?"

"Uh, sort of."

The last of the suds ran down the drain, and Dakota, sensing the end of her bath, began to shake. Susannah tightened her grasp on the leash, and calmed the dog with a few soothing words.

"If you want, I can bring Rover closer, and then we can get that two-for-one," Kane said.

She laughed. For the first time, he noticed how easily her laughter came, how light the sound was, almost like chimes. The animation in her face brought a lightness to him, too, like spreading sunshine. "Now, there's a great business idea. Almost like assembly-line dog washing." She reached over the tub for a giant hose and turned it on, blowing a steady stream of warm air on the dog. In minutes, the retriever was nearly dry.

A teenage girl breezed into the shop, dumping an over-stuffed neon-pink backpack into a chair as she did. Her brown hair, tied back in a ponytail with a blue-and-gold ribbon, swung back and forth as she bounced over to the cage holding the standard poodle. "Sorry I'm late, Suzie," she called over her shoulder. "Hey, Dakota. Hi, Fancy Pants." She cooed at the white dog, unlatching the cage and opening the door enough to give the dog a little head scratch.

Then, as if Kane was a lesser species that she had just noticed, the teenager latched the poodle's cage and sent Kane a half nod. "Oh, hi. Who are you?"

"This is Kane. Kane, meet Tess."

He greeted the girl, but she had already bent down and started petting Rover. "Do you belong to him? He's a cutie."

"No, no. *No.*"

Tess grinned when Rover perked up at the sound of Kane's voice and darted over to his side. "Seems he disagrees."

Susannah opened the gate on the side of the tub, helped Dakota down, then led the retriever over to a grooming table in the next room. Kane took Rover out to the front of the shop. With the distance of a room between them, relief whispered through Susannah. Working so close to Kane had set her on edge.

She'd been aware of his every move, of the water droplets on his skin, of the way his muscles flexed when he'd worked the soap into Dakota's coat. She needed distance from him, from the senses he'd awakened. Most of all, she needed to redouble her focus on her job—and her ultimate goals.

"Tess, do you mind finishing up Dakota and then holding down the fort alone for a little while? There's only one more appointment left for the day."

"Not at all." Tess slipped a Sudsy Dog apron over her

head and helped Susannah get Dakota into place on the grooming table, then readied nail clippers and brushes. "Let me guess. You have ten thousand errands to do for other people."

Susannah smiled, but the grin seemed to droop. "Only nine thousand and ninety nine."

"Just say no. That's what they teach us in health class." She grinned.

"That might work with randy teenage boys, but not when it comes to my sister. She's—"

"Needy. And you're too nice to turn anyone down." Tess patted her on the arm. "I know, I know, I should keep my mouth shut and respect my elders and all that."

"No, you're right." Susannah sighed. One of these days, maybe Jackie would get it and stop relying so much on Susannah. She knew she should simply stop *doing* for her sister, but that was easier said than done. She'd gotten so used to watching out for Jackie, to being both mother and father, that turning that instinct off was nearly impossible. Susannah took her apron off and hung it on a hook. "Anyway, I better get going. I'll be back to walk the shelter dogs later tonight."

"No problem. Me and Fancy Pants and Dakota will put on some Rolling Stones and have a great time. A real party." Tess winked.

Susannah was still laughing when she reached the main part of the shop, where Kane and Rover waited. "Thanks again, Kane. I appreciate your help today."

"Not a favor. A deal, remember?" He handed her the leash, collar and dog food she had given him earlier. "Thank *you* for taking my problem off my hands."

"It wasn't a problem." She smiled. "At all."

When Susannah's gaze met Kane's, a part of him wondered if she was talking about the dog. Or dealing with him. Or something else.

Dating Susannah Wilson could certainly be a great part of his vacation. She was a fiery, beautiful woman, one who had captivated his attention. By spending time with her, perhaps his days in Chapel Ridge would be a lot more entertaining than he'd expected—and come with a few extra perks, beyond a couple of days alone in the woods, time that allowed him to temporarily leave the problems of his real life far behind.

But as Kane left and the door to Susannah's shop shut behind him, he felt something brush up against his leg. Kane looked down and saw the little barrel of brown-and-white fur, right beside him, a determined stowaway. Apparently, leaving his problems behind wasn't going to be as easy as he'd thought.

CHAPTER FOUR

"You are a saint."

Susannah laughed. "Far from it. I'm just helping Jackie."

Kim Sheldon put a fist on her hip and arched a brow. Curvy and brunette, Kim brought her straight, no-nonsense approach to everything from her conversations to her jeans and in-your-face T-shirt logos. Today's read Get Your Ducks In A Row…And Keep Them Outta My Pond.

"Story of your life, Suzie." Kim reached into one of the boxes and pulled out a squat glass bowl, then placed it on the round table. "Tell me again why you're here instead of at the bachelorette party. I mean, that *is* one of the duties of the maid of honor, too, you know. To get rip-roarin' drunk and embarrass herself with a really hunky male stripper."

"I don't have a whole lot in common with those girls."

"What's to have in common? You look at the sexy guys, toss out some dollar bills and throw back some Long Island iced teas." Kim grinned. "For some people, that's the basis of a lifelong friendship."

"Jackie didn't need me there. She needed me here." Susannah opened a bag of clear glass beads, poured several dozen into the bowl, then began arranging light blue and white artificial flowers in the center. After the flowers were set, she draped silver ribbons along the edges of bowl, giving the centerpiece a touch of shimmer.

Kim put a hand on Susannah's as she reached for another bowl with her opposite hand. "She asked you to *pick* the centerpieces up, not *set* them up. So what gives with the big avoidance deal?"

Susannah sighed and sank into one of the cranberry flocked chairs. "Jackie's friends have really never been mine. Every time I'm around them, I feel like a fifth wheel. A square one at that."

"But why? You're just as accomplished as any of them."

"Kim, I *wash dogs* for a living. That's not exactly achieving my full potential."

Kim gave her friend a one-armed hug. "To the dogs, it is. They love you, and so do your customers. Heck, you started when you were eleven, and now look at you. You have your own shop, no debt, an appointment book so full it threatens to explode on a daily basis—"

"While my sister's friends are all married to doctors and lawyers and driving around town in SUVs, talking about their designer baby bags. I'm not just a bridesmaid, Kim, I'm the proverbial old maid of the group." Every time she tried to talk to her sister's friends, the conversations died midstream. Susannah felt like she had yet to experience life, had yet to reach beyond the borders of this small town.

"Jackie's friends are not that bad."

Susannah paused in filling another bowl and traced a circle into the white tablecloth. "No, they're not. I'm just grumpy, I guess. Anxious to get out of town."

"To live your life. Not everyone else's."

"Exactly." She looked up into Kim's understanding brown eyes. "I've waited so long for this chance. Now that Jackie is getting married…"

"You feel like it's your turn."

Susannah nodded.

Kim's hand covered hers again. "Maybe it was your turn a long time ago. Did you ever consider that?"

"What do you mean?"

"Jackie's twenty-two. An adult, Suzie. You stopped being responsible for her a long time ago."

Except that mantle had never left Susannah's shoulders. She'd worn the heaviness like a thick winter coat every day of her life since their parents had died eight years ago and at only eighteen herself, she'd been left in charge of fourteen-year-old Jackie. Jackie had grown up, but that hadn't stopped Susannah from worrying, from feeling as if she should stay around one more day, one more hour, and keep on watching out for her not-always-responsible younger sister. "You're right, but…"

"But you don't always take your own advice." Kim smiled. "When the wedding's over, promise me you'll stop being such a mother hen."

"Definitely. I'm going on a long, long, long trip. Three weeks in Paris by myself. You never know," she added, grinning, "I might love it so much, I might not come back."

"Leave this town forever? You?" Kim scoffed. "I don't think so. You love it here. Everyone who lives here loves you, too."

Susannah rose and stretched out her arms, spinning as she did, as if she could shake all that off. "I want to see the world, Kim. I want to see what else is out there. I want…" She heaved a sigh. "I want to experience everything."

Kim laughed. "What you want is to hit the lottery to pay for these big dreams."

Susannah lowered her arms and nodded. "Yeah, I do. But at least I can take a trip, then come back here and say

I did that, saw that, experienced this. It's a start. And it can tide me over for a long time while I'm living in an apartment and saving for the next trip. It will get me through the next four hundred poodles." She grinned, then went back to the boxes.

Kim's cell phone rang. She checked the number. "Damn. Speaking of family, that's my mom. I'm late picking her up. She has a doctor's appointment and I promised to run her over there." Kim's gaze swept the stacks of boxes, the piles of tablecloths waiting to be laid out—another money-saving step Jackie had volunteered to take on but left in Susannah's lap. "I hate to leave you with all this."

"Go, go. I'll be fine. Seriously."

"That's what you always say, you glutton for punishment." Kim gave her friend a quick hug. "Promise me you won't stay too late. I'll call you when I'm done, and if you're still here, I'll zip back and finish up with you, 'kay?"

"Sure."

Kim hurried out of the ballroom. Quiet descended over the vast room, broken only by the occasional sound of the hotel's staff working in the kitchen beyond the doors. The Chapel Ridge Hotel was small—and not much of a hotel, considering its location in the itty-bitty town. But it had a view of the lake, and because of that, the hotel did a brisk wedding and prom business.

To keep their costs low, Jackie and Paul had chosen to hold their wedding on a Friday in mid-April, before the busy season began. The owner, the father of one of Jackie's high-school classmates, had given the young couple a break on the price and as many bonuses—like a few extra days for setup—that he could.

Susannah dropped into one of the chairs, her leg muscles aching from the long day spent standing, and got busy assembling the centerpieces. The work became mindless. Dumping in the glass marbles, assembling the silk flowers, adding the ribbons. She worked in assembly-line fashion, creating four at a time—all that she had room for on the space before her.

Halfway through the chore, she started counting, then realized she had left another box in the trunk. Damn. All she really wanted to do after a long day at The Sudsy Dog was sit down and stay sitting down. Instead, she pushed off from the table and headed outside.

Once at her car, Susannah wrangled her arms around the heavy box, but the cardboard had wedged itself into the trunk and refused to budge. She turned her face up to the April sun, catching the weak rays, and wished she could insta-port herself to a beach.

"You look like you could use a hand."

Susannah started. Kane stood behind her, leaning against his rental car. He'd traded his T-shirt for a button-down shirt, this one as neatly pressed as a shirt fresh from the dry cleaners. The light blue of the oxford set off the cobalt of his eyes, and for a second, Susannah forgot to breathe. The sun bathed him in a bright golden light, casting glints across the slight waves of his short dark hair. If she didn't find him so aggravating, she'd be forced to admit he was incredibly attractive.

Okay, he *was* incredibly attractive.

"I've got it under—" She cut herself off. Hadn't she had enough of shouldering all the burden? Of doing all the work and constantly saying she was fine? Hadn't Kim told her basically the same thing just a few minutes ago? If she didn't start standing up for herself now, when was she going to? "Yes, I do need some help. Thanks."

He pushed off from the car, his strides confident, purposeful, a man who clearly commanded every situation he entered. He crossed to her, then reached inside the trunk and worked the box back and forth until it was free. From her position behind him, Susannah couldn't help but notice how well his jeans fit, hugging his body as if they'd been custom made. That sizzle of attraction ran through her again, this time at a hotter and faster pace.

"Damn," he said. "What's in here?"

"The last of twenty-five glass centerpieces. And the marbles and things that go in them."

"Feels more like twenty-five elephants." Nevertheless, Kane hefted the container easily in his grip, as if it weighed no more than a box of feathers. "Where's it going?"

"I can—" Suzie cut off the sentence, then pointed toward the building before them. He was offering to carry, and her tired arms and legs were more than willing to take him up on that offer. "Inside the ballroom here. The hotel is letting me set up early. The owners are friends of my parents and they don't have any other events in that room before the wedding."

"Why are you doing this? Isn't it normally the wedding coordinator's job?" He fell into step beside her.

Susannah scoffed. "Wedding coordinator? That's a little out of Jackie and Paul's budget. As it is, they're pinching every penny they can."

"But why you? What about Paul? Or Jackie? The brides-maids? Or the mother of the bride?"

The arrow pierced Susannah's heart with no warning, taking her breath with a searing pain. Her parents had been gone for eight years, and in all that time, she'd worked so hard to keep her emotions in check, to keep that part of herself under control.

But that one little phrase, "mother of the bride," had slammed into her with a reminder of how much she and

Jackie had lost—and how much more Frank and Eleanor Wilson had never seen happen—and never would.

Susannah swallowed hard, locking those thoughts deep in her mental closet, then pulled open the Chapel Ridge Hotel door and held it as Kane entered the building. "The, uh, ballroom is down the hall and to the right."

"And the topic is closed."

"Yep." Susannah slipped in front of him and led the way to the ballroom, then opened one of the double doors. "You can put it on the banquet table. I've got it from here. I'm almost done, anyway."

He deposited the box beside several others marked Wedding Decorations. Then he stepped back and assessed the mass of unassembled bowls, the bags of beads, the jumbled piles of waiting silk flowers. "Are you planning on doing all this yourself?"

"That wasn't the plan, but yeah, that's how it worked out. Tonight's the bachelorette party, so the other brides-maids are all taking Jackie out."

"While the maid of honor stays behind and plays Cinderella?"

Cinderella. Maybe that moniker had described her life until now, but Susannah intended to have her time at the ball. Soon. Just not today. Susannah avoided his gaze and started unpacking the box. "It's not like that. I'm not much of a partier, that's all."

He arched a brow and didn't say anything.

Susannah unfolded a tablecloth and spread it across a round table, smoothing the white surface with her palm. "I thought you were headed for the woods. For your cabin by the lake. You and your new best friend."

"I had a couple other errands to run first. Then I saw you and…here I am."

What other errand? she wanted to ask, but didn't. Again, she reminded herself she wasn't here to get to know him better, even as every instinct in her body told her this man was hiding some serious secrets. Everything about Kane Lennox spelled brooding, dark, mysterious. How on earth could gregarious, blue-collar Paul have ever hooked up with someone like Kane, a man who seemed so far removed from Paul's element, he might as well have been on another planet? "So where's your dog?"

"He's not my dog. And he's sleeping in the car." Kane met her inquisitive gaze. "Yes, I did leave a window cracked. All four of them, for that matter. I'm not completely clueless."

"I never said you were. In fact, you seem like an awfully smart guy." She reached into the box for a second tablecloth, but before she could unfurl it, Kane was there, holding the opposite end. He helped her lay the cloth on the table and palm it into shape. "You met Paul in college?"

"Yes."

"Did you get a degree in history, too?"

Kane chuckled. "No. History was my downfall. The only reason I passed it at all was Paul. In fact, that's where I met him—in Warfare Theory and Strategy."

Susannah returned to her worktable and took a seat before the mass of centerpieces yet to be constructed. "If you weren't good at history, why take a class like that? It sounds a lot more complex than World History 101."

"It was. I took it because it was my duty." At her gesture, Kane handed her a package of trim, lowering himself into the seat beside Susannah.

"For what? The army?"

He chuckled. "Sort of. My family duty. I wanted a certain type of degree, and knew which classes would best fit that, hence the Warfare Theory and Strategy class. My father is a rather exacting man, and he didn't agree *at all* with my choice of college, so I made sure all my class choices lived up to his standards."

Susannah's fingers stilled, silver ribbon suspended midway to the next bowl. "Wow. He was that hard on you? But you...you were what, eighteen already?"

"In my family," Kane said quietly, "age is never a consideration when it comes to duty. And failure is never an option. So I was very grateful for Paul's help in history."

"Never fail?" she echoed softly. She'd grown up in a family that had encouraged every achievement, no matter how small; belittled nothing. She couldn't imagine having that kind of pressure on her shoulders as a child.

Kane went on as if he hadn't heard her. "Paul sat next to me, and not only was he the class clown, something I really needed at that time in my life, but he seemed to know his history better than anyone. He saved my butt more than once."

"Paul *is* a bit of a comedian. It's what makes him such a popular teacher at the high school."

"That I can see." Kane smiled, then handed her a package of beads.

Susannah opened the bag and began pouring the clear beads into a vase. "So was your major also family dictated?"

He cocked an elbow on the table and studied her. "You really like playing twenty questions, don't you?"

"Don't you think we should get to know each other better? I mean, we are going to be latched together for the wedding."

That was her excuse and she was sticking to it. Her interest had nothing to do with the simmering attraction between them. Nothing to do with the way he studied her, or how watching him touch the silk petals had made her swallow, thinking of those same fingers against her own skin. Nothing to do with the way Kane Lennox had awakened something in her that she hadn't expected.

He laid the silk flowers in his hand down on the table. "Is that all? Just trying to get to know the guy you're going to be stuck with for a few hours at a reception?"

Nothing to do with the way looking at him made her wonder if she'd been missing out on something all these years. If Miss Responsibility should take a little vacation—before her vacation.

Susannah inhaled, and when she did, she caught the citrus notes of his cologne. The quiet undertone of man, the low, unmistakable hum of sexual current. "Of course."

Liar.

His hand inched closer to hers on the table, separated now by only the thin paper-wrapped wire stem of the faux rose. The paper rustled against her skin, nerve endings springing awake like crocuses suddenly blossoming under a new sun. "For this week, I'm here on vacation," Kane said, his voice low and quiet, as if whispering a secret meant only for her ears, "and that means I don't want to talk about my job or where I'm from or anything from my ordinary life. I just want to be Kane."

"Okay…Kane."

"And while I'm sure it would be wonderful…" at that, his voice dipped into an even lower range "…to know every last detail about you, I think it would be even more fun to maintain the mystery. So how about I remain just Kane, and you are simply—" his smile quirked up "—Susannah."

Not Susannah the sister, expected to tidy up all the messes. Not Susannah the business owner, working dozens of hours to save for a dream that seemed so far away. Not

Susannah the town daughter, who had always been so responsible, so perfect. Just Susannah—

A stranger. No expectations on her shoulders. No one waiting for her to do anything except, as Kane had said, have fun.

Fun. The one thing she'd been waiting to have nearly all her life.

The idea thrilled her. Excited her. Opened up a possibility Susannah had thought was closed to a small-town girl with a sister to raise, at least until she journeyed to the other side of the world. But maybe, for a few days at least, she could be just Susannah, and see what that would be like.

She put out her hand. "Pleased to meet you, Kane."

Kane's larger hand engulfed hers, his warm palm sending a burst of heat through her body. The insane desire to kiss him surged in Susannah's gut.

She jerked back, away from him. Whoa. This was going way beyond a simple game of pretending to be someone other than herself. Regardless, she did have responsibilities, did have people waiting on her. And did have seven gazillion beads to pour into bowls.

"I, ah, need to get back to work."

A smile crossed his face. "I recognize that trait."

"What trait?" Susannah turned to the table, opening another package of beads and pouring them into the next bowl.

Kane waited until the last bead had finished its tinkling journey into the bowl with its fellow clear friends before speaking. "Workaholic. Type A. Never on vacation. Never taking a break."

"You must have me confused with someone else, because I am definitely not—" She stopped jabbing the flowers into the beads. "Well, maybe a little. But I have a reason for all this."

In a mirror to her actions, Kane opened up some beads and filled a bowl, then began repeating her, flower for flower. "Let me guess. World domination of the dog-grooming industry? Or you're saving to launch a wedding-planner business?"

"None of the above." She slid a pile of the silver bead strings over to Kane, then demonstrated how to attach them, finishing off the centerpiece. "I'm just…saving for the future."

"I recognize that trait. The 'I'm keeping my personal cards close to my chest.' I'm like that, too."

She laughed. "I don't think we're anything like each other. At all."

"You don't." The words came out as a statement, not a question.

"For one, I don't go around barefoot on people's lawns."

"You've never gone barefoot in the grass?"

"Well, of course I've done that. But—"

"Well, I haven't." He pushed the finished centerpiece away, drew a new bowl toward him and set to work again. His work was as efficient and neat as his attire. No wasted movements or time.

"You haven't…what? Walked barefoot on grass?" Her jaw dropped. "But everyone's done that."

"Not everyone has lived the same life you do, Susannah." The beads made their plink-plink journey down, forcing a pause in the conversation.

"Did you grow up in a city or something? Live in an apartment without a yard?"

A muscle twitched in his jaw. "Something like that."

"And is that why you came here? To the middle of the country? To basically Nowhereville?"

"I came here because…" Kane paused, and drew in a breath "…this town is as far removed from my life as you can get. It's…perfect."

"That's all?" Susannah heard a hole in the sentence, though, something left out, like a puzzle piece forgotten under a sofa cushion. Or a closet door locked to keep out prying guests.

"That's all." A smile crossed his face. "And that's all I want to say today, Just Susannah."

She smiled back. "Okay, Just Kane."

But as they got back to work, Kane's words tumbled in Susannah's mind. He'd said they shared similar traits, as if he had her all figured out. But he didn't. Susannah had little in common with this neatly pressed man who clearly came from the other side of the tracks. He lived in a world so unlike her own he couldn't possibly understand her, or have anything in common with her. Or understand her driving need to work—so she could leave the very town he'd purposely sought for his vacation.

They worked for another half hour, exchanging little more than small talk about Chapel Ridge, its residents, and the fishing at Lake Everett this time of year. The bowls got filled, the flowers were placed, the tables were set, and before Susannah knew it, the room was ready. In a quarter of the time she'd expected the chore to take. Kane's cell phone rang incessantly, even though he'd turned it to vibrate. He didn't answer a single call, merely looked at the caller ID display, and then went on with his conversation with Susannah, as if the phone had never interrupted.

She rubbed at a kink in her neck. At the same time, her stomach let out a low rumble, a reminder that she had skipped dinner. Again. "Thanks for your help. I really appreciate it. You saved me hours of time."

"Did you eat yet?" Kane asked.

Her face flushed. He had heard that. "I will."

"Let me guess. Takeout, alone, at your kitchen table, or in front of the television."

"Well…" Susannah thought of lying, then found it impossible to do so when her gaze met Kane's piercing blue eyes. He had a way of looking at a woman that seemed to capture her every thought. "That's the usual approach, yes."

"Mine, too. How about we both break with tradition and—" he paused, then a slight grin came over his face "—eat together?"

"Together?" she echoed.

"No strings, no date. No 'expectations.'" He framed the words with air quotes. "Just two people sharing a table."

Her stomach rumbled again, offering an answer before Susannah could voice an objection. Exhaustion sat heavy on her shoulders, the long day, added on top of dozens and dozens of long days, catching up with her like weight on a rope. The thought of sitting alone at home—again—didn't sound as appealing as it normally did. In fact, it sounded depressing. When was the last time she'd been out on a date?

Way too long ago, that was for sure.

Besides, hadn't she vowed she was going to change her life, starting in a few days? What better way to do that than to change her habits? Step out of her rut?

Except…every time she looked at Kane, a mental alarm bell began to ring. Kane Lennox may have piqued her interest with this "Just Kane" and "Just Susannah" game, but Susannah Wilson lived in the real world, one that wasn't going to go away, not until she hopped on that plane.

Any thoughts of tangling with the fire this stranger represented should be put on hold. Set aside, for later. Or better yet, never.

Because there was something there, something that kept nagging at the back of her mind. Kane Lennox may be Paul's friend, and he may have been working really hard at coming across as just another vacationer, but something told Susannah there was more going on.

But what? It wasn't like people came to Chapel Ridge looking for hot investment properties. Or to seek out long-lost family members. The small town held no dark secrets, hidden treasures or incognito celebrities. She shook off her suspicions. Kane Lennox was here for the wedding and a few days off, nothing more. In that time frame, surely, he didn't expect to kindle anything with her or anyone else who lived in this town.

Even if a part of her wanted to kindle something—the very crazy part, the part that clearly kept forgetting a relationship was *not* on her agenda. Regardless of Kane's hotness level.

It wasn't a date, as he'd said. So she shouldn't worry one way or another about anything. About fire, or kindling or the way something stirred inside her every time Kane Lennox looked at her with that intense stare of his.

She glanced down at her jeans and T-shirt. "I'm not really dressed for dinner."

"That's okay. I was thinking something more…casual." He grinned.

"Casual?" She arched a brow. "As in what?"

"As in trust a stranger."

That was the only problem—she didn't trust him. Not even a little. And what was more—she wasn't trusting herself, or her reactions to him, a whole lot right now, either.

CHAPTER FIVE

"If this is what you call 'just dinner,' I can only imagine how fancy a real date would be."

Kane heard the tease in Susannah's voice, saw it in the way she wagged the hot dog at him, and he felt himself smile and relax for the first time in…well, forever. There was something about this woman that seemed to set him at ease, even as being with her forced him to remain on guard, to remember his place—and who he was, or rather wasn't, supposed to be.

He kept forgetting all of the above, every time he talked to her. Telling her how he'd grown up without ever stepping barefoot on the grass, how he'd never had a pet…he might as well just go around with a Hello, My Name is Kane Lennox and I'm a Billionaire badge.

But so far she didn't seem to recognize him. Most people didn't—unless they read the gem trade magazines, *Forbes* or the *Wall Street Journal.* Or if he put on a suit and got behind the wheel of his Bentley. Then he might as well advertise his heritage.

He had to rehearse his cover story better. Bored corporate exec, here for a little fresh air, some fishing. Saw an opportunity for both when Paul's wedding came up. Nothing more.

Now he and Susannah sat beneath the shadow of a red-and-white-striped umbrella, at a hard plastic picnic table, eating from paper rectangular containers filled with something called Coney dogs and French fries. A sense of liberation ran through Kane, even as he blocked his arteries with another bite, and upped his cholesterol with a second order of fries. "This is not my usual dinner," he said. And thank God for that. If he had to sit through one more dinner party of duck confit and asparagus with Hollandaise sauce, he'd scream.

"Let me guess," Susannah said, leaning back to feed an eager, tail-wagging Rover a tidbit of a hamburger patty Kane had ordered just for the dog, "you're usually eating a bowl of cereal while you watch the news. Or is it delivered pizza with a football game on the big screen?"

He bit back a laugh. He couldn't even conjure up the mental image of himself sitting on the thirty-thousand-dollar leather sofa in his vast great room, eating a greasy pizza. All his life, his homes had held a person who cooked Kane's meals, served the dinners to him on priceless china, then whisked the dishes away with silent precision, keeping his home as pristine as his business's ledgers. Before today, he'd never ordered something as mundane as a hot dog and fries, never imagined himself eating al fresco in a loud and tacky outdoor diner.

But if he told Susannah any of that, he'd raise her suspicions for sure. "Greasy pizza and football, that's me."

He was half tempted to add a few grunts, just for good measure. Manly man. Oof-oof.

She cocked her head and studied him, her deep green eyes drawing him, enticing Kane to open his world to her. "Greasy pizza, huh? Is that why you have your napkin in your lap? Why you used a fork to eat your fries?"

He looked down and realized he had, indeed, done that very thing, while all around him, people were eating the meal with their fingers. Damn. He couldn't have stuck out more if he'd draped himself in a red cape. "My, ah, mother was a big stickler for manners."

Understatement of the year, considering his mother had brought in every available descendant of Emily Post to teach young Kane decorum lessons.

Susannah laughed, and the light, airy sound again reminded him of chimes. "I guess so. Boy, did you miss out on a lot, then. Half the fun of fries is getting ketchup and salt on your fingers."

Half the fun. As he looked at her, at her smile, the light in her eyes, Kane could feel the fun emanating from Susannah Wilson like the heat from her body. She was right. He'd been missing exactly that—and had come here hoping to find that kind of fun. Thus far, all he'd found was a dog he didn't want. If he ever expected this to work, he needed to do what Susannah had said—and get a little ketchup on his fingers.

So, even though it rebelled against every ounce of decorum bred into his society blue blood, Kane put down the fork, picked up the red plastic ketchup bottle and gave it a squeeze. Nothing came out. He squeezed harder, and still the nozzle remained dry.

"Give it a shake," Susannah suggested. "Then try again."

He did as she said. Almost.

Ketchup sprayed across the fries, the tabletop, his Coney dog, and Kane's shirt, dotting everything like a crime scene. Even Rover got a glop. The dog let out a yelp, jumped back, then turned and started licking at his fur with his built-in tongue washing machine.

Kane cursed, reaching for the pile of napkins, trying to

control the tomato carnage. But Susannah started laughing. "You squeezed and shook at the same time, silly. And you did it like a man."

"Like a man?"

"Yeah, with the strength of the Incredible Hulk. It's a ketchup bottle, not a he-man contest. Here, let me help you." She reached out, took some of the napkins, and in an instant, had the table mess cleaned up.

He glanced down. "The table's good, but I look like the victim of a serial killer."

Susannah leaned forward, dipping her napkin first in a bit of water and began to dab at his shirt. Her long hair draped across her face, shielding part of her cheek, her eye, from his view. He reached up and pushed the locks back, and she paused, her gaze connecting with his. Kane's heart began to pound harder. He would have kissed her, but they were in a public place, and he swore half the town was watching them.

"I, ah, don't think that's going to do it," he said, gesturing to his shirt. "Is there a dry cleaner nearby?"

Susannah pulled back, moving to tuck her hair back, just as Kane had wanted to. A slight flush filled her cheeks. "There is, but Abe closes up shop before noon on Thursdays. It's his fishing day."

"You're kidding me. Who runs a business that way?"

"Someone who doesn't believe in working himself to death. Abe's almost seventy, and the dry-cleaning thing is only a part-time job."

"Then why doesn't he hire in some help? Then he could stay open later."

She smiled and waved at the full tables. "Look around you. This town isn't exactly overrun with people who need dry cleaning."

True, Chapel Ridge had that exact kick-back-and-put-your-feet-up air about it that had made him choose to stay here. Few people he'd seen out and about had been dressed in anything fancier than jeans and a T-shirt.

"I'm sorry I couldn't get out the stain," Susannah said, reaching out again with the napkin, then pulling back at the last second as if she'd thought better of the gesture. "I'm afraid all my dabbing only made it worse."

She hadn't made anything worse except his attraction to her.

"It's okay. I'll just buy a new shirt."

"Or you can wash that out. It'll just take a little elbow grease."

"Wash it out?" he repeated.

"Sure. Just put on some pretreatment and throw it in the washer—" She put a hand on her forehead. "That's right. You're staying in the cabins at the lake. You don't have a washer there, which means you'd have to go to the laundromat. And for one shirt, that's a whole lot of expense."

He nearly laughed out loud. What could it possibly cost to run a load of wash? A few dollars? "Yes, I'm sure it is a whole lot of expense, as you say."

She gave him a curious look. Damn. He'd been too formal. He needed to loosen up. Become more of a jeans guy. Kane cleared his throat and tried again. "Yeah, I'd rather not spend the cash, if I can help it. You know, watching the budget on vacation, and all."

"I can wash your shirt for you."

"Oh no, really, you don't have to."

"It's no trouble. How many shirts could you have brought with you for a vacation? You probably need this one, right?"

He didn't. How could he tell her he had dozens and

dozens exactly like this back home? That a shirt like this didn't come from any old corner discount store, but from a tailor Kane had known since he took his first steps? That he could flip out his cell phone and have three more custom made and in his hands in a matter of a day? "You're right," he lied. "I only have a couple of shirts with me."

"Then come on over to my house, and we'll take care of that mess."

Go over to her house. Alone. And do some laundry? Heck, right now he'd probably follow her to sort recyclables. "Sure, sounds good."

But as they got up and tossed their trash away, Kane realized every time he tried to untangle himself from his life, all he was doing was creating even more of what he already had on his hands.

A mess.

What had seemed like a good idea at the time had suddenly turned into one very bad idea. Susannah stood in the laundry room, a bottle of detergent in her hands, and tried really hard not to stare at Kane Lennox's bare chest.

The man could have been a commercial for weight machines. Or cologne. Or, heck, bottled sex appeal. Broad shoulders framed a well-defined chest, with a true washboard abdomen. What kind of workout did the guy do? Whatever his regimen, he'd make millions selling the steps to that physique.

She knew a few women who'd pay just to touch him. Present company not included. Of course.

Uh-huh. Boy, she could barely even lie to herself.

"Do you need to wash anything else? Or just my shirt?" Kane asked.

Damn. He'd caught her staring. "Just a few things," she

said, then turned back to the washer, twisting the dial until water started filling the tub. She dropped his oxford inside, added a few other items from a nearby basket, then closed the lid.

"I'm no expert at this, but don't you need some kind of soap, too?" He gestured toward the plastic bottle still in her grasp.

Heat filled her face. If Susannah could have crawled into the washing machine herself, she would have. "I, uh, forgot." She unscrewed the cap on the detergent and measured the right amount of liquid before adding it to the already churning water.

That's what she got for staring at the man's naked chest. No more doing that. Uh-huh. Easier said than done while he was all exposed like that.

"Do you want to borrow one of Paul's shirts? I'm sure he's left one or two clean ones behind. He's always doing his laundry over here. At least until yours is dry?"

"Nothing against Paul, but he's a foot shorter and fifty pounds lighter than me." Kane grinned. "I don't think anything he owns will fit."

Susannah's gaze drifted back to Kane's bare chest. He had one thing right. He definitely had more build than Paul. "Won't you be…cold?"

The grin quirked up higher on one side. "Not if you aren't."

The temperature between them arced upward, spiking three degrees, five, ten. Susannah took a step back, and bumped into the stainless steel machine. She slid to the right, but there was nowhere to go in the small room. No way to insert any distance between herself and Kane. No way to lower the charge. "Would you like some… coffee?"

He gestured toward the churning appliance. "It appears I'm your hostage, for a while, at least. Do with me what you will."

Temptation curled a tight grip around her. She wanted to kiss him—and wanted to run. Susannah hurried out of the laundry room and down the hall to the kitchen. "Decaf okay?" Because she definitely didn't need the extra stimulant of caffeine.

"Fine with me."

She skidded to a halt on the vinyl tile. New dirty dishes littered the kitchen countertops. Already? When did Jackie and Paul have time to make these kinds of messes?

Susannah knew the answer. Friends stopped by the house as frequently as birds landing on telephone lines. Like their hosts, every guest helped themselves to food and silverware, but did little more than leave the mess behind, as if some troop of elves was going to whisk it away while they were watching the latest blockbuster movie. A half-empty bag of chips sat on the table, surrounded by crumpled dirty napkins and a stack of used paper plates. There were empty soda cans, beer bottles and pizza boxes, and a nearly empty container of mint chocolate chip ice cream melting onto the kitchen table.

Insensitive. Rude. And embarrassing. Before she could pray Kane would get derailed by a sidestep into the living room, he entered the kitchen. And didn't say a word, which said ten times more than if he'd asked her what human tornado had just run through the twelve-by-fourteen room.

Susannah's face heated. "It doesn't always look like a frat house around here," she said, grabbing several of the dirty dishes on her way to the sink. She loaded them into the sink, then started running water while she loaded the coffeepot. Though what she'd said wasn't true, she still felt compelled to defend her sister and future brother-in-law's slovenly habits. Irritation rose in her chest at the renewed mess, but she tamped it down. A few more days, that was all, and then she'd be gone, and they'd be doing their own dishes.

"I'm not complaining," Kane said, but she could see shock in every inch of his face. Clearly the man lived in neater conditions than this. He moved to sit down at the table, found a stack of newspapers from that afternoon in the chair and picked them up, then stood there, as if he'd never seen a pile like that before and hadn't the foggiest idea what to do with them.

"Let me get those," Susannah said, grabbing the papers from him. She dumped the sheets into the recycle bin, then began gathering the trash and tossed it away.

Kane lowered himself into the seat, with all the care of someone placing a delicate vase on an earthquake fault. "So you, uh, live here, with your sister?"

"And Paul, even though he doesn't technically live here, he's here so much, he might as well, too. But I'll only be here for a little while longer." She bustled around the kitchen, working on the trash and the dishes in a two-prong approach. Take the pizza box to the trashcan, on the way back stop for the glasses, drop some of the dishes into the sink. Repeat the process over and over. Rover settled on a small carpet by the back door, curling himself into a furry ball before falling asleep.

"You're moving out, after the wedding?"

"Yes."

"And buying your own house?"

She laughed. "That's not in my budget, no. Dog washing doesn't pay *that* well."

"You must have a five-year plan."

She turned around to face him, putting her back to the sink. "Five-year plan? I'm just trying to get through this wedding, then get the hell out of this town for a little while before I have to return to the real world. Then I'll worry about the rest."

"That's hardly a smart strategy."

"Excuse me? You don't know me. Why do you think you can tell me how to live my life?"

"I…" He paused. "I don't. You're right. It's a bad habit of mine."

"Well, break it." She pivoted back to the dishes and began filling the sink. Regret washed over her. She'd jumped on Kane—and she rarely did that to people. He was merely being honest, and that was the one trait she valued most in others. "I'm sorry. I'm a little tense, because there's been so much going on around here lately."

"And I was completely out of line. I guess I'm just used to being in charge." He put out his hand. "Truce?"

When Susannah shook Kane's hand, electric heat jolted her senses. She broke away and returned to the sink. "If you're hungry, we can, ah, make some sandwiches."

"That would be great."

"Do you mind starting them? Then I can get these dishes out of the way." *And I can avoid looking at your bare chest, and touching you and thinking about touching you. All bad ideas, because I am totally not getting into a relationship right now.* "I know that's breaking all the rules of Hostess 101, but I can't stand a full sink." She shot him a smile, one she hoped covered every one of her traitorous thoughts.

"Sure." Kane rose, and Susannah tore her gaze away from his bare chest for the fortieth time. "Uh…where do you want me to start?"

With me. Just one kiss. Then—

"The fridge. There's ham and cheese in there. We could grill the bread. If you like. Or—" she glanced again at him and her thoughts raced one more time around the hormonal track "—not."

"Okay."

A note of doubt rose in his voice, but when Susannah looked back, Kane was in the refrigerator, searching for the ingredients. And searching some more. And some more. "Try the door," she said. "In the little compartment, above the eggs."

He lifted the clear lid, then pulled out the packaged American cheese slices. "*This* is cheese? In these little wrappers?"

She laughed. "Haven't you had American cheese before?"

He held the package in his hand, flipping it back to front, then front again, his nose wrinkling up with an expression that said he had about as much familiarity with the bright yellow slices as he did with Martians. "Oh, yeah. Uh, maybe."

Who had never tasted American cheese? Before she could puzzle over Kane's reaction, he was back in the fridge. "Where did you say I'd find the ham?"

"In the slim drawer, the center one."

He rummaged some more, then swung around, a second package in his opposite hand. Susannah paused, nearly losing the plate from her soapy grip. If there was a sexier sight than a half naked man holding sandwich fixings, she had yet to see it.

"Is this what you were talking about?"

"Uh…yeah," she said.

"*This* is *ham*." A statement, more than a question. Again, he gave the prepackaged ingredients a curious once-over. "From a deli?"

Susannah laughed. "From a grocery store. I assure you, it's good to eat. Bread's in the breadbox." When Kane remained rooted to the spot, she gave him a helpful point in the right direction. "Mayo's in the fridge, if you want that, on the door. Mustard's right beside it. And butter knives are in the drawer by my hip." She shifted to the right. Kane's gaze followed the movement, hunger darkening his cobalt eyes.

A shiver chased up her spine. So she wasn't the only one with a little heightened awareness.

The glass in her fingers slipped beneath the water, bouncing against the stainless steel sink. Susannah concentrated again on her work, instead of on Kane. He'd be gone in a few days, and so would she. Sharing anything more than a sandwich with him would be foolish.

Crazy.

Irresponsible.

And if there was one word no one would ever find on Susannah Wilson's personal résumé, it was *irresponsible*.

The glass joined plates in the strainer, followed by silverware. Soon the sink began to empty out and the pile of dirty dishes disappeared. She glanced over at Kane, expecting to see a stack of sandwiches and finding instead—

A man who looked lost.

"Need some help?"

"Uh…" Kane held the butter knife in an *en garde* position over the bread and condiments, then lowered it again. "Yeah."

Susannah drained the sink, dried her hands, then moved beside him. "Having trouble deciding between mustard and mayo or something?"

He looked down at the bright yellow bottle of mustard. "I'm just used to a…different kind."

"Sorry. This is all I had. I might have some honey mustard or maybe some Dijon in the cabinet, if you want me to look."

"No, no, I'm fine." He unscrewed the mayonnaise jar, dipped the knife into the container, then slapped a glob of the white stuff onto a slice of wheat.

"You really like your mayonnaise."

"Is that too much?" He stepped back, appraised his work. "It looks like a science experiment gone awry, doesn't it?"

"Hey, it's your sandwich."

"Cooking is not exactly my forte." He held the knife out to her. "You want to take over?"

"I think I better. I can already feel my cholesterol jumping off the charts." She shot him a grin, then, in the space of a few seconds, had two ham and cheese sandwiches assembled and placed on paper plates. She added fresh mugs of coffee, then gestured toward the kitchen table. "We can eat here, or take it outside. Rover might prefer the latter."

"Outside," Kane said. "On this trip, I want to spend as much time outdoors as I can. I spend way too many hours in an office."

An office. He'd said jewelry store earlier. Maybe Kane was a manager, or maybe she was getting too hung up on details. Susannah wanted to ask, then remembered their "Just Kane" and "Just Susannah" pact, and didn't say a word.

After switching the laundry to the dryer, Susannah led him through the kitchen and out to the deck, Rover bringing up the rear. As soon as they hit the backyard, Rover's little legs were in motion, carrying him around the grassy space, from tree to shrub, one massive scent investigation. "He's having a great time."

"I can already attest to the front yard's attributes. I'll let Rover give you the doggy thumbs-up on the back. Or is it paws-up?" Kane gave her a teasing smile.

She sat in a deck chair, easing into the thick cushion, the sandwich forgotten. For now, there was a gorgeous man smiling at her, and she was going to enjoy that. "Thanks again for your help today. I never would have finished without you."

"It was my pleasure. And believe me, I understand having too much on your plate."

Before Susannah could answer him, Kane's cell phone started chirping. Rover barked, startled by the sound, and started running in a circle. Susannah rose, helping to calm the dog. "I don't think they're going to give up unless you answer that."

"You're probably right." Kane flipped out the cell, then huffed a hello into the receiver.

Rover made a barking beeline for a squirrel running across the back of the yard. Susannah followed him, catching snippets of Kane's conversation as she went by, noting the lines of frustration in his face. Because of the dog? Or the caller?

"Leonard, I told you not to call me." Kane paused. "I know you're nervous about this deal, but you and Sawyer can handle it. A week won't make any difference. Might even bring the price down." Another pause. The lines deepened in Kane's forehead and he turned, pacing a tight circle on the deck. "No. Don't tell them a damned thing, Leonard. I'll be back on Monday, and not a minute sooner."

Susannah headed inside with the dog, to retrieve Kane's shirt from the dryer. By the time she returned to the backyard, Kane was tucking the phone away. "I'm sorry you had to step in and take over with the dog. But I appreciate it." He took the shirt from her and began putting it back on, much to her disappointment. "Thanks for washing this. It looks like new again."

"No problem." Though a large part of her wished the washer had messed up and either shrunk or ruined the shirt so she could have gotten that fabulous male view for a while longer. She gestured toward the cell. "Work issues?"

A muscle in his jaw twitched. The easygoing friendliness from earlier had disappeared and an icy tension descended over Kane. "Something like that."

"You're not the type of guy who answers a question with a paragraph, are you?" Susannah fell into step beside him as they crossed the yard. Rover found a stick, picked it up and brought it with him, ever hopeful. Kane ignored the offered game of fetch. What had that Leonard wanted that had made Kane turn on and off like a switch?

"Thanks for the sandwich, but I better get back to my cabin. Come on, Rover, time to go." He fished his keys out of his pocket, thumbed the remote on his rental car and waited for the answering beep.

"You're leaving?"

"I have…a mess I have to clean up. It seems it wasn't as easy to take a break from my life as I expected." He let out a sigh. "I don't know why I thought it would be."

Kane placed a hand on the gate of her fence, then turned back to face Susannah. A flicker of regret filled his eyes, then disappeared, gone as fast as a cloud on a sunny day.

Before she could read anything more, he pushed through the gate, climbed in his car and drove away, a man who clearly had a lot of secrets. And wasn't sharing any of them.

CHAPTER SIX

How did he get roped into these things? All his life, Kane Lennox had delegated. Prioritized. Said no to timewasters. He opened his mouth to do exactly that when Paul beat him to the punch.

"Man, I hate to even ask you for a favor," Paul said, grinning. "But you know I will."

They sat in Flanagan's Pub in downtown Chapel Ridge—or what passed for downtown, considering it was nothing more than a couple of streetlights. The shamrock-decorated barroom played country music, served peanuts and reminded Kane of the ones he and Paul had frequented years ago. The easy camaraderie the two men had had in college had been restored, as if not a moment had passed since graduation. Over a couple of beers, Kane had caught up on Paul's life, his job teaching history to high schoolers, his parents moving to Florida last year—just about everything.

When it came to his own life, Kane remained close-mouthed. What could he say, really? Life's the same. Still rich. Still overworked. No one wanted to hear those complaints.

"When was the last time you took a vacation, anyway?"

Paul asked. "I mean, with your bank account, you must go on some pretty rockin' trips."

"This is my first."

"First?" Paul let out a curse of disbelief. "Dude, in case you didn't notice, you could *buy* the island. You don't even have to rent a room there."

Kane chuckled. "The one thing I can't buy is time. Every year, I'd plan a vacation, and then a crisis would arise. My father or someone at the company would need me. And with my father..." He let out a breath. "It was complicated. I'd stay, you know, because I'd keep hoping that this time if I stepped up and played the hero for the company, he'd beat the drum and say, 'Hey, this is my son, would you look at him?' But he never did. Still, like an idiot, I kept on making those sacrifices. After a while, I just stopped planning trips. My assistant ended up taking most of them, anyway."

"That's sad, Kane. Totally sad."

He shrugged. "I'm here now. I got tired of beating a dead issue. When you called, it was like a lightbulb went off, and I said to hell with it all, walked out that door and came. Worked out great for both of us."

"And I totally appreciate it, too. I even get the whole mojito thing."

"Mojito?" Kane puzzled the word around. "Do you mean incognito?"

"Yeah, that's what I said. And I'm all for it, I mean, I've done the same thing a couple times."

"You have." It wasn't a question, but Kane put the words out there all the same.

Paul nodded, then took a long gulp of beer. "There was this time, back before I met Jackie, so, it was...well, in my wilder days. You remember those, don't you, Kane?"

A grin crossed Kane's face. "Barely."

"I know, you were a Lennox. And a Lennox doesn't party." Paul leaned over, lowering his beer and his voice. "Or at least, he doesn't if Charles the butler's watching."

"But when the butler's sleeping…" Kane added sotto voce, smiling at the shared memory of sneaking out of the dorm rooms with Paul, the only guy on campus who hadn't treated him like a leper because he'd arrived at Northwestern in a limo, and then later, with a butler for a roommate "…that's when the fun can start."

Paul clinked his bottle against Kane's. "You know it, buddy. God, there are days when I really miss those years."

"You and me both," Kane said, taking a deep pull off the bottle, the feel of the glass against his lips foreign to him. Ten years had passed since he'd drunk straight from a bottle, and even then he'd only been able to do it when Charles hadn't been around.

Because a Lennox never acted common.

A Lennox never raised his voice.

A Lennox never created a scene.

And most of all, a Lennox never did anything that would end up in the papers—except be born, get married and die. And all three of those things better be done in a dignified manner, by God, or he'd find himself on the other side of the Lennox name faster than a dog that had peed on the Aubusson carpet.

But in those months before his father had sicced Charles on him, Kane and Paul had had fun. Kane would always be grateful to Paul for that—and for the nights they had snuck out on the eagle-eyed Charles because it had provided much-needed sanity and normalcy in a life as constricting as a straitjacket.

Paul picked a few peanuts out of the small wooden bowl

on the bar, popped them into his mouth, chewed and swallowed. "So, have you told Susannah who you are?"

"No. And I'm not going to."

Paul lowered his voice. "No one knows who you are? How is that possible?"

"Nobody knows who *runs* a company, Paul. They see the ads for Lennox Gems, sure, but it doesn't say CEO Kane Lennox at the bottom or anything. As long as my father doesn't start some media frenzy, I'm fine. And I don't want to tell Susannah or anyone else who I am because—" Kane toyed with his beer bottle "—I'm tired of people who look at me as a dollar bill first and a human being second."

"Your secret's safe with me, Kane. I owe you." Paul clapped him on the back.

"You owe *me?* For what?"

"You were my sanity for getting through college, too. My old man, he thought a history degree was a waste of time. A waste of my football scholarship to Northwestern." Paul spun the bottle on the bar. "Who was I kidding, though? I was never going to play pro ball. You gotta get fairy dust for that kind of career. I needed a real plan. A real job. But my old man, he wanted the NFL or nothing. You…you understood, Kane. And I don't know if I ever told you how much that meant to me."

Kane shrugged. "You didn't have to."

"Yeah." Paul nodded, in the near silent communication of men. Then he grinned and tapped his beer bottle against Kane's. "If Susannah tries to kill me for keeping a secret from her and her sister, you will hire me a bodyguard, won't you?"

"Of course."

"Good." He unearthed some cashews this time. "And you sure you don't mind doing this favor for me tonight?

It won't be as fun as some of our midnight raids on the women's dorm rooms, but it won't be horrible, either."

"Now I know why you never went into sales," Kane deadpanned.

Paul chuckled. "Susannah's my sister-in-law, Kane. She's not a five-year-old dented Caddy I'm trying to unload. She's…nice."

"I know she is." Very nice, indeed. But Kane kept those thoughts to himself. If he spoke them aloud, Paul would be running a matchmaker service right in Flanagan's. What Paul wouldn't understand was why Kane and Susannah would be wrong for each other in the long run.

Susannah Wilson was the kind of woman men had permanent thoughts about. The kind of woman a man married. And the exact kind of woman—

His father would ship off to Europe for being "unacceptable" as a Lennox family addition.

Paul dug through the bowl of nuts again. "Damn. All the cashews are gone. And the peanuts. Larry, are you getting cheap on the nut mix again?"

"No, you're just getting greedy," the bartender said, giving Paul a good-natured grin.

"Next he'll be serving popcorn and calling it a meal." Paul pushed the bowl away, then turned back to Kane and gestured over his shoulder after the stout bartender had crossed to the opposite end. "He's a good guy, Larry is, but he's had a hard time. I went to school with him."

"What do you mean, hard time?"

"His kid's got leukemia." Paul shook his head. "'Bout breaks my heart. But Larry, you'd never know it. He's got a smile for everyone who comes in here. The town threw him a benefit a few months ago, to raise some money for the medical bills. That's what small towns are like, Kane. They're like families, only bigger."

"And without the politics."

Paul chuckled. "Trust me, small towns still have politics. Speaking of weird things in small towns, don't go running around barefoot on the lawn anymore, either. What was that about, anyway?"

"My feet were hot."

Okay, that had to be the lamest excuse known to man, but Kane wasn't going to get all honest with Paul. He had no desire to tell another guy—good friend or not—that he had had this sudden urge to feel spring grass beneath his toes. Paul would label him crazy for sure.

Paul must have agreed with the lame part because he laughed, then shook his head. "Yeah. Whatever floats your boat. But don't do it again. You'll scare the neighbors."

Kane nodded. "Are you sure Susannah wants to go out with me?"

"Let me put it this way. Jackie wants to be alone with me. Susannah lives with us, and I know for a fact she doesn't have any plans for tonight, so she should be easy to persuade. Either way, we're desperate, so if you don't get Susannah out of the house…" He put up his hands.

"You're getting married in three days, Paul."

"In all the years you've known me, have you ever called me a patient man?" Paul tipped the beer to emphasize his point. "Exactly. Nothing against Susannah, but Jackie and I just want a night alone. I need to talk to Jackie anyway. She's running through our wedding budget like it's Halloween candy. I love her, but she's got no concept of money, or taking things easy. But talking to Jackie requires a little…buttering up, if you know what I mean." Paul grinned. "So do me a favor, Kane, take Susannah out. Let her show you the sights."

Kane laughed. "In Chapel Ridge? That'll take, what, ten minutes?"

Paul rose and clapped him on the back. "Improvise, my friend. If I remember right, that was your *real* major in college. Especially when it came to fooling the butler into thinking you were behaving."

"Fishing. You want to take me fishing." Susannah stared at Kane Lennox, sure she had heard him wrong. Of all the vacationers she had met, this man looked the least like a fisherman. Especially wearing those designer shoes and pressed jeans. Granted, he'd exchanged his button-down shirts for a T-shirt and a green Chapel Ridge sweatshirt, but he still had that dressed-up air about him, despite the more casual attire.

Nevertheless, Kane was well stocked with fishing accessories. He held out a pole to her, then raised a plastic tackle box into view. "It's always more fun with two, don't you agree?"

"What about Paul? He's your best friend, isn't he? And fishing is a guy thing."

"Paul has…plans."

Susannah shot a glance at her future brother-in-law. He spread his palms up and gave her a blank look of innocence. "Plans. Sorry."

Plans? She couldn't remember Jackie mentioning anything. "Wha—"

Then over her shoulder, she caught a glimpse of Jackie, setting out a trio of candles on the dining room table. Jackie, wearing a black skirt, and a sexy red V-neck shirt, her hair long and curled.

Date hair. Date clothes. Date candles.

The lightbulb burst in Susannah's brain. Her face

heated, and she took a step back. "Oh. Those plans. Uh...I should...uh..."

"Fish," Kane finished, filling her hand with the pole and giving her a grin. "You should go fishing. With me."

"Or you can stay with us," Jackie said, with all the conviction of a low-willpower dieter in a cookie factory. "Paul and I were just going to rent a movie and—"

"Kane's *really* looking for a fishing partner," Paul cut in, taking Jackie's hand and giving it a squeeze. "You know how it is, Suzie-Q, when you go on vacation, and you want to do stuff, but you don't really know anyone to do anything with."

No, she didn't, she wanted to tell them. Because she had never been on vacation. Had never left this town. Instead, she pasted on a smile, gave the fishing pole a little shake, and grabbed her denim jacket. "Sorry I'll miss the movie," she said. "Save me some popcorn."

"Before you poke my eye out," Kane said, slipping into the driver's seat of his rental car, opposite Susannah, "let me take this and—" He took the fishing pole, rolled down the window and threw it onto the ground.

"What are you doing?"

"Disarming you. Before you blame me for what happened back there. Or...let me take all the blame, anyway."

She crossed her arms over her chest. "Were you in on the plan?"

"Well..." He swallowed. "Maybe a little. But I had no idea they were going to shove you out the door like a—"

"Houseguest who had overstayed his welcome? Like a repo man who showed up to take away the family's minivan just before the soccer playoffs? Like—"

He put up his hands. "Truce. I get the hint. And I'm sorry."

Susannah sank further into the seat. "Apparently it's me who can't get the hint."

He started the car and put it into gear, pulling away from Jackie and Paul's house. Rover settled down in the backseat, clearly content to go for a ride in the car. "Don't feel bad. Paul and Jackie are just too focused on their own merger to realize the collateral damage they're leaving in their wake."

"Either way, I won't be here to be caught in the ripples anymore."

He glanced over at her. "Where are you going?"

"Travel, see the world. As soon as the wedding's over. I'm closing my shop and getting out of town for a few weeks."

"Really? Why?"

"Because I want more. I want that life. The life everyone else seems to have and I seem to have missed." She traced a pattern along the window.

He let out a little laugh.

"What?"

"Nothing."

"You find my idea funny."

"No. Just...ironic." He took a left, not going anywhere in particular that Susannah could tell. They certainly weren't going fishing, since the fishing pole was back on Jackie's lawn.

"How so?"

"Some people," he began, seeming to choose his words carefully as he made yet another turn, "seek out the opposite of what you are looking for. They find the bright lights and big city aren't all they're purported to be, and instead, they reach for the solitude of the very life you already have."

Susannah shook her head. "I can't imagine why. There's nothing here that I want."

"Maybe so. For you." He turned down one more road, then stopped the car. They had, after all, stopped by the far end of Lake Everett. A few feet away, the still waters glistened under the moonlight, dark and tranquil, holding their secrets in an almost ebony peace. Far across the lake, the lights of the hotel twinkled, flanked by the flicker of the occasional firepit from the cabins.

"I thought we weren't going fishing."

"We aren't. But unless you have another plan, we still can't go back to your house, and I didn't think you wanted to be…well, alone in my cabin. And almost everything else in this town seems to shut down after five."

"Exactly why I want to leave and eventually move away, if I can take my business elsewhere."

Kane turned the car off and pocketed the keys, then grabbed a black leather jacket from the backseat. "Come on, let's take a walk."

Alone with Kane. In the dark. Temptation curled its grip around Susannah.

She wanted to resist. Knew she should. She had no time for a man in her life, no room for a relationship, especially one with someone who would be gone soon. "I should probably go to work. Get some paperwork done—"

He reached out and clasped her hand, cutting off her words and, with the electricity in his touch, her breath. "There's always going to be time for work. Believe me. But there won't always be a night as beautiful as this. Take it from someone who knows."

Then he got out of the car and came around to her side, opening her door before she could disagree. Rover clambered over the seat and leapt out of the car, bounding toward the lake.

Susannah stopped, drinking in the view. How long had

it been since she'd taken the time to admire the lake at night? "It's like diamonds," Susannah said softly. "The moonlight, on the lake."

"I agree," Kane said. "Did you know, like snowflakes, no two diamonds are alike? The oldest diamond is billions of years old, yet we've only been mining them for a couple thousand years."

"Wow. I didn't realize that." She followed him down the grassy path to the lake, reaching out to steady herself with a tree. Rover scrambled along with them, stopping every few seconds to unearth a new treasure, from pinecones to rocks.

"They're amazing gems, diamonds are, and one of my favorites. Cutting and polishing a stone can take away as much as half of its size. It takes a true artisan to be able to see a raw diamond and realize its potential." Kane bent over, picked up a handful of rocks and jingled them in his palm. Beneath the stars, strains of quartz glinted.

She ran a finger over the marbled seam of the largest rock, then drew back. "How do they know what shape to cut the diamond in?"

"Ah, that's where skill comes in." Kane dropped the rocks to the ground, then dusted his palms together. Rover headed off to nose at the edge of the lake, darting into the water, then back out, as if playing a game with the lapping waves. "Not just anyone can be a diamond cutter and polisher. It's a skill that's passed down from generation to generation. Fathers teach sons, grandfathers teach their grandsons."

"No mothers teaching daughters?" She grinned.

"Some. But mostly, it's about getting quiet with the stone. Looking at it, hearing what shape it should be, and being true to the stone's nature before you lay a single tool against it."

Susannah bent down, grabbed a thick rock that had likely sat at the edge of this lake since this beginning of time, and hefted it in her palm, as if it were a rare gem. "Everyone's always looking to create the next Hope diamond, is that it?"

"No, not really. What gets jewelers and people who work with gems excited is finding that next rare jewel. Or seeing the one no one else has ever seen. A red diamond, for instance, is the rarest of all. And then the public will create a demand for something like chocolate diamonds, which are diamonds with brownish tones. Years ago, no one wanted them. Now, they're the next hot thing."

Susannah replaced the rock, then rose, brushing her palms off on her jeans. "Working in a jewelry store must be romantic." She hugged her arms around her chest, a slight barrier against the cool evening breeze. Her denim jacket was too light for the midspring weather and she found herself wishing she'd dressed warmer.

He laughed. "Romantic?"

"All those couples coming in, picking out engagement rings. All those people thinking forever is just a gold band away."

Kane took off his leather jacket and draped it over her shoulders, settling his palms on her for just a second, as if cementing the coat in place. She leaned into his touch, then drifted away before shooting him a smile of gratitude. She couldn't remember the last time a man had done something so chivalrous—without being prompted.

"You sound mildly against the prospect of marriage," Kane said.

"For me, not as a rule for everyone."

"Because?"

"Because I think that not everyone ends up with the fairy tale. That's all."

"And because you have other plans."

"Exactly."

They began walking the perimeter of the lake, a slow stroll, allowing the spaniel to continue his playful game with the water's edge.

"So what would you do if you suddenly met Mr. Right? Say, while you're hiking across the Alps or touring Big Ben?"

She laughed. "The chances of that are pretty slim."

"Perhaps."

He stopped, then picked up a rock and skipped it across the serene water's surface. It bounced twice before sinking to the bottom. "That's exactly why I never tried out for the baseball team."

"You need a flatter stone," Susannah said. "That one was too round."

She bent, searching in the earth for the right rock, then when she found one, stood and put her palm out flat to show Kane. "Try this one."

"Show me."

"Okay. But I'll warn you, you're dealing with a pro here."

She turned slightly, then drew her arm back, and in one fluid movement, let the rock go. It skipped five times, bouncing in lower and lower arcs, before slipping beneath the inky water.

"Wow. You're really good at that."

She shrugged. "I told you so."

"I mean it. How did you get so adept at stone skipping?"

"I used to have a lot of time on my hands after school. Waiting on Jackie to catch up, while we were walking home."

"Was she just a slow walker?"

"No. She was what you call a social butterfly. Still is. She had to stop and say hello to everyone she saw. Instead of waiting like a third wheel, I'd go do my own thing and she knew I'd be here at the lake. I'd skip stones or climb trees or do any of the tomboyish things that my sister thought were the kiss of death."

"Kiss of death?"

"For a respectable social life." Susannah laughed. "Maybe she was right. After all, she's the one who's getting married. And I'm the one…still skipping rocks."

Kane slipped both his hands into Susannah's and turned her in the dark to face him. Beneath the silvery beams of the moon, her countenance glowed with a faint shimmer, bouncing off her eyes, her lips. She'd been wrong. It wasn't the lake that glittered with diamonds, it was Susannah. Her eyes. Her hair. Everything about her. He captured her jaw, turned her mouth up to meet his, intending only to catch her attention, but instead finding he had caught himself in the spell ten times more.

"You're much more than that, Susannah. You're…so different from anyone I've ever met."

"So plain, you mean. So—"

"So unique." His thumb caressed a lazy circle along her jawline, silky peach skin working almost like a balm to his tough exterior. To a man who had left New York jaded, overworked, sure there was no one left in the world who possessed an innocent bone in their body, she brought a sense of peace, of hope, to Kane's soul.

Susannah Wilson seemed to be the very embodiment of what women should be. Nurturing. Unpretentious. And yet, at the same time, a challenge.

"Listen, you don't have to butter me up," she said, "just because you're the best man. I'm not feeling left out of the wedding or anything like that. I know Paul and Jackie probably sold you some kind of sob story about the poor eldest sister, the spinster, as if God forbid that's some kind of crime around here. In a small town, it's like a disease not to be married. But I'm—"

"You talk too much," he said, silencing her speech with a finger to her lips.

"I—"

"I can see it'll take a lot more to shut you up," he said, teasing. Then he leaned forward and did what he'd wanted to do nearly from the moment he'd met Susannah.

He kissed her.

At first, she held her ground, unyielding to his touch, then finally she softened against him by degrees—her lips, her face, her touch. She leaned into his body, her hands ranging up his back, reaching higher, until she had him pulled against her, tight, firm.

And Kane's world exploded.

Damn. He had kissed women. Dozens of them. Women who purred against him. Women who stood still as statues. Women who made it their life's mission to cater to his every need. But never had he kissed a woman who poured herself so wholeheartedly into something so simple as a kiss.

Susannah tasted of the bitterness of coffee, mixed with the sweetness of cookies. The air held the vanilla and citrus notes of her perfume, the wave of her body heat.

His grip tightened around her, desire singing its siren song through his veins, pounding in his head. He tangled his hands in her hair, letting the silky strands slip through his fingers like a rainstorm. Knowing that for as long as he lived, this would be a kiss as unforgettable as his first.

Finally, Susannah stepped back, out of his embrace. "What…what was that?"

He grinned. "If I have to tell you, then maybe you want to repeat health class."

She swatted him gently on the shoulder. "That wasn't what I meant and you know it. Why did you kiss me?"

"Because I wanted you. Simple as that."

"I don't want a relationship."

"Did I say I did?"

"But…" Confusion warred in her gaze. "Why kiss me then?"

"Does every kiss have to lead to a walk down the aisle with you?"

She laughed. "You're in a small Indiana town. Things out here are different. We don't do too many things halfway."

He reached out and trailed a finger down her cheek, watched her sharp inhale of breath, as an echoing roar ran through his chest. "Maybe it's time you did, Suzie-Q."

CHAPTER SEVEN

THE world had turned inside-out, upside-down and sideways.

Why did Kane Lennox have to go and kiss her? Just when Susannah thought she had everything on an even keel, thought she had a plan for the days ahead, for her life—okay, maybe not her life, but at least for the next few weeks—he'd gone and added an X to an even equation. She didn't need a relationship, even a temporary one.

And she especially didn't need to be kissed by a man who made her wonder if she'd been missing out on something all her life, as if there was some great secret every other woman in the world had been holding tight—and she'd just now discovered.

Because, damn, that man could kiss.

Definitely better than her first boyfriend, Darryl Taylor. Ten times better than Tim Mills, her last boyfriend—and the one she'd dated the longest, for two years. Not that any of the men she'd dated had been bad or inattentive. Simply clearly lacking something in the experience department.

Except…more experience meant Kane had a lot of women to choose from. A lot of women in his dating past—who also must have had plenty of experience. If that was so, why would he want to date someone he'd met on vacation, a woman from a small Indiana town? Unless, as he'd said, all he wanted was a quick little fling?

Nothing more than kisses?

And did Susannah want the same thing?

"A penny for your thoughts." Kane slipped his hand into hers and began walking with her around the perimeter of the lake.

"Why are you here? Besides the wedding?"

"My job is stressful and I thought I could use a few days off. I haven't taken a vacation in...well, forever."

"Yeah, but why here? Chicago is only a few hours away. Detroit. Cincinnati. Heck, you could hop on a plane and be about anywhere but here."

"I live in a city. I wanted something different."

"And I live in the small town. I want the city. Guess we're the two proverbial mice."

"Or maybe, once you get to the big city, you'll find out that everything you ever wanted was here to begin with."

"Maybe once you spend more than a few hours here, you'll realize you were crazy for thinking there was anything more exciting than watching corn growing here."

He laughed, a deep, hearty sound that she couldn't help but echo. "Maybe."

Rover came charging up from the water's edge and ran a frenzied circle around their legs, then took off for the water again, as if trying to entice them to join him in his hunt for creatures at the lake's edge. Kane chuckled at the spaniel's antics. "Why don't you own a dog of your own?"

"I work with them all day, and that's enough for me. Plus, I want to travel, and it wouldn't be fair to the dog to just keep leaving him or her home, or boarded at a kennel. But I love dogs. They're my favorite animals in the world."

"Why? I mean, cats are cute, too, right?"

Susannah chuckled. "Yeah, I like cats, too. But there's something about dogs. You always know where you stand. They're honest. That's why I started working with them. There's none of that rubbish you get with people. Dogs are easy to read, easy to please, and they give back what they get. Honesty is important to me, and so I chose the most honest creatures on earth to be my coworkers, of sorts." She smiled.

"Maybe I should hire in a bunch of golden retrievers instead of stuffy executives."

Susannah laughed. "You might get better results. And even better, they work for biscuits."

They walked a while longer. Kane's hand captured Susannah's, as naturally as if they had always done this, always walked together. She held on to his palm, allowing herself to enjoy the little thrill that ran through her whenever Kane touched her. Out in the middle of the lake, a fish jumped, spoiling the serene surface. From far across the lake, someone turned on a stereo. With the clear night, the sounds of the song carried crisply on the air.

"Someone must have read my mind and added a little mood music," Kane said. "Would you like to dance?"

Susannah shook her head. "I have a lot of skills in life. Dancing is not one of them."

"You can't be the maid of honor and not dance."

She shrugged. "All eyes will be on Jackie, anyway."

He stopped walking, swung around her, captured her hands and then her gaze. Whenever Kane Lennox looked at her like that, a quiver began in Susannah's belly, and grew into a tingle that spread through her entire body. The breeze seemed to catch in the trees, the night birds stopped calling, the water stopped lapping at the shore. All Susannah heard was the rapid beat of her own heart, the heavy intake of her breaths. "I doubt that," he said. "Jackie may be the bride, but that doesn't automatically make her the most beautiful woman in the room."

Her face heated, and she broke eye contact with him. He didn't know the Wilson sisters. Jackie had always been the center of attention—and would be on Friday night, too. And that was fine with Susannah. Her turn was just around the corner.

Kane ran his thumbs over the back of her hands. She looked into his eyes, unable to forget his kiss from a moment ago, wishing he'd kiss her again, under this quiet veil of night.

"Dance with me, Susannah," Kane said softly, and she couldn't resist. Across the lake, the music had segued into something slow and easy, the bass throbbing out a beat as hot and heavy as their earlier kiss. "It seems they're playing our song."

"*This* is our song?"

Before she could protest, Kane slipped on arm around her waist, then put her hand into his opposite palm. She fit into his body with the ease of a missing puzzle piece, warmth seeking warmth, their legs stepping easily in rhythm, as if she'd done this all her life. "Any song that lets me do this with you is our song."

Oh, boy. She was in trouble.

Kane Lennox might be saying one thing—that he wanted nothing more than a few kisses, a turn or two around a dance floor, and she might be agreeing, but everything about this man, his charm, his easy way with her, sent Susannah's pulse racing into another stratosphere, and she simply couldn't imagine a quick entry and an even quicker exit.

Because she'd already begun to crave more. Another kiss. Another dance. And…

More? What if he stayed, beyond the wedding? What if she did? What if…

But no. That wouldn't happen. Because both of them had plans to leave town after the wedding. And this dance, these kisses, would be it. She could do this. She could have this moment of fun.

She closed her eyes and gave in to the music. To his touch. To the easy feel of his body against hers. The temptation for more rolled over her, whispering to her to abandon everything, just leave every responsible thought in her head behind.

"That's it," Kane said quietly, his voice as dark as the night. His hand inched up her back, helping her fit into his groove. "Just let yourself be, be one with the rhythm, with me."

From far off, a night bird called, his song an interruption to the one on the stereo. The sound brought her back to reality, reminding Susannah she could have a temporary reprieve from her responsibilities, but anything more was out of the question. She had a sister and a business to worry about. Until the wedding was over and until she was on that plane to Paris, her life really wasn't her own to have. Jackie still needed her—it was clear in all the bad decisions her sister kept making. And so did her business. Until then, a relationship could wait.

Susannah jerked back, out of Kane's arms. "I…I can't. This is…a bad idea."

"Dancing? Is a bad idea?"

She shook her head, trying to clear it. Of this man, of the possibilities he'd awakened. "This is more than dancing, and you know it."

"And what's so wrong with that?"

She turned away, and started heading back to his car. Rover

trotted alongside. "I really do have some work to get done tonight. If you don't mind dropping me off at the shop—"

"I do mind. You need to take time off as much as I do."

She whirled around. "Who asked you to drop into town and suddenly start telling me how to live my life? I got along just fine before you showed up."

He bit his lip and didn't say anything for a long moment. Then he nodded. "Okay. You win. I'll shut up and drive."

She grinned. "Now, that's got to be the best thing you've said all night."

He chuckled, the tense moment between them gone. "You really know how to romance a man, Susannah Wilson."

"See, that's the trouble, Kane," Susannah said with a sigh. This man had yet to hear her, really hear her. "I'm not trying to romance you. At all."

Even if a part of her kept saying otherwise.

Kane had lied.

Well, partly. He did drive Susannah to The Sudsy Dog. And he did drop her off. But he didn't go back to his cabin. He headed over to Flanagan's Pub, took a seat at the bar, and told himself several times he should go home, and instead lingered in downtown Chapel Ridge.

"So, are you a friend of Paul's?" the bartender asked.

Kane nodded. "In town for the wedding."

"He's a good guy. Him and Jackie both." The bartender put the glass he was drying on the shelf, then stuck out his hand. "Name's Larry."

"Kane." The two men shook. "I'm staying out at one of the lake cabins."

"Good fishing out there."

"So I hear."

Larry put a foot onto the stool beside him, his face drawing pensive. Behind him on the wall-mounted television, a sports commentator was droning on about spring training. "Yeah, I used to get out there all the time with my son. I miss it."

"Paul told me about him. I'm sorry to hear about all you've been through."

Larry shrugged. "It's been hard, but you know, living here makes it easier. Knock small towns all you want, but me and my wife, we got plenty of friends around here. Friends and family, they make 'bout anything easier to bear, don't you agree?"

"Yeah."

Though Kane's experience with either was slim, at least until he'd arrived in Chapel Ridge. Odd, in a matter of days, he felt closer to the residents of this town than he did to most of the executives at Lennox Gem Corporation.

"Anyway," Larry said, waving off the discussion, "you didn't come here to hear all about my problems. What can I get you?"

Kane was about to order a beer when he saw Susannah come out of her shop with three leashes in her hand—and three equally large dogs attached to the end of those leashes. "Uh, nothing, thanks. I just saw what I wanted outside."

Then he left, hurrying to his rental car to get Rover before heading over to Susannah.

"I thought you were going home," she said.

"And I thought you were going to do paperwork."

"This is one of the other parts of my job." She held up the leashes. "Walking the shelter dogs three times a day."

"Alone? At this time of night?"

Susannah laughed. "This is Chapel Ridge, Kane. Not the crime capital of the world. I'll be fine."

"If I promise not to tell you what to do with your life, how about you let me help you walk the dogs?"

She shouldn't let him. After all, "Just Kane" had this wall up she couldn't seem to see over. She understood him wanting a little privacy while he was on vacation, but she also had a nagging sense that he was hiding something—something big. And those red flags were becoming increasingly hard to ignore. "I have this under control."

"I'm sure you do. I'm simply sharing the burden." He reached over and took one of the leashes from her, brushing off her protests just as her heart did the same thing with her better judgment.

"You couldn't even walk a dog the other day."

"I'm a fast learner. Watch." He put a leash in each hand and strode forward. Except his plan didn't go the way he expected. Rover took one look at his new walking companion and let out a growl. The second dog answered with a growl of his own, and before Kane could say "stop," the two of them were circling each other with angry barks.

"I'll trade you." Susannah reached across him, took the leash of the black dog, walked that dog forward and away from Rover, then gave Kane the lead to a small white pooch instead. "You picked Dexter. He's a male, and when you put two males together—"

"They spend more time jockeying for position than getting any work done."

She laughed. "Yeah, that's pretty much it. So try this little girl." She handed him a terrier mix. "This is Sonya. She should get along fine with Rover. Just walk Rover on the far left, and I'll walk Dexter on my far right. And we'll all be one big happy family."

As soon as those words left her mouth, Susannah wanted to take them back. She barely knew this man. "One big happy family" did not describe them at all.

But Kane, if he'd noticed the phrase, didn't say anything. "The only problem is, we're outnumbered two to one, with the animals at a decided advantage."

Susannah grinned. "Do those odds scare you?"

"Nothing scares me."

"Oh, I bet some things do." She studied him, keeping her grip on the leashes firm, as they rounded a corner. She'd spent more time with Kane in the last couple of days than almost anyone besides Jackie, and yet, there were times when she felt as if she barely knew him. "Everyone is scared of something. What is it for you?"

He stopped walking and pivoted toward her. Beneath the streetlight, his every feature was outlined, his eyes seemed darker, more mysterious. "You want to know what scares me?"

Susannah nodded, mute. Her heart thudded in her chest.

Kane transferred both leashes to one hand, and reached up with the other to cup her jaw. Even as she told herself to hold back, to stay away, Susannah leaned into the touch, the warmth, the tenderness. "A woman who deserves so much more than I can give."

"I don't want anything, though."

Kane leaned in closer, his lips now a breath away. "Wanting and deserving are two different things. And what you deserve, Susannah Wilson, is the world. On a platter." Then he winnowed the gap, and kissed her again.

Her head spun, her pulse raced. She reached for him, but the dogs, impatient for their walk, tangled the leashes around Kane's and Susannah's legs and began vocalizing their desire to keep moving. She broke away from Kane.

Saved by the bark. "I think we better get going before our chaperones get too antsy."

"We probably should." He trailed a finger along her jaw. "But first, tell me, is there anything wrong with a little of that?"

"No," Susannah breathed.

"Then who says we can't do it again?" And he brushed his lips across hers before the dogs pulled him away.

And again, and again, a part of her demanded. But thankfully work—in the form of a bunch of canines—kept her on track.

Kane and Susannah headed down the sidewalk toward the town park. "We can have that," he said, referencing the kiss, "without a deep relationship. I'm only here for a few days, and so are you. I don't want to get into some big discussion about my life. Or my job. I just want to enjoy my time here, and my time with you. Is that so bad?"

Though it stung a little that Kane kept shutting the door every time Susannah knocked, she had to admit that he had a point. No getting too close, no ties in the end. "No, it's not."

Wasn't that what she wanted anyway? Nothing to bind her to this town, to her old life? So she could leave without remorse, begin a new life as soon as Jackie's wedding was over. It was exactly the type of relationship she told herself she should pursue, yet a part of herself kept rebelling, like a child who had spied the cookie jar and was now throwing a tantrum every time the treats came into view.

"Good. Because I need to ask you a favor."

"A favor?"

"I'm not quite getting what I need on this vacation and I think you're the only one who can provide what I want."

He stopped walking and turned to face her. "So I have a deal to offer you, Susannah. If you accept it, maybe we can both get what we want. What do you say?"

CHAPTER EIGHT

"YOU want me to do *what?*" Susannah stared at him. Around them, Chapel Ridge maintained its veil of silence, everyone asleep for the night, the businesses shut up, the residents tucked in their beds. As far as this corner of the world was concerned, the only people who existed were Susannah and Kane. They had waited to finish the conversation until the dogs were done with their walks and back in their kennels. Now, Susannah, Kane and Rover stood in the quiet night air outside the closed grooming salon.

"I want you to show me how to live like a normal person."

"Uh…is there a reason you don't know how?"

"I'm a…typical bachelor. Never really functioned on my own." He shifted from foot to foot, avoiding her gaze. "I want to experience life. But I'm not very good at it."

"As in…doing what?"

"Starting a fire, for one. So I don't freeze to death in that cabin. Last night was no fun, let me tell you. I'd make a really bad Eskimo." He smiled. "I want you to show me things like skipping stones. Maybe even cooking over an open flame."

"You're kidding."

"No, I'm not. And, I'm willing to pay you."

"*Pay* me?" The words rolled in her mind. Five minutes ago Kane had been talking about kissing her and, she'd thought, had been doing a very good job of trying to romance her.

Now he'd switched gears, and was offering to pay her to enhance his vacation experience. The contradictions in Kane Lennox ran deeper every second. Susannah had no doubts about his interest in her, but about his reasons for being in Chapel Ridge—beyond the wedding—she had several. About what he wanted beyond a few kisses, she had plenty more.

Could she put those doubts aside and trust him over the next few days? Without falling into the depths she saw in his eyes? Or would she be making the biggest mistake of her life by letting go of those tight reins she had on her emotions?

"I'll pay you more than enough money to make it worth your while, of course," Kane went on. "I realize this will interfere with your current job." He paused, seeming to run a mental calculator. "What do you make as a dog groomer? A hundred dollars an hour?"

"Maybe."

"I'll triple that. In exchange, you take the day off and show me what I want to see, teach me what I want to know."

Susannah nearly choked. Three hundred dollars an *hour?* More than two thousand dollars a *day?* Kane had to be joking…or insane. "Do you mean like a paid escort?"

"Well, not that kind, but yes."

"That's a ridiculous amount of money. No one pays that much for—" She stopped. "Are you rich or something?"

"I'm…I…I saved up a lot for this vacation."

"You saved up a lot for a vacation to *Chapel Ridge, Indiana?* And now you want to spend it on me? Specifically me teaching you how to do what ordinary people do every day for free?"

He didn't answer that question. "Are you turning me down?"

"No, but I'm assessing the wisdom of your offer. Not to mention your sanity in making it." And her sanity in agreeing. Every moment she spent with Kane wrapped her tighter in a spell she couldn't seem to break.

What did she have to worry about? This was all temporary. Saturday morning she'd be on a plane to the other side of the world. Surely that would be enough distance to forget him.

"Well, don't think so much. Just accept it." He reached into his back pocket and pulled out his wallet. "I assume cash is okay?"

Oh, my goodness. Kane was actually serious. When he handed Susannah a pile of hundred-dollar bills, her eyes widened. If she was frugal, she could envision these dollars becoming a jaunt over to London, maybe a quick side trip to Italy. The kernel of a savings account toward a trip to Germany or Mexico. "You carry around that much cash?"

"I'm not a fan of traveler's checks."

"Ever hear of credit cards?"

"Don't like those much, either. Cash is my way of doing business, at least on a personal level."

"Well, your ATM card must get a lot of wear." She stared at the bills in his hand, until he took her palm and placed them in hers, then she stared even more. "This is…this is way too much. You're insane."

"I only have a limited amount of time. I want my vacation to be the best it can be. And so far, all I've done is starve, freeze and find a dog I didn't want." He grinned. "The best time I had was with you. Every time I've been with you, Susannah, all I wanted to do was spend even more time with you. It didn't matter if we were washing a dog or throwing a fishing pole out the window." He took a step closer and tipped her jaw until her gaze met his. "Imagine how it would be if we had actual, planned fun together? If all I had to worry about, and all you had to worry about, was us being together? That, to me, would be a perfect vacation."

He saw Susannah's breath catch. When she looked at him like that, Kane could barely resist her. Every bone in his body longed to kiss her again, but he was afraid if he did, she really would think this offer was only for one thing— when it wasn't. Although, if he could kiss her a dozen more times over the next few days, he wouldn't complain.

"I suppose—" she fingered the hundreds "—I could have Tess take on a few extra appointments for me."

"And what about your sister's wedding plans?"

A smile crossed Susannah's face, a smile so wide it could have rivaled the sun's. And for the first time since Kane had made the crazy offer, he knew he had done the right thing.

"I think Jackie can handle her own wedding just fine, at least for a few hours a day. Apparently I have a new job."

Susannah had done some oddball things to fund her dream, but this took the cake. "You really want to do this?"

"Absolutely."

"Okay. It's your money." She handed him the shovel. "About here should be good."

He grinned, then pushed on the metal edge with his boot. The spade sank into the earth, turning up a chunk of dark brown sod. When it did, a trio of earthworms came squirming out of the ground. Rover took one look at them, let out a yelp and darted off. "Success!"

Susannah laughed. Kane Lennox made the oddest study

in contradictions in his perfect jeans and second, new, casual shirt, along with a pair of new boots Susannah had insisted he buy at the local hunter supply shop, coupled with his cocktail party mannerisms. All of them forgotten when he'd dug up a pile of worms. "You look as happy as a man who struck oil."

"I feel that happy, as crazy as that sounds." Kane grabbed the coffee can she'd brought with her that morning, then bent down and, using the lid, scooped the worms into the container. "Let's go fishing. For real this time."

Susannah watched him grab their poles, the same shiny new tackle box from the night before, and they marched on down the wooded path to the lake, Kane gleeful. She trailed along, not nearly as excited as Kane by the prospect of sitting on the dock and casting a hook into the water. She zipped her sweatshirt up, against the morning chill in the air, but Kane seemed oblivious to the low spring temperature. "You're really into this."

"Never done it before. I've heard it's fun. Relaxing."

"You've never fished?"

"I told you, I work a lot. Downtime isn't even in my vocabulary." He let out a deep breath, just as his cell phone started up again, for the fourth time that morning. Susannah had never known anyone whose cell phone rang as often as his did—and who answered as infrequently as Kane did. This time, Kane let out a curse, withdrew the cell from his jacket pocket, glanced at the number, shook his head, then tucked the phone away again. "What's first?"

"Bait your hook." She reached into the can, pulled out a worm and held up the slimy creature. "You've got to get this little guy on that tiny silver hook." She demonstrated, with a few quick nimble movements.

He arched a brow. "Not one ounce of squeamishness?

I'm impressed. I don't think any of the women I know would ever handle a worm, must less do what you just did."

"I grew up fishing. My dad loved coming here, and we used to fish together a lot." Her gaze drifted to the deep, green water, and she could swear her father's spirit still lingered here. His presence hung heavy in the budding maple trees, the rich earth, the soft whispers of the breeze. She closed her eyes and inhaled the sweet fresh air, and for a moment Susannah was ten again, spending a lazy summer afternoon with her father after his work was done for the day, learning more about life than about fishing.

Susannah opened her eyes and drank in the view again. She would miss this place. The memories that it held, the comfort she found here, like curling under a thick blanket on a cold winter's night. "Anyway," she finished, brushing off the memories before they worked their way into tears, "the main reason I'm not squeamish around this stuff is because I was the one hanging out at the lake after school. I'm not a girly-girl."

"Then you're perfect for me." He cleared his throat, as if he realized what he'd just said. "I meant for this week, of course."

"Of course."

He couldn't mean anything else, she decided. She didn't *want* him to. Did she?

No. She had plans, and those plans did not include being tied to anyone else, even a man with deep blue eyes and a teasing grin.

Kane wrestled with the wriggly worm, but after a couple of tries had it on his hook. Susannah rose and cast her line into the water, explaining her actions as she did it. "Now you try."

He leaned back, flipped the rod forward, but the hook fell short.

"Like this," Susannah said, slipping in behind him, intending only to show him, as she had been shown a thousand times before. She placed her right hand on his, her left arm on his waist. He glanced over his shoulder, bringing their cheeks together, and then, as natural as two blades of grass touching in the breeze, their lips. Had she kissed him, or had he kissed her?

She stopped keeping track because the feel of Kane's mouth against hers was agonizingly wonderful. Even as Susannah broke away and tried to get back to business, tried to ignore the dark desire lingering in Kane's gaze and his smile, a roaring zing of awareness ran through her. She knew this wasn't going to be an ordinary lesson in casting a hook into the water—because she was hooking herself, too.

If she was smart, she'd step away. Go back to show and tell. None of this hands-on instruction. Except every time her brain told her to do that, her hormones reminded her of that first kiss. And the second. And the third. Of the way Kane looked without a shirt. And then back to those kisses again. "Um, to cast a hook, you put your arm back like this," she said.

"Like this?" he repeated, his voice quiet, dark.

"Yeah." She leaned with him, his arm brushing against her chest, setting off a charge of explosions under her skin as if the fabric of her shirt and bra didn't exist. "And then you, uh, go forward, really fast, and uh, when you do, you let go of the button."

"Like this?" Kane asked again, in that same dark, deep voice, doing what she'd instructed, leaving Susannah's body behind with the movement. A whisper of disappointment whistled through her.

"Exactly." She stepped away, working a smile to her face when Kane's bobber popped up just a few feet away from her own. "You did it."

"Thanks to you. Now what do we do?"

"We wait."

He shot her a grin. "Any ideas on how to kill time?"

Oh, she had a hundred of them. None of them the usual ways she had killed time while fishing. Which had been talking, listening to music, sometimes even reading a book. But today, with Kane Lennox beside her, she didn't care one whit about catching a fish. Or watching the water. Or anything but continuing what they had started the night before.

"Why Paris?"

Of everything Kane could have asked her, that question took Susannah most by surprise. "What?"

"I noticed every poster, every decoration you have is about Paris. From all that, I assumed that was the first stop on your trip around the world. Why that city out of all the ones in the world?"

She jiggled her line a little, reeling in some before answering. Rover began digging in the dirt at the edge of the lake, trying to unearth a partially buried stick. "My parents were supposed to go on a honeymoon to Paris when they first got married, but they never did. My father's dad had a stroke just before the wedding, and my mom and dad ended up staying home to work his farmland out on County Road 9, just outside of town. Farmers work long days and never get vacations. My parents would take day trips here and there, but they never got to go on that big European trip they'd dreamed of."

"I know people like that," Kane said. "My uncle worked until the day he died. Had a heart attack in his office. Never even made it out of his chair. That's when I decided I better take a vacation and have the life I'd always wanted, even if it's only for a few days, before I ended up like him."

A smile crossed her face. "Seems we have something else in common. I never wanted a business that would consume my life like that farm did my parents'. I wanted a chance to see the world, except doing that's pretty expensive." She grinned. "Good thing I have this lucrative side job in fishing lessons."

He smiled back. "Good thing. You should consider tutoring all the clueless out-of-towners."

"Yeah, we get *tons* of those in Chapel Ridge."

He moved his rod a little to the side, pulling in the slack. "You're starting your travels with a great city."

The images of the Eiffel Tower, the banks of the Seine, the quaint bistros, all those places in Paris she'd imagined visiting and never touched, marched through Susannah's mind. "Have you been there?"

"Not as a tourist. Only on business."

"You must be pretty high up at the jewelry store to get to go to Paris."

Kane shrugged, and again Susannah could swear she detected that icy tension in his shoulders. "I suppose so."

"I'm planning on working my way through the rest of the world, one doggie shampoo at a time."

Kane reached out and clasped her hand in his own. "Paris in springtime will be a perfect way to start."

Thirty yards away, the red-and-white ball on the end of Kane's line dipped beneath the water, then popped back up again. "Hey! You've got a bite."

He began to turn the reel, but Susannah laid a hand on his. "Not yet. Give the pole a little jerk, then wait."

He did as she said. The bobber went under the water and didn't come back up.

"Feel anything?"

Kane went still. "Line's pulling."

"Now reel it in."

In slow and steady circles, Kane rolled the clear fishing line back onto the reel, inching the fish out of the water and back to the dock. A few minutes later, a six-inch bluegill dangled on the end of his line, flopping its yellow, green and blue body back and forth. "Will you look at that? I caught one. Already."

"He's big enough to eat. If you want to have him for dinner."

"No, I just want to catch them. I'm taking no prisoners." He grinned. "That's where the fun is, isn't it?" He finished pulling the fish in, then followed Susannah's instructions for removing the bluegill from the hook and releasing it gently back into the lake. The fish remained still against Kane's palm for a second, then swam off and disappeared beneath the dark surface. "Go ahead, go free," Kane said quietly. Then he cleared his throat, straightened and turned back to Susannah. "Let's do that again."

She laughed. "I can't believe you're paying me to teach you this."

"And I can't believe you're such a great instructor, with some amazing fringe benefits." He placed a quick kiss on her lips, then grabbed his pole and headed over to the bait bucket.

Fringe benefits? He'd made her sound like an insurance package or an extra vacation day. Disappointment sank like a stone in Susannah's gut, but she brushed it away. She didn't want any more than these few days.

Did she?

For the next half hour, they fished, with Kane reeling in another four fish, and Susannah catching three, throwing all of them back. After each catch, Kane was as happy as a miner discovering a vein of gold. "Had enough?"

He held up his fishing pole. "I'm ready for some marlin now."

She laughed. "You won't find those out here, but I'm glad you enjoyed the experience."

"I did." He took her hand and gave it a squeeze. "More than you know."

He leaned in to kiss her again when his phone began to ring, the sound cutting through the quiet of the lake and destroying the moment. He'd opened up more than just an old coffee can filled with worms today. All that time alone, waiting for the fish. Then the joy of finally catching one had Kane dropping his guard and opening a part of his heart to Susannah. He'd begun to feel something for her, something deeper than he'd felt for anyone before. He could practically hear the warning bells clanging. Where could he possibly take this from here? Chapel Ridge, Indiana, didn't go with Lennox Gem Corporation in New York City. And a woman like Susannah Wilson was never going to understand why a billionaire CEO had deceived her.

"I'll let you get that," Susannah said as the phone rang again. "I have to get to work so I can walk the shelter dogs. I'll catch up with you later. Okay?"

Susannah rose on her tiptoes and placed a kiss on Kane's cheek. The kiss was sweet, innocent and completely devoid of anything passionate, yet it touched a spot in Kane that he had thought New York and the business, and the world of money he inhabited, had burned away. As he watched her leave, her lithe figure moving easily up the hill and back to her car, he heard Rover let out a whine of disappointment. "I hear you, buddy. I feel the same way."

The phone continued its musical assault on his senses.

Kane fished the cursed electronic device out of his back pocket. Took one look at the silver ball and chain, then a second at Susannah and the fishing pole slung over her shoulder, and decided he couldn't do this right, not unless he did it all the way.

He turned back to face the lake, then flung the phone as far as he could. It landed with a satisfying plop, floated for a second, then sank to the bottom of Lake Everett, taking its still-ringing expectations deep into the silt.

"Suzie-Q, I need you."

"Jackie, I'm running out the door. I can't—"

"This isn't a favor. This is about Paul."

Susannah stopped in her tracks, her hand halfway to the doorknob. She knew that tone in Jackie's voice, knew it like the back of her hand. Jackie was having a crisis. Again. "What's wrong?"

"Paul called off the wedding."

"What? Why?"

A sob, a catch on the other end, then Jackie sniffled and continued. "He said…he's not ready. He thinks we're rushing. That we don't have enough money and we should wait until we've saved enough to buy a bigger house and have kids. But, Suzie, I don't want to wait. I love him."

Jackie and Paul had had this argument a hundred times over the past year. From the second Paul had slipped the ring onto Jackie's finger, he'd worried about finances. He'd calculated their budget from here to Sunday, trying to make two lean paychecks stretch further. Jackie, never one to worry about price tags or bill due dates, had argued with him more than once about the cost of the wedding.

Susannah could have saved him the breath. She'd been

trying to tell Jackie the same thing for years. But Jackie had never wanted to listen to talk about budgets and bills.

"It's just cold feet, Jackie. It'll be fine." She closed the books for The Sudsy Dog, gathered up that day's checks and the deposit slip, tucking both into her purse. Tess gave her a sympathetic smile as Susannah sent her a wave and headed out the door, mouthing a thank-you.

"I think it's more than that. Can you come over? Talk to me? I really don't want to be alone and you're so good at talking to me and making me feel better. Please, Suzie? I'm so worried."

"Aren't you at work?"

"Are you kidding me? I couldn't go back to work after Paul said that. I called in sick."

Susannah ran a hand over her face and bit back a scream of frustration. No matter how many times Susannah had tried to tell her differently, Jackie had never seemed to get the message about responsibility versus whim. "Jackie, you can't do that. You two need the money. Isn't that what this is really all about?"

"Well...yeah." She sniffled again. "But—"

"But what better way to send a message to Paul that you're on the same page as him than to keep earning your own paycheck?" Susannah paused, but got silence on the other end. She doubted Jackie was even listening. A hundred times Susannah had tried to instill a sense of responsibility, an understanding of priorities in Jackie, and gotten nowhere. Eventually it just became easier to do it all. "You should go back to work. Talk to me when you get home."

"Suzie, this is a *crisis*. How can I work when my life is *imploding?*"

She'd said the same thing last week when her dress fitting had made her feel fat. And two weeks before that when one of her bridesmaids had endured a breakup of her own. Jackie had been blessed with a patient boss, but even Susannah knew that patience could only be stretched so thin. Still, she kept all this to herself. No sense making Jackie any more upset. "Jackie, you're a receptionist at a paper company. It's not like you're in a high-stress, demanding job. Heck, after three the phone hardly ever rings over there. I'm sure you can get through the day."

"You have no sympathy at all. I can't believe you won't come home and take care of me. I need you to make me some soup and—"

Susannah leaned against her car and closed her eyes. She rubbed her temples and prayed for strength. "Jackie, I have other things to do."

"Yeah, okay." Jackie sighed. "I wish Mom was here. Don't you, Susannah? She'd make it better. She always knew what to do and say."

Guilt rocketed through Susannah. She refused to give in to the emotion. Refused to let it bother her. Refused to let it sing its siren song again.

And stop her from living her life one more time.

Kane had thought he'd have more time before they called out the bloodhounds.

He flung the newspaper into the wastebasket, but it was too late. The small headline, buried in the entertainment section of the paper—thank God for small favors—had already been burned into his memory. Gem Business CEO Missing: Family Spokesperson Says, "We're Worried."

Family spokesperson. Kane snorted. Another euphemism for Ronald Jeffries, his father's lawyer. The man called on to do all of Elliott Lennox's dirty work. Like deal with a wayward son yet again. His father had to be royally ticked off to have alerted the media.

Kane reached for his cell phone, then remembered. It had found a permanent home at the bottom of the lake. There'd be no calling home. Just as well. He wanted an escape. If he picked up a phone and called his father, there'd be a limo here in five minutes.

To drag Kane back to the life he so desperately wanted to leave, just for a little while.

He turned to enter the hardware store, when he saw Susannah coming out of her shop a few doors down. She had her keys out, her thumb on the remote for her car, when she saw him.

"Kane," she began, heading down the sidewalk to him, her steps fast, her face devoid of its earlier smile. "I can't meet with you this afternoon." She dug in her purse, then pulled out the bills he'd handed her earlier. "Let me refund your money."

He waved off the cash. "Keep it. We'll catch up later. What's wrong?"

"It's Jackie. She's in a 'crisis.'"

"I take it the world isn't coming to an end?"

Susannah laughed, and he could hear the relief explode in the sound, as if she were a bomb of stress waiting for just the right detonator. "No. Just Paul, worrying about the bills. They argued again. Called off the wedding. Again."

"This has happened before?" Then he remembered Paul's words in the bar about Jackie's spending. Clearly the issue was a source of friction between practical Paul and flighty Jackie.

"Jackie isn't what anyone would call responsible with money. And Paul probably found out that she spent too much on flowers or a veil or something silly like little plastic people to sit at the base of the cake and look like extras."

"Extras?"

Susannah nodded. "Jackie wanted to include representatives of every guest on the cake."

"Sounds to me like it'll look more like an ant farm gone horribly awry."

Laughter burst out of Susannah in a steady stream. She laughed so hard, her cheeks turned red, and her eyes began to water. "Oh, Lord, I needed that today. Thanks, Kane." She laid a hand on him, an innocent touch, the kind meant only to express gratitude, but it sent a rocket of desire roaring through Kane's body.

Susannah turned to go, and Kane knew he should let her leave. Let her deal with her family on her own. He had no need for entanglements. No wish to get involved. He was going back at the end of this week, back to a life that was as far removed from this town as Mars was from the moon.

He needed to get real here—and fast. This relationship with Susannah would never work in his world, no matter how much he might think otherwise while he was inhabiting this little slice of heaven. Except…a part of him kept on hoping the Utopia would just go right on existing.

"Susannah, wait."

She pivoted back. "Yeah?"

"Need some help? Money is one thing I'm pretty good at."

And when a smile curved across her face, Kane realized he had a problem. One all the money in the world couldn't fix.

He wanted to move the moon right next to Mars.

Jackie hyperventilated with the best of them.

Susannah sat in the kitchen with her sister, doling out

coffee and cookies, waiting for the emotional storm to pass. It turned out Paul hadn't actually called off the wedding— Jackie also had a tendency toward hyperbole—but the two of them had had yet another finances disagreement, which Jackie took as a sign of impending doom. Now, Kane leaned against the opposite corner, Rover at his feet, the two males reflecting twin pained expressions.

"What am I going to do? Paul is never going to listen to me after we get married. He's always all money this, and money that." A pile of shredded tissues lay before Jackie, beside a plate of cookie crumbs.

"Be more responsible, for one," Susannah said. "You spend money like it's pouring out of the faucet and—"

Jackie let out a gust. "I don't want to hear one more word about responsibility and boring things like money, Suzie. That's not fun. For Pete's sake, I'm getting married, not *dying*."

Kane pushed off from the countertop. "If you don't start worrying about money, you *will* die."

Susannah opened her mouth, closed it, opened it again, then finally shut it. And waited to see what Kane had to say next.

Beside her, Jackie stared at him, as if he'd just pronounced the sky brown.

Kane crossed to the table, pulled out a chair and took a seat, not swinging it around and sitting backwards like Paul did, but instead lowering himself as properly as a guest at a dinner party. "I don't mean die literally, but it'll be close to the same thing." He leaned forward, capturing Jackie's attention in that direct way he had of holding eye contact. Even Susannah found herself wrapped around his every word. "You need money to have a marriage. To have a life. Not millions of dollars, of course, but enough to pay your bills, to fund your future. Your retirement."

Jackie waved off the words. "Retirement is, like, ten million years away."

"Maybe not quite that far, but yes, you do have quite a few years. All the more reason to start saving now. Did you know that if you and Paul started putting aside just a couple hundred dollars a month, you'd retire as millionaires?"

Jackie's eyes widened. "*Millionaires?* Us? But…he's a teacher. I'm a receptionist. We can't be millionaires."

"Everyone can be a millionaire, Jackie, with the right investment strategy. You just have to be smart about your money."

"Smart? Yeah, right." She snorted, then chewed on her lip and considered that for a moment. "We'd really be millionaires?"

"Yes."

"Like, what would I have to do?" she asked, grabbing her wedding planner from the center of the table. She flipped to a blank page, poised a pen over the lined pink paper and waited for Kane's answer.

Susannah gaped at Kane, as he began to rattle off easy, step-by-step advice about 401k plans and IRAs, while Jackie scribbled. He had done what Susannah had never been able to do, in all the years she'd been talking to Jackie, thousands of words falling on deaf ears. He'd gotten her attention, and gotten Jackie to actually ask questions, take his advice, and commit it to paper. Whether she'd actually do it would be another story, but Susannah had a feeling, based on Jackie's rapt expression, that things were about to change.

At least financially.

A few minutes later, Jackie clutched the book to her chest and got up from the table. "I'm going to go call Paul, and tell him I have a…" She glanced at Kane. "What did you call it?"

"Roadmap for your financial future."

"A roadmap for our financial future." She beamed. "Maybe if he hears that, he'll see that I'm serious about money, and he won't be so worried about the wedding."

"I know Paul, and I know he'll feel better if you're both on the same page with budgets and finances," Kane said. "I think it will all work out splendidly, as long as you stick to that plan."

Jackie leaned down and gave Kane a tight, quick hug, and a kiss on the cheek. "Thank you. You really are the best man." Then she bounded off to her room, so fast, she didn't see the look of surprise on Kane's face.

"You're a miracle worker," Susannah said.

"It was nothing."

"Are you kidding me? I've been lecturing my sister about money for eight years, and yet she still spent and spent like she had an unlimited supply. It's been a constant source of friction between me and her, and her and Paul. And yet, here you come along, and in five minutes you've transformed her."

He laughed. "All I did was get her attention. Doesn't mean it'll stick, but I think once she gets married, and she and Paul have some serious discussions, things will turn around."

"If they could even turn thirty degrees, I'd be happy." Susannah rose, depositing the dishes into the sink. She ran the water over them, washed the few cups and plates, and loaded them into the strainer.

She sensed Kane behind her before she saw him. His presence, his cologne, the warmth of his body. She stilled, holding her breath, waiting for what would come next. So very aware of how alone they were now. Would he touch her? Would he kiss her? Or would he simply walk away?

He reached up and trailed a finger down her neck, a slow, easy touch that—oh, God—set every nerve ending on fire, igniting parts of Susannah's body that she didn't even know could come alive. She gripped the countertop and closed her eyes, then tipped her head to one side as Kane leaned forward, brushed the hair away from her neck and pressed his lips to the tender hollow of skin.

All thoughts of her sister, money and anything resembling reality disappeared. She forgot every reason she had for not getting involved with him. Couldn't have come up with a single sentence about why walking away from Kane before she got in any deeper would be a good idea. Because—oh, oh—he was here and he was there, and sensations were exploding in her head, along her skin.

Everywhere.

A mewl escaped her. Kane trailed the kisses down along her jaw, turning her as he did, brushing up against her lips, but not touching them. Not yet. Anticipation boiled inside her, and Susannah arched against him, her mouth open, waiting, wanting. Needing him.

His hands cupped her chin, and those eyes—those penetrating blue eyes—captured hers for a long, quiet moment. Then he leaned forward, and kissed her, slowly, sweetly, as if savoring every inch of her.

He kissed her like a composer writing a symphony. Every nerve ending sang, every touch created a concert. Susannah's arms reached around his back, held him close, as close as she could, and yet, still, it wasn't enough. Not nearly enough.

Kane drew back, an easy smile on his lips. "What do you say we get back to what we were doing earlier?"

"I thought we just did."

He chuckled. "If I remember right, I bought and paid for your services. And now that the crisis is averted, you're all mine again."

Those four words sent a tempting thrill through Susannah. "And what would you like me to teach you now?"

He closed the gap between them, his lips a breath away from hers. "To start a fire."

Then he kissed her again. And started one of his own.

CHAPTER NINE

STONES spit in a wave behind the tires of the rental car as Kane skidded to a stop in front of the cabin. Damn. He saw the guest standing on his porch and the item in her hands, both shadowed by the wooden overhang, and his instincts told him one thing.

The vacation was over.

"Wait here a second, will you?" Kane said.

"Sure." But Susannah's face showed her confusion at being left behind.

What could he say? *Sorry to tell you one thing about who I was, but the truth is about to come out? Everything I've said has been a lie, but hold on a second before you hate me, I had really great reasons for keeping my identity a secret?*

Instead he didn't say anything at all.

The dread in Kane's stomach grew as he got out of the car, Rover scrambling behind him before he could leave the dog in the car. Kane crossed to the porch of the cabin and greeted Mrs. Maxwell. He watched her face, to see if she recognized him as *the* Kane Lennox. Had she read the paper? Had she put the pieces together?

Had she, most of all, called his father? Or had his father finally found him?

"Mrs. Maxwell. Nice to see you again."

The gray-haired woman bent down and greeted the spaniel, who had yet to meet a person he didn't slobber over with a friendly greeting. Rover swished against her, his tail beating a hello into Mrs. Maxwell's floral-print housedress. "I see you made a friend with your stray. Did you give him a name?"

"I'm not keeping him. I'd hoped you might have heard about a missing dog."

"Not yet. Or at least, no one has said a word to me. I checked the *Chapel Ridge Post*, too, and there hasn't been a single lost dog ad in there all week. Pity, too. He's such a cute little booger. Someone must be heartbroken."

"Yes, I'm sure they are." So heartbroken they hadn't even noticed the dog had disappeared. "I'll hang a sign up downtown or something, then." Get to the point, he wanted to shout, but he didn't. Clearly, Mrs. Maxwell hadn't figured out who he was. To her, he was still another vacationer.

"Good idea." She straightened, her gray curls bouncing with the movement, then held out the envelope he'd seen earlier. Even from the car, Kane had recognized the distinctive white envelope and bright colors marking an overnight delivery. "This is for you. It came to the rental office, which is where all the mail for the cabins is delivered. I figured it must be important, which is why I drove it out here myself. What a lucky thing that you came home just after I got here. I was going to leave it by the door if you didn't come by, but—"

"Thank you, Mrs. Maxwell." Kane gave her a pointed look, and took the envelope.

"Oh, you're welcome." She remained standing on the porch, arms crossed. Then she looked at him, at the envelope and back at him. "Aren't you going to open it? It's probably pretty important, being one of those overnight things and all. I never get those. I can't even remember the last time a renter got one."

"I know what's in it," Kane said. "I've been expecting this." He'd known his father would find him eventually. Elliott Lennox got what he wanted. Every time.

And what he wanted—what he always wanted—was control over everyone in his life. Especially Kane.

The sharp edges of the envelope only added to Kane's resentment. When would his father see his son as a *son,* not a commodity? Notice him as a blood relative, instead of another stone in the Lennox family necklace?

Mrs. Maxwell pushed her glasses further up her nose. "Well, I suppose I better get back to the office. I have…" Her voice trailed off, then she cupped a hand over her eyes, shielding them from the sun. "Oh my. Is that *Susannah Wilson* in your car?"

He had never been in such a nosy town. In New York, people walked by and looked right through him. Sure, there was espionage and spying, but it was of the corporate kind. Not the personal kind. "Uh, yeah. She's…helping me with the dog."

"She's single, you know." Mrs. Maxwell gave him a knowing nod. "One of our most eligible bachelorettes."

"Thank you again for coming by, Mrs. Maxwell," Kane said, withdrawing a bill from his pocket and handing it to the woman.

"What's this? A tip? Oh, goodness. I don't expect a tip." She pushed the money back at him. "This isn't some big city. We don't take money for simple things like delivering someone's mail." Mrs. Maxwell shook her head and laughed. "This is Chapel Ridge, Mr. Lennox. People here do things just because."

Then she headed down his porch toward her car, sending Susannah a friendly wave and a hello as she did.

Kane marveled at Mrs. Maxwell's comment. *Just because.*

How unlike his world. He'd been wrong. This wasn't nosiness. It was more…concern. Interest. The beginnings of relationships.

What Kane had found in Chapel Ridge hadn't been simply a vacation from his job, a host of new experiences, but also a community of people who embraced each other, supported each other and welcomed strangers as if they were their own family.

Susannah got out of the car, carrying the takeout they'd picked up at the Corner Kitchen on the way over, and met him on the stoop. "All set?"

"Yes. Thank you for waiting. Just a little…business to conduct."

"For your job?"

"Yes."

"The jewelry store you work for sent you an overnight package?" Susannah cast a dubious glance at the envelope. "You must be pretty important to them if they're bothering you on vacation."

She gave him a suspicious look. Damn. Once again he had said too much, let too many details out. Twisted his cover story a little too many times. "How about an early dinner? I'm starving. And if we can get a fire started, we can break this chill."

"Sure. Do you have kindling? Matches?"

"Check and check."

"Then let me show you how to make fire. By the end of the day, you'll feel like a real caveman." Susannah grinned, then brushed past him and into the cabin.

Kane glanced down at the envelope, noting the return

address in New York. No matter what happened today, he'd already been reminded that he was still more of a prisoner of his life than ever.

A shadow had dropped over Kane's face, and had yet to disappear. Susannah watched the flames flicker across his features, and knew that envelope he'd received earlier had something to do with the change.

But what? And why?

She'd heard him tell Mrs. Maxwell he'd been expecting the delivery. Was the arrival of some work during a vacation such an annoyance? Or could the package contain bad news? Even in the close quarters of the cabin, Kane had managed to put distance between them, as if he didn't want to talk about whatever sat heavy on his mind. Susannah had thought she and Kane had drawn closer over the last few days. Close enough, at least, for him to tell her about something monumental.

Apparently, she'd been wrong.

"Are you ready for tonight?" he asked, disrupting her thoughts.

"Tonight?"

"The rehearsal. Paul is as nervous as a cat about to take a bath." Kane chuckled, lightening the tension in his face and shoulders. He slipped into his old self, or at least a closer facsimile. "When I spoke to him about it, he was as antsy as he used to be back in college before a big exam."

"Paul got antsy? He's one of the calmest guys I know—unless of course he's talking to Jackie about money."

Kane rose, hung the fireplace poker back on the rack and crossed to the small efficiency kitchen. He began unpacking the takeout bags from the Corner Kitchen, loading the packages onto the tiny wooden kitchen table. "You didn't know Paul in college. He was a little… wilder."

"And you?" Susannah asked, approaching Kane. "What were you like in college?"

"Most of the time, I was…subdued and sedate. Well mannered."

She scoffed. "Right. Show me a guy who acts like that in college. Especially when there are pretty coeds and beer around? Paul told me a few stories about his years at Northwestern. The edited versions, I'm sure, but I got the impression he went to more than a few parties." Susannah retrieved some paper plates and plastic silverware from inside one of the cabinets and brought them back to the table, then pulled up one of the two chairs and took a seat.

Kane settled into the opposite chair, and the two of them began passing the Corner Kitchen dishes back and forth, heaping mashed potatoes, homemade meat loaf, gravy and green beans baked with bacon bits onto their plates. "Paul has stories. Me, not so many."

She cocked her head and studied him. "You roomed next door to Paul. Hung out together. How could that be?"

"I…" Kane pulled a biscuit out of the paper bag, followed by a butter packet, then hesitated before opening it. "I had a chaperone, of sorts."

"You? Were you some kind of troublemaker or something?"

He scoffed. "Not at all. My father just felt like I needed a keeper."

"A keeper?" Susannah blinked. Parents still did that kind of thing in the twentieth century? It seemed impossible to believe, yet, it explained a lot about Kane. His inexperience at the simplest of life events. What kind of childhood had the man had? And why? "I can't imagine having such a strict upbringing."

"There were a lot of expectations on my shoulders." He toyed with the edge of the envelope, still unopened. "There still are, to be honest."

"Are some of them in there?"

He jerked to attention, as if he'd just realized he'd said too much. Then his gaze broke from hers and tension poured like steel into his frame.

What was with Kane? And for that matter, what was he hiding? Every time she tried to get close, tried to ask more than a few questions, he clammed up and changed the subject.

She was tired of this "Just Kane," "Just Susannah" game. She wanted more—a real connection. Even if it was only for a few days, she wanted something more satisfying than a taste of whipped cream. She wanted the whole cake.

She knew so little about him. A snippet here. A snippet there. As if he was showing her the photo album of his life, but with all the identifying details removed from the images.

Why?

Didn't he trust her? Or was he that intent on leaving at the end of his trip—and leaving all ties to Chapel Ridge behind?

"This food is great," Kane said. "Have you tried the meat loaf? Do you think the owners will sell me the recipe?"

Now they were talking *meat loaf?* She wanted to know *him,* not his preferences in the baked ground beef department. Suddenly, the past days rose to the surface, the frustration threatening to explode.

"Did you grow up in a bubble or something? Honestly, who has never had meat loaf? It was like a staple in my house, and virtually everyone else's I knew, too. Every Friday night, like it or not. When I grew up and started making my own dinners, I refused to cook it because I was so tired of eating meat loaf. Now I crave it every once in a while, oddly enough."

Kane shook his head. "My mother wasn't the meat loaf kind."

"Whoa, there's a whole lot of information."

"What's that supposed to mean?"

"It means I know almost nothing about you," she said. "I feel like I'm dealing with a crossword puzzle every time I try to have a conversation with you, Kane. I know you've never walked barefoot on grass. Had a keeper in college. Had a dad who ruled your life, and wow, here's a clue, your mom didn't make meat loaf. What the heck am I supposed to figure from that?" She rose and spun away from the table, placing her plate on the countertop. "You know almost everything about me and I…" She looked down at the dog sleeping at his feet. "I know more about this stray than I do you."

Kane shifted in his chair. Outside, birds called to each other, the breeze sent a branch scraping against the cabin window. Rover raised his head, then went back to sleep. Kane took in a breath, let it out. "You're right. I have been rather guarded about my life. And I owe you an apology for that." He ran a hand through his hair, displacing the dark waves. "If I tell you something, will you keep it between us?"

She sensed an opening in the wall, a chink about to be removed. "Of course."

"My family had a lot of money when I was growing up. So I'm not used to—" he waved around the room "—this. Any of this, especially not meat loaf. Or cheese that comes in packages, or fishing with live worms." He smiled. "I got a taste of real life, of what could be something close to it, in college when I met Paul and had brief moments of freedom. That's why I'm here. I'm far too old to keep going through life never really experiencing it. When Paul asked me to be his best man, I seized the opportunity to see the world from the other side of the fence. *Carpe diem*, and all that."

"Then, after the wedding, you plan on going back to New York, to your regular world."

"Right."

"No strings, no attachments."

His gaze met hers. Direct. Honest. "Exactly."

Whatever part of Susannah might have hoped for otherwise—if there had been a part—knew now there would be nothing more than these kisses. The dance by the lake. And whatever came of the wedding tomorrow. She should be happy, because she was leaving town herself on Saturday and knew how foolish it would be to hold on to any romantic notices of being whisked away to some hideaway chapel at the end of this week, but nevertheless, a whisper of disappointment ran through her, then settled heavy in her gut.

He wanted nothing more than these few days.

He didn't want her. And that was exactly what she'd thought she wanted, too—

Until she got it.

"So," she said, working a smile to her face, telling herself this was perfect, that people who focused on romance and dreams left themselves open to being hurt, "what else did you want to experience while you're here?"

His smile met hers, and a long moment of quiet extended between them. "One more dance, Susannah, that's all."

The minister cleared his throat. Looked at his watch. Cleared his throat a second time. "Do you have any idea where they might be?"

"No." Susannah glanced toward the front of Chapel Ridge Lutheran Church, but no one came through the doors. Jackie's bridesmaids sat in the front pews, Paul's groomsmen beside them. Up in the balcony, Mrs. Maxwell watched it all from her perch at the organ, probably taking notes for the town gossips. "Maybe they forgot?"

"Their own wedding rehearsal?" Pastor Weatherly said.

"I'll try Jackie's cell phone again." Susannah pulled her Nokia out of her purse and punched in her sister's number. Three rings and then finally, Jackie picked up with a breathless hello. "*Jackie!* Where are you?"

She giggled. "Umm…making up with Paul."

"Well, stop," Susannah whispered, heading down the aisle and out of earshot of everyone else. "You're supposed to be at the wedding rehearsal."

"Oh! I totally forgot." She giggled some more. "Uh, oh, Paul, stop, stop, honey. Oh, oooh, um, Suzie, could you please, uh, oh, Paul—"

Susannah cringed. There were just certain things she didn't want to know or hear about her sister's life. "Jackie! I absolutely refuse to listen to you and Paul have…fun. So will you quit that for five minutes and talk to me?"

"Okay, okay. I'm here. Actually, I'm in Indianapolis. So it'll be like, twenty or thirty minutes before I'm back in Chapel Ridge. Maybe, uh, more." She giggled some more.

"Indianapolis!" Susannah cast her gaze to the stained-glass images on the windows, begging for patience from the jewel-toned disciples. "What are you doing there?"

"Paul and I went down to pick up the tuxes. This is where that shop was that had the special ones I really liked, remember? And after we got them, we stopped for dinner, and then we got to talking, and then, well, we got…sidetracked. So we pulled over."

"Jackie, this is important. Don't you care? This is *your* wedding, not mine."

"Suzie, you'll take care of it for me, won't you? I'll be there soon."

Susannah ran a hand through her hair and sighed. "I don't have a choice, do I?" She hung up the phone, strode back to the front of the church and pasted a bright smile on her face. "Jackie's on her way. She'll be a little while, though. She got…tied up when they went to get the tuxes."

Pastor Weatherly flicked out his wrist. "I can't wait that long, Susannah, I'm sorry. I have a funeral here in an hour and I know you all have reservations for the rehearsal dinner, too."

"Can we reschedule? We still need to run through the wedding, at least so everyone knows where to stand. And without Paul and Jackie…"

The minister thought for a second. "I have a baptism in the morning, then another wedding before Jackie's. I just don't see another time to do this. Do we have other people who could substitute for them tonight? Then perhaps you could explain the steps to Jackie and Paul tomorrow? And if she gets here early enough tonight, I should have time for another quick run through." Pastor Weatherly looked at the women and men sitting in the pews, chatting quietly among themselves. "For tonight, all I need is a man and a woman."

Paul's single friends skulked down in the pews with that don't-look-at-me expression. Before the minister could choose a volunteer, Kane stepped over to Susannah and took her hand. "That would be us, wouldn't it?"

"Us? Are you kidding me?"

"Isn't that the job of the best man and the maid of honor? To step in as needed?"

"Uh…well…I don't think he meant literally."

But Kane was already leading her up the aisle and to the edge of the altar. "We'll do it, Pastor."

"Wonderful." He beamed at them, as if they were the bridal couple. "And your name is?"

"Kane. Kane Lennox."

"Ah, like in the Bible? The proverbial first son, who also, might I add, committed the very first murder." Pastor Weatherly gave Kane a good-natured smile. "Not that you, of course, are a felon in the making."

"Not at all, sir. And my name is spelled entirely different. Plus," he leaned forward, "I'm an only child, so there's no worry about fratricide."

Pastor Weatherly laughed. "Glad to hear it, son. Okay, Kane, you take your place to my left. And, Susannah, you can go back a few pews and make the march."

Susannah blanched. Walk down the aisle? Join Kane at the altar? This was crazy. "I really don't think that's necessary."

"Someone has to do it, and if we can at least complete this run-through, it will make everything so much easier tomorrow. Susannah, I know you'll be there to make sure everything goes smoothly for Jackie." Pastor Weatherly laid a hand on Susannah's arm. "Thank the Lord that she has had you all these years to watch out for her. You've been a wonderful sister."

"I know your time is limited, Pastor. We should get started," Susannah said, suddenly feeling hot, confined. She wanted to run from the church, from the praise the minister was heaping on her. If she'd done such a good job finishing the raising of her sister, wouldn't Jackie be here right now? Being responsible instead of being selfish?

Susannah headed to the back of the church. The other bridesmaids slipped into place before her, while the groomsmen took their places on the altar. Pastor Weatherly cued Mrs. Maxwell to begin playing the bridal march, from her perch at the organ up in the balcony. When the music began, Susannah took her first steps, clutching an imaginary bouquet. At first, she walked fast, hoping to get in, get out and make this go as fast as possible.

But then she caught Kane watching her, his cobalt eyes direct on hers, with that piercing way he had, and her steps faltered, then slowed. Her heart began to race, and her breath caught in her throat. The rest of the church dropped away, the other people blending into the background. All she saw was Kane, and the bemused smile on his face waiting for her to join him at the end of the aisle.

What if this were real? What if she were marrying him tonight? How would that feel?

Terrifying?

Or wonderful?

To see him every day from here on? To wake up to those cobalt eyes? To feel those arms around her until the day she died?

The wedding march came to a close as she made the final steps. Kane put out his hand and took hers, leading her up the two stairs to the altar. "You look beautiful when you smile like that," he whispered.

She opened her mouth to speak, but nothing came out, not so much as a breath. For the first time in her life, Susannah Wilson was totally, completely speechless.

"This is where I start the 'Dearly beloved, we are gathered...' part," Pastor Weatherly said. "And everybody tunes out for a few minutes as we go over a couple of Bible passages, sing one hymn that your sister picked out—"

"Jackie picked out a hymn for the ceremony?"

"Yes." Pastor Weatherly looked down at his notes. "'How Great Thou Art.'"

"Our mother's favorite," she whispered. And then she could hear the soft strains of her mother's voice, singing the song in church, or while she did the dishes, the stanzas carrying clear and strong, the notes lingering in the air long after she finished. How great…and, oh, how much Susannah missed those sweet vocals.

Her eyes filled with unshed tears, and the room blurred. The grief she held in check, always kept behind a firm wall, threatened to spill forward. "I…I had no idea she remembered."

Pastor Weatherly reached out a kind hand to Susannah and held hers for a long moment, his soft brown eyes telling her he understood everything. "She wanted to include Eleanor as much as she could."

Susannah smiled her gratitude to the minister, and the gesture wobbled a little on her face. For a moment, it felt as if her mother was right there, watching from the pews. Tomorrow, in the song, Susannah knew she would hear her mother's voice. What a wonderful touch, and for Jackie to think of it meant her sister was more aware of the important elements of the wedding than Susannah had thought. Her heart clenched, and she swiped at her eyes with the back of her hands. "We, um, should get started, Pastor Weatherly," she said, to change the subject, before she started crying. "You have your funeral tonight. Who died, by the way?"

"Jerry Linkheart. You probably don't remember him because he lived here before you were born, Susannah. He just moved back to town last week after he retired. Saddest thing, too." Pastor Weatherly shook his head. "It was only Jerry and his dog. Family said they haven't seen the dog in days. I guess little Bandit ran off when Jerry died. He had a heart attack at home."

"Would Bandit happen to be a Brittany spaniel?" Kane asked.

"He is indeed. Jerry loved that dog. Spoiled it rotten, from what I hear, though I suspect Bandit was just his little buddy. Either way, his sister told me she's glad it's gone. I get the feeling she's not much of a dog person. If you see it, Susannah, find the poor thing a good home, will you? That's what Jerry would want."

"I already did find the dog, or rather Kane here did. Out by his lake cottage."

The minister nodded. "Jerry lived down by the lake. Sounds like we've got Bandit. I'll call the family, see if it's okay with them if Kane keeps him. I don't think they want the dog."

Kane started shaking his head. "I, ah—"

"That would be great," Susannah cut in. Even if Kane didn't take Bandit, she would find a good home for the dog.

"Okay," Pastor Weatherly said, addressing first Kane and Susannah, then the few people in the pews, "we've got a happy ending for the dog. Let's get back to our happily-ever-after work here. We have a wedding to rehearse. After the hymn, we get to the good part. Kane, this is where you turn to Susannah."

"Uh, Jackie," Susannah corrected. No way did she want anyone thinking it was her and Kane getting married. It all felt way too realistic, standing up here, flanked by bridesmaids and groomsmen, instead of being one of the bridesmaids.

"Of course," Pastor Weatherly said. "Susannah, who is pretending to be Jackie, and Kane, who is pretending to be Paul." He grinned. "Wouldn't want me to marry the two of you tonight by accident, now, would you?"

"No," Kane and Susannah said at the same time.

Pastor Weatherly chuckled. "Well, let's pretend instead, 'Jackie' and 'Paul.' You two need to turn toward each other." He waved his hands together.

Susannah shifted her position at the same time Kane did. Acute awareness of him rocketed through her. Of where they were. Of the minister watching them. Of how easily this could, as Pastor Weatherly had said, be them getting married—

Instead of Jackie and Paul.

Would that be so bad?

Of course it would. She didn't want to get married. Didn't want to settle down. Not before she'd had her chance to explore the world, see something beyond the bounds of Chapel Ridge.

Except…she really liked Kane Lennox. His direct way of confronting problems—like the dog. Like Jackie.

Like her.

And there was something about him, something she'd glimpsed when he'd finally peeled back the layers and allowed her a peek into his world, that showed a man with vulnerabilities. Areas she wanted to know more about, even while she knew she should keep her focus on her ultimate goals, and on the fact that he was leaving and she was doing her best not to create any more ties in a life that already had too many….

She kept losing track of that resolve.

"First, I will ask each of you the same question," Pastor Weatherly said, interrupting her thoughts. "And you respond, 'I will.' Okay?"

Kane and Susannah nodded. But would she if this were real?

Before she could decide, Pastor Weatherly opened the leather-bound *Book of Common Prayer* in his hand, smoothed down the page and began to read. "Susannah, will you have this man to be your husband; to live together in the covenant of marriage? Will you love him, comfort him, honor and keep him, in sickness and in health; and, forsaking all others, be faithful to him as long as you both shall live?"

Susannah swallowed hard. Love him. Keep him. Be faithful. As long as she lived?

This was insane.

These were powerful words. *Permanent* words.

But it was all an act. Imaginary. Standing in for someone else. Not her life, not her marriage. "I will," she said, the words squeaking past her throat.

"Kane, will you have this woman to be—"

"He will," Susannah cut in. "You know Paul is going to say yes."

The minister smiled. "Of course he will. Okay, let's move on. Next, I address the congregation. Then we read a psalm, have a prayer, and read a couple of Bible passages. Then we move on to the part that gets you *really* hitched." Pastor Weatherly grinned, then turned back to Kane. "You two will have to run through these details with Paul and Jackie, but tell them not to worry if they forget. I'll be here to coach them. Kane, take Susannah's right hand in yours, then repeat after me, okay?"

Kane nodded. He reached up, took Susannah's hand in his, the touch sending a charge through her. One she couldn't ignore. Couldn't pretend was part of the act. Susannah shifted on her feet, but there was nowhere to go. Nowhere but right where she was.

"In the Name of God, I, Kane," Pastor Weatherly began to recite, "take you, Susannah, to be my wife…"

Kane's gaze met Susannah's. Butterflies raised a riot in

her gut, and she would have run from the church if he hadn't been holding her hand. "In the Name of God, I, Kane," he said, his voice soft, almost tender, "take you, Susannah, to be my wife…"

"To have and to hold from this day forward, for better, for worse, for richer, for poorer…"

Kane's hold on her hand tightened. Because he too wanted to run? Because he sensed her quivering? He ran a thumb over the back of her hand, and the butterflies roared, then began to quiet. "To have and to hold from this day forward, for better, for worse, for richer, for poorer…" On the last, a slight smile curved across his face.

"In sickness and in health, to love and to cherish, until we are parted by death. This is my solemn vow."

Kane reached up with his other hand and captured her free one. His cobalt eyes never left hers. The world closed in, leaving just the two of them on the altar. "In sickness and in health, to love and to cherish," he said, the words quietly, deliberately, "until we are parted by death. This is my solemn vow."

The last sentences seemed to hang in the air. Susannah gulped. This was supposed to be a joke, the two of them just filling in. But somewhere along the way, something had shifted, and a sense of reality had invaded the space between them.

A hush fell over the church, as if every single person was holding their collective breaths. Susannah's heart got caught in Kane's smile, in the words he'd just said.

How long had she waited to hear those very same words? For her turn at the life she'd seen everyone else have? The life she had set aside the day her parents died, so she could raise Jackie and give that gift of freedom instead to her sister?

And here in the church, for just a second, Susannah had become caught in the web of the fairy tale. She'd heard a gorgeous man pledge undying love. Even if he was only acting, Susannah closed her eyes, holding on to the fantasy for one moment longer.

Kane promising to love her. Forever.

"Now, Susannah," Pastor Weatherly said, "it's your turn. Keep holding Kane's hand and repeat after me. In the Name of God, I, Susannah, take you, Kane, to be my husband…"

Kane.

A husband. *Her* husband.

Susannah opened her mouth to speak, but the words refused to come. A rush of fear flooded her senses, and suddenly she couldn't breathe.

"Susannah," Pastor Weatherly whispered, "you're supposed to repeat what I said."

Kane's smile curved wider. "Changed your mind about having and holding me?"

"I…I can't do this," she said, spinning out of Kane's grasp. "I'm sorry."

Then she hurried out of the church and didn't stop running until she reached wide-open grass and fresh air.

The scent of freedom, the one thing she had craved for years. And refused to chance losing. Not even on an imaginary basis.

CHAPTER TEN

WHAT the hell was *that?*

Had he just gotten *married?*

Whether for real or not, for a few minutes there, Kane had been swept up into the moment and had, indeed, felt like he and Susannah were pledging to be together forever. And the crazy part?

He hadn't minded a bit.

Standing on that altar, she had looked beautiful, almost angelic. The setting sun streaming through the stained-glass windows had cast tiny rainbows across her features, like miniature jewels in her hair, on her skin.

And suddenly, his world, which had seemed so hard and cold a week ago, filled with sunshine. He couldn't imagine returning to New York, returning to work, to his penthouse apartment overlooking Central Park—

Without that.

Without her.

"Maybe that wasn't such a good idea," Pastor Weatherly said, as the rest of the wedding party began to file out of the church and head to their cars, their chattering voices expressing their surprise about what had happened. One of the groomsmen called over his shoulder to Kane that they were planning on meeting at the Corner Kitchen for the rehearsal dinner. Kane nodded agreement.

"It did seem to backfire," Kane said.

"Perhaps Susannah didn't like being in the spotlight," Pastor Weatherly said, taking a seat on the top step of the altar. He gestured to Kane to join him.

Kane suspected more was involved in Susannah's reaction. If she'd even experienced a tenth of what he had up there on that altar, of that eerie sense of reality surrounding them, as if he had on a tux and she a dress and veil instead of Jackie and Paul—then Kane couldn't blame her for running. "Maybe. Either way Jackie shouldn't have put Susannah in that situation in the first place."

"Well, that's kind of Jackie's way. She's a little…forgetful. And Susannah, well, she'd do about anything for Jackie, and she always has, ever since their parents died when Susannah was eighteen."

"Their parents are *both* dead?" Kane hadn't put those pieces together. Both her parents were gone, and at such a young age. He'd lost his own mother to cancer in college, and noticed his father had drawn even further into himself and the business. But to lose both parents—

That explained so much. Her commitment to her sister. Her emphasis on responsibility. And most of all her desire to leave, and finally live her own life.

The minister nodded. "I baptized those girls, and buried their parents eight years ago." He glanced over at Kane and read the clear question in the other man's eyes. "A boating accident. The Wilsons were fishing out on Lake Michigan when this storm came, out of nowhere. Their boat swamped when they were trying to get back to shore and they drowned."

Kane's gaze went to the doors. "Susannah was so young."

"Old enough to have her own life, but she chose instead to put that on hold and raise Jackie. Let me tell you, that girl was a handful at fourteen, bless her heart. But Susannah wouldn't have any part of breaking up her family. Jackie had lived in that house all her life, and Susannah refused to move her from there, or from the town that loved her." Pastor Weatherly laid a hand on Kane's. "After tomorrow, it's finally Susannah's turn. Even though we're all going to miss her around here, we understand why she's leaving. She deserves to have her moment in the sun."

Kane thought of the woman he had met. No wonder she was so strong. So determined. So invested in her sister's welfare. "She's never gone anywhere? College?"

"Susannah has never taken so much as a vacation. That girl has made Jackie her life." A tender smile took over Pastor Weatherly's face. "I can tell you care about Susannah, but remember everyone here in Chapel Ridge does, too. Whatever you do, do it in her best interests." He rose, laying a firm hand on Kane's shoulders before disappearing into the back of the church.

A rock of guilt sank to the pit of Kane's gut. Had Pastor Weatherly peeked inside Kane's conscience? Not five minutes before arriving at the church, Kane had been considering his exit strategy. Get out, get back to New York before he got any more wrapped up in this town, or Susannah Wilson. Staying in Chapel Ridge any longer than absolutely necessary would be a mistake. He saw no way to have both his life in New York and Susannah Wilson.

Except…

She wanted to explore the world, to leave this town. Maybe they could continue this on his turf, if she'd consider making New York City part of her itinerary.

One pesky problem remained. He had lied to her from

the moment he met her. Undoing that was nearly impossible, not without bringing him the very thing he didn't want, not quite yet.

A return to his regular life.

Or worse, the look of betrayal in Susannah's green eyes. He might not know Susannah Wilson very well, but he knew one thing. She valued honesty above everything else.

And a woman like Susannah could never love a man who lied.

"How'd it go?" Jackie said. "Sorry I'm late."

Susannah swiped at her face and turned around, grateful night had fallen and would mask her tears. "Fine."

"Were you crying just now?" Jackie leaned in close, peering at Susannah's face.

"No." Her voice betrayed her, hooking on the last syllable.

"You *were* crying." Jackie's voice lowered in sympathy. "Why?"

"I…I miss Mom, that's all. I started thinking about her missing the ceremony and it got me upset." There was a lot more emotion mixed up in those tears. Feelings about lost chances and the last few days, but Susannah kept that to herself. Instead, she reached out to her sister, clasping Jackie's hand and giving it a squeeze. "That was a really nice touch, you adding the hymn."

A smile trembled on Jackie's lips. "I wanted to surprise you. I thought you'd like it, too."

A look of understanding passed between them, of shared grief. How long had it been since the two of them had connected? On a sister level, not on a pseudo mother/daughter level? Susannah's heart swelled near to bursting. "It'll be beautiful, Jackie. Mom would have loved it."

Jackie sniffled, then rubbed her arms against the night chill. "Did the rehearsal work out all right otherwise?"

"Yep. Pastor Weatherly has a funeral in a little while, so Kane and I walked through the ceremony." Susannah didn't tell Jackie about the experience of standing at the front of the church and "marrying" Kane. About how real it had been. How…nice. How terrifying. For a moment at least, she'd forgotten what a completely insane idea marrying Kane would be. Then she'd come to her senses, thank goodness, and gotten out of there before things went any further. "I can go over the details if you want."

Jackie waved a hand. "Tomorrow morning is soon enough. Tonight, it's time to party." She grinned. "Remember, we're all meeting over at the Corner Kitchen for the rehearsal dinner? The pay-for-yourself rehearsal dinner, because Paul and I are poor, *and* we're saving our money for retirement."

Kane had gotten through to Jackie, on the financial end. Thank goodness. Nevertheless, even though Susannah had told her sister the rehearsal had made her upset because it made her miss her mother, she had really been more unsettled by Kane. She couldn't imagine sitting across from him at the Corner Kitchen tonight and acting as if nothing had happened, after just standing at the altar and hearing him feign a forever pledge. "Jackie, I'm not in much of a party mood."

"You always say that." Jackie let out a gust. "Susannah, why won't you just go? It'll be fun."

"You go. You have fun." Susannah started toward her car. "I'll go home and start the thank-you cards for the bridal shower gifts—"

Jackie grabbed her sleeve and stopped Susannah in her tracks. "No. Don't."

"You won't have time, Jackie. You know how disorganized you get with those things. And plus, you'll be back at work right after the honeymoon, and—"

"Susannah, I *want* you to have fun tonight." Jackie toed at the grass, tracing a half circle before raising her gaze to her sister's. "This is my wedding, and *I* should be doing these things."

Jackie had said the very same thing a dozen times before. Made promises she hadn't kept. Susannah shook her head. "Like being at your own rehearsal?"

"Yeah, like that."

Susannah bit her lip, refusing to get angry, to have an argument over this. "It's fine. I took care of it."

"That's the problem, Susannah. You're always taking care of me. And I let you, because it's so damned easy." Jackie turned away and crossed to a curved wrought iron bench beneath a magnolia tree. She took a seat, bracing her hands on either side, and swung her legs back and forth, leaving deep indents in the grass. "When I got to the church tonight and found out everyone was gone, and that you had already taken care of the rehearsal, I was…mad. Even though it was my fault."

"Jackie, what did you want me to do?" Susannah threw up her hands. "You weren't here. As usual. I had to do something."

"That wasn't why I was mad. I was mad at myself. For missing something I really wanted to be at. I know, I know, I did it to myself. It seems like every time I have good intentions, I do the wrong thing."

Susannah knew she could take the opportunity to jump on Jackie for all the mistakes of the past. Point out her faults, the areas where her younger sister had taken advantage. What would be the point? She'd rather hang tight to that thread of connection they'd begun to build tonight, and knit an even thicker rope. "You try, Jackie. And you're trying harder now."

"It's not enough. Not yet. I'm trying to get my life together, Suzie-Q, but you make it too easy for me not to."

Susannah rubbed at her temples. "What is that supposed to mean?"

Jackie took Susannah's hand and pulled her onto the bench beside her. She hesitated so long before speaking, Susannah wondered if Jackie would just brush off the conversation like she always did, with a joke or a distraction. Instead, she drew in a long breath, then let it out. "Ever since Mom and Dad died, you've taken good care of me. Really good care."

"That's my job, sis. I didn't want you to have to live with strangers or with some relatives in Arizona that we hardly knew."

"I know, but when I got older, you just *kept on* taking care of me." Jackie looked down at her hands. "And I let you. Because, well, I was lazy."

Susannah started to disagree. And stopped.

"I let you do everything for me, including my wedding. I shouldn't have done that." She took in a breath, let it out. "I don't want to miss any more of my wedding, Suzie. It's my wedding, not yours, and I'll only have the one. So, you are officially fired as my helper." She met Susannah's eyes and grinned.

"Fired?"

"Yep. From now on, all I want you to do is be my sister. And my maid of honor. That means, just show up tomorrow night and hold my bouquet when I'm at the altar."

Susannah leaned back against the bench, studying her sister. "What's with this sudden change of heart? I mean, I'm all for it, but—"

"Don't use that word. *But.* I'm working on being more responsible, and while I bet I'm going to screw up a lot, I'm going to try really hard. When you say 'but,' it's like you already doubt me." A tentative smile spread across Jackie's face, one that said she had her own doubts about herself but she was holding tight to her confidence. "Okay?"

"Okay." Jackie was grown up, and Susannah wanted to cry, both happy and sad, and full of love that threatened to burst from her heart. Her sister finally appreciated her, and understood what she had done—and now wanted to spread her own wings. Susannah leaned forward and drew Jackie into a tight hug. Jackie's arms went around Susannah's back, and the two of them embraced, the thread weaving together finally, bringing two sisters together again. Susannah's throat closed, and the tears spilled over, onto Jackie's shoulder. She cupped her sister's head. "Mom and Dad would be really proud of you," she whispered.

"No, Susannah," Jackie said softly, her voice hoarse. "They'd be really proud of you. Just as proud as I am that you're my sister." She drew back and their watery gazes met. "Thank you."

And with those two words, the bridge between them was finally healed.

The envelope had been a warning. The only person who had a contact address for Kane—his personal assistant, Laura—had sent the overnight message to warn him that his father had pulled out all the stops to find his son. Kane paid Laura well enough that he doubted she would talk, and either way, he hadn't given even her specific information. Just in case.

But it was only a matter of time. His father was not a man who would be denied anything, especially access to his son.

Kane paced the small cabin, Bandit running circles around his legs, unnerved by his temporary owner's continual movements. So much for a vacation. Four short days and already reality was dragging him back kicking and screaming.

Maybe it was a good thing. After all, twelve hours ago he'd been standing at the front of a church, before a minister, pledging to love Susannah till death did them part.

He had definitely *not* come here for that.

Except that moment hadn't been so bad. Or frightening. Or any of the other adjectives Kane had always associated with the thought of marriage. Maybe he could find a way to have it all. Or at least take baby steps in that direction.

For now, though, he had the envelope to deal with.

Kane crossed to the hearth and started a fire, this time with quick success. Susannah had shown him how to use a bit of newspaper to help the kindling catch the flame, then add the logs a little at a time, as well as how to operate the flue. Give him a few more days and he'd be a regular Grizzly Adams.

Bandit padded over to the fireplace and settled down at Kane's feet. Kane reached out and tousled the dog's ears. Bandit sighed and leaned into Kane's leg, tail beating a drum of happiness against the wood floor. "You like me?"

Bandit wagged some more.

He ran his hand down the dog's neck, patting the silky hair. "I've never had a dog, you know."

That apparently didn't bother Bandit, who wagged harder.

"I heard you're spoiled."

The dog whimpered a disagreement.

When he left, he'd be leaving the dog behind. Could he do that? Could he just pick up and go, and become the same old Kane Lennox again?

Did he even want to?

Kane's gaze traveled to the overnight envelope on the table.

Did he have a choice?

CHAPTER ELEVEN

"Isn't it a little early in the morning for alcohol?" Kane settled on the bar stool inside Flanagan's Pub beside Paul and ordered a coffee, waving off Paul's offer of a beer.

"I'm getting married today, Kane. *Married.*" Paul gripped the beer bottle like a life preserver. "Am I insane?"

"Do you love her?"

"Of course I do."

"Then no, you're not insane. At least not entirely." Kane grinned.

"Ha, ha." Paul took a deep gulp of the beer, made a face, then pushed the brown bottle to the side. "You're right. It is too early in the morning for beer."

Kane chuckled and signaled for a second cup of coffee. The bartender shook his head at the two men as he slid the steaming mugs across the bar. Kane thanked him. As the bartender walked away to finish drying glasses, Kane pulled out his wallet for some bills and laid enough money on the oak surface to cover the coffee and a generous tip. Kane turned back to Paul. "Did you and Jackie work everything out?"

"Kane, what are you doing?"

"Sitting here, talking to you…" Kane flicked out his

wrist. "At nine in the morning, in a bar. Reminds me of our college days."

"I meant with that." Paul gestured toward the tip, then leaned forward and lowered his voice to a whisper. "In this town, we don't leave a bartender a hundred-dollar tip. The guy is going to have a coronary when he sees that."

"Oh. You told me about what happened with his family…how he's been struggling. I know a hundred bucks isn't going to make much difference, but it should at least make his day."

Paul leaned back on his bar stool, his jaw slack. "You are *not* the same guy I knew in college."

"What, just because I'm drinking coffee instead of beer in the morning? All of us grow up, Paul. I bet you cut back, too. You have a job. Teaching kids, at that. Can't show up at school drunk or hung over, I'm sure."

"I'm not talking about the drinking. I'm talking about this…" he waved a hand over Kane "…this socially conscious, socially involved Kane."

He chuckled. "You make me sound like the next step up from Cro-Magnon Man."

"You are, compared to the rest of us guys."

Larry headed over, a pot of coffee in one hand. He started to refill Kane's mug when he spied the money, and froze. "Whoa! Dude, is that a hundred-dollar bill?"

"Yep." Kane grinned. "And it's for you."

The stout, tall man stared at the green paper. Then at Kane, then back again at the hundred dollars. "Uh…you only got coffee."

Kane smiled. "I know."

The bartender held the bill up to the light, as if he still couldn't believe it was real. "You sure? Is this really for me?"

"The whole thing. Take your wife out for dinner, pay

some bills. Relieve some stress." Kane leaned forward. "I know all about needing to relieve stress. Hope that helps."

"Yeah, it will. Thanks. I mean, *thanks*." The bartender backed up and reached for the wall phone, then started dialing. "Honey, you aren't going to believe this…"

As Larry chatted with his wife, Kane's heart swelled. Damn. Who knew giving could feel this great? And all he'd done was overtip.

Kane returned his attention to Paul. "That felt good. I mean, I give plenty of money to charities every year, but that's writing a check. This was hands-on. Maybe I should start handing out money on the street to perfect strangers."

Paul arched a brow. "Are you dying or something?"

"No. Just…" Kane drew in a breath, and when he did, he swore he could catch the floral notes of Susannah's perfume. She'd rubbed off on him, that was for sure. She and the rest of this small town. "Just enjoying my life for the first time ever."

"Well, if handing over money makes you feel good…" Paul grinned, then put up his hands. "Just kidding, buddy. I never liked you for your money, you know that."

"I do. And I appreciate it." Kane gave Paul a good-natured clap on the back. He had thought of giving his friend a healthy check for a wedding present but decided a more-personal gift—one that meant something to Kane himself—would be far better. He reached into the breast pocket of his leather jacket and pulled out an envelope. "I want you and Jackie to have this."

"What…" Paul's voice trailed off, caught in a breath. He held the envelope tight, reading the name of the travel agency on the front, then the word Jamaica beneath the logo. "*Jamaica?* But, Kane, we can't—"

"You can and you will. Life's too short, Paul. I know

you guys are tight on money and you were planning just a simple three-day honeymoon in Chicago. Nothing against that city, but you two deserve more, especially for your honeymoon. I talked to your principal and to Jackie's boss, and got you a few more days off. Two weeks, to be exact."

"Two weeks?" Paul's eyes widened. "How the hell did you manage that?"

"I, uh, offered to pay for the substitute. The principal was arguing about the cost of that until I said I'd pony up the cash. Seems small towns have small budgets when it comes to substitute teachers."

"Small towns have small budgets for everything, Kane." Paul turned the envelope over in his hand, staring at it, incredulous. "You have got to be kidding me. This is too much." Then he shook his head and slid the envelope across the bar. "We can't accept it."

Kane slid it back to Paul. "You saved my ass in college a dozen times. This is just a small way to repay you, to say thanks."

"Hey, all I did was help you study for some tests."

"No. You helped me have a life. Outside the Lennox name. That saved my sanity. Down the road it brought me here, and that saved me a second time."

"I call it even, Kane, after you talked to Jackie and convinced her saving money will make her a millionaire." Paul grinned. "Heck, I would have been happy just to have Jackie see the value of a savings account, but you've got her talking 401ks and 529s for our kids. You're a miracle worker."

Kane chuckled, then sobered. "I found something in Chapel Ridge, Paul, that taught me a lesson. Something I wanted to share with you. That's what this is really about." Kane cupped his hands around his coffee and stared into the dark liquid. "The years will pass so fast, Paul, your head will spin, and you'll wish you took the days off when you could. So do it now, while someone else is footing the tab."

Paul opened his mouth to protest again, then stopped. "Okay. But only because Jackie would kill me if I said no."

Kane laughed. "Good."

"What about you?"

"What about me?"

"Are you just going to go back to being Kane Lennox, or are you going to have a life when you get back to New York?"

Kane snorted. "You know my father, Paul. What do you think? Nothing will make him happy but me being at work twenty-four hours a day."

"Why do you try so hard?" Paul asked. "I don't want to tell you how to live your life, but why do you worry so much about what your father thinks?"

Kane spun the coffee mug back and forth. "It's complicated. He's not a bad man, just…difficult."

Paul bit his lip, closing the subject of Kane's father. "What are you going to do about Susannah?"

"Do? Nothing."

Paul snorted. "Right. I heard from my groomsmen what happened at the altar last night. Seems you two have a few feelings for each other. They said they felt like they were watching a real wedding."

Kane's mind rocketed back to that moment, to Susannah, standing beneath the jeweled light of the stained glass. To her smile when he pledged his love. Real or not, for a moment, it had been believable. Then she had run out of there, and avoided the rehearsal dinner. Avoided him. Making it clear that what had happened at that altar hadn't been real to her. Or if it had been, it had been a real nightmare. "Well, we were just acting."

Paul gave him a light elbow jab. "Maybe you're in the

wrong industry. Everyone in the pews said it was worthy of an Academy Award."

Kane thought again of the envelope. Of the warning from his assistant. His father would never approve of Susannah, and that would leave the two Lennox men even more divided than they already were. How could that do any of them, or for that matter, the company, any good? "And maybe I just need to remember my place."

Beneath the family yoke.

"Reggie is sure going to miss you," Cecilia Richards said, taking her Pomeranian from Susannah and giving the freshly groomed, caramel-colored dog a cuddle. "Are you sure I can't talk you into staying in town? Where else will I find a groomer who's as patient with my sweet little boy as you are?"

Susannah smiled. Mrs. Richards's "sweet little boy" had a temperament that usually required a muzzle and hazardous-duty pay. The Pomeranian had a hatred of all things water, and made his displeasure about his baths well known from the minute he arrived at The Sudsy Dog. Tess refused to go near him. Susannah had always been the only one who could calm Reggie enough to get him through the experience. "I'll miss him, too," she said, giving Reggie a pat and a little treat. The Pom wagged his tail, probably out of relief that the ordeal was finally over.

"You *are* coming back, aren't you? You aren't going to go to the other side of the world and stay there?"

Susannah sighed. "Yes, I'm coming back. In three weeks." As much as she didn't want to return, her bank account was only so deep, and what would be left after her trip to Paris was needed for an apartment rental.

"Oh, good." Mrs. Richards gave her dog a little nuzzling

kiss, then pouted. "But who will take care of my Reggie until then?"

"Tess would be glad to." Tess would kill her for saying that, but the girl had agreed to take any emergency appointments while Susannah was gone. The shelter dogs had all been adopted or fostered for Susannah's absence. Virtually every last detail had been attended to. Her suitcase was packed. Her last appointment was leaving, thanking her one more time as she got in her car with a growling, barking Reggie. All Susannah had left to do was clean up the shop, make her last deposit, and lock the doors.

Then after the wedding tonight, she was free. Free to finally live her own life. Free to fulfill the dream her mother and father had never had a chance to see.

As Mrs. Richards and Reggie pulled away, Susannah headed back inside The Sudsy Dog. She turned the shop sign to Closed and went into the washing room. In a few minutes, she had the tub cleaned, the supplies put away and everything put in order.

She hung up her apron and looked around at the silent rooms. She was done.

Her gaze strayed to the Arc de Triomphe poster. Tomorrow night, she would be there. Stand in that very city, seeing those sights. But for the first time since Susannah had made the decision to go to Paris, the thought didn't fill her with the same sense of joy.

"Paris is a beautiful city, especially in springtime."

She whirled around and found Kane standing behind her. Dark jeans hugged his hips, outlined his powerful legs, while a white button-down shirt stretched across his chest, beneath a black leather jacket. He'd left a couple of buttons undone, enough to give her a teasing view of the chest she knew existed beneath. A crazy part of Susannah wanted to

undo every last button, place her hands against his skin, and
do what she hadn't done that day in the laundry room. Feel
him beneath her. Taste his skin. And take this beyond a couple of passionate kisses. "What are you doing here? I
thought you'd be with Paul today."

"I was, but he's all set for a while." Kane closed the gap
between them, his purposeful strides making quick work
of the small room. His gaze connected with hers, and the
temperature seemed to rise, the tension in the room double. "He had his doubts about long-term commitment, but
they passed."

Doubts. She'd had those ever since she'd met Kane
Lennox. Doubts about who he was. Why he was here.
Whether she should get involved with him. And now,
doubts about whether she would forget him once she left
town. For a woman who hadn't wanted to leave behind any
strings, she suddenly felt very tied to this man.

Most of the lights in the shop were off, leaving only the
late-afternoon sun's rays. The last golden light of the day
cast a romantic veil over the room, washing Kane with soft
highlights, almost like he, too, were part of the scenery that
hung on her walls.

"That happens." Were they even talking about Paul
and Jackie? Desire coiled in Susannah's gut. She tightened her hold on the brush in her hand, twisting the handle against her palm.

Kane closed the gap. His gaze dropped to her mouth,
then back to her eyes. "He realized he didn't want to go on
without her."

"Good." The word escaped her on a breath.

"What happened to you last night?" Kane asked.

"I didn't want to go to the party. I, um, wasn't feeling
well." Liar. She'd felt fine. She'd been disconcerted by

him. By what had happened back in the church. And really afraid it would show on her face when he looked at her in the restaurant.

"You know what I mean." He tipped her jaw. "What happened at that altar?"

"We…" Her voice trailed off. Why lie? Why pretend? They both knew something had shifted last night, something big. "That was more than just acting, wasn't it?"

He nodded. Slowly. "I know we don't know each other well. And I know how insane that sounds. But you are the first woman I have ever met who sees me for me. Just me. And that—" he smiled "—is the sexiest thing I've ever experienced."

Her heart trilled, her pulse raced. She tried to keep the feelings tamped down, away from showing. "Well, that saves me from wearing high heels."

He laughed, then drew her into his arms. "I mean it, Susannah. You are…everything I always wanted and never even knew existed."

Now the emotion burst onto Susannah's face in a wide smile. Her arms went around Kane, and he drew her to him. She fit against him perfectly, like a lost diamond fitting into its setting. Beneath his shirt, she heard his heartbeat, the steady thump-thump matching her own. "You found that here, in Chapel Ridge, Indiana? And not in New York?"

"Exactly." He leaned down and brushed his lips against hers, tender and sweet, a slow, easy kiss. "But I don't want to lose this. I…I want you to come to New York with me. Right after the wedding."

She backed up, out of his embrace. "What?"

"Come to New York with me. I can rent you an apartment, rent you space for dogs and cats." He grinned. "Whatever you want."

New York City. The epicenter of the country, where everything happened, all the activity came in and went out. She'd be out of this small town forever. Away from its expectations, away from her responsibilities.

But…would she be trading up? Or trading laterally?

She replayed his words in her head, and heard the empty pockets in the sentences. Had he left those gaps on purpose, or was she simply missing something?

"I don't want that, Kane," Susannah said. "I want… more."

"What? A house? That can be arranged. A car? I'll take care of it."

Things. He was offering her *things*. Every single tangible item—

Except his heart.

"No, Kane. I don't want you to pay for me. For one, it's too expensive—"

"I can afford it, I assure you."

"For another, I want to achieve something big, on my own. I want…" She searched for the words she had yet to find, had yet to have time to find. "I want to see the world. Be my own person. Get out from under the shadow of Chapel Ridge. Of being the older Wilson sister. I can't do that if you're funding my move and my life." She drew in a breath and met his gaze. "I don't want to be something you treat like a pet you're boarding at an apartment nearby. If I'm living with a man, I want it to be because I *married* him."

He turned and let out a low curse. "You want everything."

"It's my right, isn't it? To want a full life? And what's wrong with that?"

"I can't give you everything. I have…expectations of my own."

"What kind of expectations could there possibly be,

Kane? I mean, you told me you work in a jewelry store, right? I understand if you work long hours and don't have a lot of time to devote to a relationship. That's, like, the story of my life."

He didn't meet her gaze. Susannah should have taken that as the first sign, but she didn't. That silly bird of hope kept trying to fly in her chest. "It's more than that. My job is beyond demanding. And that has to come first."

"Work comes first?" she repeated, dumbfounded. "This from the man who has been lecturing me all week about taking time off to have a life of my own?"

"I'd be offering you a life, Susannah. A different one from what you have here."

And then she knew. There was no possibility of this dream ever taking flight. A bittersweet smile curved across Susannah's face, and disappointment sank heavy and sour in her stomach. She'd thought she'd known him, but it turned out Kane Lennox had been a stranger all along. "Tell me what the difference is, Kane. In New York, you'd simply be paying me to be with you instead of paying me to teach you to fish."

She rose on her tiptoes and gave him a quick kiss on the cheek, then turned and walked out of The Sudsy Dog. Before she could change her mind and take what he was offering.

Which, really, was nothing she wanted.

CHAPTER TWELVE

THE stretch black limo pulled up in front of The Sudsy Dog, drawing Susannah up short. Except for the occasional funeral, prom or wedding rental, limos never drove through Chapel Ridge. And they never stopped in downtown, in front of the dog-grooming salon.

"Susannah, wait!" Kane called after her, exiting The Sudsy Dog fast on her heels.

She didn't want to stop. Didn't want to deal with anyone, not when her heart was breaking and all she wanted was to retreat to the solitude of her home.

As Kane caught up to her, his hand touching her arm lightly to keep her from leaving, a well-dressed man stepped out of the luxury car. Susannah heard Kane curse under his breath, and realized this was no ordinary limo. And no ordinary visitor.

The man in the suit had distaste and barely restrained fury written all over his features. He buttoned his jacket as he walked toward Kane, not saying a word, simply glaring. First at Kane, then including Susannah, too.

"What a surprise," Kane said, his body language reading the exact opposite. "Susannah, this is my father, Elliott Lennox." This man was Kane's *father?* What was he doing here? And in that car? Beside her, Kane had gone tense, on guard. "Father, this is—"

"Don't act like you don't know why I'm here," the other man cut in, as sharp as a razor. He turned to Susannah and a charming smile took over his face. If she hadn't just seen it herself, she'd think the earlier fury was imagined. There were layers here—layers between the two men, layers in the two men—that Susannah couldn't see. "Excuse me, miss, but this is between my son and me. If you could give us a moment?"

Everything about Elliott Lennox screamed "get away," even with the polite smile. Susannah had no desire to stand in the middle of this tense standoff, and was about to step away when Kane put his hand on her arm again. "No, she won't," he said, his tone just as sharp, insistent.

Elliott scowled. "Kane, don't drag some vacation dalliance into the middle of our family business."

Vacation dalliance? The words hit Susannah like a verbal slap. She opened her mouth to tell him off, when she remembered her place. Downtown Chapel Ridge was neither the time nor the place to stage a scene with Kane's father.

"Don't call her that." Kane's tone was even, controlled, but a growlish undertone lay beneath his words. "Susannah deserves your respect."

Elliott let out a breath of impatience and ran a hand through his silver hair. He had the same height and similar bearing to Kane, but everything else about him, from his clear disdain for the town to his instant hatred of her, seemed like he had DNA from a whole other country. "Enough of this. You've had your fun, now come back to work. For God's sake, you can't keep carrying on like this. What do you think the media will say if they find out you're here in the backwoods, living like a heathen?"

"Mr. Lennox," Susannah cut in, "Chapel Ridge is a small town, certainly nothing that would create some media firestorm for anyone on vacation. And I can't believe the jewelry store can't live without Kane for a few days."

A smirk took over Elliott's face. "Is that what you've told people around here? That you work in a *jewelry store?*" He took a step away from his son and toward Susannah. "Don't you know who he is?"

Kane's eyes narrowed. "Don't."

"This man is Kane Lennox, of the Lennox Gem—"

"I'm warning you."

"Corporation," Elliott went on, ignoring his son. "He is one of the richest men in the world, CEO of one of the biggest companies in the world. That is, if I and the rest of the board don't decide to fire him for this little embarrassment he put us through." Elliott waved at her as if she alone comprised the embarrassment he mentioned.

Then the sentences began to assemble in Susannah's mind. Kane Lennox. CEO. Lennox Gem Corporation.

One of *the* Lennoxes.

Not a jewelry store worker at all.

Susannah's jaw dropped and she stared at Kane, who started to voice an explanation, then stopped when he read her expression. The words added up, one at a time, building blocks suddenly forming into a recognizable shape. Everything Kane had said over the last few days. All the half-truths he'd told, the way he'd acted, the way he'd seemed out of place.

And then his offer—

His offer to put her up in an apartment in New York. His "vacation dalliance," taken back home to the big city. As what, his mistress? While he married some society beauty, someone who would help him expand his corporate reach?

"You…you bastard," she said, the betrayal hitting hard, slicing through her heart. "How could you?"

"Susannah, I have an explanation."

"You lied to me. Everything you said was a lie."

"Not everything, no."

"Oh, did he tell you he loved you? Or make you some ridiculous promise?" Elliott said, then snorted. "Please, Kane, don't toy with people like that. Let this poor woman be. She'd never fit in with your life and you know it." Elliott crossed to the limo and opened the door. "I'm getting back in the car. If you were smart, you would, too."

Elliott did as he said, leaving the limo door open. Waiting for Kane and his decision. Go back to New York, leaving Susannah behind. And forget this silly vacation dalliance forever.

She waited. For Kane to turn around. For him to look at her and tell her his father was wrong. That he would stay here, with her. Because she was more important than anything else. Because he loved her, and he would sacrifice anything to have her in his life.

But he didn't turn around, and he didn't say any of those things.

Susannah's heart shattered. She spun on her heel and ran to her car. Pulling away, she refused to look in her rearview mirror. She couldn't even if she'd wanted to. The tears blurred her vision.

The candles flickered in the church, bathing the room in a soft, golden glow. A hundred guests filled the pews, chatting quietly among themselves while they waited.

Susannah closed the double doors, then ducked back into the bridal room. "Everything's all set."

Jackie stood in front of the full-length mirror, adjusting

her veil, then smoothing the front of her simple spaghetti-strap, tea-length dress. "I thought I'd be nervous, but I'm not."

Susannah drew her younger sister into a one-armed hug, careful not to crinkle the satin cap sleeves and bodice of her light blue maid-of-honor dress. "That's because you're marrying Mr. Right."

Jackie smiled. "Paul is pretty wonderful, isn't he?"

"Yep." A little shiver of melancholy ran through Susannah. Her sister was marrying the right guy, beginning the rest of her life with him, and Susannah should be overjoyed for Jackie. And she was—

But she was also envious, in a weird way. Only because of that betrayal with Kane earlier. How could he have lied to her? After all they'd talked about and shared? She'd told him so much about herself, and he'd made up everything he'd told her.

Even what he felt? Had each kiss been a fraud, too?

A sharp ache ran through her chest, and tears threatened again at Susannah's eyes. She heard Kane's offer of an apartment in New York, followed by Elliott's taunting, as if he'd caught Kane doing that a hundred times before. Just one more vacation dalliance.

How stupid could she be?

"Susannah? Are you paying attention? I needed help with the straps on my shoes."

"Oh, sure." Susannah took a seat on an ottoman and bent to slip the straps into the tiny gold buckles.

"Are you all right? You're so distracted."

She rose. "Just thinking about all those last-minute details before I get on the plane tomorrow."

Jackie took Susannah's hand, her eyes misty. "I wish you weren't going away."

"I'll be back." She'd return to Chapel Ridge, to her life.

To her business. And to a decidedly empty feeling, after all that had happened with Kane. Susannah brushed the emotion away. A few weeks in Paris would help her forget.

It would.

"I know. But I'm going to miss you all the same. We've never been apart."

"We haven't, have we?" Susannah gave Jackie's hand a squeeze. "Don't worry. I'll call you every day."

"You better." Jackie swiped at her face. "Though I don't know if I'll have cell service in Jamaica."

"Jamaica?" Susannah blinked. "I thought you were going to Chicago."

"I didn't tell you?" Jackie drew back, beaming with joy. "Kane did the sweetest thing. He called my boss, and Paul's, and got us both two weeks off, then gave us a trip to Jamaica as a wedding present."

"Wow! That's generous." She chided herself for being surprised. He was a millionaire after all, probably even a billionaire. A trip to Jamaica was a drop in the ocean of money to a guy like him.

Hadn't he just proved to her that money was more important than people? In the end, he'd go back to his billion-dollar life. Who could blame him, really? When his choice was staying here with the fishing poles and stray dogs?

"Paul asked Kane why he did it," Jackie went on, "and he said that he wanted us to experience what he did while he was here in Chapel Ridge. He said he found something here he never found anywhere else." Jackie turned to the table, picked up her bouquet, then checked her reflection one more time. "What kind of experience does *anyone* have in Chapel Ridge? I mean, this has to be the most boring town in the country."

"Yeah. Nothing to offer here." Susannah pretended to

check her own reflection, the long blond hair, the plainer of the two Wilson sisters, avoiding Jackie's gaze, avoiding the truth about Kane and his "experiences," then pivoted away from the mirror. "It's almost time to go, Jackie. In a little while you'll be married to Paul."

"I can only do that," Jackie said with a smile, "if you get ready to walk down that aisle first. Can't get married without my sister standing by me, now can I?"

The only trouble? Susannah already knew who else would be waiting at the end of that aisle. And she wasn't so sure she could face him ever again.

CHAPTER THIRTEEN

IN THE PAST HOUR, KANE had been fired, disowned and written out of the Lennox family will. Twice. Now his father was trying the silent treatment. Didn't matter. Kane refused to be dissuaded. "I'm not going back to New York, not this second anyway."

Elliott Lennox didn't respond. He stood in Kane's rustic kitchen, as still as a statue. His silver hair and regal bearing made him look like a piece of art, particularly against the roughly hewn cabin's backdrop.

"I'm the best man, and that means I honor my commitment. You'd want me to do that, wouldn't you?"

Again, his father said nothing.

Kane shook his head. "What's it going to take? What do I have to do to get your attention? To get you to acknowledge me as your son?"

Elliott wheeled around. "When you start *acting* like my son, that's when I'll acknowledge you."

"Tell me a day when I didn't," Kane shot back.

"This week, for one." Elliott shook his head. "You abandoned your family. Your responsibilities. That is simply unacceptable. God, it's like you're back in college again and I need to clean up your mess."

"Is that what you're going to do? Ship Susannah off to Europe so I don't embarrass you again?"

"There was more involved than an embarrassment for the family, Kane."

Kane snorted. "What, was my involvement with Rebecca back in college going to affect some business deal for you? Her father had a one-percent stake in a competitor?"

"She wanted your money."

Kane rolled his eyes. "Right. And so does every other woman I date who you don't agree with. I swear, you'd handpick my ties if I let you."

Elliott toyed with the coffee mug before him. "Rebecca came to me over Christmas break. Walked right into my office, as bold as brass. Said she was going to marry you whether I liked it or not."

Kane chuckled. "That's Rebecca for you."

"Then she said I could stop the wedding for a quarter million dollars."

The blow to Kane's chest hit swift and hard. He stepped back, reaching for the back of a chair. "You're lying."

His father's gaze met his. "I never lie about money, Kane."

Kane thought back to how quickly Rebecca had disappeared from his life. How easy it had seemed for her to go, once she had received the buyout from his father, the offer of an overseas education. Disgust rose in his chest. "Did you pay her the money?"

"We came to an acceptable arrangement." Elliott took a sip of coffee, then held tight to the mug, not saying anything for a long time. "I was *protecting* you, Kane. You have a tendency to see the world through rose-colored glasses. You believe the best in people. I...I see them for what they are."

Kane let out a gust. "What, everyone is greedy?"

A slight smile crossed his father's face. "No. Not everyone is like you."

"Selfish and impetuous, is that it?"

"I can't say I've agreed with all your decisions, but you are more...trusting than I am. And there have been days when I wish I had some of your leap-off-the-bridge attitude."

The words took Kane by surprise. A compliment from his father—as rare as spotting a saltwater marlin in the middle of the Indiana lake. His anger dissipated, and he moved closer, seeing Elliott with new, less-jaded eyes. "You never thought of just simply taking off on a vacation? Running away from it all for a day or two? Or a week?"

"We all have those thoughts. But I had too much on my shoulders to ever indulge in them. My father, the company, your mother, you."

Kane shook his head. "You could have taken time off."

"And who would have run Lennox? Who would have made sure my father stayed in line? He might as well have been a child, given how little attention he paid to the business. To the rest of us. He spent more time at the gambling table than at the office. Someone had to step up, Kane, and that someone was me. Then I was married, a father, and years later, I had a sick wife. I had no time for flights of fancy or otherwise."

Understanding began to pour into Kane's blood. He thought back over the years, and finally saw his father's life, realizing all those hours at the office hadn't been a choice, they'd been a duty. Not to the company that bore his name, but to his family. "I had no idea."

Elliott shrugged. "I wasn't going to burden you with my problems."

"You should have. It would have helped me understand you."

Elliott shook his head. "Neither of us understands the other very well, do we? We've always been at odds. Like two bulldogs."

Kane studied the wood floor, memorizing the grain of the long, straight boards, before speaking words that had lain within him for a long time, festering. It was time he got it all out. Shared the reasons he had left New York. "I was wrong for leaving without a word, or at least answering my cell phone. The fish have it now." His father's brows knitted in confusion, but Kane went on. "I feel like I've spent my life trying to live up to some impossible standard. To please you, to do everything you've asked of me. Today is the first time you've ever complimented me, that I can remember. You treat your employees better then your own son."

"I gave you the best things in life. The best home, food, clothes, schools. Gave you a job."

"I didn't *want* any of that!" Kane swallowed the rest of his temper, then turned away and crossed to the cold fireplace.

"What did you want? A better car? Bigger house?" Elliott let out a frustrated gust. "A raise? I pay you well enough."

Kane rested his grip on the mantel, clutching the stones above the fireplace, their hard solidity providing strength. "I wanted you," he said softly. "That was all."

The room fell silent. A chair screeched, then creaked.

Kane turned around, and found his father at the table, looking older than he ever had before. His face seemed to have added wrinkles, his shoulders seemed to droop.

"You *had* me, Kane. Every day. I came home after work. And then, when you were done with college, you went to work for me. How can you say that I wasn't there?"

Kane crossed to the table, and sank into the opposite chair. "You were, but not as a father. All I wanted was the occasional hug. A few *atta-boys* here and there. Would it have been so hard to say, 'Hey, Kane, I'm proud of you,' instead of 'don't embarrass the family again'?"

Elliott turned away. "You know how I feel. I'm not some touchy-feely guy. For God's sake, that's no way to do business."

"A family is not a business, Father."

Elliott ran a hand over his face. He sat there a long time, so long, Kane was afraid he had gone back to the silent treatment. Then he swallowed hard and let out a breath before facing his son. "You know who used to say that to me all the time? My mother. She'd remind me, over and over, that family wasn't business. She told my father, too, but he didn't listen any more than I did, I guess. You get…consumed, Kane."

"Like Uncle Harold."

"That man worked himself to death. Died on the job, for God's sake." Elliott shook his head. "Should have had the sense to retire when he had a chance."

Kane arched a brow. "Know anybody like that?"

"I'm nothing like my brother." Elliott paused. "I simply haven't found anything better I want to do than go to work."

"Spend time with your family?"

"What family? You're all grown up. Your mother is…" His gaze drifted off, and Kane knew then another major reason why Elliott had poured himself into the company. "Is gone."

He looked at his father, a man he knew better as the chairman of the board than as a patriarch, and felt his heart soften. This could have been him, in a few years, if he hadn't run away to Chapel Ridge for a few days. If he hadn't taken time to walk a stray dog, dig in the earth, walk barefoot on the grass. "But *I'm* still here, Father. It's not too late, you know. You're not Uncle Harold. You still have time."

Elliott ran a hand over the cup of coffee before him, a

cup he had topped off earlier with a little bit of scotch. "Time for you and me?"

An olive branch. Kane would take it and hold on tight. If he'd learned one thing in his time in Chapel Ridge, it was that life was too damned short to waste it holding a grudge. "Do you like to fish?"

Elliott let out what might have been considered a laugh. "Fish? Are you serious?"

"As a stock report. If you want to hang around Chapel Ridge for a few days, I can show you the best fishing holes."

"Who would run the company?"

"That's the beauty of a huge company, Father. There are plenty of people to call on to take your place. Competent people that you and I hired. Trust them, and then go and relax. It'll do you a world of good."

Elliott let out a gust. "You're insane."

"No. I'm happy." Kane rose, then reached for the leash by the door and tossed it to his father. Elliott caught the lead and stared at his son. "Take some advice from a friend of mine and start with walking a dog. You might even want to try doing it barefoot. Spring grass is amazing under your feet."

"Walking a dog? You really are crazy. I can't possibly—"

"I thought the same thing. Bandit over there knows what to do. He'll lead you. And who knows…you might have fun." Kane grinned, grabbed the rental's car keys off the table, then grasped the door handle. He looked at his father, and thought about what had just transpired, and realized that he had nearly made the same mistakes as his father today. He'd tried to hold too tightly—and nearly lost everything he wanted. "I'll be back in a little while."

"Where are you going?"

"I have a wedding to go to. There's a guy I know who's

about to take the biggest risk of all, and get married, even though he makes hardly anything for money, and doesn't even have a five-year plan. He's doing it because he's in love. And if I play my cards right, I'll be doing the same thing really soon."

Then Kane hopped in his car and hurried down the lane toward the Chapel Ridge Lutheran Church, barely on time for the wedding. But hopefully not too late to get Susannah back.

Déjà vu.

Susannah stood at the front of the church, while Jackie and Paul were quiet and solemn at the altar in front of the minister, hands clasped, repeating the same words she had heard Kane say just last night. Had it been a mere twenty-four hours ago that the two of them had stood before Pastor Weatherly and rehearsed the wedding? Only a day since she believed, just for a moment, that maybe there was a future with this man?

She snuck a glance across the aisle at Kane. Her hormones betrayed her mind, jumping into action, raising her body temperature, accelerating her heartbeat. Apparently they hadn't gotten the memo that her mind was trying to forget Kane, because looking at him now brought desire roaring to the surface.

But appearances weren't everything, and she had to remind herself that this handsome package had come with a hefty package of falsehoods, too. He had lied to her, let her down and she couldn't forgive him for that.

Kane tried to catch her eye, sending her a smile, but Susannah turned her gaze away and refocused on the bridal couple.

"I now pronounce you husband and wife," Pastor

Weatherly said. He leaned in toward Paul. "You may kiss the bride."

Paul swooped Jackie into his arms, gave her a tender but passionate kiss, then pivoted her toward the church. Behind them, Pastor Weatherly introduced the new couple, and a moment later Mrs. Maxwell was playing the recessional as the several dozen guests applauded and wiped away tears.

Jackie and Paul swished down the aisle. Then Kane stepped onto the rose-covered path, his arm bent, and waited for Susannah. She pasted a smile on her face, slipped her arm into Kane's, and started walking. Just a few more minutes and this charade would be over.

Damn her body. His touch still sent a zing through her, still caused a reaction. Every ounce of her went on high alert—all those parts that had yet to forget what it felt like to be in Kane's arms. To have his lips on hers.

"You look beautiful," Kane whispered as they made their way to the back of the church.

"And you look like a liar," she snapped under her breath. She would not fall for him. Not again.

"Let me explain, Susannah."

They slipped past the double doors. As soon as they were outside the church, Susannah yanked her arm out of Kane's. "Why? You're leaving town anyway. Don't worry, Kane, I get it. You decided to fool around with the small-town girl, then leave her behind. Just one more memory in your vacation scrapbook, huh? Another *dalliance* to add to the tally?"

"It wasn't like that, Susannah."

"I heard exactly how it was, Kane *Lennox*." She headed down the granite steps of the church, unable to listen to another word. She waited on the sidewalk for the receiving line to finish, realizing then that she was stuck. She needed to ride to the reception with the rest of the bridal party, and right now, the bridesmaids were chatting it up inside the church. Just when Susannah needed to make a quick escape, too.

She was about to bum a ride off Mrs. Maxwell when a stretch white limo pulled up. A tall, thin chauffeur hopped out and opened the rear door. "Your car, miss?" he said to Susannah.

"Oh, no, this isn't for me. It's for the bride and groom."

"No, miss. This one is yours. There will be another one here shortly for them." The chauffeur waved again at the richly appointed interior of the limo—all leather, with a fully stocked bar, even a television.

"Mine? But…"

"It's yours, Susannah. I still owe you a tip," Kane said, coming up behind her, his hand at the small of her back, setting off those traitorous hormones again. "Please don't say no. The whole town is staring at you, waiting for something to gossip about anyway."

Susannah glanced over her shoulder and saw Kane was right. The guests who had turned out for Paul and Jackie's wedding—from Larry the bartender to Mrs. Maxwell—were all watching the exchange, and the unusual sight of a limo, followed by a second one rounding the corner, with undisguised interest. She had two choices. Stand here and let her business be known by all of Chapel Ridge, or get inside and at least keep the damage contained. Susannah climbed into the car, then slid over when Kane followed her.

The chauffeur shut the door, and in an instant, all of Chapel Ridge was muffled. The world closed in, becoming just her. And Kane.

"*Now* will you listen to me?" he asked.

"It seems I'm your hostage," she said, echoing his words

from a few days earlier, "for as long as it takes to get to the Chapel Ridge Hotel."

A grin curved across his mouth, then he leaned forward and brought his lips within a centimeter of hers. Her pulse raised, and anticipation pooled in her veins, warring with her better sense. "Then I better make good use of the time."

CHAPTER FOURTEEN

KANE didn't kiss Susannah, not exactly, even though every cell in his body screamed for him to. Instead, he drew back, allowing her distance and space, and prepared to plead his case. If he couldn't get her to listen in the next few miles, he'd lose her forever.

And that was the one price Kane Lennox, one of the richest men in the world, couldn't afford to pay.

"I'm sorry," he said.

She crossed her arms over her chest. Not budging an inch. "Why would you lie to me?"

"Because I wanted someone to look at me for me, not for my money. It was simple as that, Susannah."

"And what, you think so little of me that you don't think I could see past the money?"

"Past *billions* of dollars? Susannah, you're an incredible woman, but no one sees past that. Trust me. I know, because I've met dozens of people over the years and not a one looked at me and didn't see a dollar sign before my name."

She shook her head and turned to watch the town passing by the tinted windows. "I really don't think we have anything to say to each other, Kane. It's easier if you just leave me alone. We don't even have to talk to each other at the reception."

Kane ran a hand through his hair. He hadn't expected this to be easy, but knew, as the limo made another turn, that his time was running out. Small towns equaled short distances from one place to another. For the first time ever, he wished for the insane stop-and-go New York City traffic, which could have bought him a hefty half hour just to get from one side of Central Park to the other, given the right time of day.

Once the car stopped at the hotel, Susannah would bolt, and the chances of him having this kind of uninterrupted, captive audience time again were slim. "What are you going to do, Susannah, hop on that plane tomorrow and run away from the town, just like you're running away from me right now?"

She pivoted back. "I'm not running from anything. I'm going out on my own, having my life. That's not a crime."

He took her hand, running his fingers gently over the delicate bones. But she remained stiff, unyielding to his touch. "It is, if you're doing it so you can avoid the things in your life that scare you."

Her chin raised, defiant. "I'm not scared of anything."

"Oh, yeah?" With his free hand, he cupped her jaw, his touch against her cheek doing the same thing it had from the first time his palm had met her skin, offering a soothing balm to his soul. "You're scared of the same thing I am."

Her green eyes widened, their depths as rich as pure emeralds. Kane had worked with gems all his life, and never seen a single one as beautiful as the two in Susannah's gaze. "What's that?" The words were a breath.

"Falling in love. Giving up control to your emotions."

"I'm not—"

He pressed a finger to her lips, caught in the way the light blue of her dress set off the golden strands in her hair, accented the emerald in her gaze. His heart flip-flopped in his chest, and he had to hold back from kissing her. Not yet. Not until she was his again—for good this time. "You've done everything you can *not* to fall in love, Susannah. You did it for good reasons, just as, I suppose, I did, too. You were taking care of your sister. Running a business. Saving for a new life. You had no time, no room, no patience. Pick your reason. I've got a whole briefcase full of them back in New York."

She shook her head, denying it all, but the denial weakened with each shake.

"Why, Susannah?"

The limo rounded another corner, smoothly navigating the streets of Chapel Ridge. Along the sidewalks, everyone stared at the unfamiliar fancy car. Susannah toyed with the frame of the window for a long moment. "When my parents died, the family told me to send Jackie away. To let her live with an aunt in Arizona, so I could have my life. But I couldn't do that."

"Because you loved her too much."

Susannah shifted on the seat, back to Kane. She closed her eyes and sucked in a breath, then shook her head. "Because I had to hold on to what I had left, Kane. And Jackie was all I had."

A single tear slipped down her cheek, and for the first time, Kane noticed the well of emotion in her eyes, brought on by the tumultuous day. One that hadn't just changed Jackie's life, but had made a major shift in Susannah's, too. All those years of watching out for her younger sister, and now the burden was lifted, but he could see, in the pain in her eyes, that a part of her already missed the little bit of family that she'd held on to so tightly.

Kane wrapped an arm around her and drew Susannah
to his chest, folding her lithe frame into his. "You did the
right thing. It was the most selfless thing anyone could do."

"Don't you understand?" She looked up at him, her
cheek against his chest. "I did it for *me*, Kane. Because I
couldn't lose her. My parents were dead. My whole world
was gone in one day, and if Jackie was gone, too…" She
swiped at her face, clearing away newly fallen tears. "It
would have been too hard."

She'd been controlling her world, then and now. Boy,
did he recognize that trait. He'd inherited more than his
height and his eye color from his father. "I do the same
thing," Kane said. "Except I devoted myself to my job. I
said it was because the company needed me, because my
father demanded it, but really, that's an excuse. If I really
wanted to find the perfect woman and fall in love, I could
have—" a smile crossed his lips "—taken a vacation and
done just that."

Slowly, a reciprocal smile curved across her face, and
hope took flight in Kane's chest. "Have you taken many
of those? Vacations to meet the perfect woman?"

He slid a finger down her delicate nose, landing on her
upper lip. The urge to kiss her roared in his chest, thundered
in his head. "Only one. Seems the best women are in
Chapel Ridge, Indiana."

"Oooh, Mr. Maxwell isn't going to like hearing you say
that about his wife."

Kane laughed, then bent down and kissed Susannah
after all, bringing her tight to his body, holding her there
even after his lips left hers. "I mean you, silly, in case you
had any doubts."

She smiled. "I did have some. But they're starting to go
away now." She bit her lip, then met his gaze. "You were

right, Kane. Maybe I am running from love. It's just… easier when I can hold on to the reins, you know what I mean? When you fall in love, you have to let someone else have one of the reins. And that thought scares the heck out of me."

"I know exactly what you mean." He brushed the hair off her forehead and traced a line down her cheeks, then pressed a kiss along the same path. "And I was wrong to offer you what I did earlier. I was doing exactly what my father always did to me. Controlling everything, because I couldn't stand to lose you. I've realized it's easier to let you go…and open my heart."

"And take a risk?"

He nodded. "It's like having a rough diamond and deciding to cut and polish it while you're blindfolded. You could ruin it, or make it into the most beautiful marquis cut ever. You just have to trust in the stone, and your gut instincts. And my gut says that you and I together will make beautiful gems."

She smiled. "Rubies and emeralds?"

"I don't care if we end up with quartz and topaz. As long as we're together. And hey, we figured out how to fish and light a fire. I'd say after that, this getting married thing will be a piece of cake, what do you say?"

She tipped her head to smile up at him, then a second later, sat up straight, as if the words had just hit her. "Getting married? What do you mean? We just left the wedding."

Kane leaned forward and depressed the button, lowering the window separating them from the driver. "Sam, would you mind heading back to the church?"

"Certainly, Mr. Lennox."

The window went back up, and the limo did a quick U-turn.

"Kane…where are we going?"

Kane slid off the seat and onto the carpeted floor of the limousine. When he had decided that he wanted Susannah, he had moved heaven and earth to make it happen. Having the ring couriered to him, the limo set up, even asking the minister if he had time later today, assuming Susannah might say yes.

Over the years, Kane's billions of dollars had been a frustration in his life, but now he had found that it could also bring him great joy, between the people he had helped, and this.

Kane reached into his jacket pocket and pulled out a flawless two-carat red diamond ring, flanked by four same-sized white diamonds, forming a brilliant floral shape, which caught the sun and cast a rainbow of sparkles around the car. "Susannah Wilson, will you marry me?"

She gaped at the ring, then at him. "Are you crazy? I can't get married. I'm leaving for Paris in the morning and I live here and you live there and—"

He pressed a finger to her lips. "And we'll figure it all out. I always wanted to see Paris as a tourist. But we have to wait, just a few days before we leave for Paris, if that's okay."

"We do? Why?" The words came out in a little stutter, as she took in the ring, him, trying to make sense of it all.

"I promised my father a fishing trip. And believe me, by the time we get back from the church and Jackie's reception, he'll be ready to get out of the house."

She stared at him, confused. "Why?"

"I left him with the same things you gave me. A bag of dog food, a leash and a stray." Kane grinned.

Susannah laughed. "You're trying to convert the whole world?"

"No, just my corner of it." He held out the ring, his heart caught in her eyes, her answer. Never before had so much weighed on one word. "You didn't answer my question. I love you, Susannah. Will you marry me?"

"But where will we live? What will we—"

"Anything is possible."

Susannah looked into Kane's deep blue eyes, and saw the love there, a love she couldn't have believed would happen in such a short time, and felt the same emotion swell in her own heart, and knew he was right. Anything was possible. She'd met a stranger barefoot on her sister's lawn, a stranger with a secret who had forced her to get honest with herself—and had fallen in love with the man he really was.

"Yes," Susannah whispered, as he slid the ring onto her finger. "I love you, Kane."

He took Susannah into his arms and kissed her for a long, long time, loving her sweet goodness, the woman that she was, and the person she had helped him become. Then, when he finally drew back, Kane reached into his pocket and pulled out a small round globe, the kind purchased in airports and tourist shops for desks and curio cabinets.

Nothing special, nothing expensive, but to Susannah, it symbolized the heart of everything she was about. "An early wedding present," he said, pressing it into her palm and curling her hand around the colored globe. "I'll give you the world, if you let me," he said.

Susannah snuggled deeper into Kane's embrace, hearing the steady thump-thump of his heart. "I already have it, right here."

"So do I, Susannah," Kane whispered, "so do I."

Special Offers
Diamonds are... Collection

**Indulgence, luxury, diamonds…
What more can a girl want?**

*Sparkling, glittering, irresistible romances
collected into six sumptuous volumes!*

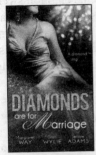

On sale 4th January

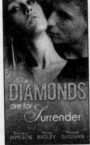

On sale 1st February

On sale 1st March

On sale 5th April

On sale 3rd May

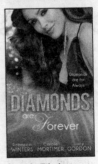

On sale 7th June

 Save 20% on Special Releases Collections

Find the collection at
www.millsandboon.co.uk/specialreleases

Visit us Online

0213/MB400

The World of Mills & Boon®

There's a Mills & Boon® series that's perfect for you. We publish ten series and, with new titles every month, you never have to wait long for your favourite to come along.

Blaze.
Scorching hot, sexy reads
4 new stories every month

By Request
Relive the romance with the best of the best
9 new stories every month

Cherish™
Romance to melt the heart every time
12 new stories every month

Desire™
Passionate and dramatic love stories
8 new stories every month

Visit us Online
Try something new with our Book Club offer
www.millsandboon.co.uk/freebookoffer

M&B/WORLD2

What will you treat yourself to next?

Ignite your imagination, step into the past…
6 new stories every month

INTRIGUE…
Breathtaking romantic suspense
Up to 8 new stories every month

Medical Romance
Captivating medical drama – with heart
6 new stories every month

MODERN™
International affairs, seduction & passion guaranteed
9 new stories every month

n o c t u r n e™
Deliciously wicked paranormal romance
Up to 4 new stories every month

RIVA™
Live life to the full – give in to temptation
3 new stories every month available exclusively via our Book Club

You can also buy Mills & Boon eBooks at
www.millsandboon.co.uk

Visit us Online

M&B/WORLD2

Mills & Boon® Online

Discover more romance at
www.millsandboon.co.uk

- 🌹 **FREE** online reads
- 🌹 **Books** up to one
  month before shops
- 🌹 **Browse our books**
  before you buy

  ...and much more!

For exclusive competitions and instant updates:

 Like us on **facebook.com/romancehq**

 Follow us on **twitter.com/millsandboonuk**

 Join us on **community.millsandboon.co.uk**

 Visit us Online   Sign up for our FREE eNewsletter at
www.millsandboon.co.uk

WEB/M&B/RTL4